High

**Will these blue-blooded grooms head up the aisle
with the woman of their dreams...
or a trophy wife?**

By
Request™

High Society
GROOMS

A BRIDE FOR THE TAKING
by
Sandra Marton

A FORBIDDEN DESIRE
by
Robyn Donald

A NIGHT TO REMEMBER
by
Anne Weale

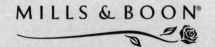

MILLS & BOON®

*MILLS & BOON and MILLS & BOON with the Rose Device
are registered trademarks of the publisher.
Harlequin Mills & Boon Limited,
Eton House, 18-24 Paradise Road, Richmond, Surrey, TW9 1SR*

HIGH SOCIETY GROOMS
© by Harlequin Enterprises II B.V., 2002

A Bride for the Taking, A Forbidden Desire and *A Night to Remember*
were first published in Great Britain by Harlequin Mills & Boon Limited
in separate, single volumes.

A Bride for the Taking © Sandra Myles 1992
A Forbidden Desire © Robyn Donald 1997
A Night to Remember © Anne Weale 1996

ISBN 0 263 83152 3

05-0102

*Printed and bound in Spain
by Litografia Rosés S.A., Barcelona*

Sandra Marton is an American author who used to tell stories to her dolls when she was a little girl. Today, readers around the world fall in love with her sexy, dynamic heroes and outspoken, independent heroines. Her books have topped best-seller lists and won many awards. Sandra loves dressing up for a night out with her husband as much as she loves putting on her hiking boots for a walk in a south-western desert or a north-eastern forest. You can write to her at PO Box 295, Storrs, Connecticut (please enclose SASE) or you can visit her on the internet at, www.sandramarton.com

Look out for
The Pregnant Mistress **by Sandra Marton**
In Modern Romance™, April 2002

A Bride for the Taking

by
Sandra Marton

CHAPTER ONE

DORIAN had barely settled into the back of the taxi, silently thanking whatever gods were responsible for finding her an empty cab during a rainy evening rush-hour in mid-Manhattan, when traffic came to a sudden halt.

She sat forward, looked out at the press of buses, cars, and trucks, then rapped sharply on the smeared glass partition that separated her from the driver.

'I've got a plane to make,' she said in the cool, don't-fool-with-me voice she'd learned worked best during the five years she'd lived in New York City.

The cabbie looked into his rear-view mirror and lifted his shoulders in an eloquent shrug.

'Is a mess, lady,' he said agreeably. 'I do best I can.'

Dorian sank back into the cracked vinyl seat. His best, she thought glumly, would not be good enough if they didn't get to Kennedy Airport within the next hour. The chartered flight to Barovnia would take off, leaving her behind.

The thought made her shudder. She was on the first decent assignment *WorldWeek* magazine had given her and, after almost two years of doing research for other reporters and little filler pieces without the coveted 'byline' every journalist dreamed of, she wasn't about to lose her chance of becoming a correspondent.

A horn blared behind them, the single sound immediately taken up by what seemed to be every other vehicle caught in the tangled snarl that filled Fifty-Seventh Street. Even Dorian's driver began to pound his fist on the horn, all the while muttering to himself in a tongue that bore no resemblance whatsoever to English.

5

Dorian muttered something too, short and succinct and not at all ladylike. The cabbie glanced into the mirror as if he'd heard her. We're in this together, the look on his face said, but that wasn't true at all. The meter was running, adding dollars to her growing frustration. He could sit here all night if he had to; at least he was earning his pay. Dorian wouldn't really begin to earn hers until she'd boarded that damned charter flight.

It would be on the apron by now, hatches open as the personal luggage of the entire Barovnian entourage was loaded aboard. The reporters themselves would travel light, but Dorian was sure the delegation would not—especially the man at the centre of it.

Jack Alexander, the wealthy and powerful head of the giant corporation that controlled Barovnian exports, would expect to travel in style—even though his destination was an isolated kingdom with one foot still planted in the ignorance and poverty of the Middle Ages. And now—now, if the newly crowned *abdhan* of Barovnia died...

Dorian slid backwards as the taxi shot into a sudden opening in the traffic. Good! They were moving again—but only as far as the next corner. She groaned and rapped once more on the partition.

'I absolutely, positively *must* get to Kennedy by seven,' she said. 'Please. Can't you do something?'

The driver threw up his hands. 'Is no my fault, miss.'

That was the motto of the day, Dorian thought glumly as she sank back in her seat. Her boss had used the same words when he'd dumped her into the middle of this situation.

She had been intent on the story she was writing, her fingers doing their usual hunt-and-peck across her computer keyboard while she tried to stretch a forty-word filler piece about the Florida citrus crop into one hundred words of journalistic brilliance, when a bulky shadow loomed across her desk. She looked up and saw Walt Hemple standing beside her.

'Got to see you, babe,' he said around the cigar that was, as always, clamped between his teeth.

Dorian nodded and got to her feet, biting back the desire to tell him for what would probably be the thousandth time that her name wasn't 'babe'. There was no point to it— 'babe' was Hemple's standard form of address for all the women staffers, a not-so-subtle reminder that, even if the law and a changed society required that *WorldWeek* employ female reporters, Walt Hemple didn't have to like it.

She followed him through the crowded newsroom to his office—a narrow cubicle perfumed with the noxious fumes of his cigar. Hemple elbowed past her, grunting as he settled into the old-fashioned swivel-chair behind his desk.

'Sit,' he said, but, as usual, there was no place to sit. Files, papers and old copies of *WorldWeek* were piled on the only other chair in the room.

Hemple folded his hands across his ample belly and looked at her.

'So,' he said after a moment, 'how's it going?'

She blinked. What kind of question was that? Hemple was not a man given to making small talk, especially not with staffers as far down the ladder as she.

'All right,' Dorian said cautiously. 'I'm just about done with—'

'What do you know about Barovnia?'

She blinked again. Barovnia. Barovnia. She knew the name, of course. It had been in the papers weeks before. *WorldWeek* had even done a piece on it.

'Not much,' she said, still cautiously. 'It's a country near the Black Sea—'

'A kingdom. A mountain kingdom in the Carpathians.'

She nodded. 'Right. I remember now. The Barovnian king died a couple of months ago, and—'

'They don't have a king. They have an *abdhan*.' Hemple grinned around his cigar. 'He's like a cross between God and Emperor of the World—an absolute monarch with the power of life and death over his people.'

Dorian nodded again. 'This is all very interesting,' she said carefully, 'but what—?'

'Read,' he said, shoving a sheet of paper across the desk.

She started to do as instructed, but Hemple clucked his tongue impatiently and snatched back the paper.

'It's an announcement from the Barovnian embassy,' he said. 'It just came over the wire. The *abdhan* may die. If he does, they'll be crowning a new one.'

'But it's a mistake. You just said the king died last month—'

'Jeez, babe, get it straight, will you? He's called an *abdhan*. How many times I got to tell you that?'

Dorian's eyes narrowed beneath their veil of dark lashes. Count to ten, she told herself, and don't say anything you'll regret.

'What I'm saying, Walt, is that this is old news. The *abdhan* had an accident a couple of months ago—'

'Having a massive coronary in your sleep after eighty-five years of being one of the world's last absolute rulers can hardly be classified as an accident, babe.'

'The bottom line is that the old man died and they replaced him, which means the wire-service story is wrong. Do you want me to phone them and—?'

'The story is one hundred per cent on the money. The old guy died, they crowned his successor—'

'Seref Baldov. Wasn't that his name?'

'Right. And yesterday there was some kind of tribal ceremony, something to do with horses. A mock battle, who the hell knows—?'

'A tribal ceremony?' Dorian couldn't quite keep the scorn from her voice. 'Hasn't anyone told these people we're on the threshold of the twenty-first century?'

Hemple's teeth showed in a smile. 'Exactly. Americans

are planning a mission to Mars and the Barovnians still play at being Cossacks. Interesting point, isn't it?'

Dorian sighed. Now she knew where this was going. A heading danced before her eyes. COSSACKS AND COSMONAUTS. Well, something like that. It didn't matter because the piece she'd write wouldn't rate a title. Walt would want a filler, some human interest thing that could be tucked in to fill space on the bottom of a page.

'How many words? Fifty?' she asked. 'A hundred?'

'So this Baldov guy,' Hemple said, ignoring her, 'the new *abdhan*, fell from his horse. He hit his head and now it looks like he may not pull through.'

Dorian nodded. 'I get the picture—although frankly I don't know why *WorldWeek's* readers should much care. Just because this little king of barbarians wants to play Mongol warrior—'

Hemple's brows drew together. 'You need to do your homework, babe. Barovnia may be backward, but it's got oil reserves that make the Arabs look like paupers, and minerals they can mine for the next thousand years—and if Baldov kicks the bucket it's also going to have a new *abdhan*.'

He didn't want a filler, she thought, he wanted an article. Not from her, of course—she'd only do the research. Someone with a name would be tapped to really write the piece.

'Interesting,' she said, trying to look as if it really were. 'OK. I'll put together what I can. How much time do I have?'

'Send me your first fifteen hundred words as soon as you can after touchdown.'

Dorian's heart gave a thump of excitement. Hemple had never sent her further than Newark on a story. Surely, he couldn't mean...

'Am I going somewhere?' she asked carefully.

'The Barovnian embassy's arranged to fly a planeload of reporters from the major media out tonight.'

Dorian swept the stack of magazines and papers into her arms and sank down in the chair.

'Are you sending me to Barovnia to cover this coronation?'

Hemple shoved a slim manila folder across his scarred desk-top. 'That's all the background the library could put together on such short notice. You can read it in the taxi on your way to the airport.'

A thousand questions were racing through Dorian's head, but there was one in particular that demanded an answer, even though only a fool would ask it.

'Walt?' She took a breath. 'It's not that I'm not—' She hesitated. Pick a word, she told herself, one that won't give away the fact that you want to leap into the air and whoop with joy. She cleared her throat. 'It's not that I'm not pleased with this assignment, but it occurs to me, we didn't send anybody to cover the last guy's coronation.'

Her boss nodded. 'Right.'

Dorian nodded, too. 'Well, then, why…?' She hesitated again, but it had to be said. 'Why now? And why has the Barovnian embassy offered to fly reporters in? I mean, why would they think we'd be interested?'

Hemple leaned forward. 'Does the name Jack Alexander mean anything to you?'

It took a few seconds to change gears. 'Yes,' she said after a moment. 'Sure. He's the head of Alexander International.'

'Uh-huh. The guy inherited millions, and he's racked up millions more on his own.' Hemple switched his cigar from one side of his mouth to the other. 'What else do you know?'

She frowned. *WorldWeek* had done a piece on the man once, when she'd first started at the magazine.…

A look of disdain narrowed her mouth. 'Our article said

he collects women almost as easily as he collects money—
except he holds on to the money.'

Walt Hemple laughed. 'I don't think we put it quite like
that but yeah, that was the general idea. Anything else?'

'No, I don't—' She nodded. 'He hates personal publicity.
His women lined up to be interviewed, but we couldn't get
a reporter past Alexander's door.'

'Not with questions about himself, no. Ask him about
Alexander International, he talks. Ask him about Jack
Alexander, he turns to stone.'

'Walt, I really don't understand. All this is interesting,
but what's the point? If you're sending me to Barovnia,
what's all this side-bar stuff about Alexander have to do
with it?'

Hemple's chair groaned its displeasure as he tilted it forward and leaned across his desk.

'Alexander International should really be called
Barovnian Exports. Sixty, sixty-five per cent of what it controls comes from there.'

'So?'

'So,' Hemple said, smiling slyly, 'it turns out that our pal,
Mr Alexander, has been sitting on a secret, babe.' He paused
dramatically. 'Mama was a Southern belle. But Daddy—
Daddy was a Barovnian. A Barovnian of royal lineage, no
less.'

It was Dorian's turn to lean forward. 'What do you
mean?'

'I mean,' Hemple said with relish, 'that Jack Alexander
was born Jaacov Alexandrei.' The sly smile came again. 'I
mean that the guy's a product of the Virginia Military
Academy, Harvard, and the Wharton School of Business—
and now it turns out that under that hand-tailored, three-
piece suit beats the heart of the guy who may become the
next *abdhan*.'

Dorian's green eyes opened wide with shock. 'What?'

'Alexander's gonna be on that plane, along with a handful

of his business buddies—American advisers, the Press release calls them. How's that grab you, babe?'

It grabbed her. How could it not? It was the best kind of story, a reporter's dream, all the most basic human interest stuff combined with something as serious as oil and gold and international dollars.

'Are you sure?' Hemple nodded, and Dorian frowned. 'Wait a minute. If this is the same Jack Alexander, the one who's gun-shy of publicity, why's he taking a planeload of reporters along with him to Barovnia?'

'The embassy made the arrangements, not him.' Hemple's eyelid dropped in a conspiratorial wink. 'And from what I've heard—on the QT, of course—Alexander made them wait until the last minute before he agreed to their plan. The guy's no dummy. There'd be no way to keep something like this off the front pages—he must figure the best way to handle things is to control the story inside Barovnia, where he's got the power, instead of having rumours leak out from the foreign embassies.'

Dorian nodded. It made sense. The only thing that didn't make sense was that this plum should be falling into her lap.

'Just think,' Hemple said, chuckling. 'All these years, companies have lived or died on this guy's say-so—and now it turns out that he may get that kind of power over people's lives. God, is that a story just waiting to be written, or isn't it?'

It was. Oh, it definitely was. But why was he giving it to her? Why?

'Here.' Hemple tossed an envelope across his desk. 'Everything you need is in there, including chits to sign for Accounting so you can take some cash with you—which reminds me, I want you to hop downstairs and buy whatever you think you'll need. Clothes, make-up—you know what I mean. The plane leaves in two hours, so there's no time to go home and get your stuff.'

Dorian nodded. 'That's OK. All I'll need is a toothbrush and a change of…' She fell silent. *Whatever you'll need. Clothes, make-up. Make-up…*

And suddenly it all fell into place.

'Walt.' Her voice trembled a little with anger; she had to clear her throat before she could continue. 'Walt,' she said, choosing her words with the greatest care, 'I'm grateful for this chance. You know I am.'

Her boss's expression gave nothing away. 'But?'

'But I'm not—I mean, I assume you haven't chosen me because I'm…I certainly wouldn't want to think that— that…'

'Because you're a woman. A good-looking woman. Is that what you're choking over saying?'

Dorian swallowed hard. 'Yes. No. I mean—dammit, Walt, is that the reason you picked me? Because you think Alexander will—will notice me?'

Hemple's beady eyes moved over her, assessing without personal interest her shiny cap of silvery blonde hair, her wide-set green eyes fringed by heavy, dark lashes, the small straight nose and full mouth.

'He'd have to be dead not to notice you, babe,' he said flatly.

Dorian flushed. She had no illusions about her looks. She was pretty, perhaps more than pretty, but it was nothing to do with her. She had inherited her beauty, she hadn't worked at it as she had at honing her reporting skills, and if she'd wanted to use her looks she'd have done so long ago. More than one city-room editor had made it clear that she could get ahead by going to bed—his bed, more specifically. She could even more easily have carved a career in TV news, where a pretty face went a lot further than ability.

But she hadn't done any of that. And she wasn't about to start now.

'Walt.' She straightened in her chair. 'I want this assign-

ment very badly. But I'm not going to take it if you think—
if you're assuming I'll trade on my—on my looks to get
anything out of Alexander. I don't work that way.' Her head
lifted until her eyes were boring into his. 'And you've absolutely no right to ask me to do something like that, either.'

Hemple's smile was bland. 'I sent you out to interview
that librarian who hit the jackpot a few months ago. Why
did I choose you, do you think?'

'That's not the same thing.'

'Because your résumé says you worked a year as a library
assistant, babe. It was a good fit, the same as it made sense
to send Joe Banks to interview that sky-diver once I knew
Banks jumped out of airplanes, too.'

'Walt, it's different. You're asking me to—'

'I'm asking you to be what you are—a reporter and a
looker, too.' He gave her a quick, hard smile. 'Unless you'd
rather I handed this over to somebody else.'

Dorian had stared at her boss, hating him for putting her
in this spot, hating herself for not being able to tell him
what he could do with his assignment, almost hating herself
for being a woman.

It had been as if Hemple had been able to read her mind.
His smile had broadened until it threatened to dislodge the
cigar, and that had been when he'd uttered the words that
almost mirrored the ones the taxi driver had used.

'Why fight reality, babe? After all, it's not *my* fault you're
a good-looking broad, is it?'

Dorian sighed as she remembered the smirk on his face
as he'd spoken. Hemple was a pig, she thought as the taxi
exited the Queens Midtown Tunnel and started along the
highway, but he was the man in charge.

She took the file folder from her bag and opened it. The
bottom line was that he'd given her an assignment, and she
would fulfil it to the best of her ability.

She would certainly not use sex to accomplish it; she'd
made that clear enough to him before she'd left his office.

Hemple had only smiled. Dorian had known what he was thinking: that if Alexander had a choice between talking to her and to a male reporter he'd talk to her.

She sighed again as she began leafing through the papers inside the folder. Even if he did, it wouldn't be because she'd gone out of her way to set things up. Certainly, she'd done nothing to glamourise herself.

She'd taken money from Accounting and dashed to a little shop on the corner where she'd bought a large carrying bag and only the basics: comb, toothbrush, underwear, a pair of jeans and a couple of T-shirts in addition to the khaki trouser suit she was wearing. Nothing feminine, nothing—

There was a sudden bang and the taxi lurched sharply to the right. Dorian cried out as the papers in her lap went flying. The driver cursed, this time loudly and fluently in Anglo-Saxon English, and pulled the vehicle off the road and on to the grassy verge.

Dorian leaned forward and hammered on the partition. 'What happened?' she demanded. 'Why are we stopping?'

The man turned and slid the glass aside. 'We have flat tyre, miss. I must change.'

She stared at him. 'How long will that take?'

He shrugged. 'Ten minute. Maybe fifteen. It is raining. Not so easy to do.'

'Well, then—can you call for another taxi to come and pick me up?'

He shrugged again. 'Sure. Can do. But other car may not come any faster than I change tyre.'

Dorian glanced at her watch. 'Do it anyway, please,' she said. 'I'm really desperate.'

He did as she'd asked, then set to work. It had gone from afternoon to night now, and the rain had turned into a steady downpour. Time passed, but no new taxi appeared.

Dorian flung open the door and stepped out into the darkness. Wind buffeted her; she felt the rain drive straight through her thin cotton jacket and trousers, felt it plaster her hair to her skull. Spray from a passing car slapped against her face.

'Miss.' She turned. The driver had risen to his feet and was standing beside her, looking at her as if she were crazy. 'I cannot fix. The jack no work. Please, we sit in taxi and wait.'

Dorian shook her head. 'I can't wait,' she said. 'My plane will be leaving.' She peered ahead into the night. 'We're almost at the airport, aren't we?'

'Yes, but—'

'That's what I thought.' She reached inside the taxi and grabbed her holdall. The contents of the file she'd yet to look at—clippings, photos—all of it lay scattered on the floor. But it was too late now. 'I'll start walking,' Dorian said. 'If another taxi shows up, send the driver looking for me, will you?'

'Miss, please, you cannot.'

'Here.' She dug into her bag for some bills and tucked them into the bewildered driver's hand. 'Maybe I'll be lucky and someone will stop and give me a lift.'

'In New York?' The driver's voice carried after her as she began marching towards the distant airport. 'It will not happen, miss, and even if it should you cannot trust. Not in this city. Please. You must wait.'

But she couldn't, not if she was going to make that plane. Dorian's footsteps quickened. The driver was right, of course. No car would stop for her. This was New York, where only the fittest survived. You could fall to the pavement in the middle of Fifth Avenue and no one would acknowledge it. And he was right about the rest, too. In this city, you couldn't trust anyone, *especially* someone crazy enough to stop to pick up a stranger.

Not that that would stop her. You couldn't be a good reporter if you were afraid of—

A horn blared shrilly, making her jump. Dorian's head lifted sharply. Go on, she thought, have fun at my expense.

A truck whizzed by, closer than it had a right to be to the verge; water splashed over her, cold as ice.

She shuddered and kept walking. How long would it take to walk a mile or two under these conditions? Twenty minutes? Half an hour? Would she make it on time, or—?

A car swept past her, swung sharply to the right, and came to a stop on the verge of the road just ahead. It was a sports car, something long and lean with a throbbing engine. Dorian blinked her eyes against the rain. Could it be…? Yes. Yes! The passenger door was swinging open.

She began running, her pace awkward in the muddy grass. When she reached the car, she paused and leaned down towards it.

The interior was dimly lit and leather-scented. Warmth drifted towards her, along with the faint strains of Tchaikovsky. There was a man at the wheel, but she couldn't see him very clearly. His face alternated between light and shadow from the headlights of oncoming cars. All she could tell was that he was tall and that his hands lay lightly—and powerfully—on the steering-wheel.

'Thank you so much for stopping,' she said, her voice a little breathless. 'You just saved my life.'

He turned slowly towards her, and for some reason her heart seemed to tighten in her breast. His face still alternated between light and shadow, but she could see that he had dark hair and eyes, a straight, handsome nose above what seemed to be a full mouth, and an arrogant tilt to his chin.

'Where are you going?' he asked. His voice was deep and soft, almost smoky. Dorian had the sudden crazy feeling that he never had to raise that voice at all, that people would do whatever they had to do to hear his words.

'You cannot trust,' the taxi driver had said. 'You cannot trust…'

Dorian touched the tip of her tongue to her lower lip. 'To—to the airport,' she said. 'But if you'd just be kind enough to take me as close to it as you can—'

'I'm going there myself. Toss your things in the back and get in.'

Dorian's heart did a funny turn again, as if someone had reached into her chest and given it a poke. It was silly, but the open door, the drift of leather-scented warmth emanating into the chill night from the car's interior, the smoky voice—all at once it seemed dangerous.

'Well?' The voice was amused now, even a little contemptuous. 'Are you going to stand out there and drown, or am I going to drive you to the airport?'

Dorian drew in her breath. What was there to fear? Men who drove expensive cars weren't likely to be serial killers, for heaven's sake. What she had to do was get to the airport and write the story of the year about a man named Jack Alexander, a man who might in hours become the absolute ruler of a country lost in the past.

'You're going to drive me to the airport,' she said briskly, and she tossed her bag into the rear of the car, climbed into the seat, and slammed the door after her.

CHAPTER TWO

DORIAN sighed thankfully as she sank into the leather bucket seat.

'It's a hell of a night for a stroll.'

She looked at the man who'd rescued her. He was smiling as he looked into his mirror and manoeuvred the car back into traffic.

She laughed pleasantly. 'Isn't it ever? I can't believe how hard the rain's coming down.' Her hair was dripping into her eyes; she put her hands to her face and shoved back the soaked strands. 'I'm afraid I'm going to make a mess of your car.'

The man beside her shrugged. 'Don't worry about it.' His foot settled more firmly on the accelerator. The engine growled as the car leaped ahead, the wiper clearing the windscreen in rhythmic strokes. 'What time does your flight leave?'

'What?'

'Your plane. I assume it must be taking off fairly soon or you wouldn't have risked life and limb on the road.'

'Oh.' She smiled. 'You sound like my taxi driver. He thought I was crazy to leave the cab.'

'That dead yellow beast on the verge was yours, then?' He nodded. 'I thought it must be.'

'Mmm. We had a flat—it was the final touch. Traffic was impossible all the way from Manhattan.' Dorian made an apologetic face as she looked down at herself. 'I really am making a mess of things,' she said. 'I didn't realise how soaked I was.'

Her rescuer glanced at her. 'You must be freezing,' he said.

She started to protest politely, but the sudden chatter of her teeth stopped her in mid-sentence.

'I suppose I am,' she said with a rueful little laugh. 'Who'd ever dream it would get chilly so late in May?'

'Well, we can warm things up a little.' He leaned forward and pushed a button on the dashboard. Warm air hissed from the heating vents and Dorian sighed with pleasure. 'Better?'

'Yes, thanks. Much.'

'There's a coat on the seat behind you. If you drape it over yourself, you'll be more comfortable.'

Dorian shook her head. 'No, thank you, that's all right. We'll be at the airport soon, and—'

'And by then you'll probably have pneumonia. Go on, get the coat.'

'Really, it isn't necessary. I'm feeling much warmer already. The heat's coming up, and—'

'For God's sake, woman, don't argue. Put the coat on.'

She stared at him. His voice had not risen; instead, it had taken on a note of command and she thought suddenly that he was a man accustomed not only to giving orders, but to having them obeyed instantly.

But not by her. It was one thing to accept a lift from a stranger and quite another to—

'You're soaked to the skin,' he said. She looked up. He was watching her, a little frown on his face. His gaze slipped over her, moving from her dripping hair to her damp face, then dropping to her wet khaki jacket. When his eyes met hers again, his face was expressionless. 'And you're cold, too.'

'I'm not. Really.'

A faint smile curved across his mouth. 'But you are,' he said softly, and suddenly she was painfully aware that her clothing must be clinging to her skin, outlining her breasts with intimate clarity.

Dorian felt her cheeks blaze. Be careful, she told herself. She'd been warned against crazies, hadn't she?

Her mouth tightened as she reached for the coat to hide herself from the man's coolly appraising gaze. He'd out-manoeuvred himself, though. Once she had the coat on, he wouldn't have much of a view to enjoy. She smiled as she snatched it up and draped it over herself from chin to toe.

'There.' His tone was light and pleasant. 'Isn't that better?'

'Perfect,' she said sweetly.

And it was. She was discreetly covered by the coat—his, she was certain, based on its size and its faintly masculine scent—and she was warm, as well…

And she'd done his bidding. He'd manipulated her into doing what he'd first commanded.

She blinked. Why on earth had she thought that? Besides, what counted was that she was warm again. The little tremors that had raced through her body had stopped. And it would have been stupid to have risked a chill at the start of her first big story…

'So.' He stretched lithely, shifting his weight in the bucket seat. 'You still haven't told me what's so urgent that you were willing to risk a night-time walk along the highway.'

'I did tell you.' Dorian's tone was politely neutral. 'I've a plane to catch.'

'Let me guess.' Her rescuer gave her a quick smile. 'You're off for a long weekend on the beach at Cancun.'

She laughed. Was that where people went for a weekend in his world? 'No,' she said, 'not hardly.'

'Martinique, then.'

'Not Martinique, either.'

He sighed. 'Ah, that's too bad. I was going to recommend a little place I know on the north side of the island—they serve the best rum punch this side of paradise.'

And he'd just love to take her there. Was that what came next? Dorian sighed inwardly. She knew all the moves by now, after five years of living in New York. You'd meet a

man, there'd be a little chit-chat about dinner, or the newest
nightspot, and then—as if the idea had just sprung into his
head—he'd invite you to visit it with him. She'd passed up
invitations to the Hamptons, to Miami, once even to Lake
Tahoe for fun and games.

But Martinique? That was new to her list. Apparently the
stakes were higher in this man's league. Still, why wouldn't
they be? Everything about him spelled M-O-N-E-Y. Dorian
stole a glance at him, her eyes taking in longish but expen-
sively cut dark hair, the well-tailored suit, the Rolex Oyster
glinting on his wrist. Yes, she thought a little disdainfully,
he would know the best place on Martinique—and in half
a dozen other pricey spots in the Caribbean.

She looked at the dashboard clock. Her mouth twisted. In
a little while she'd meet Jack Alexander, and she had no
doubt but that he would be much like the man seated beside
her: wealthy, very sure of himself, good-looking—and never
hesitant about turning on the charm for an attractive woman.

And yet—she stirred uneasily. And yet there was something else about the man driving this car, something she
couldn't quite put her finger on. It had to do with the way
he'd spoken to her, with the way he seemed to have forced
her into a corner moments ago. It was as if a core of steel
lay hidden just beneath the silken exterior.

She glanced at him again. There was something in the
way he held himself, too, head high and shoulders straight,
with just the slightest touch of arrogant pride to the set of
his mouth. It was there in the way he drove this expensive
car—a Porsche Carrera, she was fairly certain—with a skill
and assertiveness that almost bordered on aggression, as if
the caution of the slower-moving drivers on the rain-slicked
road was an insult to his masculinity.

Her gaze fell on his hands, lying lightly on the steering-
wheel. They were tanned and well cared for, yet she was
quite certain they would be strong and powerful, that they
would not only be able to elicit the best from an automobile,

but from anything else they touched. From a woman, she thought suddenly. A woman would respond to him as the car was—with eagerness and pleasure—and all at once she found herself wondering what it would be like on Martinique, wondering if flowers scented the air along the beach…

'…where you're going, if you want to make your plane on time.'

Dorian turned towards him, afraid to breathe, afraid she'd somehow spoken those last insane words aloud. But she hadn't; he was watching the road, the car was moving more slowly, and she realised that they'd turned off the highway and on to the road that traversed the airport.

'Excuse me? I—I didn't hear what you said.'

'I said, you'd better tell me where you want to be dropped off, if you want to make your flight.'

Her brows rose a little. She'd been wrong, then. He'd been gallant to the end; he'd given her a lift, flirted probably no more than his male ego demanded, and now he was all business. In fact, now that she looked at him, she could see that he'd undergone a subtle change in the last few minutes. That soft, sexy smile had been replaced by a certain grimness, and the hands that lay on the steering-wheel gripped it almost tightly.

But then, he had a plane to catch, too. Dorian felt a little twinge of something that surely couldn't have been regret. She sat up straighter, took the coat from her lap, and tossed it into the back seat.

'Of course. You can drop me off at—at…'

Where? Her breath caught. It was a damned good question, and she had no answer. She had no idea where to get the flight to Barovnia. Walt Hemple hadn't told her.

'Well?' Her rescuer slowed to a crawl. 'Look,' he said impatiently. 'I've a plane to catch myself and not a hell of a lot of time to do it in. Where shall I drop you?'

Her mind spun in frantic circles. What now? She glanced

at the dashboard clock. Ten minutes? Ten minutes to make
her flight. No, she thought grimly. Not her flight. Her career.
If she missed that plane, she might as well never show her
face at *WorldWeek* again.

'Come on, lady,' the stranger said. 'Where do you want
to go?'

'I don't know,' she admitted.

His dark eyes narrowed. 'You don't know? What in hell
is that supposed to mean?'

'It means—it means he didn't tell me,' she said a bit
shakily.

His expression grew even more grim. 'He didn't tell you?
You mean, you agreed to go away with some guy for the
weekend without…?'

'No!' Dorian's eyes flashed with green fire. 'I certainly
did not. And I resent the implication.'

His mouth seemed to soften a little. 'It wouldn't be so
extraordinary, would it?' He smiled. 'A beautiful woman
going away with her boyfriend for a couple of days, I mean.'

Some of the stiffness went out of her spine. 'No. I just—
you had no right to assume—' She broke off. What in
heaven's name did it matter *what* he assumed? He was a
stranger; she would never see him again after this. She
sighed and looked at him. 'I'm not going away for pleasure,'
she said. 'I'm flying out on business.'

'Ah.' His smile tilted. 'As am I.'

'And it's—well, it's an important trip. But my boss forgot
to tell me where my plane would be leaving from.'

His smile broadened. 'The problem's easily solved. Take
a look at your ticket. The name of the airline will be on it.'

His suggestion gave her hope—until she remembered that
all Walt had handed her was the library material and petty-
cash voucher.

Dorian blew out her breath. 'I don't have a ticket.'

'I see. You're supposed to pick it up at the counter,
hmm?' He shrugged before she could say anything. 'Well,

call your boss and talk to him.' He reached for the cellular phone.

'No,' she said quickly, stilling his hand. He looked at her, brows lifted, and she gave him a nervous smile. 'You don't know him. I—I don't think he'd be very happy to find out that I'd screwed up.'

The stranger frowned. 'But it's his fault, surely.'

Dorian sighed. 'You don't know my boss. He might not see it that way.' Her shoulders rose and fell in a little shrug. 'This job I've been sent on is important, you see. It's hard to explain, but—'

'You don't have to explain.' He made a sound that was not quite a laugh. 'I know all about important jobs, and how they have to be dealt with even when they seem damned near impossible.'

Dorian nodded. 'Impossible,' she repeated—and all at once, to her horror, her eyes filled with tears. She blinked them back quickly, but not before he'd seen their tell-tale glitter.

'Hell!' His brows knotted together as he undid his seatbelt and moved towards her. 'No job is worth that.'

'This one is.' She swallowed hard. 'You don't under-stand—'

'I told you.' His voice was harsh. 'I *do* understand, better than you could possibly imagine.' His frown deepened, and then he began to smile. 'What if you just forgot about it?'

Dorian stared at him. 'What do you mean?'

'Your job.'

'Just—walk away from it?' She shook her head. 'I couldn't.'

'Why not? Where is it written that one must do whatever one is told?'

She gave a puzzled laugh. 'But that's what having a job is all about,' she said, watching him closely. 'You do what you have to do.'

He moved closer to her. 'What I said about Martinique

is true, you know.' His eyes searched hers; he gave her a sudden, swift smile. 'We could have a late supper at that little place on the beach, then go for a walk in the moon-light.'

Dorian shook her head. So, she hadn't been wrong about his intentions after all. He'd been coming on to her all the time, just waiting for the right moment to make his move.

Still, she'd never had an invitation to any place as exotic as this. His line was different, she had to admit that—so different that it made her want to smile, something that had seemed impossible only seconds ago.

'I don't think so,' she said lightly.

He clasped her shoulders. 'Give me one good reason why.'

She smiled. 'Well,' she said, still in the same light tone of voice, 'it's pouring cats and dogs.'

He shook his head. 'Not in Martinique.' His hands moved slowly from her shoulders to her face. 'Believe me, I wouldn't dream of letting it rain in Martinique tonight.'

He looked deep into her eyes, and suddenly she wasn't smiling any more. No, she thought crazily, no, he wouldn't let it rain. He would make the moon come up, the stars fill the skies. He would—he would...

His gaze dropped to her mouth. 'Let me take you to Martinique, kitten.'

Dorian swallowed drily. 'Kitten?'

'That's what you looked like, standing there in the rain.' His gaze met hers. 'A little wet kitten, with its fur all matted down, needing somebody to dry it and cuddle it until it purred again.'

He cupped the back of her head; his hand gentled the silken strands of her hair that had dried in soft curls on the nape of her neck.

Dorian gave a little shudder. He was good at this, her brain said in a sharp whisper. He was very good. The way he was watching her, as if only she and he existed in the entire universe. The smile that promised pleasure. The soft, smoky voice that surely sounded as if he'd never said any of these things to another woman—it was all part of an act, one he'd probably used a dozen times before.

And yet—and yet...

'Sweet little kitten.' Her breath caught as he bent to her and pressed a light kiss to her damp hair. 'Say you'll come with me.'

Dorian shook her head. This was insane. It was—it was...

His mouth brushed her temple, then the curved arc of her cheek. 'Don't,' she said. At least, that was what she thought she said. But all she heard was the whisper of her own sigh as she lifted her face for his kiss.

Her heart pounded wildly as his lips met hers. Her hands crept to his chest, the palms flattening against his jacket.

'Say yes,' he whispered against her mouth, and all at once she wanted—she wanted...

A jet roared overhead, the sound filling the small, enclosed space like a peal of thunder. Dorian's eyes flew open. She stared at the stranger blankly, and then sanity returned. She pushed against him; he let go of her, and she scrambled back against the door.

'So much for gallantry,' she said. Her voice trembled.

For a long moment his face was expressionless. Then, finally, the corner of his mouth lifted in a cool smile.

'And so much for playing the reluctant maiden.' He turned away from her and shifted into gear. The car plunged off over the kerb and shot down the road. 'Have you figured out where you want to go yet, or are you still suffering from amnesia?'

Dorian's chin rose. 'You can drop me off at the International Arrivals building,' she said coldly. 'I'm sure I can get the information I need there—not that it matters now.'

His smile was like ice. 'Yes. You've probably missed your plane to Timbuktu or wherever it is you were going.'

'Barovnia,' she said, her tone curt. 'That's where I was going until you—' She cried out as the car came to a sudden halt. 'Are you crazy? I could have gone through the wind...'

'Barovnia? Did you say you're flying to Barovnia?'

'I said, I was *supposed* to fly to Barovnia.' She lifted her bag into her lap and folded her arms across it. 'But I won't be doing that now. *WorldWeek* will just have to get its news from pool reporters.' She swung towards him as he began to laugh. 'I suppose that seems very funny to you, that I'd be worried about missing a plane to a—a primitive little kingdom?'

His laughter stopped as abruptly as it had begun. 'If you think it's so primitive,' he said softly, 'why are you going there?'

Dorian stared straight ahead of her. 'Don't you mean, why *was* I going there?'

'All right. Why were you?'

All her anger came swelling up inside her. 'To report back to my editor on—on what it's like to watch a nation of poor peasants turn a man who's never done a useful day's work in his life into a little tin god.'

'Really.'

His voice was soft as the rain, as menacing as the night, but Dorian was too far gone to hear it.

'Yes, really. I know you can't understand why I'm upset. And I suppose, in a way, you're right. After all, nobody's really going to miss that report except me. I mean, what does the world give a damn about Barovnia? But I'm going to lose my...' She gasped and clutched at the dashboard as the car leaped forward. 'Dammit, must you drive like a lunatic?'

'I'm only trying to be helpful, Miss... What did you say your name was?'

'Oliver. Dorian Oliver. And it's too late to be helpful. While you were—while you were mauling me, my plane took off.'

The stranger flashed her a quick, cold smile. 'Relax, Miss Oliver. Your plane is still on the ground.' The tyres squealed as the car skidded to a stop. She watched, bewildered, as he got out of the car, came around to her side, and flung her door open. 'Do you have your Press pass, Miss Oliver?'

'Yes. Of course. But—' She caught her breath as he leaned into the car, caught hold of her arm, and tugged her unceremoniously out into the darkness. 'Would you mind explaining exactly what you're doing?'

He clasped her arm tightly as he marched her forward towards a building marked 'North Passenger Terminal'.

'I'm saving your job for you,' he said grimly.

He pushed the door open and tugged her into the lighted interior, and then he paused. There was a cluster of men near by, large men, all of whom had, apparently, been watching the door—and waiting, Dorian saw with some surprise, for their entrance. The stranger turned to her. 'Wait here,' he said in that same commanding voice he'd used to her before.

Dorian wanted to tell him what he could do with the order, but there was no time. He stepped forward and said something to one of the men, and then he turned to her again.

'This gentleman will escort you to the plane, Miss Oliver.'

'The plane?' Dorian stared at him. 'What plane?'

The stranger's lips drew back from his teeth. 'The plane to that primitive little kingdom. There's no other plane that could possibly interest you, is there?'

She knew what he was thinking, and she met his cold smile with a contemptuous stare. Had he really ever believed she'd given a moment's thought to all that nonsense about Martinique?

'None. But how did you…?' Dorian put her hand to her mouth. Lord. Oh, lord. That air of authority. The wealth. The dark good looks. Was it possible? Had she spent the past half-hour with Jack Alexander—and had she, then, blown any slim chance she might have had of getting an interview with the man?

She ran her tongue over lips that had gone dry. 'Are you,' she whispered, 'I mean, it occurs to me that you—could you possibly be…?'

He let her stammer and then, mercifully, he saved her from further embarrassment.

'Let me help you, Miss Oliver.' His voice was silken. He stepped closer to her, until he was only a whisper away. 'Will I be the new *abdhan*? That's what you want to know, isn't it?'

Dorian swallowed hard and nodded. 'Yes.'

He watched her for a long, long moment, his handsome face devoid of all expression, and then he gave her a smile that was colder than the rain.

'How could I be? The king of a primitive little country would have to be a barbarian, would he not?' He caught hold of her wrist; she felt the sudden, fierce pressure of his fingers on the fragile bones. 'He'd have to be a complete savage. Isn't that right, Miss Oliver?'

'Please.' Dorian grimaced. 'You're hurting me…'

He almost flung her from him. 'Relax, Miss Oliver. I can assure you, I am not the *abdhan*.'

She watched as he turned and strode away from her. The cluster of men who'd waited politely throughout the interchange fell into step around him. Within seconds, they'd vanished into the depths of the terminal.

'Miss?' She turned, startled. The man who was to guide her to the plane had come up beside her. He was as soft-spoken as he was huge. 'We must hurry.'

Dorian nodded. 'All right. Just one thing. That man—who is he?'

Her escort took her bag from her as they began walking. 'Didn't he tell you?'

She shook her head. 'Is he a friend of the new *abdhan*?'

The man frowned. 'There is no new *abdhan*, miss. There is the anointed one, and there is the *abdhazim*—the Crown Prince, the next in line for the throne.'

'Well, that's what I meant. The *abdhazim*. Is he—was that man a friend of his? Is he part of the delegation?'

Her escort smiled for the first time. 'Yes. You may say that. He is part of the delegation.'

She had expected the answer. Still, it made her feel sick to her stomach to have it confirmed.

Her rescuer was a friend of Jack Alexander's, the man who never let reporters get near him. He was the *abdhazim*'s friend, and she had made an enemy of him.

Good work, she told herself with a sigh. Oh, yes, good work.

Dorian Oliver, girl reporter, was off to one hell of a great start!

CHAPTER THREE

STUPID, Dorian thought as her burly escort led her through the terminal, stupid, stupid, stupid! Her first shot at success, and what had she done? She'd damned near obliterated it—and that without having even left the United States! Given enough time, who knew what wonders she might manage?

'This way, please, miss.'

Her escort's hand pressed gently into the small of her back. He was hurrying her towards the boarding area.

Well, she thought grimly, at least he wasn't marching her out to the car park. For one awful moment, that had seemed a real possibility. Still, she wasn't on the plane yet. There was still plenty of time for things to change.

The man who'd picked her up on the road had probably reached Jack Alexander's side by now; he was probably telling him that Dorian Oliver of *WorldWeek* had already made up her mind about Barovnia and about him.

The things she'd said flashed through her mind like poisonous darts. She'd called the kingdom primitive, its people peasants, and Alexander himself—Dorian winced. Had she really called him a little tin god?

And if her words were being repeated to Alexander, who knew what might happen next? It was no secret that the next *abdhan* of Barovnia had no great love for reporters, not when it came to his private life. For all she knew, he was at this very minute listening to her rescuer's story, his face darkening with displeasure as he heard himself, and his people, described in such ugly terms.

'What's this fool's name?' he would demand, and the stranger would tell him.

'Oliver,' he'd say, 'Dorian Oliver,' and a big, silent man

who might easily be the twin of the one at her side right now would be dispatched to wait for her, to bar her admittance to the Press section of the plane.

'You are not welcome on board this flight,' he would say, and how would she explain any of it to Walt Hemple, or even to herself? She was a reporter, for God's sake, she was supposed to exercise discretion, to say the right thing at the right moment and not run off at the mouth, especially to someone she'd never laid eyes on before...

'The steward will seat you, miss.'

Dorian started. They had reached the boarding stairs; her escort was smiling politely as he stepped away from her.

'Have a pleasant trip, Miss Oliver,' he said.

She nodded. 'Yes. Yes, thanks very much.'

The steward greeted her pleasantly. 'Your Press pass, please,' he said, and she handed it over, still half expecting a hand to fall on her shoulder.

But none did. The steward gave her an empty, mechanical smile, handed back the pass, and suggested that she might find a vacant seat back in the last few rows.

Dorian nodded. 'Thanks,' she said, and she set off down the narrow aisle, making her way carefully over outstretched feet and overstuffed shoulder bags that had pushed their way out from beneath the seats under which they'd been stored, saying hello to the few reporters she knew, trying not to gape at the famous faces interspersed in the crowd.

'Hey, Oliver,' a voice called out. 'Here's a seat, lover, you can sit on my lap.'

Dorian looked at the man from the *Mirror*. 'No, thanks,' she said sweetly, without missing a beat, 'I'd just as soon not share it with your belly,' and everybody chuckled.

'Oliver. Hey, Oliver. How come they hold the plane for good-lookin' broads?'

'Because bald guys aren't ''in'' this year,' she said airily, and there was more good-natured laughter all around.

Her sense of elation had returned by the time she settled

into a seat. It felt wonderful to be among these people, to be on assignment along with the best her profession had to offer. As for the bantering, Dorian had grown used to it a long time ago, and she understood it, too.

Journalists—except for fools like her editor—didn't care if you looked like Quasimodo or Marilyn Monroe, so long as you got the job done. But journalism had always been a male-dominated profession. And, because of that, there were still certain rites of passage you had to endure before being accepted into its ranks.

Learning to trade one-liners, for instance. The newer you were, the more you had to prove you could smile and deliver as good as you got. Dorian had honed her skills on her very first job, back in Buffalo, New York, and she was still pretty good—on her better days, anyway.

She sighed as she tucked her bag beneath the seat. But this hadn't been one of her better days. First Walt Hemple, that ass, had all but asked her to seduce Jack Alexander so that she could get *WorldWeek* an exclusive. And then the man in the sports car had come on to her with a line so polished that it had—that she had...

There was no point in trying to pretend she hadn't responded to him. She had, even if it had only been for a second. Well, that was easily explained. She'd been worried sick about missing her flight—and he'd been an expert seducer. 'Let me take you to Martinique' indeed! She blew out her breath and turned her face to the window. Lord, what nonsense.

'Oliver. Hey, Oliver! Why didn't you strip down before you took that shower?'

Dorian smiled and shot back an appropriate answer, and then she turned to the window again. The rain really was heavy, falling as steadily as when she'd first climbed into the stranger's car. Her gaze drifted up to the black sky, to where the landing lights of an approaching plane burned a path into the darkness, and suddenly his voice was in her head, soft and smoky and filled with promise.

'We could go for a walk in the moonlight.'

That was what he'd said. But it was such a corny line. Such a...

Was it raining in Martinique, or was the moon painting a beach with its silvery light? What would have happened if she'd said, yes, take me there, take me with you...?

'Good evening, ladies and gentlemen. On behalf of the Barovnian delegation and the crew of Global Airlines, we welcome you aboard. The captain has asked that you extinguish all cigarettes and...'

Dorian sat up straight and clasped her hands together in her lap. Thank goodness. The plane was moving, heading towards the runway. It was time to get to work.

She had a job to do, and—come hell or high water—she was going to do it well.

The flight seemed endless. Dorian picked at her dinner, passed on the game of pinochle that started across the aisle, and tried not to let the snoring of the man beside her drive her crazy.

What time was it, anyway? She had no idea. Her watch had stopped working, courtesy, no doubt, of its exposure to rain, and the steward had done a vanishing act. All she knew was that she'd been crammed into this narrow space long enough for her toes to have pins and needles in them, for the card game to have ended, and for silence to have finally descended like a curtain over the Press section.

But she was surprised when the seatbelt sign blinked on and she felt the plane tilt gently earthward. It was a nine-hour flight to Barovnia. Surely, they hadn't been in the air that long?

The steward materialised out of nowhere, hurrying quickly up the aisle. Dorian leaned across the motionless

hulk of the reporter asleep beside her and caught hold of
the man's sleeve.

'Excuse me,' she whispered. 'Are we in Barovnia already?'

He shook his head. 'No, miss, we're not.'

'But it feels as if we're coming in for a landing.'

'Yes. Mechanical troubles. Nothing to be alarmed about,
though, I assure you. We'll fix things up and—'

'But where are we?'

Was it her imagination, or did he hesitate? 'Somewhere
in Yugoslavia, I believe.'

'You believe? Don't you know?'

'I really can't say any more, miss.' He gestured towards
the curtain that walled off the Barovnian delegation from
the Press section. 'Security, you know.'

Dorian sighed. 'Once we've landed, can we at least get
out and stretch our legs?'

'Sorry. All passengers will have to stay on board.'

No, Dorian thought a little while later, not all passengers.
It was the Press that had to keep to their cramped quarters
while the plane was on the ground. The steward opened the
front cabin door so that a fresh breeze drifted in, but the
Barovnians—the bigwigs, Dorian's seatmate called them
when the gentle touchdown roused him from his sleep—
were free to get out and move about. She could see them
through the smudged windows, a little knot of men in dark
business suits standing incongruously in the middle of nowhere, caught up in animated conversation witnessed only
by the grey dawn and an airport hangar that had clearly seen
better days.

Dorian frowned. What kind of place was this, anyway?
The runway was all but deserted, save for a couple of small,
light planes that stood off to the side, and it was badly in
need of patching.

Whatever mechanical problems had brought them down
must have been significant, otherwise why would the pilot

have landed at such a desolate spot? And yet—her frown deepened. And yet, no mechanic had so much as come near them. Not even the pilot had emerged to take a look at his craft.

There was no one on the apron at all, except for that cluster of men in dark suits.

All Dorian's instincts went on alert. Something was up, she was certain of it, and, whatever it was, the Barovnians were doing their damnedest to keep it from the planeful of reporters.

Dorian unbuckled her belt. The steward would have some answers, and, by heaven, if she couldn't get them from him, she'd—she'd—

Suddenly, a man stepped from the shadow cast by the plane; he'd apparently just emerged from the cabin. He said nothing, did nothing, but at the sight of him the little knot of conferees fell silent, seemingly commanded by his presence.

Dorian's brows rose. Well, she thought wryly, he was, indeed, an impressive sight. For one thing, he was dressed differently from the others. No dark business suit for him. He wore, instead, a white open-necked embroidered shirt of some silky-looking material, close-fitting black trousers, and knee-high black leather boots. An ancient leather jacket hung casually from his shoulder.

And he wore it all very well. He was tall and lean, with shoulders powerful enough to strain the seams of the shirt. He looked—he looked…

His face was in shadow, yet something about him reminded her of the man who'd rescued her from her broken-down taxi back in New York. No. It wasn't possible. Her rescuer had been the epitome of sophisticated urbanity, but this man—this man was…

Dorian caught her bottom lip between her teeth. Masculine. Fierce. Sexy. He was all of that, but the only other word she could think of to describe him seemed far more accurate.

He was dangerous. A funny tingle danced along her spine; she thought, suddenly, of a story she'd done on a new exhibit at the Bronx Zoo—and of the magnificent black leopard that had been its centrepiece, a creature lithe and splendid in its beauty, yet frightening to look upon because there was no mistaking the tautly controlled power contained within its hard-muscled body.

Dorian went very still. The man was stepping forward, moving out of the plane's shadow. Her heart slammed against her ribs.

He, and the man who'd driven her to the airport, were one.

She watched as the Dark Suits moved towards him. One of them spoke and the others nodded; there was a lot of gesturing, a lot of talking, and then he held up his hand, and they fell silent.

Dorian swung towards her seatmate, who had already laid back his head and closed his eyes, and jabbed him in the shoulder.

'Who is that?' she whispered.

'I'm too tired for guessing-games, Oliver.'

'Come on, take a look. Who's that out there?'

He groaned as he hunched forward and peered past her. 'The Barovnian Ambassador.'

Her heart sank. Dear lord, the man she'd insulted was the Ambassador. Well, she wasn't really surprised. She had seen the deference in the other men's behaviour. He had to be someone important—

'Or do you mean the other guy, the chargé d'affaires? Or the chief legate to the UN? They're all out there, Oliver, even a couple of Alexander's American advisers,' her seatmate said grumpily. 'Which man are you talking about?'

'That one,' she said, twisting towards the window again.

'The one wearing the riding boo…' He was gone, vanished as if by magic. 'He's gone,' Dorian said slowly.

The reporter beside her sighed. 'Goodnight, Oliver. Wake me when we touch down in Barovnia.'

'One last favour. Just tell me which man is Jack Alexander?'

Her seatmate yawned loudly. 'You don't really expect to find Alexander standing around out there?' He yawned again and settled back in his seat. 'Old Jaacov is tucked away in a private compartment up front, sleeping the sleep of the angels. Which is what I intend to do, Oliver. If you wake me again, it'd better be for a damned good reason.'

There already was a damned good reason for staying awake, Dorian thought. Mechanical troubles, the steward had said, but there still wasn't a mechanic in sight—there was only that cluster of men, drawn tightly together, in what appeared to be deep conversation.

She stirred uneasily. Something was up, but whatever was happening, the reporters would be the last to know—unless they found out for themselves.

Her pulse thudded as she got to her feet. The cabin was in darkness, window shades pulled against the pale morning light. Everyone was asleep—at least, they seemed to be, and the steward was nowhere to be seen.

Still, she had to be careful.

She moved quietly, slipping towards the front of the cabin and the door that stood ajar. Her heels clinked lightly on the metal boarding stairs and she held her breath, waiting for someone to shout a warning. But the steward hadn't heard her, and neither had the Dark Suits. They were on the opposite side of the plane—she could see them if she leaned out a little—and they were too caught up in conversation to notice anything else.

Dorian peered to where the ghostly hangar loomed against the lightening sky. Its door stood open. The interior was dark. The only thing she could see was the glint of metal and—and a figure, a tall figure wearing an embroidered white shirt.

She looked around quickly. No one had noticed her yet. There was an open stretch of ground between the plane and the hangar, but if she moved quickly enough... There was a story here, she was sure of it, something that would give her the angle she needed, that would separate her first dispatch from everyone else's.

Besides, what was the absolute worst that could happen if she got caught? A dressing-down from someone in the Barovnian delegation? Hell, any reporter worth the name had lived through that and worse. You were supposed to go after stories aggressively, and if you stepped on toes while you did, well, that was just part of the game.

Still, her adrenalin was pumping as she slipped out from the shadow of the plane. The hangar suddenly seemed a million miles away; her breath was whistling in and out of her lungs by the time she reached it.

She stepped inside the door and flattened against the wall. Her eyes swept the cavernous space. Yes. There was a plane, a small, sleek jet. But the man she'd followed—he was nowhere to be seen.

The jet blocked her view of the rear of the hangar. He was probably back there somewhere. She'd just have to check.

Dorian swallowed. There was a sharply metallic taste in her mouth. It was fear, but there was nothing to be afraid of. After all, what could possibly—?

A sudden loud whine filled the hangar. She spun around, hand to her throat, and as she did the whining noise increased until it was a roar.

Dorian's eyes widened. The plane—*her* plane—was—oh, God, it was moving. It was moving! It was racing down the runway and—

A hand, hard as steel, fell on her shoulder, the fingers biting sharply into her flesh.

'What in hell are you doing here?' a harsh, angry voice demanded.

She swung around again and stared into the furious face of the man she'd been following.

'The—the plane,' she stammered. 'It's leaving!'

His mouth curved downwards. 'I asked you a question, Miss Oliver. What in God's name are you doing here?'

Dorian shook her head. 'Didn't you hear me? Our plane—it's taken off. It's left us behind.'

He laughed coldly. 'A brilliant assessment. I suppose these are the superb sorts of intellectual skills that make you the fine reporter you are.'

'Dammit, don't you understand?' She twisted away from his hand. 'The plane to Barovnia just took off.'

He looked at her for a long, silent moment, and then he nodded. 'Yes.' His tone was clipped. 'It did exactly that.'

'But—but how could it? How could that happen? Didn't they know that we—?'

'How did you get off that plane?'

'The same way you did. I simply—'

She cried out as he caught hold of her again. 'There's nothing simple about it, Miss Oliver. You were told to stay on board.'

'Let go of me. Do you hear me?'

'You were given orders.'

'I don't take ''orders'',' Dorian said sharply.

His mouth thinned. 'So it would seem.'

Dorian's heart was slowing as things began to fall into place. There'd been a mistake, that was apparent. The plane had taken off without them, and if her absence hadn't yet been noticed surely his would be. The plane would turn around and come back for them in just a few minutes.

'Pretty sloppy security,' she said smugly.

'Yes.' His voice was grim. 'My thoughts precisely.'

'I mean, if they didn't notice that *you* were missing—'

'Didn't anyone try to stop you from leaving, Miss Oliver?'

'It's going to make a terrific story, though. "Two left behind at..."'' She cried out as his grasp tightened. 'You're hurting me!'

'Two? Is that all your report will say? Just, "two"?' He stepped closer to her and his voice became a purr. 'No names, Miss Oliver?'

'I don't know your name,' she said, gritting her teeth against the pressure of his hand. 'And even if I did—'

'Don't you?'

'I only know that you've been the perfect gentleman from the moment we met.' She forced a cold smile to her lips. 'Manhandling me in the car, manhandling me now—'

'You're lucky that's all I'm doing.' His face darkened. 'Just why the hell did you follow me?'

'I didn't follow you. Not exactly. I just knew something was going on.'

His hand fell away from her. 'Did you.'

His tone was flat, turning the question into a statement. Dorian felt a chill tiptoe up her spine. In the excitement, she'd almost forgotten why she'd come after him in the first place, her conviction that something was happening that no one was supposed to know about.

Now, the feeling returned. She'd been right; something was going on.

But what? And what part did this man have in it?

Her chin rose in defiance. 'Yes,' she said, bluffing, 'and you might as well give me the details.'

He gave a short, sharp laugh. 'An exclusive interview, is that it?'

'Why not?' Dorian looked outside. The sun had risen; the sky was a pale, cloudless blue. 'We've plenty of time. The plane's not in sight yet, and—'

He laughed again and put his hands on his hips. 'Isn't it?' he said, as if she'd made some clever joke.

She hesitated. There was something in the way he was watching her that made her feel uneasy.

'For a start, who are you, anyway?'

'I thought you already had all the facts, Miss Oliver.'

'I never said that.' She trotted after him as he turned and began walking further into the hangar. 'What I meant was that there was time for you to tell me—'

She gasped as he swung towards her and caught her by the wrist.

'Exactly what do you know?'

'What do I...?'

'I've not time for games,' he said brusquely. 'Answer the question, dammit. What do you know?'

Dorian swallowed. 'Well, well... I know that we didn't really have mechanical problems.'

'And?'

'And—and...'

She fell silent. He stared at her for a long moment, and then he laughed.

'I should have known it was a bluff.' He let go of her and turned away. 'The answer's no,' he called over his shoulder.

'No?' What did that mean?

He stopped alongside the plane and ran his hand lightly along the burnished silver fuselage. 'No, I will not give you an interview.'

'But we have time before the plane comes back for us,' she said when she reached him.

He stepped to the wing and peered upwards. 'They won't.'

'Who won't?' Dorian ducked beneath the wing and scrambled after him. 'For goodness' sake, Mr—Mr whatever your name is, can't you speak in whole sentences? Who won't do what?'

He took his time, patting the silver skin as if the plane were a live creature, and then, at last, he turned to her.

'My name,' he said coldly, 'is Prince. Jake Prince.' He folded his arms across his chest. 'And what they won't do, Miss Oliver, is turn that plane around and come back for us.'

Dorian laughed. 'Oh, but they must. They can't just—'

'They can and will.' His voice was grim. 'The plane will go straight on to Barovnia.' He glanced at the little jet. 'And so will I.'

'In that, you mean? But I don't understand.'

'Then let me clarify things,' he said, his eyes never leaving her face. 'And let me do it in whole sentences, just so we're both certain you get the message.'

Dorian's cheeks reddened. 'I didn't mean—'

'Your colleagues—the ones who had brains enough to stay on board that plane—will land in Barovnia in a couple of hours.' He stepped beneath the jet, bent down, and removed the locking pins from the landing gear. 'It may take me a little longer,' he said, frowning as he walked slowly around the plane and scanned it, 'but I'll be there in plenty of time for a late breakfast.'

She stared at him. 'But—but what about me?'

He turned and looked at her. 'What about you?'

'You're not...' She took a deep breath. 'You're not thinking of leaving me here. You wouldn't do that, would you?'

'Wouldn't I?' He gave her a quick, wolfish smile. 'Have I mentioned that I'm of Barovnian ancestry, Miss Oliver?'

'No, you haven't. But what's that got to do with—?'

'I was born in that "primitive little country" you hold in so much contempt.'

Dorian paled. 'Look, just because I said some things—'

'Which makes me a barbarian. Wasn't that what we agreed?'

'No.' She shook her head. 'No, we didn't. It was you who said that. I never—'

'Reporters,' he said, his mouth twisting as if the word were bitter on his tongue. 'You're all alike—you think you can stick your noses in where they don't belong and never pay the consequences.'

Dorian drew in her breath. 'Look,' she began, 'I'm only doing my job. Your people invited the Press to come along on this junket. If you wanted to keep things from us, you—'

'And there's another thing. I did not manhandle you.'

'Mr Prince—'

'Not that I didn't come damned close.'

'What's that supposed to mean?'

He moved quickly, like the panther of which he'd reminded her. He was next to her before she could react, his hands on her shoulders as he drew her to him. '*This* is what I did,' he said, and his mouth dropped to hers in a quick, almost savage kiss. It lasted only an instant, and then he stepped back and gave her another of those cold, terrible smiles. 'Now,' he said softly, 'do we understand each other?'

'You're despicable,' she whispered. 'You're—you're…'

He laughed when she sputtered to silence.

'Don't tell me you've run out of adjectives, kitten. Where's the journalistic skill you're so proud of?'

Her eyes flashed with indignation. 'Don't you dare call me that again, dammit!'

'If you don't want to rot in this God-forsaken place,' he said briskly, as he turned away, 'you'd better get a move on. I want to be airborne in five minutes.'

'You're the most—the most horrible…' She caught her breath. *You'd better get a move on.* She touched the tip of her tongue to her lips. 'You'll—you'll take me with you?'

He turned, his hands on his hips. 'Tell me how to avoid it,' he said unpleasantly, 'and I'll be happy to oblige.'

Dorian nodded, trying not to let herself look as surprised—and relieved—as she felt.

'You're quite right. Deserting me here would only be bad publicity for—'

She gasped as he caught hold of her wrist. 'Just remember something. This is no cushy chartered flight.'

'Let go of me, please.'

'And I am not a steward, or one of your fellow reporters.' His eyes swept across her face. 'It would be a waste of time to try using that pretty face to get what you want, Miss Oliver. I'm not about to fall for the same nonsense you use on everybody else.'

'I get the message,' she said stiffly. 'Now, if you'd let go—'

'Just remember something. Once you set foot in that plane, you're nothing but an unwelcome passenger.'

Dorian stared at him, enraged. What a cold, unforgiving bastard he was. But what choice did she have?

'As I said before, Mr Prince,' she said finally, 'you're a true gentleman.'

He stared into her eyes while the seconds ticked away, and then he let go of her.

'Let's get started, then.'

He turned towards the boarding stairs. Dorian made a face at his retreating back as she massaged her aching wrist.

There were certain irrefutable truths about Jake Prince. He had lots of money. He could, when the occasion demanded it, turn on the charm. And he was, without question, the best-looking man she'd ever met.

But none of that was enough to make up for the fact that he was, first and foremost, an insolent, egotistical son of a bitch—and she could hardly wait for the moment she could shove that fact directly under his handsome, arrogant nose.

CHAPTER FOUR

SUNRISE was different when you saw it from the cockpit of a jet streaking across the sky. Dorian had seen the rising sun paint the towers of Manhattan in pale gold; she'd watched it blaze across the wheaten plains of her native Minnesota. But nothing had prepared her for the transfiguring glory of morning viewed from this lofty height.

The sun was a fierce golden ball, burning away the last remnants of the night. Below, mountain peaks burst into flames that spilled down into the valleys and banished darkness.

Dorian sighed. It was a breathtaking way to greet the day. It was just too bad that she had to share it seated beside Jake Prince—however, considering the circumstances, she supposed she had to be grateful she was sitting here at all.

He had not said a word to her since they'd left the ground, but then, he didn't have to. The set of his jaw, the stiffness of his spine spoke volumes. He resented her presence, and he had no intention of pretending otherwise.

She thought of those last moments in the hangar and how it had seemed he might leave her behind.

It hadn't been such an unreasonable fear. The truth was, she had no way of knowing what this man would do. He was not only a stranger, he was an absolute enigma, the more so as time passed. Each time she thought she had him figured out, he changed—almost before her very eyes—into someone else.

Who was Jake Prince, really?

Initially, Dorian would have had no difficulty describing him. He was a man used to money. The car, the clothes, the pricey watch were clearly all second nature. He had a smooth, sexy line and dark good looks that had to be appealing to many women. He was a man who had been handed all of life's goodies on a silver platter.

But there was, it seemed, quite another side to him. He was a man of influence and power in the Barovnian delegation. What she'd witnessed on the runway was proof enough of that. As for that easy charm he'd used on her when they'd first met—it gave way quickly enough to a steely determination.

He was not a man to be crossed, she thought, remembering again those moments in his car and the hangar.

She gave him a quick glance from under the dark sweep of her lashes. What was the great secret he'd been afraid she might know? What was he doing, making this very private flight to Barovnia? She had asked him about it the moment they were airborne, and his response had been direct, cold, and condescending.

'Don't waste your breath and my time, Miss Oliver. I've no intention of providing you or your magazine with bits of titillating gossip.'

Dorian's reply had been as swift as his. '*WorldWeek* doesn't deal in gossip, Mr Prince,' she'd said. 'We're a news magazine. We provide information to our readers. If you'd ever bothered reading an issue, you'd know that.'

'Your publication is like every other glossy scandal sheet, Miss Oliver. It's not interested in fact.' His lips curled with distaste. 'You start out with preconceived notions, and you look around until you find something to support them. Then you print some trivia you label significant—and God knows how many fools rush out to plunk down their money just to be misinformed.'

'Has it ever occurred to you,' Dorian demanded, 'that *you* might be the one who's misinformed? I'm a reporter, Mr Prince, not a—a scandal columnist. And my magazine—'

'There's nothing to debate. I am not going to be interviewed.'

Lord, the arrogance of the man! Dorian swung towards him. 'I hate to disappoint you, Mr Prince,' she said with saccharine sweetness, 'but I'm not interested in interviewing you, necessarily. I'm only interested in…' Dorian frowned. 'Which reminds me—what's your relationship to Jaacov Alexandrei, anyway?'

'Perhaps you didn't understand me, Miss Oliver. I'm not going to give you any information at all.'

'But that's—that's ridiculous! Surely you can tell me what part you play in the delegation. Are you one of his American advisers? Are you an old friend? Are you some sort of Barovnian representative?'

Prince ignored her questions. 'As for this little trip of ours,' he said coldly, 'I wouldn't waste time planning on ways to work it into your dispatches to your magazine.'

'And what, exactly, is that supposed to mean?' she demanded.

'It means that this flight—and my part in it—are, for the moment, not for publication for *WorldWeek's* eager readers.'

'You can't be serious.'

'I've never been more serious in my life. This flight is strictly off the record.'

'This may come as a surprise to you,' she said through her teeth, 'but there are laws about a free Press.'

'In the United States, yes. But—in case you haven't noticed—you're not in the United States any more.' He'd looked directly at her then, his face a hostile mask. 'I suggest you spend the rest of the flight thinking about what that means.'

And Dorian had done just that as the plane droned through the sky. Could he really keep her from filing whatever story she chose? At first, she assured herself that he could not. Barovnia might be still languishing in the Middle Ages, but she was an American citizen and a member of the Press, at that. She'd write what she damned well wanted.

But could she file it? She shifted uneasily in her seat. She had no idea what kinds of facilities she'd find in Barovnia, but if the Press's access to telephones and telegraphs was controlled or limited by the government it might be impossible to send stuff back to New York without interference.

What was so hush-hush about this flight, anyway? Dorian glanced at the man seated beside her. Why was Jake Prince at the controls of this little jet instead of in the cabin of the Barovnian charter?

She blew out her breath. And yet those weren't the million-dollar questions. The big one—the one that really needed answering—was the one that was at the heart of everything that had happened in the past hour.

What part did Jake Prince play in this story?

Dorian had come up with some theories, but each had holes.

Was he a Barovnian diplomat?

It hardly seemed likely. No diplomat would behave with as little tact as this man.

He might be one of Alexander's American advisers. But what American adviser would be powerful enough to say that he'd be the one to decide what a member of the Press could write?

And he really didn't seem terribly American. There was something about him, an air of masculine insolence he wore like a badge of honour, that suggested he hadn't come of age on the same side of the Atlantic as she had.

Dorian frowned. Jake Prince was an enigma. What sort of man could command a clutch of diplomats with a look? Or climb aboard a sleek, fast-moving plane and handle it with the same nonchalant ease he'd handled his sports car? Whatever he was, he was certainly not simply the rich, handsome playboy she'd written him off as at first.

Dorian's heartbeat stuttered. Prince. Jake Prince...

No. No, he couldn't be. It was impossible. She couldn't have got so lucky.

'…belt secured?'

She looked up, startled. 'Did you—did you say something?'

He nodded. 'I asked if your belt was secured.'

Her brain was spinning. Prince, she thought, *Prince*…

'Dammit, lady, it's not a very difficult question. Is the belt closed?'

'Yes. Yes, it is.' She touched the tip of her tongue to her lips. There had to be a way to keep the conversation going. 'Uh, why do you ask?'

He gave a negligible shrug. 'Just a precaution.'

'Just a precaution,' she repeated foolishly. Later, she would remember that simple statement and wonder at her inability to pick up on the meaning hidden within it. But just now she was too busy concentrating on what fate might have dropped into her lap to pay attention to reality.

'There's nothing to worry about, Miss Oliver. Just sit back and relax.'

Silence filled the cockpit again. Think, Dorian told herself, think! Keep him talking. There's got to be something…

She cleared her throat. 'I—uh—I suppose flying a plane like this takes a lot of training?'

Prince nodded. 'Yes.'

'It—umm—it must take a lot of skill.'

'Some.'

'And—uh—experience.'

'Right.'

It was all she could do to keep from groaning. Yes. Some. Right. At this rate, it would take the entire flight before she got a whole sentence from him.

She cleared her throat again. 'Have you been flying long?' He glanced across at her and she smiled politely. 'I mean, did you take it up recently, or have you always done it?'

It was, she knew, an inane question and yet, to her amazement, it did the trick. Jake Prince gave her a genuine smile—and an entire sentence in response.

'What you're asking is, do I really know how to handle this aircraft. Is that the question, Miss Oliver?'

Dorian clasped her hands in her lap. 'Yes,' she said, smiling back at him. 'That's right.'

'Well, you can breathe easy. I've had more than a thousand hours in planes like this one.'

'Is that a lot?' she asked pleasantly. 'I don't know anything at all about flying.'

'It's enough.'

He fell silent again, and Dorian's brain began whirling. Keep him talking, she thought furiously. Don't let him stop now.

'Well, that's good to hear. I've always wondered why airlines don't give passengers information about their pilots. You know the sort of thing I mean.' She gave a little laugh. 'Name. Place of birth. Experience.'

'Would it make you feel better if I said I've been flying since I was eighteen?'

He was clever, she had to give him that. He'd managed to neatly evade the two questions that really mattered. Still, it was the first bit of personal information he'd given her.

'Have you?' She smiled. 'You've been flying for quite a while, then?'

He nodded and shifted his long legs under the console. 'Almost twenty years.'

Her smile expanded. Another bit of information. Jake Prince was almost thirty-eight. How old, she wondered, was Jaacov Alexandrei? If only she hadn't left all that stuff from the research file on the floor of the taxi...

'Well,' she said brightly, 'that's interesting.'

His head swivelled towards her. 'Is it?'

'Oh, yes, absolutely. I never—I mean, it's so unusual to meet someone who knows how to fly...' Why was he watching her with such sudden intensity?

'Really?' He smiled politely.

'Really.' She hesitated. 'So, what else do you do? Besides fly, I mean.'

He leaned towards the console. 'I work,' he said, tapping his knuckle lightly against a gauge.

'At what?' His head came up, and she swallowed drily. Careful, she thought, careful, careful... 'I mean, I've never met anyone who—who knew how to fly before. I just wondered if you'd learned as part of—part of your job, or—or...' Why was he looking at her that way? Dorian's tongue felt as if it were tangling in her mouth. 'Or in the air force, perhaps,' she said desperately. 'Lots of young men learn to fly in the air force.'

'No, I took private lessons.'

If only she had her notepad, she thought furiously. Or her tape recorder. But both were tucked inside her bag, lying uselessly beneath her empty seat on the chartered jet. But it would be OK. She had a good memory. All she had to do now was find a way to get him to confirm her most important suspicion.

'In the good old USA.' He glanced over at her. 'That's the answer to your next question, isn't it?'

It took all her effort not to smile. Whoever Jake Prince was—even if he was the headline catch of a lifetime—he was, when you got right down to it, like every other human being in the world.

He loved to talk about himself and about his own interests. If she'd used her head and realised that from the start, she'd have—

'Unless, of course, you made the assumption that a country as primitive as Barovnia wouldn't have airplanes.'

Dorian looked up quickly. He was still smiling pleasantly, but an edge had crept into his tone.

'Why, no—no, I didn't make any assump—'

'Stop talking rubbish, Miss Oliver.'

She blinked. 'What?'

His smile fled, leaving his face cold and hard as granite. 'Do you think I'm a fool? All this charming chatter, the pretty smiles—I told you it wouldn't work on me.'

'But I wasn't—'

'Please, don't insult my intelligence.' He leaned towards the control panel again and tapped his finger against a dial. 'I know how you people operate.'

'You people?'

'I've dealt with reporters before. I know better than to trust them.'

'Mr Prince, I don't know what kinds of reporters you've known, but *WorldWeek* stands for honest reporting, and I—'

'Do you know what an oxymoron is, Miss Oliver? It's a figure of speech, using words that contradict each other.' He gave her a tight smile. 'Military intelligence, for example. Or holy war.'

Dorian's chin lifted. 'Look here, Mr Prince—'

'But my favourite is "honest reporting".' His smile grew even more grim. 'So before you toss out whatever lies you think will get you a scoop or an exclusive or whatever in hell it is you and your pals would sell your souls for—'

There was a bang, and a sudden, shrill whine filled the cabin. The plane began to shudder, and all at once Dorian's argument with Jake Prince didn't seem terribly vital.

'What's wrong?' she demanded.

Prince didn't answer, but then, Dorian thought wildly, how could he? He was flicking switches on the control panel with a swift precision that was, in itself, terrifying.

'Mr Prince? What is it?'

'We've lost an engine.'

'We've—we've lost an engine?' Her gaze fell to the sweep of mountains below, to their snow-capped peaks rising razor-sharp against the blue sky, and her heart seemed to stop beating. 'Are we going to crash?'

Prince shook his head. 'No. We can make it on one engine.' He hit another switch, and the plane steadied itself.

Dorian closed her eyes. 'Thank God,' she whispered. 'For a moment there, I thought—' Her words tumbled to a halt. The plane was losing altitude, heading slowly but steadily downwards. She swung towards him, her eyes wide. 'We're going down.'

He nodded. 'Yes.' His eyes never left the windscreen. 'Make sure that belt's tight, Miss Oliver.'

'But you said—'

'I know what I said.' His mouth narrowed into a grim line. 'This plane is designed so that it can fly on one engine—but, considering what lies ahead, I think prudence is the better part of valour.'

Dorian looked from Jake Prince's granite-like profile to the mountains ahead. Her hand went to her throat. They made the mountains that had preceded them seem insignificant, and she knew, without question, that he was right.

'I see.' Her voice shook a little. This was it, then. She was in a plane with a man she didn't know, in a place she'd never been, and they were about to crash.

'No.' His voice was clipped. 'You don't see. We're not going to crash.'

'You don't have to pretend,' she said quietly. 'Whatever's going to happen will happen.'

He reached across the narrow cockpit and put his hand over hers. Instinctively, she let her fingers curl into its comforting strength.

'There's a plateau ahead—do you see it?'

He jerked his chin towards the south and she followed the gesture.

'You mean, that little patch of grass?'

Prince nodded. 'We can set down there.'

'It doesn't look very large,' Dorian said softly.

His hand tightened on hers. 'Trust me, Dorian. I've landed in less space than that.' He gave her a quick smile. 'It'll just be a little bumpy.'

The ground was rushing up faster and faster. Dorian swallowed, then returned his smile as bravely as she could.

'Then I suppose it's a good thing we didn't have dinner service on this flight, isn't it? I'd hate to spill coffee all over my lap.'

He grinned. 'We'll have champagne on our next flight together, I promise.' He gave her hand one last squeeze, and then he clasped the control yoke. 'Just think positive thoughts,' he said, 'and before you know it we'll be down safe.'

Dorian nodded, but it was too late to think anything. The earth was coming up to meet them at an alarming speed. At the last minute, just before the wheels touched down, she closed her eyes tightly. There was a wrenching thud, a rushing noise, and then—and then silence.

'Dorian?'

She sat absolutely still, half afraid that if she opened her eyes she would see something awful.

'Dorian. Are you all right?'

She swallowed. 'I—I think so.'

She heard the clink of metal, the whisper of fabric, and then the touch of a hand on her face.

'Dorian. Look at me.'

Her eyes opened slowly. Jake was bending over her, his face dark. With anger, she thought—but then, suddenly, he blew out his breath and dropped to one knee beside her.

'You're all right,' he said.

She nodded. 'I think so. Yes. Yes, I'm fine.' She laughed shakily. 'Just a little scared.'

His hand stroked her cheek lightly. 'You've a right to be scared.'

She swallowed. 'Actually, it's more like terrified.'

He smiled, and she thought suddenly that it was a very nice smile, and that he had not smiled at her that way since—since just before he'd kissed her that first time at the airport.

'You should have trusted me,' he said. 'I told you I'd get us down in one piece.'

Dorian looked at him. Why should I have trusted you? she wanted to say. After all, you don't trust me.

But he was right not to trust her, wasn't he? Just before the engine had conked out she'd been playing games, trying to wheedle a story out of him while he—he had made her a promise and kept it.

Still, he hadn't been entirely truthful with her. She didn't know who he was. Although she had an idea. A damned good idea.

Her eyes lifted to his. 'Mr Prince?'

He smiled again. 'Yes?'

She touched her tongue to her lips; his gaze followed the gesture, then returned to hers.

'Considering the circumstances...' She paused. 'I—I—I have a question.'

'Yes,' he said softly, 'so do I.'

He bent and kissed her, his mouth warm and seeking against hers. She drew back in surprise and his arms went around her and gathered her close. Her lips parted. She told herself it was to whisper a protest, but when she felt the first brush of his tongue against hers a soft sound came unbidden from the back of her throat. Her hands came up; she leaned into him and caught hold of his shirt, clutching it tightly in her fingers, and the race of her heart and the pound of her blood obliterated all reality.

It was he who ended the kiss. 'Kitten,' he whispered.

Dorian's eyes opened slowly. He was holding her a breath from him; she knew that the flush of desire that crimsoned his cheekbones must be matched by her own.

It was hard to talk, at first. 'Jake.' She stared into his eyes. 'I didn't mean...'

He smiled. 'At least you've answered my question,' he said softly. 'I was going to ask if you didn't think it was time you called me Jake?'

Dorian hesitated. 'Is that—is that really your name?'

'What do you mean?'

'Well, it occurred to me that—that you just might be...'
She swallowed. 'I was wondering if you might be the
abdhan of Barovnia.'

Desire left his face. He looked at her coldly as he stepped
back and rose to his feet.

'I suppose I should have expected that. A good reporter
never stops thinking about her story, does she?'

'It's a logical question, Jake. You can't blame me for
thinking—'

'Let me put your mind at ease, then. I am not the *abdhan*.
And the only thing you'd better think about is that we've
got to get out of here, and fast.'

She frowned. 'Shouldn't we wait with the plane? How
else will the search party find us?'

Jake moved past her into the cabin. 'There won't be a
search party.'

'Don't be silly. Once you put out an SOS—'

'I'm not going to draw my people in here, Dorian.'

'In where?' she said, staring at him. 'What in heaven's
name are you talking about?'

'We've come down in the middle of the Askara
Wilderness,' he said as he pulled open a locker and reached
inside it.

'What does that mean?'

'It means,' he said grimly, 'that you're going to get the
chance to take a long, hard look at a primitive territory
inhabited by barbarians.'

Dorian got to her feet and put her hands on her hips.
'Very funny. But I've apologised for that remark too many
times as it is. It's time you stopped trotting it out at every
opportunity.'

'There's nothing even remotely funny about our situation.' He was stuffing things into the sack as he spoke. Two
lap blankets. Chocolate bars. A couple of cans of Coke.

'This is a place where it's impossible to tell the good guys from the bad. So, unless you want to risk researching what it's like to be the night's entertainment, you'd better get your pretty butt in gear and follow me.'

Dorian blinked. 'You're joking.'

Jake looked at her. 'Do I look as if I'm joking?' he asked coldly.

No, she thought, he didn't. But he couldn't really be serious. A primitive territory? Bad guys you couldn't tell from good guys? Barbarians?

And all at once she understood. The engine malfunction had been real enough—instinct told her that Jake Prince wasn't the sort of man who'd fake something as dangerous as a landing on a plateau the size of a breadboard—but the rest was nonsense. He'd seen his chance to make her eat her words about primitive countries and barbarians, and he'd leaped at it. This was payback—an exhausting hike to Kadar, the capital of Barovnia, which was probably an hour or two away—and he'd have had the last laugh.

Well, he could just take his nasty little scheme and shove it.

Dorian smiled sweetly. 'Are you ready to leave?'

Jake nodded as he snugged the sack shut and hoisted it on his shoulder.

'Yes. The Cristou Mountains are just ahead, and—'

'Well, then, have a good trip.'

He straightened and stared at her. 'What?'

'I said, have a good trip. I'll stay here and wait.'

Jake's eyes went flat. 'For what? I've just told you—'

'I know what you told me.' She shrugged lazily. 'I'll take my chances with the—what do you call the people who inhabit this place?'

'Dorian. Listen to me.'

Her smile fled. 'No,' she said, shaking her head, '*you* listen for a change. I know what this is all about. I know what you're up to. You're determined to make me eat my words about—about—you know, the primitive country thing, and—'

'Do you really think I'm that petty?' he asked quietly.

For a second, her resolve faltered. But then she looked into his cold eyes, and her spine stiffened.

'I'm not budging. If you're going, you go alone.'

'Get up, Dorian.'

His voice was ominously soft. But she was tired of being intimidated by this man. It was time to put a stop to it.

'No. I'm not going with you.'

'Get up!'

She stared at him. He looked suddenly dangerous, and she thought again of the panther, but it was too late to back off.

'I'm not taking orders from you, Jake.'

He stepped closer. The look on his face made it difficult not to shrink back in defence, but she held her ground.

'I've no time to play games,' he said.

'Good. Then you'll stop all this foolishness, turn on the radio, and call for help. Or must I do it my—?'

She cried out as he bent towards her, but he didn't touch her. Instead, he reached for the microphone and ripped it from the console.

'Hey,' she said. Doubt crept into her voice. 'What'd you do that for?'

'Just in case you get any ideas. I told you, I don't want my people drawn into this place. Now.' He straightened and stared down at her. 'Are you coming with me or aren't you?'

Dorian gave a nervous laugh. 'Come on, Jake. Don't you think you're carrying this a little too far…?'

Her voice drifted to silence as he pushed open the door. 'Good luck,' he said, and then, to her absolute astonishment, he dropped lightly to the ground and trotted off across the silent meadow.

CHAPTER FIVE

OBVIOUSLY, Jake didn't know when it was time to admit he'd lost the game.

Dorian blew out a breath. It had taken a moment to figure out, but once she had it all fell into place. Jake had expected her to swallow his fanciful tale of bogeymen and danger, and when she hadn't he'd been caught short. That arrogant male pride of his had kept him from admitting that he'd invented the story, and so he'd marched off across the meadow without so much as a backward glance.

She shaded her eyes with her hands and watched his receding figure. The only question now was what would happen next. How long would he let her stew in her own juices before he came back to collect her? Because that was what he'd have to do. Despite all the dramatics with the radio, there would undoubtedly be a search party on the way, and he couldn't very well let it find her alone.

Dorian smiled. She could just imagine him trying to explain his way out of that situation.

'Jake Prince went off and left me here,' she would say bravely, first for her rescuers and then for the media. 'I suppose he thought he would be safe, leaving a defenceless woman alone in a—a wilderness. I guess he thought he would never be found out. I mean, he kept reminding me that no one knew I was on board the plane with him.'

She laughed softly as the dark forest swallowed him up. 'Sorry, Jake,' she murmured as she settled in to wait. 'I'm afraid you've underestimated me.'

She wondered again how long it would take him to come

trudging back. He had, at best, only minutes to play with—
and then, she thought smugly, he would have to admit de-
feat.

At first, she watched the forest, waiting for the first sign of
Jake's return, but after a while that got dull and so she
kicked off her shoes and sat down in the open doorway,
gazing around the plateau instead, watching the grass and
the few spring wild flowers that had already blossomed bend
under the gentle whisper of the breeze.

But none of that made time move any more quickly. It
seemed to have come to a standstill, and she told herself
that it was only because her watch had stopped working.
When you couldn't see the minutes change, they seemed to
drag. She remembered a day last winter when the newsroom
clock had gone on the blink and everybody had joked about
not knowing whether they'd put in eight hours or eighteen
without its pulsing digital face to read.

But it did seem as if Jake had been gone quite a while.
How far would he push this nonsense, anyway? She began
to think about what excuse he'd offer when he had to come
back and face her, and gradually she decided that only one
had any possibilities at all.

All right, he'd say in a brusque, no-nonsense voice, I
misjudged where we came down. This isn't the Askara
Wilderness at all. There's a road just beyond those trees and,
surprise, surprise, Kadar is an easy couple of miles away
and you won't mind just going for that brief stroll with me,
will you, Dorian?

She smiled. 'Really, Jake,' she said into the silence.

Her voice seemed loud, almost unnatural, an alien presence intruding on the warm air, and she felt a faint stir of
uneasiness. What a strange place this was, this deserted sea
of grass. There wasn't any sign of life out there, not even
a bird or an insect.

And the silence. It was so total. So complete. So—so
penetrating.

Jake would probably tell her there was no such thing, that the phrase was—what had he called it? An oxymoron. But how else could you describe such quiet? It *was* penetrating. She could hear it drumming in her ears, feel the heaviness of it in each breath she took.

If only Jake would come back.

Dorian caught her bottom lip between her teeth. Just so she could tell him what she thought of him, of course. That was why she wanted to see him come striding across the meadow, so she could look him straight in the eye and say, Jake Prince, you damned fool, don't you think you've…?

What was that?

Her heart leaped like a frightened rabbit, lodging somewhere between her throat and her breasts. Something was out there. She'd heard it, a sound, a low sound, like—like…

'Jake?' she whispered.

She waited, pulse thudding, but there was only silence. That terrible, unnatural silence. It took all her courage to lean forward and peer cautiously out of the door. But there was nothing to see. Of course there wasn't. There was nothing out there but grass. The endless grass, stretching to the dark, dark trees.

Dorian wrapped her arms around herself.

'You're playing straight into his hands,' she muttered to herself. If she kept this up, she'd be a basket case by the time Jake returned, and that was what he wanted, wasn't it? He'd stalked off and left her here because she hadn't fallen for his silly stories; he had to be counting on her going to pieces while he was gone, then doing something ridiculous when he reappeared, something she would never be able to live down.

She blew out her breath. What she had to do was concentrate on something else. On—on what had happened so far. Jake had said she couldn't write about their flight, but who was he to give orders? This whole thing would make terrific copy. The mysterious flight. The forced landing. And Jake. Jake would make the best copy of all.

Did he really think she couldn't write about him just because he'd refused to give her any information about himself? A smug little smile curled across Dorian's mouth. She knew enough about the enigmatic Mr Prince to make *WorldWeek's* readers forget their morning coffee.

Jake Prince, the arrogant, opinionated mystery-man of the Barovnian delegation, spent the morning alone with this reporter. Although his relationship with Jack Alexander, the man who may well be the next Barovnian abdhan, *is not clear, it is obvious that he has the power to influence many of the policies the* abdhan *will…*

And he knew something. Something big. She was sure of that. He was hiding a secret, the kind that would make a name for the journalist who unearthed it, and she was determined to be the one who did.

Dorian frowned. It wouldn't be easy, though. Jake had said he'd tell her nothing, and he didn't strike her as the sort of man who ever went back on his word. He was harsh, he was hard. He was insolent and cold and totally unapproachable, but she couldn't imagine him saying something and not following through…

And he'd asked her to go away with him, a lifetime ago, before he'd known who she was or where she was going. What would have happened if she'd said yes? Would he have given up his role—whatever it was—in the delegation for a night with her? Would they have walked along the beach in the moonlight? Would he have taken her in his arms and kissed her and kissed her until they sank down into the sand, until…?

Oh, God!

There it was again, that sound. Dorian felt the blood draining down to her toes. There was definitely someone out there, just as Jake had said. Why had she ever thought he'd made the whole thing up? He wasn't a man who played get-even games: if he were, she'd still be standing at the airport, trying to figure out how to tell her boss she'd been blackballed from the flight to Barovnia.

The sound came again, carried on the breeze, this time accompanied by a metallic clank, like a bell pealing mournfully in hell.

Dorian moaned, jammed her fist against her lips, and scooted deeper into the plane. Whoever was out there was coming closer. And that sound—that pitiful, keening sound, was enough to—to...

Her shoulders hit the wall, and she turned her face to it. 'Jake,' she whispered, 'Jake, please...'

There was a scrabbling sound at the door, and she swung towards it, her fists upraised in defence and terror in her heart...

It was Jake, Jake silhouetted in the doorway. She uttered a sob and flew to him, wrapping her arms tightly around his neck, savouring the comfort of his embrace as his arms closed around her.

'What is it?' he demanded. His voice hoarsened with concern. 'Are you hurt? What happened?'

She shook her head as she burrowed deeper into his arms. 'No,' she said, her voice shaky and muffled against his shoulder. 'I'm all right now.' She could hear the steady thud-thud of his heart, smell the sunlight and the meadow grasses in his scent, and she knew suddenly that she had never in her life felt this safe before.

He held her for a long moment, and then he clasped her shoulders, drew back, and looked into her face.

'I shouldn't have left you,' he said grimly. 'Hell. I knew it the minute I—'

'It was my fault,' she said breathlessly as she peered past him. 'I should have believed you. Oh, Jake, there's someone—there's someone...' She went stiff in his arms.

'Dorian? What...?'

A black and white cow stepped delicately out of the trees

and into the meadow, mooing plaintively to the sound of the brass bell that hung from its neck.

Suddenly, all Dorian's pent-up rage came tumbling out. Her boss had humiliated her, Jake had humiliated her, and now this—this stupid beast had finished the job.

She drew a deep breath and wrenched free of him.

'You—you rat,' she spat. 'You worthless bastard. You— you...'

Jake's brows rose. 'I take it you're feeling better,' he said drily.

'The hell with you, Jake Prince.' She slammed her fist against his chest. 'Lying to me, making me think that—that there were things out there...'

He caught hold of her wrist before she could hit him again. 'There *are* things out there,' he said tightly.

'Cows,' she said, spitting out the word as if it were a curse. 'That's what's out there. Cows!'

Jake glanced over his shoulder. 'Yes.' There was no humour in his voice. 'That's right—which means we've more reason than ever to get out of here now.'

'Oh, please! I've milked far too many cows to run from one now, Jake. I hate to tell you this, but the party's over.'

A quick smile twisted across his mouth. 'Cows, Miss Oliver? At *WorldWeek* magazine?'

'At home, in Minnesota, not that it's any of your business.' She gritted her teeth as she twisted uselessly against his hand, then raised her reddened face to his. 'All right, you've had your fun. You filled me full of lies and I swallowed just enough of them to go to pieces over nothing. Are you satisfied?'

Jake's mouth curved downwards. 'I'll be satisfied when we've got the hell out of here,' he said. He glanced down at her feet. 'Go on, get your shoes on and let's get moving.'

'Uh-uh.' Dorian shook her head and crossed her arms over her breast.

'Uh-uh?' He went very still. 'What does that mean?'

'It means,' she said with great precision, 'that nothing's changed. I am not budging from this plane.'

He smiled. Although it was not really a smile, she thought suddenly. It was—it was just a drawing back of his lips, a quick flash of white teeth, and it sent a shiver down her spine.

'I could have been almost to the pass by now,' he said softly, so softly that she had to strain to hear him.

The pass? What pass? What was he talking about?

'...stupid enough to come back for you.'

Dorian tossed her head back. 'I see.' Her voice was sugary. 'You came back for me.'

Jake's eyes narrowed. 'Yes. But I'm beginning to wonder why I bothered.'

She smiled. 'Why, Jake. You came back because you're a gentleman. We both know that. Everything you've done, from the moment we met, has proved how gallant you are.'

A muscle knotted and unknotted in his jaw. 'Don't be clever, Dorian,' he said softly.

'Why *did* you come back?' She gave him a wide-eyed, innocent smile. 'Come on, I'm sure you can come up with something creative.'

'Maybe I don't want your blood on my hands.'

'That's it? You can't do better than a hackneyed old bit like that?'

'Dammit, woman! I've no time for games.' He took a step towards her and then, with a swiftness that stole her breath away, he gathered her to him and kissed her.

It was a kiss unlike any she'd ever experienced. There was no gentleness in it, no tenderness; there was, instead, a wild, fierce passion that should have been terrifying.

But it wasn't. She felt the raging heat of his body as he held her to him, felt the questing demand of his mouth on hers, and before her heart could manage a beat she was on fire.

'Yes,' he said against her mouth, and he drew her closer

until there was nothing in the universe but him, nothing but the feel of his lips, the heat of his hands, the urgent need of his hard body.

She was trembling when the kiss was over, and unsure of which of them had ended it. Her eyes opened slowly and focused on his face, and she knew that it had been he who'd ended it.

That she'd responded to his passion was humiliating enough, but this knowledge—that he had been able to think, to stop what was happening even while she was drowning in a whirlpool of desire—was devastating. She took a deep breath, then laid her hands against Jake's chest.

'You can let go now,' she said. Her voice was steady despite the fact that inside she was a churning mass of warring emotions. 'You've made your point.'

A muscle ticked at the corner of his mouth. 'Have I?'

'You Tarzan, me Jane. That's the message, isn't it? Big, brave man comes back to save terrified woman.' She forced her eyes to meet his. 'I suppose you thought I'd fall into your arms with gratitude.'

He drew her close to him again and she could feel the evidence of his desire.

'You know what the message is, Dorian.' His voice fell to a husky whisper. 'I should have taken you in my car, back in New York.'

Stunned, she stared into his insolent, unsmiling face, and then she balled her hands into fists and pushed against his unyielding chest.

'You bastard! Who do you think you are? How dare you—?'

'I could have found a motel for a few hours, and you'd have come to me, all quicksilver passion and desire, and to hell with the rest of the world.' She began to struggle against him; his hand slid up to the column of her throat and he cupped her face and held it still. 'I could take you now, just as easily,' he said, his eyes fixed on hers, 'in this plane...'

'You…you son of a bitch. You—you—'

'Or outside, in the meadow, with the sun heating your skin and the grass beneath you.'

He bent to her and she struggled to turn her head, but he was strong, far stronger than she'd imagined. His mouth touched hers, gently, almost lazily, his kisses slow, druggingly sweet, and, to her horror, she felt the tremor start within her again, felt her bones turning to honey.

Images blazed behind her closed eyelids: Jake, beautiful in his nakedness, his shoulders blotting out the sun as he came down to her; Jake, touching her flesh with slow, intimate knowledge, putting his mouth and tongue to all her secret places…

Dorian groaned softly, and instantly a triumphant smile curved across his mouth.

'That's right, kitten. Think of how it's going to be when I finally take you.'

The smug words set her free.

'And that's exactly what you'd have to do to make love to me,' she said, her eyes meeting his. 'You'd have to take me, Jake, because I'd never go to you willingly.'

He laughed. 'Making love is just a fancy term for what we both want, Dorian.' Her hand shot up and he caught hold of her wrist, his fingers like steel on the fragile bones. 'Temper, temper,' he said softly.

She stared at him, her breasts rising and falling quickly, as if she'd just run a mile.

'I hate you,' she said in a low voice. 'Do you understand?'

His teeth glinted in a quick, cold smile. 'I'd love to continue this discussion, but I'm afraid we're running out of time.'

Dorian tossed her head. 'Don't tell me we're back to that!'

'Last chance,' he said. 'Either you come with me willingly, or—'

'Or?'

'If I have to drag you out of here, it won't be pleasant for either one of us.'

'I'll wait here, thank you.' She wrenched free of him and leaned against the bulkhead. 'The search party ought to be here soon, and—'

'Are you stupid?' He reached out and caught hold of her wrist. 'There won't be a search party. I told you that.'

'You told me lots of things, and they were all lies.'

Jake's mouth whitened. 'I am a lot of things, Miss Oliver,' he said softly. 'I am, perhaps, some of the things you've called me. But I am not—and never have been—a liar.'

She stared up into his cold, furious face, and, for the first time, real doubt crept into her mind. She knew little about Jake Prince and what she knew she didn't like—but would he lie? 'Do you think I'm that petty?' he'd once asked, and all at once she was fairly sure she knew the answer.

But if he wasn't lying, then his stories about bandits and barbarians were true. And if they were, then—then right now, this very minute…

'Yes,' he said, reading the growing fear in her eyes. 'That's right. We've pushed our luck as far as we can. Any minute now it's going to start running out. Now, get your shoes on and let's get the hell out of here.'

He let go of her and turned towards the open doorway. Dorian stared after him while her brain worked furiously. Which was it? Was he telling her the truth? Were there men out there—cruel men, who got pleasure from rape and things that might even be worse? Or was it all a hoax? Was there nothing out there more harmful than a cow?

'Well?' Jake looked at her, his face dark. 'Which will it be? Do I throw you over my shoulder and carry you, or are we going to do it the easy way?'

Would he carry her, if she refused to go with him? Yes. He probably would. And if she was right—if there was a search party on the way, or if Kadar was a stone's throw from here, that was not quite the way she'd want to make her entrance, draped like a bag of laundry over Jake Prince's shoulder.

It didn't really matter if he was telling her the truth or not. The walk to Kadar would make terrific copy. That was reason enough to give in and go with him, wasn't it?

'All right.' Jake moved swiftly towards her. 'That's it. You've had your chance—'

'No,' she said quickly. 'I mean, I've—I've decided to go with you.'

His eyes fastened on hers. 'But you still don't believe me,' he said softly, 'do you?'

'Does it matter?'

The muscle moved in his jaw again. 'No.' His voice was chill. 'No, it does not. Just so long as you do as you're told, we'll get along just fine.'

Dorian shrugged her shoulders, then bent down to get her shoes. 'I'll do whatever makes sense,' she said.

When she straightened up again, she found Jake watching her, his hands on his hips.

'You've pushed and pushed,' he said softly. 'And now I'm warning you, Dorian. Don't push me any further.'

She flushed. 'I might give you the same message.'

'You're to stay right behind me,' he said, ignoring her remark, 'and you're not to say a word. Is that clear?'

'Yes, sir.'

Jake's mouth tightened. 'We're going to make straight for the trees. Once we're in the forest, try to put your feet exactly where I've put mine.'

Her mouth opened in the start of another quip, but she thought better of it.

'OK.'

He nodded. 'Let's go, then.' He took her hand and drew her towards the door, and then he stopped. 'One last thing.

If anything happens to me, don't stop. Just keep heading for the trees. That way, you'll stand a chance of making it.'

The words, and the way he said them, stopped her short. 'Jake,' she breathed, 'Jake, wait a minute…'

He bent and kissed her, hard and fast, then drew back and gave her a quick smile.

'OK,' he said. 'Down the steps and let's hit the ground running.'

And, since he still had her by the wrist, that was what she did.

The trees were further away than she'd thought. She was panting by the time they reached them, and she put out a shaky hand.

'You've got to let me stop and catch my breath,' she gasped.

'Shut up,' Jake hissed.

She groaned as he tugged her after him until they were well within the dark forest. Branches whipped into her face and pulled at her hair like witches' claws. When he finally whispered that they could take a break, she sank back against a tree trunk and drew great gulps of air deep into her lungs.

'Better?' His voice was low.

'Yes,' she puffed, and then she was sorry she had answered because it made him take hold of her hand again and push her deeper into the woods.

This time, she didn't waste breath begging him to stop, she just kept going, stumbling on rubber legs. It was all beginning to seem brutally real. Jake's behaviour was more than cautious. He was—he was behaving as if the forest really might be dangerous.

They stopped suddenly, and his arm snaked around her and drew her tightly into the hard curve of his body.

'Stay perfectly still,' he hissed into her ear.

Dorian did more than that. She stiffened, her body becoming rigid. There were sounds in the brush. Voices. Voices. Men's voices, speaking in a strange language. There was a guttural savagery to the voices that—that…

She buried her face in Jake's shoulder and he held her close, his hand stroking her hair, until the voices faded away, and then he squeezed her hand.

'OK,' he whispered. 'Let's move.'

Each footstep sounded like a gunshot, each snapping tree branch like a whip. All she could pray now was that she'd been right, at least, about Kadar: that it was not terribly far, that reaching it would be an easy walk.

They came out of the forest suddenly, stepping with no warning from darkness into sunlight. Ahead lay an endless plain with a single, badly rutted dirt road angling across it.

Dorian blinked. 'But—but where is Kadar?' she asked in a breathy whisper.

It seemed to take forever until Jake answered. 'Do you see that mountain?'

She did. It rose like a tiger's tooth far in the distance.

'Yes,' she said. 'But—but you don't mean…' She swallowed. 'You can't mean…'

'I do mean.' For the first time, there was a quality that just might have been compassion in his voice. 'Those are the Cristou Mountains, Dorian.' He put his arm around her shoulders and drew her closer. 'And Kadar,' he said softly, 'is on the other side.'

CHAPTER SIX

DORIAN glanced up at the sun. It had been high overhead when they'd begun their trek; now, it was midway towards the horizon. How long had they been at this, anyway? A million hours, by the feel of things. She was weary and sweaty, and the sole of her right foot felt as if it were slowly turning into hamburger. Her thin, low-heeled pumps had been designed for pavement, not for narrow dirt roads.

Jake had set an unrelenting pace, one she'd had trouble matching. But she'd been determined to do it, driven as much by pride as by the cold chill that seemed to have settled between her shoulder-blades, the feeling that some-one might just trot out of the forest and come after them.

After a while, keeping up with him had become impos-sible. He had a long-legged, lean-hipped stride—it took al-most two of her steps to match one of his—and finally she'd asked him if he could please slow down a little. By then, she'd fallen in just behind him and he hadn't even bothered looking back when he'd answered her question with one of his own.

'Can't you keep up?'

She hadn't been able to see his face, but then, it hadn't been necessary. His tone had oozed cold disdain.

So much for compassion, she'd thought grimly, and she'd tossed back a quick response that had nothing at all to do with the truth.

'Of course. I was just hoping I could have more time to enjoy the scenery.'

That, she'd noted with satisfaction, had caught his atten-tion. Jake had stopped dead in his tracks and swung around to face her.

'In case you hadn't noticed,' he'd said coldly, 'this is not a guided tour.'

'No,' Dorian had answered, trying not to let him see that she was breathing hard. 'But it will be part of the dispatch I file.'

'I told you, you aren't going to be filing a story about this.'

Her smile had been sweet enough to lure an ant colony into a trap.

'So you keep saying. But I will, eventually. You know that.'

'Really?'

His voice had become a threatening purr and she'd hesitated, suddenly wary of angering him in this desolate place. But then she'd looked into that hard, implacable face and her courage had come back in spades.

Who was Jake Prince to think he could give her orders?

'Really,' she'd said, very calmly and very quietly. 'Please don't forget that it's my job to tell *WorldWeek*'s readers about things that will interest them.'

Jake's eyes had gone dark. 'No,' he'd said in a chilly voice, 'I won't forget it, Dorian. Not for a minute.'

And then he'd turned abruptly and marched on, never so much as sparing a glance to see if she'd followed him or not.

Dorian made a face as a branch snagged her cotton jacket. As if she had a choice, she thought as she wrested it free. How else would she find her way to Kadar, if not trailing ten paces to the rear of Jake Prince? Her mouth turned down. Ten paces to the rear was how he preferred it, too. She was certain he was the kind of man who liked his women docile and valued them slightly less than his favourite polo ponies.

She wondered, once again, just how long she'd been trudging along in Jake's footsteps, following him mindlessly down this road like some—some servant girl out of another

century. Yes. That was how she felt—as if they were marching not only towards Mount Cristou, but away from the
present.

She had never seen a place where there were no signs of
the modern world. Even back in Minnesota, where the plains
stretched on unbroken for miles, there were bits of man's
handiwork to remind a visitor that the land had been tamed.
Cars. Telephone poles. Houses.

But there was none of that here; there was just this ribbon
of dirt stretching towards the mountains. And it was eerily
free of other travellers. They hadn't seen or even heard anyone since those awful moments in the forest.

A little shiver danced up Dorian's spine. She'd asked Jake
who those men were, just before they'd started walking towards Kadar.

'Were they bandits, do you think?'

His answer had not been encouraging. 'One side's the
same as the other, as far as we're concerned,' he'd said
grimly.

She was more than willing to agree. If hearing those guttural voices hadn't been enough to convince her that Jake
had been telling her the truth all along, then the feel of this
strange countryside would have done it. Maybe it wasn't the
sort of proof reporters were supposed to look for, but then,
some of the best journalists she knew talked about having
a 'nose for news', which was just another way of saying
they'd learned to trust their instincts.

Dorian sighed. Actually, hers hadn't been too dependable
lately. Kadar, by the looks of things, was certainly more
than a couple of hours' walk. And if she'd waited for the
search party she'd been sure was coming, those men would
have found her by now.

But staying behind hadn't been an option. Jake had come
back prepared to take her off the plane by force, if necessary. Would he have done that? she wondered. Her gaze
moved over him as he strode along the road ahead of her.

Yes. Yes, he would have. He would have tossed her over his shoulder or tied her and gagged her: he would have done whatever he damned well had to do to get what he wanted. For all that earlier sophisticated polish, Jake Prince was a man clearly in his element. Dorian smiled a little, remembering that she'd thought he might be Jack Alexander.

He wasn't, of course; she knew that now. Not just because he'd denied it—if Jack Alexander had been travelling incognito, he'd never admit it to a reporter—but because the last few hours had been convincing proof. The head of Barovnian Exports would be a man at home in skyscrapers and penthouses, a man used to the power of the boardroom and the pleasures of the bedroom, and the thought of him enduring in surroundings such as these was almost enough to make her laugh out loud.

But Jake—Jake was at home here. Not that she wasn't damned sure he was as familiar with the boardroom as Jack Alexander. That air of cool authority could only belong to a man accustomed to being in charge.

As for women—Dorian's gaze moved over him again. The afternoon had grown warm, and he'd taken off his leather jacket and stuffed it into the sack he carried. His shirt, damp with sweat, clung to his body, moulding itself to his shoulders and back so that it accentuated the play of muscle beneath his skin.

Suddenly, unexpectedly, she remembered how it had felt to be in his arms, to taste his mouth, to feel his heart beating against hers...

'...what you're feeling, Dorian.'

She looked up, startled. Jake was standing dead ahead, his hands on his hips, watching her with a narrow-eyed intensity that sent her pulse rocketing.

'What?'

'I said, if you don't answer my questions and let me know how you're feeling, you won't be able to blame me for pushing you too hard.'

The breath puffed from her lungs. 'Did you—did you ask me a question?'

He nodded. 'I asked if you wanted to take a five-minute break.'

Tell him you don't need to, she thought—but what was the sense in being stupid? She nodded, and Jake pointed to some flat rocks off to the side of the road.

'Are you all right?' he said when he sank down beside her.

She wasn't. There was a persistent ache in her right foot, but somehow the thought of admitting weakness to Jake was worse than enduring the growing discomfort.

'Fine,' she said with a quick smile.

She watched as he slipped the sack from his shoulder and unzipped it. Water, she thought, please, let there be a Thermos of water inside.

Jake held his hand. 'Have a piece of chocolate.'

She shook her head and opted for honesty. 'I'd rather have something to drink.'

'Later. For now, eat the chocolate.'

She had a sudden vision of that moment when he'd packed the sack. 'Soda,' she said. He looked up. 'There are some cans of Coke in there. I saw you put them in.'

He nodded as he unwrapped the chocolate. 'Yes. Maybe we'll open one later.'

'Why? I mean, if we're thirsty now—'

'*We* are not thirsty now,' he said coldly.

Dorian drew in her breath. 'OK,' she said, 'OK, *we're* not. *I* am. Do you want me to—to prostrate myself for a miserable drink?'

His expression grew very still. 'That's the second time you've accused me of being a petty dictator,' he said softly.

Her eyes met his. 'If the shoe fits…'

'The fact is, we may have a better use for those cans.'

She laughed tiredly. 'Be sure and let me know what it is when you figure it out, will you?'

'There's a village just ahead,' he said, ignoring her gibe. 'I want to be long past it by nightfall.'

'Nightfall?'

'Yes. We'll camp in the foothills.'

'But—but…'

'But what?' He smiled unpleasantly. 'Surely you didn't think we'd cross those mountains and reach Kadar today?'

She hadn't thought, and she didn't want to, even now. A night, spent in this desolate place? A night alone, just she and Jake? A tremor went through her, of fear and of something more.

'Tomorrow, then. We'll be at Kadar tomorrow,' she said quickly. 'Right?'

Jake gave her a long, steady look, and then he zipped the sack shut and stood up.

'Ready to go?'

'No…'

Dorian sighed. He was already striding down the narrow road. She rose slowly and dusted off the seat of her trousers with her hand. 'If you don't answer my questions…you won't be able to blame me for pushing you too hard,' he'd said, but he hadn't meant it. She stared after him, tempted, for the moment, to call him back and tell him she needed a longer rest.

But she had no wish to show any signs of vulnerability to a man as unfeeling as Jake Prince. Instead, she firmed her jaw and fell in behind him.

She was debating whether it would be better to take off the miserable shoe and go barefoot by the time Jake announced another halt. She smothered a groan as she collapsed to the ground and kicked off the offending shoe.

'What's wrong?'

His voice was sharp. With concern, she thought in surprise—but then she looked up and saw the way he was watching her. It wasn't concern at all. Not for her, anyway. He was just worried that she'd put them off schedule.

'Nothing,' she said, defiance glinting in her eyes.

Jake cursed as he dropped the sack to the ground and squatted beside her.

'Let me see your foot,' he said angrily, pushing her hand aside.

She caught her breath when he touched his fingers lightly to the tender flesh, and then he sat back on his heels and glared at her.

'When did this happen?' he demanded.

'Don't worry about it.'

'I asked you a question, dammit.'

'You asked me one before, too. ''Are you ready to go?'' you said, but you didn't wait around to hear my answer.'

Jake looked at her in silence, then got to his feet. 'Get up.'

She moaned softly. 'Not yet. Please, let me just—' She gasped as he swung her up into his arms. 'What are you doing? I can walk.'

'And you will,' he growled as he strode into the trees that grew beside the road, 'after we take care of your foot. The village I told you about is just over that rise. I'm going to leave you for a while and go on ahead.'

'Leave me?' The thought was terrifying. 'No. Don't do that.'

He shifted her weight in his arms. 'I won't be gone long.'

'Jake, please—let me go with you.'

'It's out of the question.'

'Why?' Her gaze swept across his face, taking in the grim set to his mouth, the harsh thrust of jaw, and those cold, determined eyes. 'Just give me one good reas—'

'OK. One, your foot hurts and you might as well rest now as later, and—'

'But I'll manage.'

'And two,' he said, ducking his head as he made his way

through a thicket of flowering wild cherry, 'we made a deal, you and I. I said I'd take you with me to Kadar—and you promised to do as you were told.'

'I did not. I said I'd do what seemed sensible,' she said quickly. 'And it isn't sensible to leave me alone here.'

He came to a stop and looked down at her, his eyes steady on her face.

'Are you afraid?' he asked softly.

'No,' she said quickly. 'No, of course not. I just—I just…'

'Nothing will happen to you here, Dorian.'

'You can't guarantee that, Jake. Anyone might—'

'I'll check the area thoroughly.'

'But why must you leave me here?'

He smiled. 'Do you speak Pragavic?'

She shook her head. 'No.'

He smiled again. 'I didn't think so.'

'Yes, but—but I could keep still. I wouldn't have to say anything.'

His smile became a grin. 'You? Somehow, that's hard to imagine.'

'I would, though. They'd never suspect that—'

'Of course they would.' His hand slipped up and cupped the back of her head. 'Your hair, Dorian. Your eyes—you're different. Everything about you is different.'

He was different, too, she thought suddenly. She had never known a man like him, a man at home in two such different worlds. She had never known a man who looked like him, either, with a hard masculinity that seemed only to enhance his beauty. Because he *was* beautiful. That tall, regal bearing. The handsome face, with its faint layer of dark stubble. And his eyes—she could see them clearly now. She had thought they were black, or even brown, but they weren't. They were something in between, a dark, midnight hazel that—that…

Say something, she told herself. Say anything.

But it was Jake who spoke, his voice low and intimate. 'Do you really want to be with me?'

It seemed hard to draw breath into her lungs. She had been afraid of being left alone when she'd made her admission, wondering who—or what—was in the woods. But Jake's whispered question had given her words an entirely different meaning and suddenly the air became charged with electricity.

That he'd still try and play such a game in the midst of danger infuriated her.

But that she felt herself responding to it infuriated her even more.

'I—I…' She drew a deep breath. 'Of course. That way, I can get some background information about—about the people in this place. For my articles, I mean.'

Jake's face changed to stone. 'How conscientious you are,' he said coldly. He lowered her to her feet and stepped back. 'Stay here and don't move. Not an inch, do you understand?'

'But—how long will you be gone?'

His smile was quick and humourless. 'As long as it takes,' he said, and then, like a shadowy ghost, he melted into the trees and vanished.

In truth, he wasn't gone very long at all. And when he did reappear he seemed to materialise out of nowhere.

'Here,' he said, dropping a bundle of clothing in her lap. 'Get those things on, and be quick about it.'

She frowned. 'What is all this?'

'What does it look like?' he snapped. 'A skirt and blouse. A shawl. And a pair of sandals. Come on, will you? We've only another couple of hours of daylight.'

She rose slowly. 'Where did you get this stuff?'

'From one of the village belles.' A cool smile twisted across his lips. 'Not your style, hmm?'

'But why? My clothing is torn, but it's still wearable.'

Jake laughed. 'I know this is going to break your heart,' he said, 'but truthfully I didn't give much thought to whether or not your outfit needed replacing.'

'Well, then...?'

'You look different from the women we'll see.'

That was what he'd said just a little while ago. But the words had had a softness then. Now, it was an indictment.

'We haven't seen anybody yet.'

'We will, once we reach the mountains, and the fact that you don't speak either Pragavic or Barovnian—'

'Barovnian?' She shook her head. 'Why would anyone expect me to speak that?'

'I can take care of that by saying my wife is mute,' he said, ignoring her. 'But the rest is impossible.'

Dorian's eyes widened. 'Mute?'

'Maybe we can get away with the colour of your hair and eyes,' he said thoughtfully. 'My country is small, and has been invaded often.' His eyes swept over her and a look of faint distaste settled on his face. 'But there's no way to explain your Western clothes—especially that trouser suit.'

'Jake, for heaven's sake—why will you have to make excuses for anything once we get to Barovnia?'

'We're wasting time,' he said in clipped tones. 'Change your clothing.'

'But—but you haven't explained anything.'

He caught hold of her shoulders. 'Dress yourself, Dorian, or I'll do it for you.'

Their eyes met and held. A flush of anger rose along her cheeks and she shrugged free of him.

'You really belong in this part of the world,' she said coldly. 'It suits you perfectly.'

His smile was grim. 'Does it?'

'Oh, yes. All that charm is just a cover-up, isn't it? You'd much rather give a woman orders than anything else.'

'You're wrong.'

Dorian tossed her head. 'I don't think so.'

'But you are.' He laughed softly as he reached out and caught her face in his hands. 'Giving a woman orders is sometimes necessary, but there are other things I much prefer doing.'

Colour flooded her cheeks again. 'I wonder,' she said evenly, 'does Jack Alexander know what kind of cold-hearted bastard you are?'

Jake's smile vanished, like a light suddenly extinguished. 'He knows all there is to know about me, Dorian.'

'And he still wants you around?' She grimaced. 'But then, why wouldn't he? He's probably the same kind of rat you are.'

'No.' His voice was very soft, almost a whisper. 'He isn't. He's far worse than I am.' He looked at her for a long moment, and then he let go of her and turned away. 'You have two minutes to get out of what you're wearing and into the clothes I've given you.' He glanced down at his watch. 'Two minutes, Dorian.'

She stared at his back, at the straight spine, the arrogantly held head, and she knew that he meant what he said.

Her fingers flew over buttons and hooks, until her khaki suit lay at her feet and she was dressed in the soft black wool skirt, embroidered blouse, and dark leather sandals Jake had brought for her.

The clothing fitted well enough; it was even handsome, in its own way. Why, then, did it make her feel so uncomfortable?

'Thirty seconds, Dorian. Twenty. Ten—'

'I'm ready,' she said quickly.

Jake turned around, his gaze moving slowly over her. She felt it linger at the slight swell of her breasts visible in the scooped neckline of the blouse, felt it feather across the narrow waist of the skirt. When he looked up, he was smiling.

'Yes,' he said softly, 'yes, you'll do. You'll do fine.' She watched as he buried her khaki suit and shoes underneath a rock. 'Now, let's see that foot.'

She started to tell him that her foot would be OK in the thick-soled sandals, but one glance at his determined face and she knew it would be useless to argue.

'It's fine,' she said, propping her foot on his knee as he knelt before her.

Jake pulled a strip of soft flannel from the sack, made a pad of it, and slipped it between the sole of her foot and the sandal. His hands were strong, yet surprisingly gentle. Without warning, she thought of how they would feel on her breasts...

'All right.' He rose quickly. 'Let's go. I don't think we'll cross anyone's path until morning, but, if we do, remember who you are.'

She stiffened, reacting as much to the unexpected vision of a moment ago as to his air of authority.

'This is ridiculous,' she said. 'I don't have to—'

'You are mute.' His voice was harsh. 'And you are my wife. Do you understand?'

'No, dammit, I do not understand.'

'There's no time for explanations. Just do as you're told.'

'Why?' Her eyes flashed green sparks. 'Because that's how the men of your country treat their women?'

Jake's eyes narrowed. 'That's as good a reason as any.'

'Well, I have news for you, Jake Prince. You may belong in this part of the world, but I don't. And I am not your woman. I—'

She cried out as he reached for her and pulled her into his arms. His mouth dropped to hers and he kissed her with a harsh, unforgiving passion that left her breathless.

'You are what I say you are, until we reach Kadar,' he said when he lifted his head. 'Is that clear?'

She blinked back the angry tears that rose in her eyes. 'Absolutely.'

He gave her a long, steady look, and then he nodded and turned away.

'Let's go, then,' he said and, after a moment, because there really weren't any other choices, Dorian fell in behind him.

CHAPTER SEVEN

DORIAN blotted her forehead with a corner of her shawl, spat out a mouthful of dust, and did her damnedest to keep up with Jake.

None of it was easy. The shawl was getting soggy with sweat, she felt as if she'd swallowed half the dirt road, and Jake—Jake was marching along as if he didn't care whether she could stay with him or not.

No. That wasn't exactly true. He'd asked her, when they'd started, if her foot felt all right, and he'd asked the same question half a dozen times since in a way that implied that he expected her to be the worst kind of burden.

'It's fine,' she'd kept saying, which was true enough. The improvised pad, and the thick leather sandals, had solved the problem. Eventually, he'd stopped asking. Now, he simply glanced back from time to time, checking her presence the way you would check to see if a stray dog was still following you.

'Let's go, let's go. Can't you move any faster?'

She glared at his sweat-soaked back. No, she thought, not without wings. I'm exhausted and sweaty and I hate you for what you've done to me, dressing me in this—this cheap costume out of a bad operetta, treating me as if I were your property, making veiled references to danger ahead when the truth was the danger was long past, and all because you're determined to make me look and feel foolish.

Her mouth tightened. God, how she ached to tell him all that and more. Jake Prince was a man with no heart and no feelings. He was a robot, damn him; that was why he could keep such a killing pace.

But why would she give him the satisfaction of telling

87

him what he already knew? He *knew* he held all the cards until they reached Kadar; she had to follow where he led and do what he ordered, her only comfort the knowledge of what she would write when she finally got to a typewriter.

Jake Prince, a barbarian in a barbaric land, gives new meaning to the word 'uncivilised'. If Jack Alexander has any plans to bring Barovnia into the twenty-first century, he would be well-advised to oust Mr Prince from his circle of advisers...

And if that's what Jake was, then Alexander was a fool.

'Come on, Oliver. Your feet are dragging.'

Dorian looked up. Jake was standing on the road ahead, glaring at her, his hands planted firmly on his hips.

More than her feet were dragging, but she'd be damned if she'd let him know that.

'What's dragging is these sandals. Do all the women in this God-forsaken place have feet the size of ox carts?'

'Be grateful I got you sandals at all.' His gaze raked over her. 'And get that shawl up on your head.'

'It's wool. It's too warm to wear in this sun.'

'Get it on. You're supposed to look like a peasant.'

'I am sweating to death under this thing,' she said when she reached him. She yanked the shawl from her shoulders. 'Look, if you don't believe me.'

Jake smiled coldly. 'What's the matter, Oliver? Haven't you ever worked up an honest sweat before?'

'You don't know—'

'But then, you wouldn't have to, would you? Sitting at a desk all day, wielding a poison pen, isn't very taxing.'

'I see. Now I'm going to get a lecture on the honesty and decency of physical labour.' She glared at him as she shoved her damp hair behind her ears. 'Well, before you get carried away, I suggest you consider what *you* do for a living as opposed to what you might be doing.'

His face darkened as he caught her shoulders. 'What in hell is that supposed to mean?' he demanded.

'You're hurting me!'

'Answer the question, Dorian. What did you mean?'

'Just that I doubt very much if being an adviser to a man like Jack Alexander improves the condition of the world any more than my work does,' she said as she twisted in his grasp.

He stared at her for another few seconds and then he dropped his hands to his sides. When he spoke, she could hear a faint weariness in his voice.

'Just get that thing on your head.'

'Come on, Jake. We haven't seen a soul. Anyway, you didn't worry about what I was wearing before.'

'There were no alternatives before. Now pull the shawl up.'

'But—'

'Dammit, woman, are you a slow learner or just a fool?' He took a quick step towards her until they were only inches apart. 'Good wives are not argumentative. And ones who are mute are not argumentative at all.'

'That's ridiculous. There's no one here to—'

Jake reached out and caught her by the wrist. 'You are my woman, Dorian,' he said in a harsh whisper. 'And women know their place here. Do you understand—or must I give you a lesson?'

Tears of rage and frustration glistened in her eyes. 'I hate you, Jake, do you know that?'

His smile was grim. 'Hearing that just about breaks my heart. Now, get that scarf up over your head. Further. Further, dammit.' When it hung down over her forehead, half covering her eyes, he nodded with satisfaction. 'Keep it that way,' he said, and he swung away from her and set off towards the mountains again.

She stared after him, hating not just him, but his long-legged stride and the dirt and the itchy shawl, too.

'You just wait until I file my first dispatch,' she called out. 'You just wait...'

Jake didn't bother turning around. Why would he? Her threat was meaningless. They were miles from a telephone or fax machine. Besides, he'd said he would censor whatever she tried to send out, and the more time she spent with him, the more certain she was that he had the power to do it.

For the time being, at least, he was in command.

Grim-faced, she marched on.

The road grew narrower. It began to slope upwards, the angle increasing steadily. Dorian was breathing hard now, even panting a little, and her legs ached. Jake had to know that she was pushing herself to the limit and beyond, but he didn't slow down or give any quarter.

That was OK, she thought darkly. She could keep it up as long as he did, and if she needed anything to keep her going all she had to do was remember what he'd said about being his woman until they reached Kadar. And if that didn't do the trick, remembering how he'd kissed her certainly would.

Her mouth still felt the imprint of that kiss. It had been bruising, even degrading. It was a kiss that had had nothing to do with passion and everything to do with dominance. It had been a graphic, almost brutal reminder of her status.

She was a woman, dependent for her survival on a man she barely knew, in a place that time had forgotten.

Well, she had a message for Jake Prince. He could swathe her in wool like a badly wrapped package, he could treat her with disdain, he could pretend that they'd both fallen into the thirteenth century—but she was still herself inside, where it really counted. She was Dorian Oliver, and she could handle whatever he dished out.

Suddenly, it became important not just to follow ten paces to the rear, as she had all morning, but to match Jake stride for stride. Her footsteps quickened until she was at his side. Jake gave her a quick glance and if she hadn't been breathing so hard she would have laughed aloud at the look on his face.

'You'd be better off behind me,' he said.

'I'm better off right where I am,' she puffed, and she slogged along beside him, gritting her teeth and letting her hatred for Jake give her the strength to continue.

And it worked, even after her legs turned to lead and her lungs to flame. It worked, even when Jake plunged off the dirt road on to a twisting trail where the brambles and tree branches seemed determined to draw blood from any patch of exposed skin. After a while, she had to drop back because the trail was only wide enough for one, but that was just as well.

She was completely exhausted and disorientated. Her eyes focused singularly on the path at her feet while she tried not to think about her aching muscles, thirst, and…

'Bognia dovitch?'

The guttural voice startled her and she went careering into Jake's back. She collected herself, stood on tiptoe, and peered over his shoulder.

Ahead of him—oh, lord—ahead of him were two of the biggest, most wicked-looking men she had ever seen. They wore trousers and shirts similar to Jake's, but theirs were encrusted with filth. Knives with sharp, curving blades gleamed in their waistbands.

Her eyes went from the fat one with the piggy face to the tall, broad one with the moustache. Quickly, she covered her face with the shawl so that only her eyes showed.

'Saletsa?' Pig Face said, and, although she had no idea what the word meant, the way he was looking at her terrified her.

Jake said something to the men in that same rough tongue, and then he reached back and grasped her wrist, snarling something guttural to her as he dragged her up to stand beside him. She shook her head and all three men laughed.

Dorian's heart fluttered. The sun was dipping towards the horizon, but she knew that wasn't why she suddenly felt so cold. She looked past Jake. Pig Face was grinning at her. She cast her eyes down, glad to be wrapped in concealing layers of dark wool.

The conversation went on and on, and she needed no translator to warn her that parts of it were about her. Jake was laughing as much as the strangers were; she caught her breath when his hand left her wrist and moved casually over her body.

'*Shnoi voritch*,' he said, and she knew that he was staking claim to her.

'*You are my woman, until we reach Kadar.*'

The words that had so angered her hours before were her only solace now. But—would the deception work?

Jake barked a command at her, put his hand into the small of her back, and shoved her forward. Pig Face laughed as she brushed past him, her eyes cast obediently towards her sandals. Jake barked again and she came to a halt, waiting, trembling, watching out of the corner of her eye as he and the strangers grasped each other's forearms. The two men strode off, vanishing down the trail, and Jake moved up towards her.

'*Gastia*,' he snarled as he elbowed past her, and she fell in dutifully behind him.

She made no attempt to catch up to him this time. Instead, she shuffled along, eyes downcast, trying to breathe past the lump in her throat that was her stomach, trying not to look back over her shoulder to see if Pig Face and his friend had really vanished. Time dragged by, an hour, perhaps more, until finally, *finally*, Jake stopped and turned around.

'Wait,' he said softly.

She watched as he trotted down the trail. There was nothing but silence; then, just when she'd almost given up hope, he reappeared.

'It's OK,' he said. 'They're gone.'

'Gone?' she whispered.

Jake nodded. 'Yes.'

A sob of relief burst from her throat. 'Oh, God,' she whispered. 'Jake—Jake...'

He caught hold of her. 'It's all right, kitten,' he said softly. 'Everything is OK now.'

She wanted to answer, to say something clever—one of the one-liners she did so well—but all that came out of her was another sob. Jake looked at her for a long moment, his dark eyes sweeping over her face, and then he sighed and drew her close to him.

'Come here,' he said gruffly.

His arms tightened around her and she burrowed against him, seeking the warmth and strength that were so much a part of him. She was safe now, she would be safe so long as he held her.

How could that be? the journalistic sceptic within her whispered, but Dorian was too drained to care.

The moments ticked away like heartbeats, and then Jake drew the shawl from her head and let it fall to her shoulders.

'I've pushed you hard,' he said.

Dorian wanted to laugh. What was the point in denying it, when they both knew that it was his arms and his strength that were keeping her on her feet?

'A little,' she whispered.

He sighed. 'I had no choice, kitten. This was the only safe place I could think of to spend the night.'

She looked up, noticing their surroundings for the first time. They were in what seemed to be a rocky bowl. Grey stone slabs rose all around them.

The place looked desolate, but strangely enough it gave her a feeling of comfort—until she remembered.

'Jake.' Dorian gave a little shudder. 'Those men...'

He drew her head to his chest. 'Don't think about them.'

How could she not think of them? She would never forget them, not as long as she lived.

'But—will they come after us?'

'They'd have trouble finding this spot, I think.' She felt the rise and fall of his chest and he chuckled softly. 'Besides, I doubt that they're much interested in you any more.'

'They were, though.' She drew back and looked at him. 'I knew it!'

'Uh-huh. So I told them they could have you.'

Her mouth dropped open. 'You did what?'

He laughed at the look on her face. 'I said you were all theirs—if they really had use for a woman who had no teeth.'

'No teeth?' she said in horror. Her fingers went to her mouth.

'And no nose.' He smiled modestly. 'Hell, kitten, I thought that was a nice touch. A woman with no teeth is one thing, but a woman without a nose...'

Dorian swallowed. 'I—I don't understand,' she whispered. 'No nose? No teeth?'

'I told them I'd cut your nose off myself.'

'But—but why would they believe you?'

'Because that's still the penalty for adultery among some of the hill tribes.' He grinned. 'I said I'd knocked out most of your teeth for disobedience before that, and you really weren't much of a beauty any more, and that was why I was taking you to the bridal market at Quarem where I could, perhaps, sell you to a blind man—unless they wanted to buy you now and save me the trip.'

'And—and they didn't,' she said shakily.

Jake's smile turned grim. 'No. Fortunately for us, they didn't.'

'But—but how—you can't mean things like that still happen?'

He let out a deep sigh. 'It's not easy to take a country from the Dark Ages into the future,' he said. 'People—and customs—lag behind.' There was a moment's silence, and then he stepped back and smiled at her. 'Now,' he said briskly, 'how about supper?'

Dorian sighed. 'Do we still have some chocolate left?'

He nodded as he eased the sack from his shoulder and dropped it to the ground.

'Chocolate,' he said, digging into it. 'A packet of mints.' He looked up and grinned. 'Two boiled potatoes. Two hard-boiled eggs. And a loaf of black bread.'

'That stuff wasn't on the plane.'

Jake chuckled. 'You didn't really think that high-fashion outfit you're wearing was a two-Coke job, did you? I traded one can of soda for this feast.'

She smiled as she plopped down beside him. 'It *is* a feast,' she said. 'I'm starved.'

He handed her a potato. 'How's your foot?'

'My foot? Oh, it's fine.'

'Are you sure?'

'Uh-huh. These shoes did the trick.'

He smiled wryly. 'The ox carts, you mean?'

Dorian smiled, too, and then she cleared her throat. 'Jake?' She hesitated. 'What—what's Barovnia like?'

His smiled faded. 'I thought you knew what it was like. Backward. Barbaric. Primitive.'

Patches of colour rose to her cheeks. 'I guess I deserve that. But I only got this assignment a couple of hours before I was due at the airport. And, you've got to admit, Barovnia's not a country that's in the news very much.'

'You mean, it isn't a household name.'

'Well...' She looked at him, relaxing as she saw his lips twitch in a faint smile. 'Exactly. I doubt if most people had ever heard of it, until the death of the *abdhan*.'

'You're right.' He sighed as he picked up an egg and began shelling it. 'And it's ironic as hell—I mean, the old man spent his entire life doing his damnedest to keep Barovnia out of the world's eye, and now...'

Dorian pulled a slice of dark bread from the small round loaf. 'Did you know him?' she asked softly.

Jake nodded. 'Yes.'

'What was he like?'

He shrugged. 'Dedicated to his people; a believer in the old ways…I didn't know him all that well, actually. I hadn't seen him in years. Not since I was a boy.'

'And the new *abdhan*, the one who's been hurt? Do you know him, too?'

There was a silence before he spoke. When he did, his voice was gruff.

'Seref and I were playmates when we were kids.'

'Then you must be very worried about him,' Dorian said stiffly.

Jake nodded. 'Yes. Being cut off like this, without any way to find out how he is…' Suddenly, his eyes turned cool. He gave her a long, steady look, and then a tight smile angled across his mouth. 'You're good at this,' he said softly.

She stared at him. 'Good at what?'

'It's quite a technique, Miss Oliver.' He gathered together the remnants of their meal, then got to his feet. 'The sweetly concerned voice, the innocent face—I suppose I should be grateful you don't have a tape recorder tucked into your pocket.'

It took a few seconds to realise what he meant. Once she did, Dorian rose quickly and hurried after him.

'You're wrong, Jake,' she said honestly. 'I wasn't even thinking about *WorldWeek* just now. I was just interested in—'

'I'm sure it works like a charm most of the time—especially on men.' His tone was clipped; he was moving quickly, deeper and deeper into the rock-strewn valley, peering into shadowed clefts as he spoke. 'But I can promise you that it won't work again.'

'Jake, please—' She gasped as he whirled around and caught her by the shoulders.

'I told you before, Dorian. Don't push me. And don't underestimate my intelligence, either.'

'I wasn't. I mean, I didn't. I just…' She ran her tongue along her lips. She really hadn't been thinking of the magazine at all while they'd been talking. That, in itself, was troubling; why hadn't she been taking mental notes for a later article? 'I wasn't thinking of *WorldWeek*,' she said honestly. 'I suppose—I was only trying to make sense of things. Try and see it my way, will you? Yesterday, I was in New York, where everything was familiar, and now—now…'

'Now, you're in the middle of nowhere with a man who could give you the interview you're longing for.'

'Jake, please—'

'Just how far would you go to get that interview?'

His voice had gone soft, not with promise but with menace. She felt her pulse give a nervous flutter, but she forced herself to meet his gaze head-on.

'Let go of me,' she said quietly.

'Just think of the article you could write. "Innocent girl reporter, raped by Barovnian barbarian…" Or would it really be rape, Dorian?' His teeth flashed as he gathered her against him; she felt the quick, hard heat of his body against hers. 'No,' he said softly, 'I don't think it would.'

'I know what you're trying to do, Jake.'

He laughed. 'I'd be disappointed if you didn't.'

'You're just—you're just trying to scare me.' He was succeeding, too, she thought shakily, but she couldn't afford to let him know that. 'We both know Jake Prince isn't the kind of man who'd—'

Jake laughed again. 'You don't know a damned thing about Jake Prince.'

'I know that the man I met back in New York wouldn't use sex as a weapon.'

'No.' His mouth twisted. 'But that's not who I am any more, Dorian. I'm someone else entirely, someone who doesn't have to live by any laws but his own.'

'Are you telling me I was right, then?' It was getting hard to keep her voice steady. 'Are you saying that Barovnians are animals?'

He went very still. She waited, barely breathing, while the seconds dragged by, forcing herself not to look away from his flat, cold stare. Then, with no change of expression, he let go of her and stepped back.

'It will be dark soon. We'd better get settled in.'

She watched as he turned and began making his way up the sloping hillside. She was shaking now, in the aftermath of the last awful moments. It was impossible to really think he'd have taken her by force, but the tautly controlled violence in him had been real enough; it had been basic, almost primitive, and it had stunned her.

'Let's go,' he called, his voice rough with impatience. 'In another few minutes you won't be able to see an inch beyond your nose.'

She blinked. He was right: the sky was already a soft charcoal against which the rocks stood out in dark—and threatening—relief.

Dorian blew out her breath and started climbing up towards him.

'Can't we build a fire?' she said.

Jake shook his head. 'Not unless you want guests dropping in for a cup of coffee.'

No, she thought with a shudder as she followed after him while he peered into dark crevasses and under rocky ledges, she certainly did not. When finally he grunted his approval, she was glad to see that he'd picked a spot protected on three sides by large boulders.

'This should do,' he said, tossing the two small blankets to her. 'Put one of those under you—the ground is still chilly this time of year.'

'Won't you need one?'

He shook his head. 'I have my jacket. It's enough.'

He dropped to the ground, ignoring her completely. She watched as he leaned back against a boulder, crossed his long legs at the ankle, and tucked his hands into his armpits.

Dorian sighed. She spread one of the blankets on the ground, lay down on it, and draped the second blanket over herself. Jake was right about the chill; within minutes, she felt it seeping into her bottom and into her legs. She rolled on to her belly, wrapping herself in the blanket, trying to find a bit of ground that didn't have sharp rocks protruding from the soil.

He'd been right about nightfall, too. Darkness had swallowed them up; it was a moonless, starless night, and the blackness was so complete that it was almost disorientating.

Where was Pig Face? she wondered suddenly.

Far from here, she hoped. Very far from here.

Something shifted stealthily just below them. There was the scrabble of claws, a faint stirring sound, a tiny squeal.

'Jake?' she whispered.

He sighed. 'It's probably a mouse, Dorian, and it's not the least bit interested in us. Just shut your eyes and get some sleep.'

She rolled on to her side and cradled her head on her arms. He was right. She needed sleep—she was exhausted, weary to the very marrow of her bones. And tomorrow wouldn't be any easier. Tomorrow...

An animal cried out into the night, its voice rising like the shriek of a demented soul in torment. Dorian gasped and struggled upright.

'Jake? Did you hear that?'

'Lord.' His voice was hoarse with weariness. 'It was a wild dog.'

'No dog in the world ever—'

'A wolf, then. They hunt at night. Now lie back.'

'A wolf?' Her voice rose into the darkness. 'A wolf? Are you serious?'

'Oh, for God's sake!' Jake's arm snaked out and wound around her waist. 'Come here,' he demanded, tugging her towards him, 'and shut up so we can both get some rest.'

'I can't,' she whispered.

He turned her to him and drew her closer, until she was lying back in the protective curve of his arm, her body pressed against the hard warmth of his.

'You can. Count chickens or sheep—or covers of *WorldWeek*, with your byline on it,' he added drily. 'Think about whatever will comfort you enough so you can sleep.'

'Nothing will. I—I…'

Dorian yawned. Lord, she was so tired. Beside her, Jake's breathing slowed; she felt the warmth of it soft against her temple. How could he have fallen asleep so easily? 'Count sheep,' he'd said. Sheep. Or bylines. Or *WorldWeek* covers.

Covers. Covers, with her name prominently displayed…

Long moments later, she was still awake. It wasn't going to work. Think about whatever was comforting, Jake had said, but Jake didn't—he didn't…

Think about whatever was comforting.

Dorian's eyelids drooped. Jake, she thought dreamily, Jake…

And then she was asleep.

CHAPTER EIGHT

IN JAKE PRINCE'S Footsteps: a first-person account of an impossible journey, by Dorian Oliver, WorldWeek Magazine. Entry One: we go through the Cristou Mountains via the Tomma Pass...

The sun beat down on the trail that wound like a grey ribbon towards the cleft that divided the massive mountain. High overhead, vultures wheeled in the sky, waiting and watching for any creature that might succumb to a mis-step or to the sudden death of an avalanche.

Dorian tried not to think about that. She tried, too, not to think about the way her breath was wheezing in and out of her lungs or how the muscles in her calves burned with fire. And she tried most especially not to think about how far they'd come or how far they had yet to walk.

What was the point? Jake wouldn't give a damn if she fell on her face; he'd only stand over her and tell her to either get moving or be left behind...

And if she really knew how many endless miles they had yet to cover, she might just do that.

The one thing she wasn't concentrating on was the scenery. Not that it wasn't spectacular: the craggy mountain peaks rising around her, still gleaming under snowy mantles, the puffy clouds that seemed close enough to touch, the occasional glimpse of a white-bearded mountain goat—it was all beautiful, even exotic. But you had to lift your head to really get a look at things, and lifting your head took energy.

Dorian had little energy left.

Jake, damn the man, had enough for both of them. He was still moving along ahead of her as if he were out for a

101

morning's stroll, just as he had been from the beginning, his easy stride effortlessly eating up the miles.

Air puffed in and out between her parted lips.

Entry Two: We will be at the Barovnian border soon, according to Jake. Up this slope, then down the other side, and—finally—we will be in Kadar, although I keep thinking of what Jake said yesterday, about my keeping mute once we reach his country. I must have misunderstood him. I would ask, but my reluctant guide and I have not spoken in hours…

It had been early morning when exhaustion, hunger and a night spent sleeping on the rocky ground had combined to produce the kind of disorientation that had led to the incident that had ended in their mutual silence.

She had come awake slowly, rising from a deep, peaceful sleep.

'Mmm,' she'd murmured while she stretched languorously.

She ached—her back felt stiff, and so did her legs—but her head was comfortably cradled on a hard yet yielding pillow. There were noises in the background, not the distant sounds of traffic that penetrated her apartment windows almost twenty-four hours a day nor even the drone of the clock-radio. What she heard were bird calls, piercingly sweet and clear.

'Mmm,' she sighed as she snuggled more deeply into the warmth of her bed.

'Good morning, kitten.'

The voice was soft as silk, sweet as honey. Something touched her temple—a butterfly's wings, gentle and cool.

'Did you sleep well?'

Jake, her sleep-fogged brain whispered. Jake…

She came awake immediately, eyes opening wide and fastening on the dark, intense ones looking down into hers. Jake was holding her closely in his arms; her cheek was against his shoulder, her mouth almost at his throat. Her arm was curled around his waist. They were as intimately entwined as—as lovers, sharing the same space, even the same breath.

Waves of colour beat across her cheeks. God! Had they slept this way all night? Desperately, she tried to remember. The pitch-black night; the quavering bark of the wolf; Jake, pulling her into his arms...

Jake smiled. It was a slow, sexy smile, and it sent heat pulsing through her veins.

'I've never shared my bed with a kitten before.'

Had they...? Had she...? No. No, she would have remembered if Jake had made love to her. His kisses would have burned her flesh, his touch would have turned her body into flame.

His smile grew softer, hinting at secrets yet to be shared. 'You have a very expressive face, kitten,' he said in a hoarse whisper. His finger traced lightly along the contours of her mouth, and she had the sudden, almost overwhelming desire to touch her tongue to his skin and taste its heat. 'I can almost read your mind.'

'Jake.' Was that papery croak hers? 'Jake, please...'

'What?' He moved, tilting her head back, and smiled down at her. 'What were you going to ask me?'

His eyes were dark and filled with promise. His mouth was inches from hers. She remembered suddenly how he tasted: clean, smoky, cool. And she wanted—oh, she wanted...

He bent and brushed his lips over hers ever so lightly, the kiss like the touch of a butterfly's wings.

'Kitten.'

Dorian closed her eyes as his mouth found hers again. His lips moved on hers, seeking response; she whimpered as he shifted, rolling her gently so that she lay back against the warm earth. Their bodies touched, and she could feel his desire for her.

'Jake...'

'I want you,' he whispered. She caught her breath as his hand stroked her body. 'I've wanted you from the beginning, Dorian. You know that.'

And she wanted him. It was pointless to pretend she didn't. She'd wanted to be with him, to go with him that very first night...

His hand slipped under her blouse; she gasped as he cupped her breast. The heat of the sun was on her face, but it was the heat of Jake's fingers against her skin that set her trembling.

'Such a beautiful kitten,' he whispered. 'So soft, so sweet.' Her lips parted as his mouth closed on hers again. Their breath intermingled and Jake groaned and gathered her closer.

He kissed her deeply, passionately, while his fingers stroked her nipple. Her head fell back in supplication as he kissed the long column of her throat, the soft rise of her breast. Her body felt molten, as if it had been waiting for the moment when Jake's touch would shape it and claim it as his own.

'Do you want this?' he whispered, and she answered by sighing his name and linking her arms around his neck. She drew him down to her, her fingers tunnelling into his dark hair.

Somewhere high in the pale blue sky a bird of prey cried out in fierce exultation, its pagan cry mingling with Jake's growl of triumph as he moved over her.

'Tell me that you belong to me,' he said in a fierce whisper. 'Tell me that you are my woman.'

And, as suddenly as she had become fire in his arms, Dorian became stone.

'*You are what I say you are, until we reach Kadar.*'

The words—Jake's words—echoed inside her head. Oh, God, she thought, and she began to tremble, not with desire but with disgust for herself, for what she had almost let happen.

Jake lifted his head and looked down at her. 'Dorian?'

'Let me up,' she said quietly.

His eyes fixed on hers. 'Kitten—what's wrong?'

Everything, she thought. I've just behaved like a fool. No. I behaved like a—a slave-girl, being seduced by her master.

Years of trading verbal barbs as a journalist came to her rescue.

'You said you'd never awakened with a kitten in your arms, Jake,' she said coldly. 'Well, I've never awakened with a tomcat in mine—and it's a species I don't much care for.'

Jake went absolutely still. 'What is this all about, Dorian?'

'An experiment,' she said, forcing herself to meet his eyes. 'I thought it might be interesting to try—'

His hand closed lightly on her throat. 'Something different? Like a barbarian, perhaps?' His voice was deadly soft and dangerous.

'Let go of me,' Dorian had said calmly, although she knew he must feel the leap of her pulse under his fingers.

After a long, long moment he'd given her a cold, terrible smile.

'I am like the wolf, Dorian. Left to my own devices, I bother no one. But force my back against the wall, and you risk the danger of my fangs.'

It had taken all her courage to smile back. 'What is that, Jake, some quaint Barovnian proverb?'

'Simply a reminder of your own vulnerability.' While she'd still been struggling for a response, he'd rolled away from her and risen to his feet. 'Go on into the bushes and do whatever you have to do,' he'd said coldly, and she'd known that this, too, was a reminder—a reminder of their complete isolation. 'We've miles to cover before nightfall.'

They had not exchanged another word in the hours since, not even after they'd finally reached the mountain and begun climbing.

Entry Three: The mountains in this part of the world are like none I've ever seen. They are incredibly high and treacherous. Although the Tamma Pass has been a steady climb, the going has been uneventful—except when rockslides from past avalanches block the way, but I scramble over them behind Jake, clutching at rocks and boulders, sometimes falling back a step for each two I take. I long to ask how much further there is to go, but I won't. It's becoming like some awful game, waiting to see which of us will be the first to break the silence…

'…if you need it.'

She looked up, startled by the sound of Jake's voice. He was standing a few yards away, looking back down the trail towards her, his face set, devoid of expression.

Dorian drew a deep, gasping breath. 'Sorry,' she said, pushing the hair from her eyes. 'I didn't quite get that.'

'I said, we can take a break, if you like. Unless you'd rather keep going…?'

She knew what he expected her to say, what her own pride told her to say. But she was beyond such foolishness; besides, she'd won the game of who-speaks-first, and that was enough for the day.

'I'd just as soon stop for a break,' she said, and without further hesitation she sank down into the grass, fell back, and closed her eyes. Moments later, she sighed. 'Do we have much further to go?'

'Another mile, perhaps. And then—'

'And then we'll be in Barovnia,' Dorian said, thinking how amazingly beautiful the name could sound when it marked the end of their journey.

She felt the brush of Jake's leg against hers as he sat down.

'Yes. Barovnia.'

She opened her eyes and looked up at him. His face was an emotionless mask, his voice without feeling, which was surprising for a man almost at the end of a difficult journey.

She watched him from under her lashes. He was sitting with his legs crossed beneath him, looking out over the valley, but she had the feeling that he wasn't really seeing any of it.

'Jake?' She hesitated. Would he be civil after what had happened this morning? Well, she had nothing to lose by trying. The worst he could do was give her more of the silent treatment. 'Jake? What's Kadar like?'

She was surprised to see a faint smile tilt across his mouth.

'Primitive,' he said.

Dorian bristled. 'Look, I've apologised and apologised—'

'I'm quite serious. I don't mean that it's uncivilised—my people's culture is ancient and beautiful, and the city itself is a handsome mix of old and new.' He sighed. 'But it hasn't the amenities it should have in today's world.' He looked at her. 'Oh, there's electricity, even a telephone service that works most of the time—but there aren't enough physicians or hospital beds, there are horse-drawn carts on the roads and veiled women in the streets…'

'Veiled women?' She shook her head. 'But Kadar is the capital of a European city, not a Middle Eastern one.'

Jake smiled thinly. 'There's a saying in my country: "Barovnia is the tie between the continents and the chasm that separates them."'

'"My people—my country."' Dorian looked at him. 'I don't think I've ever heard you say that before.'

'I told you, I was born there.'

'Yes. But somehow I thought you saw yourself as part of the West.'

'I'm an American,' he said sharply.

'And a Barovnian, as well?'

Jake shrugged. 'It's difficult to explain. Sometimes I feel—I feel…' He blew out his breath. 'I told you, it's hard to explain.'

'You don't have to. I understand.'

He laughed. 'No, you don't. How could you, when I don't understand it myself?'

'Well, I know how *I* feel, when I go home for a visit. I always wonder if it will feel strange to be in Minnesota again. Am I a mid-westerner, I think as the plane takes off, or am I an easterner?'

'And? Which are you?'

She smiled. 'I'm still trying to figure that out.'

Jake smiled, too. 'Somehow, I can't quite see you as a mid-west farm girl.'

'But I was, for almost nineteen years. And then…'

'And then?' he prompted, stretching out beside her and propping his head on his hand.

'And then,' she said with a little shrug, 'I decided to see if all those high-school English awards I'd won had any meaning. So I packed up my typewriter and headed east.'

'Where you found fame and fortune at *WorldWeek*,' he said.

'Where I found a weekly pay-cheque that would disgrace a beggar,' she said with deliberate lightness, 'and an old-boy system that might just let me wangle a byline in a hundred years or so.'

'And you decided to stay.'

She smiled wryly as she sat up and wrapped her arms around her knees. 'Of course.'

'Well, that's certainly logical,' Jake said with a little laugh. 'After all, if the pay's bad and the chance for advancement's even worse, what else could you have done?'

Dorian rested her head on her knees. 'What do you do for a living, Jake?'

There was a moment's silence. 'This and that,' he said finally. 'I'm in the export business.'

'And you're successful?'

He shrugged. 'I suppose you could say that, yes.'

'Did you work hard to get where you are?'

His mouth tightened. 'Some would say no.'

'But you say…?'

'I say—I say I took a small, family-owned company and made it into an international firm.'

She nodded. 'And was it easy?'

Jake laughed. 'Hell, no. It was hard work.'

'But you loved every minute of it?'

His eyes darkened with suspicion. 'What is this, Dorian? The game of twenty questions?'

'It's an explanation,' she said. 'I love what I do, the same as you. And I want to carve a niche for myself, the same as you.' She picked up a loose stone and examined it intently. 'And I will, some day. All I need is a chance.'

Silence fell over them, broken only by the soft whisper of the wind.

'I suppose you expect these reports you'll file from Barovnia will give you that chance,' Jake said finally.

Dorian lay back and rested her head on her arms. She had thought a lot about her dispatches while they were climbing through the pass, and the more she'd thought, the more she'd realised that what she'd write—what she'd *really* write, not the fanciful copy she'd composed in her head to make the time pass more quickly—would not, when you came down to it, be that different from everyone else's stuff.

Her assignment had been Jack Alexander. That was the simple truth of it. Walt Hemple had chosen her because he'd hoped she'd catch Alexander's eye, and, even if she'd balked against setting out to deliberately do that, she'd certainly hoped to interview the man.

But whatever chance she'd had was long gone. She'd spent the past two days a million miles from the next *abdhan*. He would have said all he had to say to the other reporters by now; they would have filed their stories, enough of them so that the Western Press was probably on overload. Anything she would write would only be superfluous.

Even Jake's solo flight, which had seemed so mysterious

and promising, didn't seem that way any more. She still didn't know why he'd made it, but what did it matter? It was too late for it to have any effect on what was happening in Kadar. After all, if death had come to Barovnia's ruler and Jack Alexander was crowned *abdhan*, the ceremonies could certainly go on without Jake.

It was only this journey across the wilderness that might prove interesting—but not newsworthy. It had nothing whatsoever to do with the man of the hour.

The bottom line was that she was out of the action, and there was nothing she could do about it.

'Well? Is this Barovnian jaunt your ticket to success?'

Jake's voice was rough with impatience. She looked up at him and smiled wearily.

'To tell you the truth, unless Jack Alexander suddenly fell into my lap with the offer of an exclusive interview, my stuff won't even raise an eyebrow in New York.'

Jake got to his feet and stood with his back to her. 'I wouldn't count on that,' he said softly.

She laughed. 'Oh, I'm not. What I'm counting on is a hot meal and a hot bath. Or a hot bath and a hot meal—I haven't decided in what order I want them yet.'

He stuffed his hands into his rear trouser pockets. 'Well, you'll have plenty of time to decide. We've at least another day's journey before we reach Kadar.'

'What?' Dorian scrambled to her knees. 'But you said—'

'I said the city was on the other side of the mountain—and it is, more or less.'

'Dammit, Jake, why did you lie to me?'

'I didn't lie,' he said mildly. 'I just thought it best not to let you worry about the distance we had to cover.'

'Then what *is* on the other side of the mountain? You said there was a town…'

'There is. It's called Quarem.'

'The place where they have the bridal market?'

Jake nodded. 'It's a rough place. I'd skirt it altogether, if

I were alone. But I can't ask you to go without food much longer, and we'll need horses to get through the valley.'

'The valley?' She stared at him in bewilderment. 'What valley?'

'The valley of the Two Suns. Crossing it will take us a day and a half or so, and then we'll be in Kadar. There will be some risks, but they should be minimal, assuming you can remember your instructions.'

Dorian stared at him. Their brief truce was ending; she could hear that clipped, authoritative tone seeping back into his voice as he spoke.

'What instructions?' she asked warily.

Jake turned to her. 'You have an amazingly short memory for a reporter,' he said softly. 'Have you forgotten that you're my adoring, mute little wife?'

Her face coloured. She was his woman. No. Of course she hadn't forgotten, not after what had happened this morning.

But he never had explained why it would be necessary to keep up the farce once they were safely inside Barovnia.

'You're to defer to me at all times,' he said, bending and picking up the supply sack. He looked at her as he slung it over his shoulder. 'Keep the scarf low on your forehead. We'll do something about the way you're dressed. No respectable man would let his wife be seen in such mud-spattered, torn clothing. Just remember not to talk, not to lift your eyes unless I tell you to, and—'

'And not to breathe.' Dorian rose and faced him, her hands on her hips. 'Listen, Jake, I am not going to be led into that town like a—a donkey unless you do some explaining.'

He glowered at her. 'Haven't you been listening? You will do exactly as you are told.'

'I most certainly will not.'

'Listen to me. There are things you don't understand.'

'Then explain them.'

His face turned cold. 'They're none of your business.'

'Well, then, I'll tell you what. When we get into town, you go your way and I'll go mine. I'll find a telephone and—'

'No!' His voice was razor-sharp. 'No,' he repeated. 'You will not do that.'

Dorian's chin jutted forward. 'Give me one good reason why I shouldn't.'

Jake drew in his breath. 'Dorian, I need—I need time...'

'For what?' she said impatiently. 'For God's sake, there *is* no time. You should know that even better than I do. Jack Alexander is probably going to become the tin god in this little part of the world, and—'

His eyes narrowed. 'Is that what you think he'll be?'

'More or less. What would you say?'

Jake blew out his breath. 'I'd say the man's been asked to assume an out-of-date responsibility no one in his right mind would want.'

She looked at him, surprised by the impassioned words. 'Surely that's not Jack Alexander's opinion?'

'Of course it's his opinion,' he growled. 'He doesn't belong here.'

'Then why has he come?'

'What do you mean, why? He's come because he has no choice.'

Dorian's eyebrows rose. 'That's ridiculous. Everyone has a choice.'

'Everyone has *responsibilities*,' Jake said, his eyes blazing into hers. 'I know it's not a popular word in today's world, but it's the truth.'

'Even so—how awful could it be for someone like Alexander to become the ruler of Barovnia? There was always the possibility—'

'Each time you cross the street, you know there's a possibility you might get hit by a car. But you don't dwell on it, do you? If you did, you'd never leave your flat.'

'Come on, Jake,' she said with a little smile, 'that's not the same thing at all. One is—well, it's a disaster that might happen, while the other—'

'Being dragged away from the life you know *is* a disaster.' Jake swept out his hand in a gesture that took in everything. 'I don't belong here, dammit! I have a life of my own.' He drew a ragged breath. 'I have freedom...'

'You?' Dorian became very still. 'You, Jake?'

Their eyes met, and a dark flush rose along his cheeks. 'I'm—I'm just putting myself in Jack's place,' he said quickly. 'I know how he feels, of course. He's told me. I mean, we grew up together, and I've always—we've always...'

Jake clamped his lips together and turned away, but it didn't matter. She didn't have to see his face to know the truth. It had been right in front of her all along, she'd even bumped against it a few times—and yet she'd ignored it.

Jake Prince and Jack Alexander were one and the same man.

The realisation was dizzying. In one instant, everything in her life had changed. It was as if a fairy godmother had suddenly stepped down from the top of Mount Cristou, waved her magic wand, and changed the meadow grasses into gold.

Dorian could hardly breathe. A byline, she thought. A column! Hell, she'd get the Pulitzer!

Her gaze went to Jake, standing rigidly ahead of her. She could write about this, too, about the reluctance of this once and future king, about his desperate wish for freedom and privacy warring with his inbred sense of responsibility.

Her eyes swept over that proud, straight back. She could see the terrible tension in him, that stiffness of muscle and spine that told her his face would have taken on that cold arrogance that could be so frightening.

But he wasn't like that. Not really. She thought of how he'd soothed away her fear yesterday. She remembered how he'd protected her against Pig Face, with a combination of wit and guts and brash determination—and she remembered, too, how he'd taken her into his arms last night when fear of the unknown had set her teeth chattering, how he'd kissed her and touched her this morning.

Had he wanted her as a woman, not as a conquest? Had he turned to her for the most basic kind of comfort, knowing that soon he would not be a man but a king, that he was about to assume a burden so awesome that she could barely imagine the weight of it?

Jake, she thought, and her heart gave a strange little lurch. Jake...

She whispered his name as she reached out and laid her hand lightly on his shoulder. His muscles were bunched, taut as steel, and suddenly nothing in the world mattered but easing away his sorrow and his loneliness.

'Jake,' she said again, 'please. Don't turn away from me. Talk to me. Tell me how—'

His breath rasped as he spun around and grabbed hold of her.

'God, but you're good,' he said hoarsely. 'It's an art, you know, making someone believe you're concerned when actually you're busy composing a story inside that beautiful head.'

'No! I wasn't doing that. I wasn't even thinking of—'

'Come on.' His smile was cold and hard. 'We both know the truth. You've been after the intimate details about Alexander from the start. If only you hadn't followed me off that charter plane...'

'What's that got to do with anything? I still don't know why you were flying off into nowhere.'

'No. You don't.' His grasp tightened, until she could feel the press of each finger through her blouse. 'What went wrong this morning, Dorian, hmm?' His mouth twisted. 'Did you lose your courage at the last minute? Hell, I'll bet you've done your best investigations in the sack.'

'You—you bastard! You—you—'

'Out of words again, sweetheart?' Jake's eyes turned black. 'Just be sure you're out of them when we get to Quarem.'

Her heart seemed to shrivel within her breast. The anguish and concern she'd felt minutes ago hardened to ice.

'Don't threaten me, Jake.'

'There are a thousand things that could happen to you between here and Kadar.'

'Such melodrama,' she said, trying not to let him hear the fear in her voice. 'Don't you think you're overdoing it a bit?'

'There are tribes in my country that still deal in stolen women, Dorian. I'll bet you didn't know that.' His smile slashed across his face. 'Harems have been outlawed for years, but they still exist. And blondes always sell well.'

'Stop this.' Her voice quavered a little; she hated herself for it, and for the sly smile it brought to Jake's face.

'And then there's the bridal market at Quarem.' She tried twisting away as his hand came up to her hair; he caught some pale golden strands in his fingers and rubbed them together, as if they were silk. 'You'd bring a good price there—even if I had to have your tongue taken out first.'

Oh, God! She was trapped, trapped in a place that knew nothing of freedom, the captive of the next *abdhan* of Barovnia, a man who held the power of life and death—a man who was ruthless enough to use that power.

'You can't get away with this, Jake,' she said breathlessly. 'I know women don't have equal status in your world, but—'

She cried out as his hand swept over her, moving possessively over her hips, her buttocks, sweeping up the curve of her waist until it reached her breast.

'You're wrong.' His voice was dispassionate; it was as if he were talking about the worth of a horse or a favourite hunting dog. 'Women are very important. They're property—valuable property.' His hand cupped her breast, his thumb brushing lightly across her nipple. '*You* are property,' he said coldly, as his other hand pressed against the base of her spine and brought her closer to him. 'And you belong to me, for as long I want you.'

'When I'm free—when I get to Kadar, I'll tell the world about you,' she said hoarsely. 'I'll tell them everything, Jake. Everything!'

He laughed. 'Tell them whatever you damned please.' She struggled as he gathered her to him, but his strength overpowered her. His mouth dropped to hers; she felt the coolness of his lips, the brush of his tongue—and somewhere deep within her, in the marrow of her bones or the pulse of her blood, some dark passion uncoiled and sent heat licking through her body.

She swayed in his arms and Jake made a ragged sound in his throat as he gathered her to him, holding her so tightly that she could feel the race of their hearts intermingling.

For a moment, they were alone in the world.

And then Jake lifted his head. He clasped her shoulders and put her from him. Dorian's eyes opened slowly and met his; for one instant, she thought she saw her own confusion mirrored there, but then a harsh smile curled across his mouth and he stepped back.

'Tell them whatever you want,' he said softly. 'Don't leave anything out.'

He turned and stalked away while she stood trembling, her arms wrapped around herself for comfort. Halfway up the trail he swung around and faced her.

'Get that scarf up,' he said.

Dorian didn't move. After a moment, Jake put his hands on his hips.

'Well? Are you coming—or do I leave you for the vultures?'

When she stood her ground, he shrugged, turned his back

to her, and started walking. Within seconds, he'd disappeared from sight.

High overhead, as if on cue, a wild cry rent the silence. Dorian looked up at the dark shapes soaring on the wind.

Tears of rage and frustration rose in her eyes.

'Damn you, Jake Prince,' she said softly.

Her whispered words rose like smoke into the air. After a moment, she drew the scarf over her head and set off after him.

CHAPTER NINE

THE pass merged with a dusty, unpaved road at the base of the mountain. Jake was waiting for Dorian as she skidded down the last steep section. He caught her in his arms, but there was nothing welcoming in his embrace.

'No more lagging behind,' he snapped. 'From now on, I want to know where you are at all times.'

'Is that so?' she said coldly.

'And I don't want to hear a word out of you. Have you got that?'

Dorian wrenched free of him. 'Come off it, Jake. The macho act gets tiresome after a while.'

'Behave yourself,' he said in a soft, ominous tone.

'Or?'

'Or you might just turn our little adventure into something you'll never forget.'

'You're very good at making threats. Let's just see how good you are at keeping promises—like the one you made me about getting us to Kadar.'

Jake smiled grimly. 'Just do as you're told and everything will be fine.'

He didn't know how right he was, she thought as he clasped her elbow and tugged her unceremoniously into place beside him. Everything *would* be fine—just as soon as she notified *WorldWeek* that she was coming in with the story of the decade. Walt had wanted her to find a way to wangle an interview with the next *abdhan*. What he'd meant was, get this story even if you have to go to bed with the guy, and she'd told him where he could shove that idea.

Dorian smiled. In the end, what she'd done was a lot more creative.

118

She'd trotted across half of forever with the publicity-shy Jake Prince or Jack Alexander or whatever in hell he wanted to call himself, learning more about him in two days than others had in years of trying.

No other reporter's story would be able to hold a candle to hers. She would get the full treatment when the news of her exclusive broke, but she didn't want it to happen in Kadar. She wanted it the minute they came trudging through the Valley of the Two Suns. She could see it now: TV cameras. Radios, microphones—she wanted it all.

And she knew exactly how to set it up. All she needed was two minutes alone with a telephone, once they reached Quarem.

Jake glanced at her. 'Keep that scarf up.'

'I thought you said there were blondes in Barovnia.'

'What did I tell you about giving me a hard time?'

'Forgive me, my lord,' Dorian said pleasantly, and she pulled the shawl high up on her head.

He gave her a glowering look. 'That's better.'

Of course it was, she thought gleefully. It was perfect! Not her ridiculous compliance: if he thought she'd believed all that stuff about the horrors that awaited her in Quarem, he was crazy.

No. What was perfect was the story she was bringing with her—and the fact that Jake, in his pitiful male arrogance, still thought she had no idea that he was the *abdhan*.

Did he really think she was that simple-minded? Was she supposed to accept the explanation that he'd been talking about his buddy, Jack Alexander, and not about himself when he'd said all those things about why he didn't want to be *abdhan*?

And the things he'd said… Dorian rolled her eyes. She'd almost fallen for that touching little speech he'd made—all that stuff about freedom and responsibility. But once she'd been marching down the trail after him again, all the loose ends had begun to knit together.

Jake had not been flying *to* Barovnia aboard that private little jet. He'd been *fleeing* from it, in a last-minute panic.

It was so obvious, once she thought about it. He had never wanted to give up his easy Western lifestyle for the rigours of being *abdhan*, but somehow the Dark Suits had talked him into it. And then, midway to Kadar, he'd balked.

'Land this plane,' he'd demanded, or something like it, 'and have a small jet fuelled and waiting for me.'

And the Dark Suits had done it. Of course they had! Who among them would have dared argue with the next *abdhan*—the *abdhazim*—even if he was trying to refuse the throne?

Jake's voice intruded on her thoughts. 'Quarem is just ahead,' he said. 'You are mute, Dorian, remember?' When she said nothing, he cursed softly. 'Dammit, do you hear me?'

'I can't speak if I'm mute,' she said sweetly.

He caught her by the shoulder and spun her towards him. Her pulse thudded when she saw the dark fire in his eyes. This trip wasn't over yet; she had to be careful not to push him too far.

'Well, it's the truth, isn't it? You have to make up your mind, Jake, if you want me to speak or not.'

A muscle bunched in his jaw. 'You're to answer me if I ask you a question,' he said finally. 'Just keep your voice down and that scarf over your mouth, and no one will know the difference.'

She nodded and they began walking again. Oh, yes, she thought, it was easy to see why the Dark Suits would have felt cowed by Jake Prince. And it was a cinch to figure out why they'd looked so unhappy as he talked to them on that runway in the middle of nowhere.

'I'm leaving,' he'd said, and there they were with a plane-load of reporters and no Crown Prince. Heaven only knew what story they'd fabricated to explain his disappearing act. They were probably stonewalling it like champions.

As for Jake's rage at finding her on his heels—well, it was one thing to do a disappearing act, but having a journalist peer over your shoulder when you were doing it guaranteed notoriety. Just what a man who loathed personal publicity would want, she thought wryly.

Because of her, he'd had to rewrite his script. And it wasn't finished yet. That was why he was determined to travel incognito. Who knew what story the Dark Suits had come up with? Jake would have to contact them just to make sure their stories coincided, which meant that he'd have to use the telephone once they reached Quarem.

Well, that was right down her alley. Let him phone Kadar as fast as his fingers would dial. When he was done, she would call Walt. And then—

Jake's hand closed around her wrist. 'We're coming into the town.'

She looked up and her stomach did a funny lurch. She had expected—what? Houses. Roads. Something not terribly modern, but recognisably Western.

But Quarem didn't meet that description. It looked, she thought, exactly as a town in Eastern Europe might have looked five hundred years before. Half-timbered houses lined narrow, dusty streets. The men she could see were dark and rough-looking, and the women had an air about them. They looked worn, almost defeated.

The realisation made her feel frightened—and rebellious.

'Remember,' Jake said, 'no talking, except to me.'

'Oh, yes, master. I understand.'

'Keep that shawl over your head.'

'Certainly, sir. Is there anything else, sir?'

Jake cursed softly and pulled her against him. 'Yes. Remember to keep a civil tongue when you speak to me.'

'Or what?' She glared at him. 'Will you sell me at the bridal market?'

His smile chilled her. 'Don't be stupid. You'd bring a lot more money from the Tagor.'

She laughed. 'You're getting desperate, Jake. The Tagor, indeed! You're making all this up!'

'Behave yourself,' he said softly, 'or you just might get to meet him.'

Dorian grimaced. Who was he kidding? No matter how backward Barovnia might be, slaves, bridal markets, and bandit kings just didn't exist any more. Still, it was hard not to feel a growing sense of unease as he led her deeper into Quarem. Close up, it looked even more uncivilised and menacing—like Jake.

Two days of travelling on foot through rough terrain had honed his appearance to a menacing edge. Dark stubble covered his cheeks and chin, and dust covered his once-shiny boots. He looked like a man who had squared off against trouble more than once and had yet to find out what it was to lose. And yet—and yet she had to admit that none of that detracted from his good looks. If anything, it only emphasised them.

He was sexy and dangerous-looking, and it was a powerful combination. That was probably why she'd made such an ass of herself this morning. Jake, the bastard, had surely counted on it. How better to control a woman than to kiss her into submission? And how better to make a journalist forget her objectivity than to make her your lover?

But it would not happen again. Two more days, Jake had said, and then they'd reach Kadar. And when they did…

His arm slipped around her waist. 'Stay close to me,' he murmured.

She blinked, then caught her breath. They had reached the centre of Quarem, and, despite what she'd already seen, the reality of the market itself was staggering.

The square was cobblestoned and thronged with people and animals. Staked-out pigs and sheep competed for space with wooden cages of squawking chickens and ducks. Smells filled the air, cardamom and cinnamon and coffee mixed with the muskier tones of goat and horse. And the noise, the overwhelming cacophony of voices haggling in a language she'd never heard before...

Jake seemed to sense her confusion. He slipped his arm lightly around her shoulders.

'It's all right,' he said softly.

'My God,' she whispered. 'It's so—so—'

'Different? Yes. But I warned you it would be.' He drew her closer and she let him. 'Just keep moving. That's it. We want to look as if we belong here, remember?'

She nodded as she walked along beside him, her eyes taking in everything she saw: women, some in Western dresses years out of fashion, others dressed as she was, and some few bundled head to toe in shapeless jellabas; men, dark-eyed and fierce, most of them looking as if they'd just laid down their weapons to come into town...

But no telephones. Not that she could see, at any rate.

'Jake? Isn't there a phone?'

She felt him stiffen beside her. 'So you can contact your magazine?'

'So we can let people know we're all right.'

He shook his head. 'I'm sorry to disappoint you, Dorian, but there's no phone here.'

None for her, at any rate, she thought grimly. But surely Jake would find a way to contact the Dark Suits and warn them, not just that he was still alive, but that he was en route with a journalist in tow.

Well, two could play that game. If he found a phone, so would she. And, when she did...

'What we need is food. And horses. Then we'll take care of getting you a change of clothing.'

She looked at him as if he were crazy. 'With what? We have no money.'

'I have a pocketful of *czelnys*—more than enough to buy what we need. Just stay close to me.'

Stay close to him? She almost laughed. What else would she do? she thought as they went from stall to stall while

Jake purchased provisions for the trip through the Valley of the Two Suns. She still wanted to find a telephone, but she wasn't about to dash off on her own to do it, now that she'd seen Quarem. The place was—it was alien. And—and…

A whisper of alarm danced along her skin. Someone was watching them. She looked up carefully. A huge man with a beard and turban was looking at her from across the narrow street.

She bowed her head quickly and drew her scarf closer around her. It had slipped a little, and she wondered if he'd seen the paleness of her skin or the colour of her hair. There'd been something in the way he'd looked at her…

When she looked up again, he was gone. Dorian let out a sigh of relief.

'Dorian?' Jake's voice was low. 'What's wrong?'

'Nothing,' she said quickly. 'Are we—are you almost finished?'

He nodded towards the next stall. 'We're just going to stop here to buy a change of clothing.'

The sense that she was being watched returned. Her gaze flew beyond Jake—and there was the bearded man! Dorian clutched at Jake's arm.

'Please—can't we leave now?'

His mouth tilted at the corners. 'I'm touched at your eagerness to be alone with me, kitten,' he said drily, 'but surely you can survive another few minutes in the company of my countrymen.'

'It's not that. It's—there's…' Her voice faded away. The man had vanished again.

'Look, I haven't time to play games. If there's something you want to say, say it.'

She stared at him while her brain shrieked at her to tell him about the bearded man. But what, exactly, was there to say? That she'd seen the same face a couple of times and panicked?

'Well?' he said, his voice rough with impatience.

Dorian swallowed drily. 'I—I was only going to say that I'm tired.'

Jake's brows drew together as he looked at her. His gaze moved over her face, lingering on her shadowed eyes and trembling mouth, and she waited for him to say something scathing. Instead, to her surprise, he sighed and pulled her into the curve of his shoulder.

'I know. But the next part of our journey will be easier, I promise.'

She closed her eyes for an instant as she let herself lean into him. How could it still feel so right to let him hold her close?

'I hope so,' she mumbled into his jacket. 'I've about had it with camping out under the stars.'

Jake laughed softly. 'OK. Tell you what. You stay here while I buy the horses. How does that sound?'

As if he was heading for a telephone, she thought breathlessly. She drew back and gave him what she prayed was an innocent smile.

'It sounds—it sounds like a good idea.'

His eyes narrowed. 'I assume you're not foolish enough to even think about taking off without me.'

'In a crowd like this?' She shuddered delicately. 'Believe me, Jake, I won't move an inch.'

Except to dog your footsteps… And what harm could come to her if she did that? He was going for a phone, she was certain of it.

'And you're not afraid to be alone for a few minutes?'

But she wouldn't be alone, not the way he meant. Not if she followed after him…

'Dorian?'

She shook her head. 'No. Of course not. I'll—I'll be grateful for the chance to rest.'

He gave her a long, assessing look, and then he nodded. 'All right. I won't be long, I promise.' Clasping her arm, he drew her to a stall where the counters overflowed with woollen and cotton clothing. She watched while he spoke to the heavy-set proprietor and pressed several coins into her hand. The woman peered past him at Dorian and nodded.

'OK,' Jake said when he turned back to her, 'it's all taken care of. I've explained that you're from a distant hill country. I told her that you don't understand our language and that you have an unfortunate handicap that keeps you from speaking normally, even in your own tongue.'

Dorian grimaced. 'What a charming description. What does she think of me?'

'She thinks you are a woman who needs looking after.'

'I'll bet!'

'I told her that I'm concerned for your welfare in this village of scoundrels. She promises she will take good care of you while you choose trousers and a shirt for me and a jellaba for yourself, and that she will see to it you don't wander off and get yourself into trouble.' He laughed softly as he bent and kissed her cheek. 'Get that look of outrage off your face, my beloved wife,' he whispered, 'or I'll trot you down to the marriage broker.'

Dorian gritted her teeth as Jake strolled away. Go on, she thought, enjoy yourself. I'm the one who's going to have the last laugh once we reach Kadar. In fact, once I've made this call...

The vendor caught her hand as she started to step out after Jake.

'*Bobska? Bobska, nasht vadai.*'

Dorian looked at her helplessly. The woman was taking her responsibilities seriously, dammit! Jake was almost at the end of the street; soon, he'd fade from view.

She shook her head urgently and pointed after him. But the woman only smiled gently without relinquishing her grasp in the slightest.

'*Nasht vadai.*'

'Stay here,' she was saying.

Dorian rose on tiptoe. Jake was at the corner, he was turning it…

'Dammit!' The word exploded from her lips. She swung towards the woman. 'You must let go of me. Let go, do you hear?'

The dark, liquid eyes widened. 'You—you English, *bobska*?'

'No. Not English, I'm American. I…' Dorian caught her breath. 'You—you speak my language,' she whispered.

The woman nodded. 'My *menya*—my cousin,' she said proudly. 'In Chicago.'

'Listen to me.' Dorian looked around, then moved closer. 'Do you have a phone? A phone,' she repeated sharply when the woman looked blank. 'You know. Hello? How are you? A phone!'

'Your man say you no speak, *bobska*.'

'He's not my man.' Dorian's jaw shot forward. 'He—he's taken me from my people.'

'Ahh.' The woman frowned. 'Bad, take womans.'

'Yes. And I must contact them and tell them what he's done. A phone.' She mimed putting a receiver to her ear. 'Do you have one?'

The woman shook her head. 'Office,' she said, pointing down the street. 'Tele—tele…'

'There's a telegram office in Quarem?' The woman nodded and Dorian smiled in triumph. So. That was where Jake had gone. She had been right; two could, indeed, play at this game. 'Do you have pencil and paper? Pencil and paper,' she repeated, miming writing on the palm of her hand with her finger.

The woman frowned. 'No-o…' Her eyes lit. 'Wait,' she said, and she turned and moved quickly along the narrow aisle. She was back in seconds, clutching a soiled paper sack and a tiny pencil stub. 'Pencil, paper,' she said proudly.

Dorian printed *WorldWeek's* address, then hesitated. What message could she send Walt that would tell him everything but have no meaning for anyone else? A smile curved across her mouth. She bent over the paper as the shawl slipped from her head to her shoulders.

'Assignment completed,' she wrote. 'Emperor of World in pocket. Arrive two days, Valley of Two Suns.' She signed it, 'Blondie.'

'Can you send this for me?' she said urgently. 'I—I have no money. But I'll pay you back after—after my family comes for me.'

'I do.' The woman's mouth narrowed. 'Bad man, take womans.'

Dorian nodded. 'He—the man with me—mustn't know.'

The woman nodded, too, as she took the note and stuffed it into her pocket. '*Bobska* take,' she said, pointing to the garments on the shelves.

Dorian nodded. 'Bless you,' she said breathlessly, 'you're right. This, then,' she said, pointing to a dark blue caftan. 'And—and this. And…'

The hair rose on the nape of her neck. She straightened slowly, and as she did she saw the other woman's eyes widen.

'*Vostaritch*,' she muttered, nodding her head surreptitiously at something behind Dorian.

From the look on her face, whatever she saw was not good. Dorian took a deep breath, then swung around.

Her throat constricted. It was the bearded man, only now he was on horseback. And he was not alone—two others, as big and as ugly as he, rode with him. He smiled, showing a mouthful of discoloured teeth, and said something that made the men with him burst into laughter.

'*Bobska*!' The woman from the stall shoved her, hard. 'Go,' she said urgently. 'Go, *bobska*!'

Dorian didn't hesitate. She spun away and raced blindly down the narrow street, driven by a terror so primal that it drove all rational thought out of her head. All she knew was that she had to reach Jake before the hoofbeats and that awful male laughter caught up with her.

A small herd of horses was staked just ahead, but would she find Jake there? If he'd gone to send a telegram, then she'd have to face whatever rode behind her alone.

There was no time to think about it. She ran towards the horses. It was her only chance. Jake had to be here. He *had* to be…

'Dorian?'

She fell into his outstretched arms, sobbing his name, burrowing into his embrace while she gasped for breath.

'Dorian.' His voice was rough with concern. 'Kitten, what is it?'

A tremor went through her. 'A man,' she huffed. 'A horrible man. He—he was watching me.'

'Where?' Jake grasped her shoulders and held her from him. 'Dorian. Tell me where you saw him!'

'Everywhere! And now—now he's got other men with him…'

Her words tumbled to a halt as Jake stared past her. She watched as his face changed. His eyes turned cold, his mouth narrowed—and she knew. Oh, God, she knew…

'Get behind me,' he said softly.

'Jake. Jake—who is he?'

'Dammit, woman, did you hear what I said? Get behind me. Now!'

She did, then stood trembling as she peered over his shoulder. There they were—the bearded man and his friends—looking as evil as death as they urged their horses slowly forward.

Jake said something. She couldn't understand, but there was no mistaking the intent. His voice was harsh, angry—and protective. Instinctively, she reached out and put one shaky hand on his shoulder, and he reached up and covered her fingers with his.

One of the men pointed to them, threw his head back, and laughed.

'Go to hell, you fat son of a bitch!' Jake snarled.

The bearded man snapped out a word, and the laughter stopped. He moved forward, his horse dancing with almost obscene delicacy beneath his weight, and said something.

'No,' Jake said. 'No, goddamn you!' He added something in Barovnian.

The man with the beard reached slowly into his waistband. Dorian cried out as he drew out a black revolver. Jake reached back and drew her into the curve of his arm.

'It's going to be all right, kitten,' he said softly.

But it wasn't. She knew that as soon as one of the men moved off, trotting to the small herd of horses. He grasped the staked-down reins of a large black stallion, jerked them free, and led the animal back to them.

'*Itsai*,' he snapped.

Jake took the reins slowly. 'I want you to do as I tell you, kitten.'

'Jake, please—what do they want?'

The bearded man stabbed his heels into his horse's flanks and moved quickly forward, snarling a command.

'They want us to go with them.'

'But where? Why? I don't—'

'We have no choice. They're armed—and they have many, many friends. We wouldn't stand a chance of a snowball in hell against them.'

Dorian began to tremble. 'What do they want?'

'*Itsai*!'

Jake snarled something in return, and then he leaped on to the back of the stallion and held his hand out to Dorian.

'Come,' he said softly.

She put her hand in his and scrambled up ahead of him. His arms closed around her as the other horsemen surrounded them, and the little party began moving out of Quarem.

'Jake?' Dorian swallowed hard. 'Please, you have to tell me what they want.'

He took a deep breath. 'Remember what I told you about the bridal market, kitten?'

'I thought—I thought you were joking about that.'

'No,' he said grimly. 'I was never more serious.'

'Does he think you brought me to sell? Well, tell him you didn't. Tell him—'

'I did.' His arms tightened around her. 'But he doesn't believe me. He's taking us to his leader.'

'But why? What does his leader have to do with anything?'

'*Itsai! Itsai!*'

The man riding alongside reached out and slapped his hand on the stallion's flank. The horses broke into a swift gallop, and Jake drew Dorian more closely into his arms.

'Their leader is the Tagor,' he said.

Hysterical laughter rose in her throat. There it was again, that ridiculous name. But Jake—Jake wasn't smiling, she thought as she tilted her head back and looked at him. He was cold-eyed, narrow-lipped—he looked—he looked…

'Jake?' Dorian drew in her breath. 'Why are they taking me to him?'

Jake's arms tightened around her. 'I won't let anything happen to you,' he said in a harsh whisper.

She felt very cold suddenly. 'Please, tell me the truth. Why is the man with the beard taking me to the—the Tagor?'

He put his mouth to her ear before he spoke, so that his whisper seemed to travel into her very bones.

'He wants to give you to him as a gift.'

Dorian waited. She waited for the punch-line to the joke, she waited for Jake to say he'd only been teasing; she waited for some terribly clever rejoinder to come dancing into her head.

But all that happened was that her heart began beating

faster and faster, as if it were trying to keep time with the
stallion's thudding hoofbeats, and finally the only thing that
seemed to make any sense at all was to bury her face in
Jake's neck and cling to him for her very life as they gal-
loped wildly across the alien landscape.

CHAPTER TEN

DORIAN had once interviewed a young woman who'd been unfortunate enough to have been held hostage for more than twelve hours by a bank robber who'd locked her in a lavatory while he negotiated with the police.

'You must have been terrified,' Dorian had said.

The woman had nodded. 'Oh, yes, I was. It was the worst experience of my life.'

'But how did you get through it? What did you do to make the time pass?' Dorian had asked, and the woman had got a defensive look on her face.

'Well,' she'd said after a pause, 'once I realised there was nothing much I could do to change things, I slept.'

Dorian had been incredulous. The woman slept? Slept through those terrifying hours? No, she'd thought firmly, that was impossible.

Now, as they rode slowly towards the mountain encampment of the Tagor, she wondered if perhaps the woman had taken the only reasonable action.

Her mind was doing dreadful things, conjuring up scenarios that might take place once their captors turned them over to the Tagor. The imaginative scenes were vivid, frightening, and all shared an ending that was filled with violence and degradation.

Jake felt her move restlessly in his arms, and he drew her back against him.

'We'll be all right,' he whispered, his breath stirring the damp tendrils of hair on her cheek.

For some reason she didn't understand, the tender reassurances in his voice brought a lump to her throat. She wanted to fling her arms around his neck and beg him to hold her to his heart, not because of what might lie ahead, but because being close to him suddenly seemed all that mattered. All she could concentrate on now was the solace of Jake's embrace, the steady beat of his heart beneath her ear, the coolness of his lips as he brushed them against her temple.

'Close your eyes and get some rest,' he said softly as the horses picked their way through a rock-strewn valley.

She protested that sleep was impossible. But little by little fear and fatigue worked against her, until finally her head fell back against his shoulder and her eyelids drooped shut.

'That's my girl,' Jake whispered. She felt the soft press of his mouth against her hair. She thought of the woman hostage she'd interviewed, and then, mercifully, she drifted off into nothingness.

She came awake with dizzying swiftness, awakening not in a sweet, sensual haze as she had that morning, but to a formless terror, a sudden nightmare of such awful proportions that it made her gasp and jerk upright.

'Jake?' she said, and instantly his arms tightened around her.

'Easy, kitten. I'm right here.'

A tremor went through her. 'I—I was dreaming,' she whispered. Images flashed through her mind and she buried her face in his shirt. 'It was awful.'

'Trust me, Dorian. Everything will be all right.'

She nodded and waited for her heartbeat to slow. Everything would be all right, Jake had said, but she wondered if that could possibly be true. Her dream had been ugly, but reality was little better.

She sat up and looked around. The horses were moving in a line through a rocky defile, with the black stallion in the centre of the little procession. It was late afternoon: the sun was low in the sky.

'Jake? Will we be there soon?'

It was a child's question, but Jake understood the despair behind it. He nodded as he drew her back against him.

'Yes. I think so.'

Dorian hesitated. 'What—what will happen to us?'

She felt him draw a deep breath. 'I suspect we'll be cleaned up a bit and then taken to see the Tagor.'

She smiled for the first time. 'Cleaned up a bit? What for? I mean, judging by the way our escorts look and smell, soap and water isn't a priority item around here.'

'I know. But the Tagor prides himself on his civility and sophistication.'

She tilted her face up questioningly. 'You sound as if you know him.'

'No. We've never come face to face. But I've heard of him.' He gave her a tight smile. 'He's rather well-known in this part of the world.'

'Well,' she said, trying desperately for a light touch, 'he can't be very sophisticated if he believes in stealing women.'

There was nothing light in Jake's reply.

'He'd never dream of stealing you, kitten,' he said grimly. 'But accepting you as a gift from his men—well, that's different.'

Bitter-sweet laughter rose in her throat. 'I see,' she said. 'The Barovnian version of Emily Post, right? Lesson One: Never look a gift horse in the mouth.'

Jake blew out his breath. 'I guess you could put it that way.'

'But he won't really—I mean, surely not even in Barovnia...' She hesitated. 'I suppose I shouldn't keep saying things like that. I know that we're talking about a bandit here, not a typical Barovnian.'

'There's no reason to pick your words now,' Jake said gruffly, 'not when we've just been kidnapped so you can be presented to the Tagor like a Christmas present.' He laughed bitterly. 'Hell, who have I been kidding? My country has one foot planted so firmly in the past that it will take everything short of dynamite to blast it loose.'

'Yes, but—'

'And I've always known it. It's just that I'm uncomfortable admitting it, even to myself.'

'I understand.'

Jake sighed. 'No,' he said after a pause, 'no, kitten, you don't.'

I do, though, she thought. I know who you are, Jake, I know that it wasn't selfishness or cowardice that sent you fleeing your duty—it was desperation. I know how torn you've been by the decision you had to make…

'Then explain it to me,' she said softly.

A bitter smile flashed across his face. 'Why? So you can write an exposé about the doubts of—of one of Jack Alexander's advisers?'

For a moment it was hard to think why he would think that. *WorldWeek*, and the articles she'd been sent to write, were the last things in her mind.

In the real world, the one that lay beyond these mountains, she would have given him a clever answer, one that would have made him smile even while it established the adversarial relationship of reporter and subject.

But this wasn't the real world; it was a place where life had suddenly taken on special meaning, and there was no room for anything but the truth.

'No,' Dorian said softly. 'I—I just—I just want to know about you, Jake.'

His eyes darkened. 'Kitten…'

'*Javai!*'

The sharp command caught them both by surprise. The little column was coming to a halt; they had entered a broad meadow pocked with canvas tents and grazing horses.

'*Javai!*'

The behemoth was standing beside the stallion, glaring up at Dorian with his massive arms outstretched. She couldn't understand his words, but his message was precise and clear.

'Get off,' he was saying. 'Get off and I'll catch you.'

Jake slipped from the saddle before she could move and said something sharp and authoritative. Dorian held her breath while the two men stared at each other. Then, with an unpleasant laugh, the bandit waved his meaty hand in the air and stepped back.

She felt her heart begin to beat again as Jake looked up and held out his arms. She dropped into them without hesitation.

'Jake,' she whispered feverishly, 'I beg you, don't do anything that foolish again. I'd have survived—'

'But I wouldn't.' His voice was raw. 'If that son of a bitch so much as touches you—if anyone touches you—'

He fell silent, but not before the same electric message flashed between them again.

'*Sinza!*'

The giant stepped forward and so did Jake, but before either man could make a move a woman covered head to toe in a black jellaba pushed between them, barked something as she clamped a hand around Dorian's wrist, and began tugging her towards a nearby tent.

'Wait a minute,' Dorian said quickly. 'Hey! Did you hear what I said? Just wait a—'

Jake shoved past his guard. 'Go with her, kitten,' he said

quietly. 'She's only going to give you a chance to eat something and get cleaned up.'

Her lip trembled. 'But—but where will you be?'

'In another tent, doing the same thing.' He touched his
hand to her cheek and she fought back the desire to bury
her face in his warm flesh and sob out her fear. 'Hey,' he
said with a little smile, 'just this morning, you couldn't decide if it was a bath or a meal you wanted most. Now, our
host is about to provide both. Besides, a little soap and water
and some food will help you regain your strength.'

She looked past him to the sullen-faced men who had
gathered to watch the show, to the swaddled women scattered among them, and to the tents that stood like huddled
animals against the overhanging mountains. Her gaze returned to Jake, standing close beside her, and suddenly she
knew that she could find all the strength she would ever
need deep in his dark eyes.

She would be as brave as he was, she thought, and she
lifted her head proudly and smiled back at him.

'Don't forget to wash behind your ears,' she said, and
then she turned and followed her jellaba-draped guard to the
tent.

Some food, Jake had said, and a little soap and water, but
this interlude was not going to be that simple. Her first surprise came when her escort peeled back the tent flap and
shoved her inside.

The interior was surprisingly spacious and not anywhere
near as barren as she'd expected. A heavy fall of white
gauzy fabric separated it into two rooms.

Dorian looked around slowly. The one she was in was
quite handsome. Intricate woven hangings were draped on
the walls, their colours rich and bright. This was, apparently,
a dining area: a pleasant scent of coffee and spices hung in

the air, softly faded carpets lay underfoot, and there was a low wooden table off to the side.

The woman poked her in the back and urged her towards the table. She waited until Dorian sat, cross-legged, on the rug before it, and then she clapped her hands sharply. A girl stepped through the tent door bearing a basin of scented water, soap, and a towel.

'*Fladai*,' her guard barked.

Dorian obliged, washing her hands and face, then blotting herself dry with the towel. The woman scowled at the girl, who scampered off. The flap opened again and a troupe of girls stepped inside, their hands laden with platters, their eyes gleaming with interest as they looked at the mysterious stranger.

The food was placed before her and Dorian stared at it. She wanted to treat this meal with casual disdain. But the sight of it made her realise how hungry she really was. She devoured the warm, flat bread spread with sweet butter, the tiny meatballs, the nuts and raisins, and she drank three cups of hot, sugary coffee before she sat back and sighed with contentment.

The woman in the jellaba clapped her hands and the platters were whisked away.

'*Fladas*,' she said, motioning towards the rear of the tent.

One of the girls hurried ahead and pulled aside the heavy curtain. Dorian rose to her feet and moved forward slowly, gaping at what awaited her.

A little soap and water, Jake had said, and that was what she'd expected—a bucket of water and a bar of coarse soap. But what she found was a huge wooden tub with high, sloped sides. Steam curled from its depths, along with the faint scents of sandalwood and oil of roses.

The woman pointed to the tub. '*Fladas*,' she said irritably.

Dorian nodded. 'Yes, I agree. A *fladas* sounds like a great idea.' She gave a meaningful look at the woman and the girls. 'But I prefer my baths in private, if you don't mind, so if you'd all please get out…?'

'*Fladas*,' the woman snapped.

'Listen, I get the message. And I'm telling you, just take your little retinue and—hey. Hey!' Dorian's voice rose in indignation as the woman grabbed hold of her, but it was useless. The girls swarmed around her like bees, buzzing with laughter as they peeled off her dirty clothing, whispering with delight when they saw her fair skin. In seconds she was naked, and the woman in the jellaba pointed sternly at the tub.

Dorian tossed her head and marched towards it with as much pride as she could manage, considering the circumstances. She stepped in, then lowered herself gingerly into the hot, scented depths. Despite herself, she gave a little sigh of pleasure, leaned back, and rested her head against the rim.

Her guard slapped her hands together and the girls rushed forward and snatched Dorian's scattered clothing from the floor. The woman looked at Dorian and said something.

She smiled sweetly. 'I've no idea what you're saying, you old witch.'

The woman put her hands on her hips and stared at Dorian. A moment passed, and then her brows rose.

'*Syet*,' she commanded, putting her hand to her nose. She made a dreadful face, then pointed to the clothing. '*Octa*,' she said with disdain, and she made a sweeping gesture to the tent door.

'Throw it out, you mean?' Dorian had to laugh. 'By all means. Please do.' She sat forward quickly. 'So long as you have something else I can put on.'

As if on cue, one of the girls stepped forward, a long

length of white cotton draped in her arms. The woman made a long, harsh-sounding speech, but all that mattered was the one word Dorian understood.

Jellaba. That was what the length of cotton was, and it was for her. It looked clean and soft; even the sight of it lifted her spirits. With a weary sigh, she sank back into the tub and waved her hand, mimicking the other woman's gesture.

Where was Jake now? she wondered as she washed herself with a bar of sweet-smelling soap. He'd been right about the food and the soap and water making her feel better. But—but had those same things been in store for him? She, after all, was being gift-wrapped. But Jake—Jake could be nothing but a detriment to these men, and he'd insulted them, too, he'd challenged their power...

'The hell with this!' she said, and she rose abruptly, sending a cascade of water sloshing on to the carpet. Her guard rushed forward, waving her hands while she barked commands, but Dorian ignored her. She stepped from the tub and snatched a towel from the hands of one of the girls, who'd gone from giggling to gaping.

'I want to see Jake,' she demanded angrily as she dried herself. The woman looked at her blankly, and Dorian said something sharp and pointed as she tossed the towel aside and snatched the clean jellaba from the girl holding it. She pulled it over her head, fluffed her fingers through her wet hair, and stalked through the hanging curtain.

Her stunned guard caught up to her at the tent door. She said something and grasped Dorian's arm, but Dorian wrenched free.

'Did you hear what I said?' she demanded. 'I want Jake.' The woman looked blank, and Dorian stamped her foot. 'I don't know how to say it in your language, dammit. I want my man!'

'Do you, kitten?'

She whirled around at the sound of Jake's voice. He was standing in the open doorway, and she hesitated only a heartbeat before she flew to him and threw her arms around his neck.

The woman said something in a sharp, high voice, but Jake ignored her and gathered Dorian close.

'Oh, Jake.' Her voice quavered a little. 'I was afraid—I was afraid...' She drew back and clasped his face between her hands. 'Did they hurt you?' she whispered.

He smiled. 'Well, the razor they gave me felt as if it's been used to shave a regiment.'

Dorian smiled back at him. 'Lady Macbeth over there probably used it to shave her moustache.' Her eyes swept across his face. 'Are you really OK?'

'Yes, kitten, I'm fine. They gave me a bowl of lamb stew and a bucket of soapy water, and—why are you laughing?'

Why *was* she laughing? Considering what might await her, there was nothing remotely funny about their situation. But Jake was here, she was in his arms, and that was all that mattered...

'Lamb stew and a bucket of water, indeed,' she said lightly. 'I guess it pays to be the Tagor's gift.'

Jake's smile faded. 'The Tagor,' he said softly. He waited a moment, then clasped her shoulders. 'Remember what I told you about not saying a word and letting me do all the talking?'

'You mean, you want me to pretend to be mute? But all these people know I can—'

'What I mean is that you're to speak only when spoken to and take your cues from me. Can you do that?' She nodded, and he put his hand under her chin and lifted it. 'Listen to me, kitten,' he said softly. 'You mustn't underestimate this guy's intelligence, or his power. He's absolute ruler here—'

'Like the *abdhan*,' she said, her eyes on his.

Jake's mouth twisted. 'No,' he said harshly, 'not like the *abdhan* at all. The *abdhan* is trapped by his power. If he weren't—if he weren't…'

His mouth dropped to hers with a sudden wild hunger. Dorian's lips parted beneath his; she rose on her toes and pressed herself close to him—and suddenly a beefy hand clamped down on her arm and dragged her from Jake's arms.

The bearded behemoth glared at the two of them with fury in his eyes. He snarled a command and pointed to the door.

'OK,' Jake said softly, 'this is it, kitten. It's show time.'

It seemed a strange way to describe what lay ahead, she thought. But once they'd stepped inside the tent of the Tagor Jake's choice of words seemed to make absolute sense.

The tent was large, draped inside with billowing lengths of crimson silk that added to the sense of enormous size. The Tagor seemed even more enormous. He sat on a carved chair that stood on a elevated platform, his huge body wrapped in what looked to be yards of embroidered cloth.

Their bearded escort thrust them into the centre of the tent, bowed, then backed out of the door, leaving Jake and Dorian alone with the Tagor.

Jake glanced at Dorian. 'Get your head down,' he whispered fiercely.

'Why? You're not bowing to him. Why should—?'

She caught her breath as Jake put his hand on her head and shoved it down.

'You're female,' he said sharply.

'Well, it doesn't take brains to figure that out, Jake. If I weren't female, nobody would have bothered offering me up to him,' she muttered, eyes on the lush rugs that carpeted the floor.

'Dorian, dammit, shut up!'

The Tagor barked something at Jake.

'What's he saying?' Dorian asked.

'He says you are very beautiful.'

She sighed. 'That's only because I don't have a moustache.'

'He says, too, that you need to have some respect beaten into you.' Jake's mouth twisted. 'I told him that I agree.'

'What? Listen here, Jake…'

The Tagor spoke again and Jake laughed politely.

'What's he saying now?'

'He says he will be happy to do the job for me. He will make you into a loving, obedient woman.'

'And? What did you tell him?'

'I told him that he would need God on his side to succeed where I have not.'

Dorian's head came up sharply. 'I thought you told me everything would be all right.'

'It will be, dammit. Get your head down and shut up!'

'It *won't* be, if you play along with him.'

The Tagor growled a command. Jake caught Dorian's arm and drew her forward.

'Sit,' he said, pointing to a small, low stool before the throne.

'I don't want to sit, I want to—' She gasped as Jake shoved her on to the stool. The Tagor gave a booming laugh and motioned Jake closer.

The men entered into a long conversation. Dorian kept her head down, but every now and then she risked a quick glance from under her lashes. The Tagor kept pointing at her and Jake kept shaking his head. She could tell, from his tone and demeanour, that he was being politely but coldly firm about something.

About her, she thought with a little shiver. But—but this was ridiculous. The twenty-first century was on the horizon, and here she was, sitting like a polite lump of dough while her fate was being debated, and no one had yet asked her what she thought about it.

'Jake? Excuse me. Jake?'

Jake spun towards her, his eyes dark with barely suppressed anger.

'What is it now?' he snapped.

'I think I have the right to know what's going on. I mean, this discussion is about me, isn't it?'

'Dorian, dammit to hell, what did we agree?'

'I know,' she spat. 'I said I'd keep quiet. But you speak his language, Jake. You could translate for me. You could explain to him that—that no one does this kind of thing where I come from—'

'Listen to me. If you don't want to end up as his newest toy, you'll look down at the floor and keep still!'

She stared at him. 'You wouldn't let that happen to me,' she whispered. 'Would you?'

'Yes,' Jake snarled. 'I damn well would. It would be no more than you deserved. It would...' He fell silent. 'All right,' he said grimly, 'here it is without any sugar coating. If I can't talk my way out of this, he'll kill me and give you to his men.'

'What? You're not serious!'

'I'm dead serious. I've explained that we're from America—'

'Doesn't he wonder why you can speak his language?'

'I told him that I was born in this part of the world, that you were my fiancée and I was having trouble with you so I took you to the bridal market as a joke.'

Dorian gave the Tagor a sidelong glance. 'Some joke,' she said shakily.

'I said I'd hoped it would scare you into behaving as a woman should.'

'I just don't see how that's going to get us out of this,' she said in a small voice. 'Why would that keep him from—from…?'

'Because,' Jake said patiently, 'I've presented it all as if it were a puzzle to solve. He's bored, Dorian. Hell, who wouldn't be, when all you have to do is snap your fingers to get whatever you want?'

For just a moment she forgot everything but Jake.

'Power can be exciting,' she said softly, 'it can be a challenge.'

Jake's eyes narrowed. 'That's simplistic nonsense.'

'It isn't. If you—'

The Tagor snarled. Jake turned and listened.

'He says,' he translated, 'that he permits us this behaviour only because you are a foreigner and a barbarian. He says he allows us to behave in his presence as we would behave in the presence of our own king so that he might learn something of our country.'

'I hope you told him that *he's* given the word ''barbarian'' a whole new meaning.'

Jake sighed wearily. 'The bottom line is that he's given us permission to stand in his presence and to look towards him. Not *at* him. Don't push our luck.'

The Tagor grunted and motioned Jake closer. After a long time, Jake inclined his head, made his way back to Dorian, and took her arm.

'Smile and curtsy.'

'Curtsy? Americans don't—'

'Just do it, dammit! That's it. Now walk with me—backwards, *backwards*! Good girl.'

She took a deep breath as they stepped outside. Night had fallen: the meadow was black, except for the blazing lights of a hundred camp-fires.

'Jake? What's going to happen now?'

As if in answer to her question, the bearded giant stepped towards them. But he didn't touch them this time; instead, he motioned them towards the tent opposite the Tagor's.

The tent's furnishings were sparse. Except for a tumble of blankets, and a hissing kerosene lamp atop a small table, it was unadorned.

Dorian turned to Jake as soon as they were inside. 'Well? What will he—?'

Jake clamped his hand over her mouth and pointed to the shadow of their guard, silhouetted on the tent door. She nodded and followed him through the tent's shadowy depths.

'Please,' she whispered, 'tell me what happens next?'

'He was very understanding, kitten. He told me he's dealt with some difficult women himself.'

She tried to laugh, although the sound she made was, despite her show of bravado, choked and false.

'What did he do, have them beheaded?'

Jake put his arms around her. 'He assured me that all such a woman needs is a Barovnian husband.'

'Yes. I can imagine.' Dorian shuddered. 'Shoeless in the winter, pregnant in the summer, and an occasional beating as a reminder of who's boss.'

Jake laughed softly and tilted her face up to his. 'I'm not sure about the shoeless thing, and the beating is ridiculous—but the rest isn't a bad idea.' He bent and kissed her, a long, sweet kiss that stole her breath away. 'Not a bad idea at all.' His hand slipped down her spine, lightly tracing her vertebrae. 'As for bringing a recalcitrant woman into line, I've always found that long, slow loving is the best method.'

Dorian shuddered beneath his touch. 'I can't—I can't think when you—when you—'

He smiled. 'Exactly. That's why the Tagor reminded me of an old Barovnian proverb: "A husband who wishes his wife to behave sees to it that she can feel but not think."'

'And—and what did you say?' she whispered.

His mouth took hers again in a kiss that grew deeper and more passionate as it went on, until finally he cupped her face in his hands and drew back, just far enough so that he could see into her eyes.

'I said that he was absolutely right,' he whispered, 'that it was clear to me that what you needed was a good Barovnian husband. We agreed that you must have one.'

Dorian's heart plummeted. 'My God,' she whispered. 'Jake, how could you? If he—if he tries to take me as his wife, if—if—'

She fell silent. Outside the tent, the sound of soft drums and flutes began rising on the cool night air.

'You've got it all wrong, kitten. The Tagor told me he thanked his men for their thoughtful gesture—'

'For me, you mean?'

He nodded. 'Yes. He hated to turn down such a gift, but he says he has far too many wives already.'

'Then—then what…?'

Jake lifted her face to his and kissed her until she was breathless.

'But he will see to it that you have a Barovnian husband,' he said softly. 'In fact, he's determined to take care of it tonight.'

She knew what he was telling her—it was in Jake's eyes, it was in the sudden leap of her blood. Still, she had to put the question to him.

'And—and who will my husband be?' she whispered.

Jake smiled, just as he had the night they'd met, when

he'd asked her to go away with him and—for the swift beat of her pulse—she'd wanted to say that she would.

'Who?' she repeated.

He drew her close and kissed her deeply, and then he whispered against her lips.

'Guess.'

CHAPTER ELEVEN

HE HAD kissed her and kissed her, and he was still holding her in his arms. Maybe that was why she couldn't think coherently. Maybe that was why she'd thought he'd said—he'd said—

'This is—it's a joke, right?'

Jake smiled wryly. 'Life is full of surprises, kitten. For instance, I never dreamed I'd propose to a woman in a tent in the middle of a camp filled with bandits.'

Dorian swallowed with effort. 'Come on, Jake. You and the Tagor decided that—that you'd teach me a lesson...' She waited for him to say something, but he didn't. He just went on looking at her with that little smile curled across his mouth and a look in his eyes that she could not quite define.

'You're—you're serious,' she whispered after long seconds had crept by. 'You really told that—that awful man that we'd—'

'I didn't "tell" him anything, Dorian.'

'I don't—I don't understand.'

'The Tagor sees himself as a civilised man. That's why he's agreed to let me keep you.'

'Keep me?' she said, staring at him.

'Yes. I told you, he thinks you're my fiancée. That means I have certain rights and obligations.'

'My God! If that's his idea of civilised—'

'But he's not about to wish us *bon voyage* and send us on our way.'

Dorian swallowed drily. 'He's not?'

'The way he sees it, you're a desirable woman. All you need is some taming. If I don't exercise my rights and perform my obligations, someone else will. You get your choice, lady. Me—or one of the Tagor's men.'

She stared at him. 'But that's—that's crazy!'

A strange half-smile twisted across his mouth. 'Like it or not, kitten, he holds all the cards. It's either do as he says—or do as he says.'

Dorian nodded slowly. Marriage, she thought, marriage—to Jake. Not that it would be a real marriage, of course. But marriage...

The ceremony would, no doubt, be exotic and colourful, something she could write about for *WorldWeek* that would probably sell more copies of the magazine than ever before.

I Was the Bride of the Abdhan, by Dorian Oliver.

Her heart gave an unsteady lurch in her breast. Jake's bride. What a ridiculous idea...

'Well?' She looked up. Jake was watching her, and suddenly she wished the lighting was better so that she could see beyond the shadows and into his eyes. 'What's it going to be, Dorian?' He gave a little laugh. 'The barbarian you know—or the one you don't?'

'Don't say that,' she said quickly.

'Why not?' His voice was brusque. 'It's what you're thinking, isn't it?'

'Jake, for God's sake, I'm only thinking that—that getting married is—is—'

'Yeah.' The air puffed from his lungs. 'I know exactly how you feel.'

No, she thought, watching him, he didn't. How could he, when she didn't know how she felt herself?

Marriage. Marriage, to Jake...

'It's a hell of a thing,' he said as he bent over the kerosene lamp and turned up the flame, 'being forced to go through a farce like this.'

There it was again, that little constriction within her chest. But why?

'Yes,' she said slowly, 'it is, isn't it?'

'The ceremony won't be binding, of course. We won't have to bother with an annulment, in case you were concerned about that.'

'I understand.'

But she didn't. She didn't understand why she ached so, why she wanted to take a step forward and touch him.

'We can forget it ever happened, once we get out of here.' Jake turned and looked at her.

Why was he making an issue of it? She understood the situation. If they had to go through with a charade to save their necks, then that's what they'd do. And then it would be over; it would have no meaning in her life or his.

She nodded her head.

'Good,' he said gruffly. 'In the morning, when we leave— '

'In the morning?' A little note of panic threaded through her voice. 'What do you mean, in the morning? Must we stay the night?'

'We have no choice.'

'But why? If we go through with the ceremony...'

'Use your head, Dorian. What would he think if a newly married couple denied themselves the pleasures of their wedding night?'

He smiled, and a little stab of pain twisted into her heart. This was a game to him, she thought, a game, but to her— to her...

'I know this must seem amusing to you,' she said stiffly. 'But I'm finding it anything but funny.'

'Dammit, will you listen?' His hands tightened on her and

he shook her. 'If the Tagor so much as suspects that we've played him for a fool, he'll give you to one of his men—or maybe to all of them. He'll make me watch—and then, when they're finished, he'll cut out my heart. Is that blunt enough for you?'

It was blunt enough to turn her knees to water. 'Oh, God!'

Jake nodded grimly. 'Exactly. So we'll do whatever we can to convince him that we treat this marriage as seriously as he does.'

'Dammit, Jake, how do we do that?'

'We make it obvious that we're happy as hell about to-night's little shindig.'

'How? Do we laugh all the time? Do we go out there skipping? I don't understand what you expect—'

'I'll show you, then,' he said, and he pulled her into his arms and kissed her.

It took no great imagination to figure out what he was doing. His kisses were deep, almost bruising. When he was finished, her lips would be pink and swollen, her cheeks flushed. She would look like a woman eager for the marriage bed.

Jake drew back a little and looked at her. 'You're not co-operating,' he said softly.

'I don't have to,' she said a little unsteadily. 'And I don't want to...'

He gathered her closer and kissed her again, and still she stood immobile in his arms.

'Kitten,' he whispered. 'Kiss me back.' His mouth moved along her cheek, to her ear, and a tremor went through her. 'We have to be convincing, remember?' Her eyes closed as his tongue brushed the sensitive skin behind her lobe. 'How will it look if my bride is cold as stone?'

'I'm not—I'm not...' She whimpered softly as his hand

swept over her, across the curve of her hip, up over her midriff, and cupped her breast.

'You see?' His voice was hoarse and low. 'It isn't so difficult to pretend to feel desire for me, kitten, is it?'

'Jake. Jake, don't...'

She groaned into his mouth as his hand slipped inside the deep neck of the jellaba. His fingers were hard and rough against her flesh; she felt her nipple leap to his touch, felt the answering leap of flame deep within her womb.

Jake's breath sighed against her skin. 'Yes, kitten. That's the way.'

Outside, in the darkness, the sound of the drums quickened, until their pulsing beat matched the race of Dorian's heart. Her hands crept up Jake's chest, to his shoulders; she moved blindly against him, and her mouth opened to his kiss.

The women came bursting into the tent, laughing as they wrenched her from his arms. The dour-faced one who had supervised her bath and her meal peered into Dorian's flushed face and clapped Jake on the back.

'She says that you look like a woman ready for her man,' he whispered as they took her from him, and Dorian knew that he was right.

They took her to the women's tent, where she stood trembling while her attendants stripped her of the jellaba and rubbed her skin with scented oil. They brushed her hair until it gleamed like pale gold, and while they fluttered around her they laughed softly and nudged each other.

Dorian had never been the kind of girl who'd spent much time thinking about marriage. She'd assumed, if pressed, that she'd fall in love some day and marry, but it had all been hazy, the kind of misty stuff that would come with the future and wasn't quite as important as the present.

But she knew what her wedding day would be like. The church would be decorated in yellow and white. Her father would give her away while her mother looked on with teary eyes; the girls she'd grown up with would be her brides-maids, and all the people who'd ever mattered in her life would be waiting to see her come down the aisle.

Certainly, she'd never imagined a wedding like this. To be given away by the Tagor when he'd just as soon give her to any—or all—of his men, in a place of dark tents and wine-red carpets, where the guests were as likely to carve each other up as toast the happy couple, was beyond her wildest dreams.

'*Tastavai, bobska, tastavai.*'

'Turn around,' they were saying. They were saying other things, too, the kind of off-colour jokes bridesmaids might make, she was certain of it. Well, at least that crossed cultural barriers. There were sexy jokes, and bridesmaids, there was a bride—and there was a groom.

'*Bobska. Vrostovia, simsaja, eh?*'

Someone handed her a pair of wispy silk underpants and she stepped into them. A bridegroom, she thought. Jake. Jake was to be her bridegroom.

'*Bobska. Tsisenjai.*' She looked up, bewildered. One of the women clucked her tongue impatiently. '*Tsisenjai,*' she said, and she grabbed Dorian's arms and lifted them over her head.

Jake. Jake. She was marrying Jake…

Her heart skipped a beat as they slipped a cotton gown over her head. Hands moved lightly across her body, smoothing the gown at her hips, then working at its rear closure. One of the women bent and placed a pair of delicate leather sandals before her, and Dorian stepped into them. At last, her attendants stood back and nodded their heads.

'*Da, bobska,*' one of them said softly.

Someone put a hand in the small of her back and propelled her through the curtain to the rear of the tent. The tub was empty now, and beside it stood a standing oval mirror. Giggling, the women urged her towards it.

Suddenly, the last thing Dorian wanted was to see herself in her wedding gown. She shook her head as they pushed her forwards.

'I'm sure this is the latest in wedding finery,' she said with forced lightness, 'but it doesn't much matter to me what I look like. For all I care…'

Her eyes met her reflection in the mirror, and she fell silent.

The gown was beautiful by anyone's standards. It was made of white eyelet, with a low, off-the-shoulder neckline that emphasised the curve of her throat and breasts. The sleeves were short and puffed, and the bodice fitted snugly at her waist before becoming a swirling, ankle-length skirt.

A lump rose in Dorian's throat. 'Oh,' she said softly. 'It's—it's lovely.'

One of the women stepped forward and placed a slender wreath of pale yellow and white flowers on her hair. She smiled and said something, and Dorian knew she must be asking if the bride was pleased with how she looked.

'Yes,' she murmured, 'oh, yes. I look—I look—'

To her horror, her eyes filled with tears. She looked like a woman on her way to the arms of her beloved. But that was a lie. What was going to happen in the next few minutes wasn't real, it had nothing to do with love…

'Bobska.' The dour-faced woman leaned forward and pressed her cheek to Dorian's. 'Oskavit,' she said, and Dorian could only hope that it had been a traditional offering of good fortune.

She was going to need it.

*   *   *

It was quiet when she stepped from the tent, and very bright despite the hour. Bonfires ringed the encampment, and an ivory moon hung in the sky. A balalaika whispered a poignant song into the night, and ahead—ahead, a carpeted path stretched towards the brightest fire of all, where the hulking shape of the Tagor waited.

Dorian's heart began to pound. She couldn't go through with this, not even if it meant—

'Kitten.'

She caught her breath as Jake stepped out of the shadows. He was smiling, and it was a different smile from any she'd ever seen on his face before. It was tender and welcoming, and when he put out his hand she hesitated only an instant before she took it. His fingers laced through hers and he led her forwards through the darkness and towards the Tagor.

She moved slowly, her sandalled feet whispering against the soft carpet, her eyes on Jake's face. No, she thought, this was not the wedding she'd imagined would someday be hers. But it *was* her wedding. Hers, and Jake's.

He had been dressed for this occasion, too, in a silky black shirt, leather vest, and close-fitting woollen trousers. His boots had been polished until the dust of the trail was not even a memory.

He looked both civilised and barbaric—he looked like the Jake Prince who'd picked her up along the road a lifetime ago and he looked like the man who would be *abdhan*. But most of all, most of all, he looked like…

Her heart thudded. He looked like the man she had fallen in love with.

No. It was out of the question. They were adversaries; they'd been that from the start and they still were. Hadn't she wired ahead and arranged to turn him into a headline? Hadn't he carefully kept his identity secret from her?

But all of that had nothing to do with the simple truth.

She loved him, she loved Jake Prince or Jack Alexander or the next *abdhan* of Barovnia—she loved him in whatever guise and identity he chose, because no one part of him was indistinguishable from the others.

He was an adventurer and a man who sat behind a desk, he was a dreamer and a doer—and she loved him. And, because she did, she could not go through with this sham. It was bad enough to go through with a pretend marriage to a man who meant nothing to you, but, when you loved the man, how could you participate in such a lie and ever face yourself—or him—again?

She came to a stumbling halt just as they reached the Tagor. 'Jake,' she whispered urgently, 'I can't do this!'

'You can, kitten. You must!'

'No. Jake, no. Please—'

The Tagor spoke. Jake nodded and turned to Dorian. 'He asks if I have lied to him. He says if you have no love in your heart for me, you must tell him so now.'

Her throat constricted. 'Jake. Tell him—tell him...'

Jake cupped her face and gave her a gentle kiss. 'Don't lose your courage now,' he said softly.

His voice was as loving as his kiss. But she knew it was only meant to deceive the Tagor.

The Tagor! In her selfishness she had almost forgotten him. Her glance flew to the chieftain. He had changed his clothing for the wedding, but everything else about him was the same as she remembered, especially the stern, unyielding cast of his swarthy face.

Was she crazy? If she didn't go through with this ceremony, the Tagor would give her away like a party favour. Worse, he'd kill Jake. And a world without Jake was not a world worth living in.

'Kitten?'

Dorian looked straight at the Tagor. 'Tell him I am eager to be your wife,' she said quietly.

Jake put his arm around her waist and drew her close to his side as the Tagor spoke.

'He says that the joining of two people is not to be taken lightly,' he translated, while the chieftain's deep voice rumbled. 'He says that life is a long journey that should not be taken alone. Man and woman should undertake this journey together.' Jake paused. 'He asks if I love you.'

Dorian looked at him. 'And what did you say?' she whispered.

Jake's eyes met hers. 'I said that I love you with all my heart.'

Of course. What other answer could he have given, if they were to get out of this in one piece?

'Now he asks if you love me.'

Her mouth trembled. 'Yes. Tell him I say yes, that I will love you always.'

Jake's arm tightened around her. 'He says, then, that you are mine, and I am yours.'

She swallowed. 'You mean—it's over? We're husband and wife?'

'Yes.' He turned her to him and his hand cupped her cheek. 'We're married, kitten.'

Married. *They were married*!

A shout rose up from the assemblage, and Jake smiled. 'We're getting comments from the sidelines. They want me to kiss the bride.'

Dorian smiled, too, and blinked back the tears burning in her eyes.

'Then do it,' she said lightly.

Jake bent to her and kissed her. It was a kiss meant for the crowd, and they responded to it with good-natured laughter and a smattering of applause. Off in the distance, the balalaika began playing again, joined now by a drum and tambourine, and suddenly Jake swung her up into his arms.

'Jake? What are you doing?'

'Claiming my bride,' he whispered, and his mouth dropped to hers again.

The crowd cheered and parted for him as he strode through it, and all the while he never stopped kissing her. It was part of their performance, she knew that; she told herself that she was only doing her bit when she wound her arms around his neck and kissed him back. The charade would end once they'd left the bonfires—and the crowd— behind.

But it didn't end; it changed, instead, so that by the time they'd reached the darkness of their tent Jake was kissing her with a hungry passion. He lowered her to her feet slowly, letting her body slide down the hard length of his, and she knew without question how much he wanted her.

Not that it was a surprise: he'd wanted her from the start—he'd been honest about that.

Now they were alone, a million miles from reality.

Why wouldn't he want to play this game to its end?

She wouldn't let him, though. To let him make love to her would only make their parting more difficult. It would only make forgetting what had happened this night impossible.

That was what her head was telling her. But her body wasn't listening to her head—it was responding wildly to Jake's touch, to his taste and smell, it was warming under the soft stroke of his hand, quickening under the cleverness of his fingers.

His mouth was hot and open against hers. She made a little whimpering sound as his tongue explored hers. Slowly, inexorably, her hands lifted to his head and her fingers curled tightly into his dark hair.

Jake shuddered at her touch. 'Yes,' he whispered.

Her head fell back as he bent to her and pressed kisses against her throat. His teeth bit gently at the swelling flesh above her gown's neckline.

'I've never wanted a woman as I want you,' he whispered. He cupped her buttocks and brought her tightly against him. 'Feel what you do to me, kitten.'

She felt it: the heat, the hardness. And she wanted that, she wanted the tightly leashed power of him in her arms and in her body, she wanted...

'This is our wedding night, kitten. How can we deny what we feel on a night such as this?'

Dorian felt the sharp sting of tears. 'Our wedding night,' he'd said. But it wasn't that at all; it was only a sham. But if she let him take her, if she let him make this a night she could never forget...

'Tell me you want me as much as I want you,' he said softly.

'No. Jake, I—I can't.'

His fingers were moving down her spine; she felt the coolness of the night air on her skin.

'Jake, you mustn't. Please—'

But her whispered protest was meaningless; it hadn't the power to stand up to his kisses or his caresses. Her gown floated to her ankles like a gentle snowfall. She moaned softly as Jake's hands began moving over her.

'I can feel your desire, kitten,' he said softly. She stood, trembling, while his fingers brushed lightly across her budded nipples. 'Here,' he said, 'and here...'

She cried out as he touched the dampness of her womanhood. 'Oh, Jake. Jake, I—I can't...'

'You can.' His whispered words were fierce. 'You're my wife, kitten. You belong to me now.'

'You belong to me.' How barbaric those words had sounded, only a little while ago. Now—now, they sent a tremor of longing spiralling through her. If only she did belong to him. If only—if only all of this were real. If only…

A match hissed in the darkness. She blinked. Jake stood in a pool of golden candle-light, watching her.

'Ah, kitten,' he whispered, 'you're so beautiful.'

Was she? Suddenly, she wanted to be beautiful, she wanted to be everything Jake could ever desire in a woman.

He took her hand and drew her gently to him.

'Undress me,' he said softly.

Her fingers shook as she undid the first button of his shirt and then the next. Jake caught his breath as she touched his skin; he clasped her wrist, brought her hand to his lips, and pressed his mouth to her palm. His clothing fell away as hers had, until finally he stood proud and unashamed in the candle's glow.

He was beautiful, too; she wanted to tell him that. But how could she talk when his hands and mouth were searching out all her secrets? She was a creature made of crystal and air, shimmering with light and desire, and when he drew her down with him into the darkness she was trembling.

'Dorian,' he whispered. 'My wife.'

His kisses were flames burning her skin everywhere, his whispers promises of pleasures yet to come. Moaning, she moved against him, her body on fire, her hands learning the hardness of silken skin stretched taut over muscle.

When he entered her she cried out, a long, keening sigh that broke from her throat in wonder. Trembling, she called out his name and he held her close, his body shaking, too, as he fought for control.

'Slowly, kitten,' he whispered into her throat. 'We have the whole night for love.'

A night. What was one night, when she wanted forever? And they *had* forever, she thought suddenly. There were things to sort out, but Jake—Jake...

'Ohhh.'

Her cry rose into the darkness and was captured in Jake's kiss. I love you, she thought—and then she was beyond thought: she was adrift in the night and the darkness, guided only by the sweet, fierce power that filled her.

The tent was dark when she came awake, stirred from sleep by his caress.

'Mmm,' she sighed, her mouth pressed to his throat.

Jake kissed her. 'Sleepyhead,' he whispered as his hand moved over her, his fingers stroking lightly across her nipples. 'So you're finally awake, hmm?'

Dorian smiled. 'How could I not be?' Her breath caught as he trailed his fingers down her belly. 'It's very hard to sleep when you're—when you're doing that...'

'It's hard to sleep when you're in my arms, kitten,' he whispered. 'It seems a shame to waste this night.'

This night. Was he telling her that this night was all they had?

'Dorian—I don't know if you realise how different things will be, once we reach Kadar.' She heard the rasp of his breath. 'You'll be Dorian Oliver again, *WorldWeek*'s reporter on the scene—'

'*WorldWeek*?' She smiled into the darkness. 'What's that?'

Jake kissed her. 'And I—I'll be—I'll be...'

'You'll be the *abdhazim*.'

He went still in her arms. 'You know?'

She sighed. 'Yes.'

'When…?'

'I don't know, exactly. I thought that's who you were, at first, and then you convinced me otherwise. But when we were on the way to Quarem…'

Her breath caught. Quarem. The telegram. She had to tell him about the telegram…

'Dorian.' He stroked the hair back from her face. 'These last few days with you—they've meant everything to me. I never dreamed my last hours of freedom would be so sweet.'

'Your last hours…?'

'Yes. My advisers almost went crazy when I told them I was going to fly into Kadar alone, but—'

'Is that what you were doing? I thought—I thought you'd changed your mind about becoming *abdhan*.'

'How could I change my mind about a responsibility?' He kissed her gently. 'I just wanted the luxury of being Jack Alexander a little while longer.'

Dorian touched his cheek. 'Or Jake Prince.'

'No, love. I never expected to be lucky enough to be a man named Jake Prince—or for these days to have been so special.'

Her heart lifted at those simple words. 'Have they been?' she whispered.

He rolled to his side and took her with him, holding her close in the hard curve of his arm. There was a silence before he spoke again.

'When I was eighteen, I met a woman. I met her at a party, one of those university madhouses where there are too many people, too much noise, and too much booze. I wasn't much for that kind of thing, but I'd let my room-mate talk me into going.' He drew in his breath, then expelled it. 'I'd been having a bad time. I'd just lost both my parents in an accident—'

'At eighteen? How painful that must have been.'

'I suppose I was feeling sorry for myself, and very much adrift. I'd always had this strange division in my life because my father was a Barovnian diplomat, part of the royal family, and my mother was an American. Losing them made me feel as if I'd lost the only solid ground I had. So there I was, vulnerable as hell, and there *she* was, this woman, a little older, very beautiful—and very understanding.'

'But she hurt you, didn't she? I can hear it in your voice.'

'We became lovers. We were inseparable for a couple of weeks.' He drew his arm from under Dorian's head, sat up, and wrapped his arms around his knees. 'And I trusted her. I told her things—I talked about how hard it was to live in two different worlds, about the tragedy of the poverty that still plagued my father's birthplace...'

Dorian sat up, too. 'And?' she asked softly.

'And,' he said, his voice hardening, 'about a month after the affair ended, everything I'd said was splashed across four columns in the sleaziest of the tabloids—including some not-so-subtle references about what it was like to go to bed with—I think her phrase was "a magnificent savage" like me.'

'Oh, Jake!' Dorian put her arms around him and pressed her cheek to his back. 'It must have been horrible.'

'Yeah.' His voice was gruff. 'But it was a lesson, and I never forgot it, a lesson about reporters—and about women.'

His words drove a knife into her heart. The telegram, she thought, the telegram!

Perhaps it hadn't been sent.

'Jake—are we—are we going to Kadar through the Valley of the Two Suns?'

He turned and took her into his arms. 'Just listen to this

woman,' he said, drawing her down beside him. 'She wants a geography lesson at a moment like this.'

'Jake, please—it's important.'

The old woman hadn't spoken English very well, had she? Perhaps she hadn't really understood.

'This is more important,' he whispered.

Perhaps there wasn't a telegraph office in Quarem after all. Perhaps...

Jake bent to her, and she was lost.

When she awoke next, grey light was filtering into the tent. Jake was fully dressed and leaning over her.

'I've been out scouting,' he said quietly. 'Our pals are still sleeping off the party. I want to get going before they awaken and change their minds about letting the guest of honour leave.'

She dressed quickly, then crept after him out of the tent and through the silent encampment. A herd of horses was grazing just beyond the tents. Jake held up his hand and Dorian stood still while he moved in among the animals. Minutes later, he emerged on the back of a white horse.

'Give me your hand,' he said, and he swung Dorian up behind him.

'Jake?' She put her arms around his waist and leaned close to him. 'When will we get to the Valley of the Two Suns?'

'Why do you keep asking me that?'

Because I've betrayed you, she thought. No. She hadn't, not really, she'd only been doing her job. But it was too much to explain now.

'Dorian?'

'I must talk to you,' she whispered. 'Before we reach the valley.'

Jake hesitated. 'We'll make a stop before then, OK? Now, hold on tight, kitten. We're going to ride hard.'

They rode for what seemed like hours. How could she tell Jake about what might be waiting for them? What could she say? No matter what she said, he wouldn't like hearing it, but he'd understand. He had to understand.

The mare reared wildly as a shattering roar filled the air. Dorian ducked as an enormous dark shadow swooped over them.

It was a helicopter.

'Jake,' she shouted, 'Jake, look...'

But he'd already jumped to the ground. He clasped Dorian around the waist and brought her down beside him, and then he began waving his arms over his head.

The 'copter dipped down for a closer look, then settled slowly to the ground ahead of them. The engine whined to silence as a handful of men tumbled out and trotted to where Dorian and Jake stood.

'My lord!' The tallest of the men dropped to his knees. 'Thank God you are all right!'

'Get up, Kasmir. I'm happy to see you got my message.'

'From Quarem. Yes, it reached us yesterday.' The man smiled. 'It is good that you remembered this ridge.'

'How is my cousin? Is he—?'

'He lives, my lord, but in a coma. The surgeons say we must wait.'

Jake nodded. 'Well, then,' he said briskly, 'let's get going. I'll want to see him as soon as possible.'

Dorian moved closer to Jake's side. 'You told them to meet us here?'

'Yes.'

'Then—we're not going through the valley?'

Jake's mouth twisted. 'No.'

'But you told me—'

'I know what I told you. But it made more sense to arrange to be met here.'

She nodded. 'Because—because you didn't trust me.'

He thrust his fingers through his hair. 'Dammit, Dorian, does it really matter now?'

'Yes, it does,' she said. She thought of the anguish she'd suffered, thinking he was going to walk into the trap she'd set. 'Why didn't you tell me the truth when I asked how we'd be entering Kadar?'

His mouth turned down. 'As long as we're asking questions, why did you keep asking?'

'My lord.' Kasmir stepped forward. 'I would suggest that Miss Oliver had a very special interest in your point of entry.' He looked at Dorian, his eyes as cold and flat as a serpent's. 'An army of reporters and photographers awaits you at the Valley of the Two Suns, my lord. They have been there since last night, at Miss Oliver's direction.'

Dorian shook her head as Jake swung towards her. 'No,' she said quickly, 'that's not so.'

'It is, my lord. I myself saw a copy of the wire.'

'Well, yes, I mean, I sent it.' Dorian flung out her arms as Jake stared at her. 'But—but I sent it before—before—Jake, don't look at me like that! I was going to tell you.'

'When were you going to tell me?' He caught hold of her and drew her aside. 'When the first flash bulb exploded in my face?'

'No!'

He thrust her from him as if she were something evil and poisonous. 'Keep the hell away from me,' he said in a soft, terrible whisper. 'Do you understand?'

'Jake, please, you have to listen. After—after last night…' Her voice fell to a whisper. 'After what we shared…'

'What we shared was a bed,' he said coldly. 'And if you plan on detailing the more intimate aspects of our adventure for *WorldWeek*'s eager readers, I'd suggest you remember that every word you write about me will only make you look like the whore you are.'

The blood drained from her face. 'You can't really think...'

'Jaacov?'

The woman's voice was as soft as silk, but it silenced them both. She stood in the open door of the 'copter, a slender figure swathed in gold silk, her dark eyes fixed on Jake.

'Alana,' he whispered. He moved towards her quickly, a smile curving across his mouth. 'Alana, sweetheart, what are you doing here?'

The woman smiled, too, a smile that lit her beautiful face.

'How could I not come to you, Jaacov, when you have been away so long?'

Jake swept her into his arms and she wound her slender arms around his neck as he lifted her off the ground.

'Alana,' he said—and Dorian turned away.

'Oh, God,' she whispered.

Beside her, Kasmir smiled coldly. 'It is a sight to warm the heart, is it not, Miss Oliver?'

'Who—who is she?' Dorian asked unsteadily. But she knew. In her heart, she knew! 'Things will be different when we reach Kadar,' Jake had said...

'She is Alana Vadrovna—the betrothed of the *abdhan*.'

CHAPTER TWELVE

'YOU,' the grey-haired RBC-TV anchorman said, raising his glass of red wine in Dorian's direction, 'are one hell of a reporter.'

'Indeed she is.' The TNT-TV news commentator smiled. 'You've pulled off quite a coup, Miss Oliver.'

The leggy brunette from the Pyramid Network flashed her perfect white teeth. 'If you'd just give us a hint about the *real* Jack Alexander,' she said coyly, 'just a little colour for background information, of course…?'

The TNT-TV commentator shifted as close as the minuscule table in the bar of the Hotel Kadar would permit. 'Just some background material from an ''unnamed source''. We wouldn't violate your confidence.'

'No.' The brunette showed her white teeth again. 'You can count on that, Dorrie dear.'

'It's Dorian,' Dorian said.

The brunette's silken eyebrows lifted. 'Pardon?'

'My name.' Dorian's smile was all sweet innocence. She was tired of being buttered up by everybody from a stringer for *Der Spiegel* to the publisher of *The Times*. They, at least, had been less obvious than this trio. 'You keep calling me Dorrie—I'm called ''Dorian''. And I'm afraid you'll just have to wait until *WorldWeek* prints my article. I know my boss would be as livid as yours if I gave away an exclusive.'

Dorian's colleagues looked at each other. The fatherly gentleman from RBC frowned, announced his sentiments with a word that would have shocked his nightly viewers, and then belted down his third Scotch and soda of the evening.

'Well,' he said, 'this damned news blackout can't last forever.'

'It can last as long as Jack Alexander wants it to last,' the brunette said grumpily.

'You mean Jaacov Alexandrei,' the TNT-TV commentator said. 'Hell, now that he's ensconced in that medieval pile of stone up the road, he's sure as hell not Jack Alexander any more.'

'He's not even Jaacov Alexandrei,' the RBC anchor muttered. 'He's the *abdhan*, and he's not about to let us forget it.'

'He's not the *abdhan*,' Dorian said. They all looked up, startled, as if they'd forgotten her presence. 'He's still the *abdhazim*.' The three faces remained impassive. 'I mean, his cousin is still alive.'

'We know what you mean,' the brunette said with a condescending smile. 'What we don't know is why the bastard's clamped a lid on all information coming from the palace.' Her smile took on a crafty edge. 'But we suspect it might have something to do with you, sweetie, and that little sojourn in the wilderness you and he had.'

Dorian looked at the expectant faces. The false smiles were gone now, replaced by looks of sly speculation. She cleared her throat, then pushed back her chair.

'Well,' she said brightly, 'I think I'll call it a night.'

Was it her imagination, or did conversation pause as she made her way out of the hotel's café to the lobby? She couldn't tell any more; after a week of being her colleagues' centre of interest, Dorian had begun to feel mildly paranoid.

She stabbed her finger at the lift button. It had started the day she and Jake had been found. By the time the helicopter had whisked them to Kadar, the clutch of newspeople who'd been waiting at the Valley of the Two Suns had somehow been alerted to the fact that they were to be denied the story of the *abdhazim* and the reporter, so they'd been waiting to pounce on Dorian as she entered the hotel.

She'd begged off answering any questions, but her swollen eyes and trembling mouth had not gone unnoticed. And when word had come down from the palace that the *abdhazim* had decided that all news would from now on be cleared through his ministers the rumour mill had gone to work full tilt.

'What went on out there between you two?' people kept asking, although their nudges and winks made it clear that they really didn't require answers.

The lift doors opened and Dorian stepped inside. Walt had asked, too, during their first phone conversation, in words less subtle. It had been his very first question. Dorian had closed her eyes wearily and before she could answer the line had gone dead.

The lift shuddered to a stop and she stepped into the hotel corridor. Walt would be phoning soon for an update and she didn't want to miss his call. She was going to tell him what she'd been telling him for three days now.

She wanted to go home.

Not because of the rumours circulating around her; she was a big girl, and she could survive those. And not because she couldn't bear being in the same city as Jake. No. It was nothing as foolish as that.

The key trembled in her hand as she inserted it in the lock. She just—she just wanted to go home so that she could get started writing her story.

That made sense, didn't it? Everyone was waiting around to see if the *abdhan* would survive or if the *abdhazim* would be enthroned in his place, but she was weary of waiting. It wouldn't change her story: she had the goods on Jake

Prince, and she'd tell it to the world as soon as she sat down at her word processor.

Her room was dark and quiet, and she sighed as she closed the door and tossed her room key on the desk. There was a tiny balcony, and she walked slowly to it and stepped outside.

Kadar lay softly lit and silent around her. Jake had said she would find the city with one foot in the past and one in the present, but he had not told her that she would also find it beautiful and exotic—but then, that depended on your perspective, didn't it? If you were virtually a prisoner inside the grey stone walls of the castle, as Jake was, exotic beauty didn't have much meaning.

Not that she felt the least bit of compassion for him. Why should she? Only a fool would feel compassion for a man like Jake Prince. Jake, or Jaacov Alexandrei, as he was now called, had no soul. And no heart.

And she had never loved him.

It had taken a lot of pain before she'd realised the truth; she'd wept into her pillow that first night in this room, wept until she'd had no tears left, but somewhere between the last fading star and the rise of the sun it had come to her.

Jake had hurt her pride, but not her heart. She had fallen in love with love, but not with him.

She'd been thrown into a dangerous yet romantic situation, with a handsome, virile man—a man to whom she'd been physically attracted, and the result had been inevitable. Who could blame her? Exhaustion, fear, the disorientation of having gone from a world she knew to one she'd never imagined had warped her perspective.

She had let him make love to her, and she'd romanticised it by telling herself it was love.

But it hadn't been love. It had been sex.

Dorian sighed as she stepped back into her room. How

she could have let herself think, even for a moment, that she loved him was beyond her. What was there to love in a man like that? He was an arrogant, egotistical bastard who didn't care about anybody's feelings but his own, a man with an appetite for women and a hatred for reporters. As for the story he'd told her about the woman who'd betrayed him—who cared? Even if it were true, it didn't give him the right to treat people as he did, nor to treat her as he had.

He was, in short, an insolent barbarian who'd been given power by the fortunes of birth. He had no scruples about using people and then discarding them, but her turn was coming.

The pen, she thought with a little smile, was a mighty instrument indeed.

Jake could keep the lid on the news while she was here in Barovnia, but as soon as she reached the States the ball would be in her court. She was a reporter, and she had one hell of a story to tell. And, while she would not pepper the column she wrote with personal details, no matter what Jake thought, she would write about the man as he really was.

Selfish. Vain. Imperious. Unfeeling.

Jake Prince, A Scoundrel Among Men: A First-Person Account, by Dorian Oliver.

Yes, she thought as she brushed her teeth, that headline would do for a start. And the sooner she got started on writing the article that would accompany it, the better. Walt could fly someone in to replace her. He could—

The phone shrilled, and she snatched at it.

'New York's burning up with rumours, Blondie,' Walt said without preamble. She knew he was trying to talk fast enough to elude whoever might be monitoring the call. 'You should hear the stories going around about you and Alexander.'

Dorian closed her eyes. 'I can imagine.'

'Nope.' Walt chuckled. 'You can't. Some of them are pretty creative.'

'Why do I get the feeling you're not doing anything to stop them?'

He laughed. 'Hey, it's all free publicity, right? We're gonna outsell *Time* and *Newsweek* combined.'

'Walt?' She took a breath. 'I was thinking. Why don't I head back to New York tomorrow?'

'Now, Blondie, we've been through this. You hang in there until we see if the *abdhan* kicks the bucket.'

'But why? It won't change anything.'

'Of course it will. If your travelling companion becomes *abdhan*, your story will have even more kick.'

'I really don't see—'

'What's going on there, Oliver?' Walt's voice grew suspicious. 'You thinking of doing a deal with somebody else?'

'No. No, it's nothing like that. I just—'

'Good. Because you work for *WorldWeek*. You just remember that.'

'Walt.' Dorian stared at the receiver. 'Walt?'

The phone was dead. She sighed as she hung it up and then she rose slowly and walked to the balcony again.

All right. She could survive another few days. Maybe she'd start getting her notes together. Actually, there was nothing to stop her from starting the article now, while she cooled her heels in Kadar.

Her mouth hardened. Just wait until the world read the truth about Jaacov Alexandrei, who treated women like property, who took what he wanted and to hell with anyone else...

Who'd held her in his arms when she needed comforting, who'd made her cry out his name over and over during their long night together...

Dorian began to tremble. And all along, *all along*, the son of a bitch had been engaged to be married; he'd had a bride waiting for him in Kadar—one of his choosing, not simply one for the taking.

If only she hadn't seen Jake slip away from that charter flight! If only she hadn't followed him! She would have missed this story and what it was going to do for her career, but that would have been better than this, better than the pain that kept knifing through her heart...

A sob burst from her throat. Who was she kidding? She'd cried that first night and every night since, and, no matter how she concentrated on hating Jake, she couldn't stop wanting him.

She spun away from the balcony, hurried into the bedroom, and threw open the wardrobe door. Her career was important, but not as important as her sanity. She had to get control of her life again, and she could not do that here, in a place where Jake Prince was Emperor of the World. She was going back to New York, where she belonged, and if Walt Hemple didn't like it he could just go to hell.

It turned out to be easy to slip out of the hotel unnoticed. Her fellow journalists had turned the café into a clubhouse, which meant that the lobby was deserted when Dorian stepped from the lift. The taxi she'd called was waiting just outside.

'The airport, please.'

'Airport, *da*,' the driver said, and with the careless disregard for speed limits of taxi drivers everywhere he wove through the quiet streets of the city, on to the one main highway, and delivered her with more than an hour to spare before the late-night flight to New York.

She began to feel better as soon as she entered the terminal. She would be home soon, among all the things that were familiar, and what had happened to her in this country would be nothing but a memory.

Her steps faltered as she approached the ticket counter. Jake would be a memory, too. How long would it take to purge her thoughts of him? A month? A year?

A lifetime...

'*Bobska*?'

She looked up, startled. The ticket clerk was smiling pleasantly. Dorian smiled in return.

'Sorry. One-way to New York.' Dorian pushed her credit card across the counter. 'Charge it, please.'

'You have luggage, miss?'

'No. Just a bag.'

'Passport?'

Dorian nodded. 'Yes. Here it is.'

The woman took the little blue booklet and opened it. Her face creased in a frown. After a moment Dorian cleared her throat.

'Is there a problem?'

The clerk looked up. 'Is no entry stamp, miss.'

'No entry...' Dorian blew out her breath. How could there be an entry stamp, when she had not entered the country through Customs? 'No,' she said, 'no, there isn't. But I came in legally, I assure you.'

The clerk frowned again. 'Must be stamp, miss.'

'I didn't come in the usual way. I—I...' She bit down on her lip. How could she explain? Someone had done a rough translation of the local Press's coverage of Jake's unorthodox entry into Barovnia; she had not been mentioned. The clerk's English was limited and Dorian's Barovnian non-existent. Explaining would take half the night, by which time the plane would have left.

'Look, is there a supervisor around? A supervisor.

Someone in charge.' Dorian leaned forward. 'Don't you have a boss?' she asked desperately.

'A boss!' The clerk smiled. 'You wait, please.'

She waited five minutes, then ten, and when she was almost ready to stamp her feet with frustration a man came strolling out from an office down the hall.

'How do you do?' Dorian said with a fixed smile. 'My name is Dorian Oliver, and—'

'The reporter?'

Her smiled wavered a little. Had the rumours spread outside the circle of reporters? Had she become a household name among the Barovnians, too?

'Yes,' she said briskly, 'that's right. There's a slight problem with my passport, but I thought, if you'd just phone my Embassy. I know it's late, but I'm sure there's an emergency number, and—'

'There is no problem, miss.'

Dorian let out her breath. 'Well, that's good news.'

'Please.' He smiled and inclined his head. 'If you'll just come into my office and make yourself comfortable—'

'But my plane…' Her gaze flew to the wall clock as he took her arm and led her down the hall. 'It leaves in three quarters of an hour.'

'Make yourself at home, please, Miss Oliver. I'll take care of the problem immediately.'

'But…'

The door swung shut after him. Dorian stared at it, and then she stalked across the room and sank down on an institutional plastic sofa.

Now what? She'd heard endless stories from foreign correspondents about how many hours, if not days, it could take to get through red tape, especially in out-of-the-way little countries.

She pushed back her sleeve and looked at her watch. Ten more minutes had slipped by.

'Come on,' she said through her teeth, 'come on!'

Five minutes passed, and then five more, and finally Dorian slapped her hands on her knees and stood up.

'OK,' she said grimly, 'enough is enough!' She stalked to the door and grabbed the handle—but it wouldn't turn. Her brow creased; she twisted it again and again. 'Hey!' Her voice rose. 'Hey! Open this door, will you?' She waited, but there was only silence. 'Do you hear me?' Furiously, she pounded both fists on the door. 'You open this door right now,' she yelled, 'or I'll—I'll…'

She fell back as the door swung open. 'Or you'll what?' Jake said coldly.

For a moment she was too stunned to speak. Then, gradually, she felt her brain begin to function again.

'Jake,' she whispered. 'What—what are you doing here?'

He stepped into the room and slammed the door behind him. 'I'm not the one answering questions, Dorian. You are.'

'Did—did that foolish man call you? I didn't ask him to do that; I asked him to call—'

'The Embassy. Yes. I know.'

'Then why did he call you?' Her chin lifted. 'Was my name on a list? Are you trying to stop reporters from leaving the country?'

He strode past her, leaned back against the desk, and folded his arms across his chest.

'Why are you sneaking out of Barovnia in the middle of the night?'

Colour striped her cheeks. 'I am not sneaking out in the middle of the night.'

Jake crossed his feet at the ankles. 'It's almost one a.m. If that's not the middle of the night, what is it?'

Her chin lifted in defiance. 'Early morning.'

A quick, cool smile flashed across his face. 'I'd almost forgotten how clever you are with words, Dorian. Now that we've done with the pleasantries, perhaps you'll answer my question. Why are you leaving Barovnia?'

She stared at him. 'I don't have to answer that.'

'No,' he said, nodding his head, 'no, you don't. You can just sit here until the sun comes up, and—'

'I'll have missed my plane by then.'

He shrugged lazily. 'There'll be another.'

But not until midday, she thought in sudden desperation. And I can't stay here any longer, Jake, I can't...

'I can't,' she said, a little breathlessly. 'My—my boss wants me in New York immediately.'

Jake's teeth flashed in a quick smile. 'Your boss told you to stay here until your job was finished. I may not have the phrasing exactly right, but—'

'You *have* been tapping my phone!'

'Why are you running away, Dorian?'

Their eyes met. 'I'm not.'

Jake reached into his pocket and held out her passport. 'And why,' he asked softly, 'are you trying to use this when you know it's illegal?'

Dorian glared at him. 'My passport isn't illegal.'

'Really? That's not what Mr Sojac tells me. He says you have no entry stamp.'

'Of course I haven't. How could I, when I never entered the country through Customs?'

'No.' His eyes grew cold and hard. 'You never entered to the applause of your colleagues, either, but then, it was just your hard luck that I managed to spoil your plans.'

She stared at him, her breasts rising and falling with the rapidity of her breathing. She could feel her anger slipping away; it was being replaced by bleak despair, but she mustn't let that happen.

So what if he thought she'd betrayed him? The truth was that *he* had betrayed her, and in the cruellest sort of way. She had to keep remembering that, remembering how she despised him...

'Jake.' She cleared her throat. 'Please. Don't do this.'

'Don't do what?' He opened the little blue book and peered into it, leafing idly through the pages as if he might come across something interesting. 'What a pity,' he said. 'You don't seem to have done very much travelling.' He looked at her. 'Don't you like to travel?'

'Dammit, Jake—'

'But then, of course, travel is expensive.' He frowned as he flicked the passport shut. 'Well, not to worry. Now that you're about to become a hotshot columnist, your boss will send you anywhere you want to go. The Far East. South America. Paris, London.' His face darkened. 'Of course, you want to be sure he doesn't try to send you where you're not welcome.'

'What is it, Jake? Do you want me to beg?' Her voice was steady, but her hand shook as she held it out to him. 'If you've any decency at all, you'll give me my—'

'Decency.' His voice caressed the word. 'And what would you know of decency, Dorian?'

'Give me my passport!'

He smiled coolly. 'If you want it that badly, come and get it.'

'Jake, dammit!' Dorian slammed her hand against the desk. 'This isn't a game!'

'Sure it is. And you play games so well. Don't you want to play another?'

'You—you—' A word burst from her lips as she flew across the room. 'Give me that!' she demanded.

Jake laughed as he raised the passport over his head. 'Give you what? This?'

Tears rose in her eyes. 'I hate you, Jake Prince,' she panted as she stretched for the little blue booklet. 'Damn you to hell!'

'No,' he said, and suddenly he wasn't laughing any more, 'no, Dorian, you can't damn me to hell.' He caught her wrists in his hands, spun her around, and backed her against the desk. 'You already did that once, you see; you don't get a second chance.'

Her breath sobbed in and out of her lungs as she struggled against him. 'Let go of me, Jake! I swear, if you don't, I'll— I'll—'

'You'll what? Call the cops? The militia? The king?' He laughed. 'Don't waste your time, Dorian. I *am* the cops. And the militia. And the king, in effect, remember? I'm all those things—and I'm also the man you betrayed.'

'*I* betrayed *you*? That's a laugh.'

'You're damned right you betrayed me.' He let go of her wrists and clasped her shoulders in his hands. 'You set me up. You fed me little titbits of sex and sweet compassion, so you could lead me like a lamb to the slaughter.'

'No. That's not true.'

'Are you trying to pretend you didn't send a telegram to *WorldWeek*?'

'I was only doing my job. But you—'

'And what a job you did,' he said coldly. 'Setting me up for the cameras—'

'That's a lie!' Angry tears rose in her eyes and she swiped them away with her hand. 'I tried to warn you—'

'When, Dorian? Just tell me that!'

'I *did* try! I tried to tell you during the night, when you awakened me. And—'

'Yes.' Jake shifted his weight, so that his body brushed

lightly against hers. 'I remember waking you. I remember it very clearly.'

She remembered too, oh, yes, she remembered. His kisses. His whispers. The feel of his hands and his mouth…

'And—and then the next morning,' she said quickly. 'I kept saying I said I had to talk to you. I was going to tell you about the telegram I'd sent.'

'So what? Maybe you'd decided you'd made a mistake, calling for the reserves. Hell, you'd drawn stuff out of me that would make for quite a story. Keeping it an exclusive would have made it more valuable.'

Dorian stared at him. 'You're a fine one to talk,' she whispered. 'You—you used me, Jake. I was just—I was a toy, something to play with…'

Her throat constricted. What was the point in this? Jake hated her, and she—she hated him. Nothing they could say would change that, and if it was hard to stand this close to him without reaching out and trying to smooth away the tiny lines at the corners of his mouth and eyes it was only because—because…

Her heart fell. It was because she loved him, and she always would, despite what he'd done to her. If there was a special place in hell for a man who'd treated a woman as Jake had treated her, then there had to be a place there, too, for a woman foolish enough to go on loving such a man.

Tears rose in her eyes, and she turned her head away.

'Please,' she said in a choked whisper, 'let me go home.'

'Why? So you can get back to New York and write your story? What are you going to call it, *The Lady and The Barbarian*?'

'No. I—I won't write anything like that. I'll just—I'll write about—about a man who—who…'

She fell silent. She would not write this story at all, she thought, and the realisation came as no great surprise.

Perhaps she'd known it all along. She would never write about Jake. How could she, when no matter what she said or how she said it she would violate not just his privacy, but the precious time they'd shared?

Jake clasped her chin and forced her to look at him. 'About a man who what? What's your story for *WorldWeek* going to be about?'

Dorian took a deep breath. 'Nothing. There'll be nothing in the magazine.'

'I see.' He glared at her. 'So you sold out to the highest bidder. Who was it, Dorian? American TV? The British penny papers? I hear *Stern* pays damned well.' He jerked her head up. 'Who'd you sell your soul to?'

'No one.' She met his eyes. 'I'm not going to write anything at all. I know you don't believe me—'

'You're right, I don't.'

'So I'll sign a release, or whatever it is you call it. Just have your lawyers send it to me—'

She cried out as his hands slipped to her shoulders and he half lifted her to her toes.

'What kind of fool do you take me for? You go off to New York, and it's too late for me to do anything. No, Dorian, you're going to have to do a lot better than that.'

'What, then?' The tears she'd tried so hard to stop began to trickle down her cheeks. 'What do you want from me, Jake? What can I do to prove that—that I'd sooner die than hurt you?'

The admission hung between them, drifting in the air like smoke from a dying fire. Dorian wanted to call the words back, but it was too late. Jake's hands slid from her shoulders to curve lightly around her face.

'I'll tell you what you can do,' he said, his voice suddenly soft and gentle. 'You can kiss me.'

'No. Jake, no. Don't. I don't—I can't...'

He bent his head and brushed his mouth lightly over hers. It was a soft, gentle kiss, and she tried to turn away from it, but he held her fast, his lips moving over hers tenderly, sweetly, and, despite her determination not to reveal herself to him more than she already had, she gave a little sob and swayed towards him. Her arms linked around his neck as he gathered her to him, and she returned his kiss with the same tenderness and passion.

They stayed that way for a long, long time, lost in each other's arms, and then, finally, Jake drew back.

'Did you really think I'd let you leave Barovnia so easily?' he asked softly.

Dorian leaned her forehead against his chest. 'Why are you doing this?' she asked in a broken whisper.

'Because I want to hear you admit the truth.' He held her from him and looked into her eyes. 'You're in love with me.'

Her eyes filled with tears. 'This isn't fair,' she whispered. 'You have to leave me something, Jake. My pride, at least.'

He smiled. 'Why should I, kitten? You haven't left me anything but days and nights of anguish.'

'Don't.' She sighed as he drew her against his heart. 'Don't lie to me. There's no reason.'

'You're right, there isn't. That's why I'm going to tell you the truth.' He took her face in his hands and kissed her mouth. 'I love you, kitten.'

Wild joy filled her heart—but then she remembered.

'No,' she whispered. 'You don't.'

'Don't I?'

Dorian closed her eyes. 'I've seen Alana, remember?'

Jake's brows rose. 'Alana?'

She looked at him. 'Yes. And if you're going to tell me that a prerogative of royalty is—is having both a wife and a mistress, I'm not interested.'

He smiled. 'That's a very old-fashioned notion, kitten.'

Her mouth trembled. 'Didn't I ever tell you, Jake? I'm an old-fashioned girl.'

'Very well.' He let go of her, reached into his pocket, and held out her passport. 'Go on,' he said, 'take it. It belongs to you.'

Well, what had she expected? He was the *abdhazim* and Alana was the bride he'd chosen. Carefully, eyes downcast so that he would not see the tell-tale gleam of tears on her lashes, Dorian took the passport from him.

'Thank you.'

'You're welcome. What are you going to do with that, now that you've got it?'

Dorian looked up. 'You know what I'm going to do with it. I'm going to go back to the States.'

He nodded. 'That's a good idea. I'll be doing the same thing in another few weeks, when my cousin's fully able to resume normal activities.'

'The *abdhan*'s all right, then?'

'Yes.'

She smiled tremulously. 'I'm glad,' she whispered. 'Now you won't have to be *abdhan*. You can go back to your old life.'

Smiling, he reached out and touched her hair. 'Well, with some modifications, I suppose. I've agreed to spend part of the year here, to help Seref modernise our country.'

'Good. I mean, I know that's important to you.'

'And then, there's my marriage.'

Dorian swallowed past the lump in her throat. 'Yes. Your marriage.' She turned away. 'I wish you only the best, of course.'

'Of course.' His voice was solemn. 'Well. I suppose I'd better get back to my people. When I got the call that you were trying to leave, we'd just got word of Seref's recovery. The celebration is still going on.'

She nodded. Don't cry, she warned herself fiercely, as he started to turn away, don't you dare cry!

'But I suppose I should warn you, though…'

'Warn me?'

'Yes.' Jake looked at her. 'They won't accept your passport.'

She blinked. 'What do you mean?'

'Well, it's not stamped.' He frowned, but she could see the laughter in his eyes. 'You're in the country illegally, and that's a serious offence.'

'But—but we've been through all this! I *am* here legally!'

He shook his head. 'Nope,' he said, leaning back against the door and folding his arms over his chest, 'you're not. And your passport lists you as Dorian Oliver.'

'Of course it does. That's my name!'

He smiled lazily. 'No, it isn't. Your name is Dorian Alexander. Or Dorian Alexandrei.' He laughed. 'Or maybe even Dorian Prince.'

A tremor went through her. 'Jake. What are you talking about?'

He reached for her and drew her to him. 'We're married, kitten. You're my wife.'

'No. No, I'm not. It wasn't legal. You said so yourself.'

A sly smile tugged at the corners of his mouth. 'I lied.'

'What?'

'Well, what else was I going to do? You had to agree to that ceremony, or it would have been the end of the line.' He tilted her face to his. 'Besides, when a man finds love, he'll do anything to keep it.' His smile became a grin. 'Even get married.'

'Married?' she whispered. 'We're really married?'

He laughed softly. 'Don't look so upset, darling. We can

take our vows again, if you like, in a proper setting with all the trimmings.'

'But—but what about Alana?'

Jake nuzzled her throat. 'What about her?'

'Well, you can't marry the both of us, not even in Barovnia.' She frowned and the tip of her tongue touched her lip. 'Can you?'

'Not unless I want Seref to take me out and shoot me.'

Dorian stared at him. 'Seref?'

'Alana is just what Kasmir said she was, sweetheart. She's the betrothed of the *abdhan*. The three of us grew up together, but it's been special between the two of them for a long, long time.' He smiled. 'I'm going to warn Seref that he and Alana had better have enough little princes and princesses so I never have to worry about becoming the *abdhan* again.'

'Oh, Jake. I thought…' She shook her head. 'Why did you let me think we were going to the Valley of the Two Suns?'

Jake's mouth twisted. 'I suppose—I suppose I didn't trust you. I was going to explain…'

'But there wasn't time.'

He nodded. 'Exactly. Can you forgive me?'

Dorian smiled. 'I'll forgive you,' she whispered, 'if you forgive me.'

He kissed her, and she sighed. 'That last night, though—I kept hoping you'd tell me the truth about yourself, but you didn't.'

'I wanted to. But if anyone in camp had recognised me, all bets were off. They might have held us for ransom; they might have decided to slit our throats.' He gathered her tightly into his arms. 'It was a burden I couldn't share with you, kitten. Do you see?'

She nestled into his embrace. 'What I see,' she said softly, 'is that you've protected me from the minute we met.'

'And I'll go on doing it for the rest of my life, if you'll let me.'

He kissed her deeply. After a long time Dorian stirred.

'Have you forgotten, my *abdhazim*, that your people are waiting for you?'

Jake swung her up into his arms. 'How do you feel about keeping to the old ways, sweetheart?'

Dorian smiled. 'You mean, you want me to quit *WorldWeek*?'

'No.' He took a deep breath. 'No, love, I wouldn't ask that of you.'

'But you can,' she said softly. 'You see, I'd much rather be at my husband's side than at my desk in New York.'

'You really are an old-fashioned girl,' he said, smiling. 'Who would have dreamed it?'

She linked her arms around his neck. 'But I'd never agree to walk ten paces to the rear of my husband.'

'No,' Jake said. His smile broadened. 'I didn't think you would.'

'And I'd never promise to remain mute.'

'The custom I had in mind is a little bit different, kitten. It's one that says that the *abdhazim* brings his bride to his castle and shows her to his people, so they can all see how beautiful she is.'

'Ah. Well, that sounds lovely.'

Jake kissed her. 'And then,' he whispered, 'he takes her to his rooms, and he makes love to her until the sun is high in the sky.'

Dorian sighed and laid her head against his shoulder.

'Sometimes,' she said softly, 'the old ways are very definitely the best.'

Robyn Donald has always lived in Northland in New Zealand, initially on her father's stud dairy farm at Warkworth, then in the Bay of Islands, an area of great natural beauty where she lives today with her husband and an ebullient and mostly Labrador dog. She resigned her teaching position when she found she enjoyed writing romances more, and now spends any time not writing in reading, gardening, travelling, and writing letters to keep up with her two adult children and her friends.

Out this month!
Forgotten Sins **by Robyn Donald**
In Modern Romance™

A Forbidden Desire

by
Robyn Donald

PROLOGUE

HE REFUSED to look across the crowd of people dancing beneath the intense, dark Fijian sky, but a frown half hid his hard blue eyes. He resented this awareness, this almost psychic summons, mainly because he was accustomed to thinking of himself as a restrained man, easily able to control the emotions that prowled in the cage he'd fashioned for them five years ago.

For some reason, tall, slim Jacinta Lyttelton rattled the bars of that cage. It didn't help that she was completely unaware of her power, or that he didn't know why the hell she possessed it.

Ignoring a woman who'd been trying to catch his eye for the past four days, he let his gaze roam to the pillars on the edge of the dance floor.

Heat gathered inside him. Yes, there she was, clad in one of the neat, not quite fashionable dresses she wore in the evening. She was standing alone and watching the dancers, looking interested rather than wistful.

The day before, as he'd sat talking to her mother in the shade of the leaning coconut palms, the same insistent tug at his senses had pulled his gaze away from the older woman's thin, lined face and along the hot white coral sand.

'There's Jacinta,' Mrs Lyttelton had said, smiling, her face alight with pleasure.

To his dazzled, suddenly feral eyes Jacinta had appeared as an embodiment of the fecund extravagance of the tropics, a glowing, sumptuous creature whose hair collected and intensified the sun's rays, a woman gleaming in the soft, humid air like a spirit of fire and desire.

An urgent hunger had slowed and thickened his blood.

5

Although he'd tried to summon his usual ironic detachment to combat it, the violent physical reaction swamped both will-power and discipline.

He'd been disappointed and relieved when she got closer and the fiery goddess turned into an almost plain woman, tall, too thin, her breasts hidden by a large, faded cotton shirt, only her long, lightly tanned legs hinting at that promise of hidden passion.

Watching her now, he felt his gut clench and his body spring to painful life as he was gripped by the unmistakable burgeoning of desire. Thank God the torches that flamed around the dance floor cast enough shadows to hide his response.

The flaring light touched her pale skin with fire and licked with adoring incandescence across the aureole of her hair. The previous day she'd worn the thick, tumbling curls pulled back in a practical ponytail, but tonight she'd left it unharnessed, and the bright abundance shouted an invitation.

Dragging his eyes away, he concentrated his blue gaze on his hand on the table, saw with astonishment the rigid curl of his fingers as he fought for control. Within inches of those dark fingers flowers lay in artful, casual glory—vivid scarlet hibiscus, frilled and suggestive, and the cool, smooth stars of frangipani, their creamy restraint belied by the sweetly pervasive, erotic perfume. He wanted to crush them in his hands—he wanted to pick them up and heap them on a bed for her and take her on it for long, passionate hours until she surrendered completely and eagerly to his will.

A couple of hundred years ago he'd have believed that Jacinta Lyttelton had bewitched him. Oh, he'd always been susceptible to brilliant colouring, but the women he desired had invariably been beautiful, with a certain mysterious allure that excited the explorer in him.

Jacinta possessed neither. Skin of translucent ivory and

big hazel eyes—even a soft, red, inviting mouth—were dominated by a straight, high-bridged nose and subdued by a round chin. Good legs and delicate ankles and wrists didn't compensate for the hollows at her collarbone, the angular body. Apart from that astonishing colouring, he thought, trying to be coolly dispassionate, she had no presence.

His bizarre reaction—the urge to carry her off to the nearest bedroom and stamp his imprint on her so starkly that she never looked at another man—was a sexual aberration, a primitive, freakish eccentricity caused by some delusion.

Which was just as well, because she had enough to deal with at the moment. One glance had told him that her wheelchair-bound mother was dying. He had no idea why mother and daughter had chosen to stay at this expensive resort hotel in Fiji at the hottest time of the year, but Mrs Lyttelton was enjoying it and the affection between mother and daughter was obvious.

His eyes narrowed as one of the hotel guests, a tall, brawny Australian with shoulders as wide as a barn door, approached the woman in the shadows.

A primal jealousy fogged his brain; he was on his feet and halfway across the room before he realised he'd moved. Even as he told himself that he was behaving like a fool he felt an unusual aggression tighten his muscles and fill him with unrepentant hostility.

The Australian didn't even see him; grinning, he said something that brought a smile to that soft red mouth, and turned to go out onto the beach.

Jacinta waved a hand and turned back to her survey of the dancers.

Relaxing his headlong pace, he watched the man go out into the dark night, but his skin was tight and the heavy, hungry need that prowled though him snarled softly, thwarted of legitimate prey. Noiselessly he walked up to her, some savage part of him enjoying the little jump she gave when she became conscious of his presence.

'Would you like to dance?' he asked, masking his emotions with the smile he knew was one of his greatest assets.

She looked startled, but after a moment said, 'Yes. Thank you.'

He wanted her to stumble, be heavy on her feet, not know the steps. But she was like the wind in his arms, a fragrant, spice-scented wind, swaying seductively through the languid flowers of the tropics, warm, flowing silkily against him.

Every cell in his body shouted in triumphal recognition. Anger at his helpless response cooled his voice. 'Is your mother not well enough to come tonight?'

'She's just tired.'

The faint huskiness beneath her voice smoothed across his skin like silk velvet. 'Is she enjoying the holiday?'

She looked swiftly at him, and then away again. The thick curls moved slightly as she nodded. 'She's having a wonderful time,' she said quietly. 'Everyone's been so kind.'

Because he couldn't trust himself to say anything that wouldn't increase her distress, he remained silent. Unfortunately that meant his mind could concentrate on the multitude of signals his rioting senses relayed—like the fact that her eyes were actually green, and that the hazel effect came from little gold flecks embedded in the cool depths...

Like the curve of her brows, slightly darker than her hair, and the deeper colour of her lashes as they lay on her skin, casting mysterious little shadows...

Like the tiny creases at the corners of her mouth that gave it an upward tilt...

Like the faint scent of her skin—pure essence of enchantment, he thought grimly.

Like the brush of her breasts across his chest, and the sleek strength of her long legs as they negotiated an elderly couple enjoying themselves enormously doing what looked like a forties jitterbug.

Anger—sheer and hot and potent—only fuelled his runaway response. Of all things, he despised being at the mercy of his emotions; it had been five years since he'd felt such an elemental hunger, and even then he hadn't been tormented by this intense immediacy, this compulsion.

Thank God he was leaving tomorrow. Once back in New Zealand and deprived of nourishment, this obsession would starve and he'd be his own man again.

CHAPTER ONE

'MY COUSIN Paul,' Gerard said in his pedantic way, 'is the only man I've ever known to decide that if he couldn't have the woman he loved he'd have no other.'

To hide her astonishment Jacinta Lyttelton gazed around Auckland's busy airport lounge. 'Really?'

Gerard sighed. 'Yes. Aura was exquisite, and utterly charming. They were the perfect match but she ran away with his best friend only days before the wedding.'

'Then they couldn't have been a perfect match,' Jacinta pointed out, smiling a little to show she was joking. During the nine months she'd known Gerard she'd learned that he needed such clues. He was a dear, kind man, but he didn't have much of a sense of humour.

'I don't know what she saw in Flint Jansen,' Gerard pursued, surprising her because he didn't normally gossip. Perhaps he thought some background information might smooth her way with his cousin. 'He was—I suppose he still is—a big, tough, dangerous man, bulldozing his way through life, hard-bitten enough to deal with anything that came his way. He was some sort of troubleshooter for one of the big corporations. Yet he was Paul's best friend right from school, and Paul is a very urbane man, worldly and cosmopolitan—a lawyer.'

Jacinta nodded politely. Perhaps Aura Whoever-she'd-been liked rough trade. 'Friendship can be just as mysterious as love. Your cousin and Flint must have had something in common for it to last so long.'

The same taste in women, to start with!

Her eyes followed a small Japanese child, fragile and sol-

10

emn but clearly at home in such surroundings, her hand lost in that of her mother.

My biological clock, Jacinta thought wryly, must be ticking away. Twenty-nine wasn't over the hill, but occasionally she was oppressed by a feeling of being shunted quietly out of the mainstream, banished to float peacefully and dully in a backwater.

'I could never understand it,' Gerard said, for the fourth time turning the label on his cabin bag to check that he'd addressed it. 'She and Paul looked wonderful together and he worshipped her, whereas Flint—oh, well, it doesn't matter, but the whole sordid episode was incredibly hard on Paul.'

Being jilted would be incredibly hard on anyone. Jacinta nodded sympathetically.

Gerard frowned. 'He had to pick up the pieces of his life with everyone knowing and pitying him—and Paul is a proud man. He sold the house he and Aura were going to live in and bought Waitapu as a refuge—I suppose he thought he'd get some peace half an hour's drive north of Auckland—but then Flint and Aura settled only about twenty minutes away! In a vineyard!'

Jacinta composed her face into a sympathetic expression. Gerard's loyalty did him credit, and this wasn't the time to tell him that things had changed. Nowadays guilty couples didn't retreat to some far-flung part of the world and live in abject, if happy, retirement.

'When did this all happen?' she asked.

'Almost six years ago,' Gerard said in a mournful tone, fiddling with his boarding pass and passport.

Almost six years! Jacinta said mischievously, 'What about that exquisitely beautiful woman you pointed out to me in Ponsonby a couple of months ago? You didn't exactly say so, but you implied that she and Paul are very good friends.'

Gerard blinked and stood up. 'He's a normal man,' he

said austerely, 'but I doubt very much whether Paul intends to marry her. She's an actress.'

As well as being kind, loyal and pedantic, it appeared that Gerard was a snob.

A voice on the communications system announced that passengers for Air New Zealand's flight from Auckland to Los Angeles should make their way through the departure gate.

Gerard bent down and picked up his bag. 'So don't go falling in love with him,' he directed half seriously. 'Women do, and although he doesn't like hurting people he's broken hearts these last five years. Aura's defection killed some essential compassion in him, I think.'

'Don't worry,' Jacinta said dryly. 'I'm not planning to fall in love.'

'Not until you've finished your Masters,' he said, and to her astonishment bestowed a swift peck on her cheek. 'I'd better go.'

She hoped she'd concealed her startled response. 'Have a great trip, and I hope your research goes well.'

'It will, but thank you. Enjoy the summer,' he said, 'and work out exactly what you want to do for your thesis. Have you got the books?'

'Yes, and your list of suggestions to mull over.'

He nodded and turned away, tall, slightly stooped, his fair hair shining in the lights. Watching as he made his way through the people, Jacinta thought he always seemed out of place except when he was lecturing. Anyone looking at him would immediately pick him as an academic. If his projected book was a success he might turn out to be one of the youngest history professors in the country.

At the gate he turned and waved. Smiling, she waved back, waiting until he'd disappeared before turning to go down the escalator to the car park.

An hour and a half later she opened the car door just a hundred metres from a glorious beach, and unfurled her long, thin body and legs.

Sun-warmed, salt-tanged, the air slid into her lungs—smooth as wine and just as heady. The big grey roof of a house loomed above the dark barrier of a high, clipped hedge—Cape honeysuckle, she noted, eyeing the orange flowers—and the lazy mew of a gull smoothed across the mellow sky.

New Zealand in summer; for the first time in years, anticipation coiled indolently through her. Not that it was officially summer—November was the last month of spring—but it had been a weary, wet, grinding winter and she was eager for the sun.

A half-smile lifted the corners of her controlled mouth as she unlatched the gate and walked up the white shell path, amused at how pale her narrow feet looked. Ah, well, a few walks along that sweep of sand she'd seen from the hill would soon give them some colour. Although she turned sallow in winter her skin loved summer, gilding slowly under layers of sunscreen.

The house was huge, a white Victorian villa superbly settled in a bower of lawns and flowery borders, sheltered from the small breeze off the sea. The scents of the garden and newly mown lawns were concentrated into an erotic, drugging perfume.

She hoped that the man who owned all this appreciated it.

'My cousin Paul,' Gerard had told her when he'd suggested she spend the summer at Waitapu, 'was born into old money, and because he's both hard-headed and very intelligent he's added considerably to the paternal legacy.'

Obviously. The house and the gardens bore the unmistakable sheen of affluence.

A bead of sweat gathered on each of Jacinta's temples. Before leaving town she'd clipped back the hair that reached halfway down her back, but during the drive the curly, slippery tresses had oozed free. Tucking a bright ginger strand behind one ear, she walked up three steps onto a wide, grey-painted wooden verandah and knocked at the door before turning to admire the gardens more closely.

She must look madly out of place here, Jacinta thought wryly, dressed in clothes without a vestige of style. And although she was tall enough to be a model she hadn't been granted a model's grace.

Her green-gold gaze roamed across the felicitous mixture of trees and shrubs, lingering on the slim grey trunks of a giant cabbage tree, each smooth branch topped by a sunburst of thin leaves. At its feet nasturtiums and Californian poppies struck sparks off each other.

The soft wind of the door opening dragged her smiling attention away from a gaudy orange and black monarch butterfly. With the smile still lingering, she turned. 'Hello, I'm Jacinta Lyttelton…'

The words dried on her tongue. She knew that handsome face—the strong jaw and arrogant cheekbones—as well as her own. The intervening months hadn't dimmed the brilliance of those eyes, a blue so intense they blazed with the colour and fire of sapphires. Yet in spite of that clarity they were oddly difficult to read.

Suddenly aware that the trousers she wore were five years old and had been cheap to start with, and that her tee-shirt had faded to a washed-out blue that did nothing for her, Jacinta realised she was standing with her jaw dangling. Clamping it shut, she swallowed, and tried to repulse a sudden, insistent warning of fate advancing inexorably, mercilessly on its way, crushing everything in its path.

'Welcome to Waitapu, Jacinta.' His deep, flexible voice wove magic, conjured darkly enchanted dreams that had dazzled her nights for months.

Fortunately her numbed brain jolted into action long enough to provide her with the location of their previous meeting.

Fiji.

The lazy, glorious week she and her mother had spent on a tiny, palm-shadowed resort island. One night he'd asked her to dance, and she'd been horrified by her fierce, runaway response to the nearness of his lean, big body. When the music had stopped he'd thanked her gravely and taken her to the room she had shared with her mother before, no doubt, rejoining the seriously glamorous woman he was on holiday with.

And for too many weeks afterwards Jacinta had let herself drift off to sleep on the memory of how it had felt to be held in those strong arms, and the faint, evocative fragrance that had owed nothing to aftershave—the essence of masculinity...

An embarrassing flash of colour stained her high cheekbones.

Damn, she thought helplessly. How unfair that this man was Paul McAlpine, her landlord for the next three months.

Hoping desperately that her weak smile showed nothing of her chagrin, she said, 'I didn't know you were Gerard's cousin.' She tried to sound mildly amused, but each word emerged tinged with her discomfiture.

'Whereas I,' he said, 'had a pretty good idea that the Jacinta I met in Fiji and Gerard's Jacinta had to be the same person. He mentioned your height and was rather poetic about your hair. It didn't seem likely there'd be two of you about.'

He was the most handsome man she'd ever seen in her life, the impact of his strong, regular features emphasised by his startling colouring. Not many men of his age had hair the warm ash blond of childhood, so close to gold, and blue eyes without a trace of green or grey, and those who did were usually afflicted with pale brows and lashes that made them look pallid and juiceless. Paul McAlpine's were a brown so dark they were almost black.

On that hot, enchanted Fijian atoll he'd smiled—a smile

both utterly compelling and completely trustworthy. It had been almost too good to be true, that smile.

No sign of it now. The chiselled mouth was straight and the narrowed eyes aloof.

Jacinta's face set. Gerard's Jacinta? He'd merely repeated her sentence construction; of course he wasn't implying that she and Gerard had some sort of relationship. Nevertheless she felt she should make it very clear that Gerard was simply a good friend.

Before she could do that, Gerard's cousin said smoothly, 'Unfortunately there's been a hitch in plans. You can't stay in the bach because penguins have moved in.'

Wondering whether she'd heard correctly, she stared at him. 'Sorry,' she said inanely, wishing her brain hadn't fogged up. *'Penguins?'*

'Little blue penguins are quite common around the coast. Normally they nest in caves, but sometimes they find a convenient building and nest under the floors.'

Surely he couldn't be serious? One glance at those eyes— so cool they were almost cold, limpid and unshadowed— told her he was.

'I see,' she said numbly. Until that moment she hadn't realised how much she wanted to get away from Auckland. A kind of desperation sharpened her voice. 'Can't they be removed?'

'They have young.'

Something about his glance bothered her, and she stopped chewing her bottom lip.

He added, 'And they're protected.'

'Oh, then I suppose… No, they can't be disturbed.'

'They make gruesome noises when they return to their den at night—like a demented donkey being slaughtered. They also smell of decaying fish.' He met her suspicious glance with unwavering self-possession. 'Would you like to go and smell them?' he asked.

Unable to think of a sensible reply, Jacinta shook her head.

'You'd better come inside,' Paul McAlpine said.

Within seconds Jacinta found herself walking down a wide hall and into a beautifully decorated sitting room. Windows opening out onto an expansive roofed terrace looked over a lush lawn bordered with flowers and shrubs, with glimpses of the sea through sentinel pohutukawa trees.

Jacinta thought fiercely, I am not going back to town.

It would be like returning to prison.

And where had that thought come from?

'Sit down and I'll get you some tea,' Paul McAlpine said with remote courtesy, and went through another door.

Reluctantly Jacinta lowered herself into a very comfortable armchair and contemplated her legs, almost as ungraceful as her too-thin arms. Why on earth had she chosen to wear trousers of such a depressing shade of brown?

Because they were the best she had and she couldn't afford new ones. What did it matter? She didn't care what he or anybody else thought, she told herself sturdily, and knew that she lied.

'Tea'll be ready soon,' Paul McAlpine said, startling her with his swift reappearance.

Averting her eyes from his broad shoulders, and the way his well-cut trousers hugged muscular thighs, Jacinta swallowed. She even thought she could smell the elusive male fragrance that still infiltrated the occasional dream.

With a shock strong enough to be physical, she braved the icy brilliance of his eyes.

'Don't look so tragic, Jacinta. I have a suggestion to make.' There was a faint, barely discernible undertone to the words, a hint of cynical amusement that startled her.

Especially as she hadn't realised she was looking tragic. Taken aback, certainly, but 'tragic' was altogether overstating the case. Her hackles rose as he sat in the chair opposite her, so completely, uncompromisingly self-sufficient that her spine stiffened and she angled her chin in mute resistance.

Jacinta had no illusions about her looks; she knew that her height and thinness and the clearly defined, high-bridged nose that dominated her face were not redeemed by thick, violently ginger hair, or green eyes hazed with gold and set beneath straight, dark copper brows. Accustomed to feeling out of place amongst the chic women she saw everywhere, she was nevertheless outraged that Paul McAlpine should make her feel the same.

'Yes?' she said, aware that she sounded curt but unable to alter the tone to her usual confidence.

'I have several spare bedrooms,' Paul McAlpine told her. 'You're more than welcome to use one. My housekeeper lives in a flat at the back, so you won't be alone in the house with me.'

No sarcasm sharpened that beautiful voice, nothing even obliquely hostile glimmered in those blue eyes, but the skin pulled tight on the nape of Jacinta's neck as a shiver of cold foreboding slithered the length of her spine.

'That's very kind of you,' she said warily, 'but I don't think—'

He smiled. It was a smile that had probably stunned more women than she'd had showers. Silenced by its impact, she had to swallow when her words dried on her tongue.

Calmly, almost blandly, he said, 'If you feel awkward about living here with me I'll stay in a flat I own in Auckland.'

'I can't drive you out of your house,' she said, feeling both irritated and awkward.

His dark brows inched inwards. 'I believe that you had to move out of your flat, and as Gerard's sold his apartment you can't go there. I spend quite a lot of time either travelling or in my flat in Auckland; a few extra nights there won't be much of a hardship.'

What would it be like to own several houses?

After one swift, circumspect glance Jacinta realised she didn't have a chance of changing his mind. Thoughts churned around her mind, to be promptly discarded. She didn't have enough money to stay in a motel or rent another flat; the main advantage of Paul McAlpine's bach had been that it was free of charge.

He watched her with eyes half hidden by his lashes, waiting with a sort of vigilant patience—the remorseless tenacity of a hunter—that intimidated her in a way she didn't understand.

For heaven's sake! She was letting the aftermath of one dance ten months ago scramble her brain entirely.

With enormous reluctance she finally said, 'Then—thank you. I'll try not to get in your way.'

'Gerard said you're starting on your thesis.'

'Did he?' she said non-committally. 'What about Christmas?' she asked. 'Will the penguins be out from under the bach by then?'

'It's unlikely.' An enquiring eyebrow lifted. 'Were you planning to stay in the bach over Christmas?'

This would be her first Christmas alone. Through the lump in her throat she said raggedly, 'Yes. My mother died only a week after we came back from Fiji.'

'I'm sorry,' he said quietly. 'That was hard for you.'

Looking away, she nodded, swallowed and went on, 'I never had the chance to thank you for your kindness to her in Fiji. You left the day before us, and I—'

'I wasn't kind,' he interrupted. 'I liked her very much, and admired her gallantry.'

'She liked you, too.' Jacinta paused to steady her wobbly voice. 'She really enjoyed talking to you. It made her holiday. She was so determined I shouldn't miss anything…'

Cynthia Lyttelton had insisted Jacinta use the facilities at the resort, pleading with her to swim, to sail, to go snorkelling. 'Then you can tell me all about it,' she'd said.

Because the resort staff had been kind and attentive to

her mother, Jacinta had given in. When she'd returned, salt-slicked and excited, after her first snorkelling expedition, Cynthia had told her about this man who had joined her beneath her sun-umbrella—handsome as Adonis, she'd said, and funny, with a good, sharp brain.

Gently, he said now, 'She told me she didn't have long to live. I gather she'd been ill for a long time, yet she was completely without self-pity.'

'She had arthritis, but she died of cancer.' I will not cry, she averred silently, clenching her jaw against the onset of grief.

'I'm so sorry,' he repeated, and she knew he was.

So many people—considerate, well-meaning people—had told her that her mother's death must have been a blessed relief to them both. She'd understood that they were giving her what sympathy they could, but although often in great pain Cynthia had enjoyed life, and she hadn't wanted to die.

And Jacinta still mourned her loss.

She nodded, and they sat without speaking for some moments while she regained control of her emotions.

Eventually she looked up, to meet a gaze that rested on her face with unsettling penetration. Instantly his lashes covered his eyes, and when they swept up again there was nothing but that vivid, unrevealing intensity of colour, hiding all emotion, all speculation. His sculptured mouth had thinned to a straight, forceful line.

A firebrand plummeted to the pit of her stomach. Instinct, so deeply buried in her unconscious she'd never known of its existence, stirred, flexed, and muttered a warning.

What am I getting into? she thought.

Common sense, brisk and practical, told her she wasn't getting into anything, because she wouldn't allow herself to. Paul McAlpine might look like every woman's idea of a dream hero, with his golden hair and athlete's body and disturbing mouth, but she didn't have to worship at his shrine if she didn't want to.

'I usually have a quiet Christmas,' he told her. 'Anyway, it's almost two months before we have to think of that. Our tea's probably ready, but if you'd like to come with me now I'll show you where the bedrooms are and you can choose one.'

Stiffly she got to her feet and went with him in and out of five superbly furnished bedrooms, all with both double-hung and French windows leading onto the encircling verandah. Just like something from a glossy magazine.

Jacinta refused to be impressed. In the end she chose one with a view of the sea solely because it had a long, businesslike desk on one wall.

'This one doesn't have its own bathroom,' Paul told her, 'but there's one right next door.'

'It'll be super, thank you.' Outside, the verandah had been furnished with a lounger and several chairs. Below the wooden balustrade flowers frothed and rioted. The room was pleasantly cool, with a daybed in one corner and an elegant Victorian dressing table, less ornamented than most of its kind. 'It looks lovely,' Jacinta finished sincerely. 'Thank you.'

'It's nothing.'

The negligent disclaimer was delivered in a deep voice, its obscurely equivocal intonation setting her teeth on edge.

She was being paranoid.

Well, it was probably normal. Although earlier that year she'd endured an unpleasant experience with a man, eventually her suspicions regarding masculine intentions must fade. Unfortunately it wasn't going to be a speedy process. Even with Gerard, who couldn't have been nicer, she'd found herself searching for sinister motives.

And now she was doing it again. Possibly because Paul McAlpine was so—so—well, so gorgeous. Her nervousness didn't mean she sensed anything ulterior; it arose from her physical awareness of him, which was her problem, not his. Behind Paul McAlpine's air of calm, confident good humour was simply that—calm, confident good humour.

Any ordinary woman would be jittery and a bit over-whelmed when confronted by one of the favoured few, a golden man with everything, including a presence that automatically made him a man to be noticed.

Exhausted, and therefore easily influenced, she simply needed time and peace to catch up with herself again. And here, in this beautiful, peaceful place, she'd get them.

Especially if her host was going to be away a lot.

They were halfway down the hall on the way to the kitchen when he said, 'Gerard tells me he's doing research for another book. I thought he'd just finished one.'

'Yes, but he found out that an old rival of his is intending to move in on his territory so he thought he'd better get going on this one and pre-empt him. Even in the academic world things can get rough when it comes to ego and staking claims.'

'I see. Is he planning to spend all his leave in the archives?'

'I think so. It was organised in such a rush that I'm not too sure of his plans.'

One eyebrow arched in a manner that showed only too clearly what Paul McAlpine thought of that, but he said nothing more. As she accompanied him Jacinta thought acidly that it was impossible to imagine this man ever doing anything on impulse.

In the spacious, very modern kitchen he introduced her to his housekeeper, a large-boned, blue-jeaned woman in her late thirties called Fran Borthwick, who smiled at her and said, 'Welcome to Waitapu. The tea's ready. Where do you want it?'

'I'll take it into the conservatory,' Paul said serenely, lifting the tray.

Jacinta returned the housekeeper's smile and went with him.

The conservatory, a delicious Victorian folly, was equipped with rattan furniture upholstered in muted stripes. Jungly tropical growth sprouted from splendid pots; in one a huge frangipani held up white and gold flowers, their sweet scent reminding Jacinta forcibly of the week she'd spent in Fiji.

'Would you like to pour?' Paul McAlpine invited, setting the tray on a table.

Jacinta's gaze lingered too long on his elegant, long-fingered hands—hands that promised great strength as well as sureness. Resenting the mindless response that shivered across her nerve-ends, she said, 'Yes, of course,' sat down and lifted the teapot.

He liked his tea without milk and unsugared. Spartan tastes, Jacinta thought as she poured, then set down his cup and saucer.

It was an oddly intimate little rite, one that seemed right for the old-fashioned house and teaset. Ruthlessly ignoring the niggling edge of tension that sawed at her composure, she drank her tea and made polite conversation, wondering as she listened to his even, regulated voice whether authority and imperturbable good humour was all there was to Paul McAlpine.

No, he wouldn't have reached the top of his profession without intelligence and, she suspected, ruthlessness.

No doubt with women, too. The lover Gerard had pointed out that day in Ponsonby was a woman so beautiful she'd dazzled. However she was not the woman who had been with Paul in Fiji.

Perhaps he was promiscuous. Was that what Gerard had been hinting at with his reference to broken hearts?

Her quick revulsion at the idea was a warning, as was her conviction that he was too fastidious for crude promiscuity. All she knew about him was that he'd been kind to her mother, he'd been jilted—and he'd had two lovers in ten months.

And he danced well.

When his cool voice broke into her memories she jumped guiltily, and had to pull herself together to answer his question about her degree.

'I majored in history,' she said.

'Yes, of course. Gerard's speciality. That's where you met him, I suppose?'

It was impossible to accuse him of prying. He must, she thought—surely irrelevantly—be hell in a courtroom. Any witness would be lulled into a sense of security by that lazy, calm voice that expressed nothing more than interest.

But he must have heard the reservation in her voice when she replied, 'I—yes.'

Dark lashes almost hid his eyes. 'I believe he offered you bed and board in his apartment. That must have been very convenient.'

Tautly she responded, 'He realised that things were—difficult—where I was living, and very kindly told me about a flat a friend of his wanted looked after while she took up a scholarship in England.'

For a moment the classically shaped mouth straightened, but when she looked again it was relaxed, even curved in a slight smile. 'Flatmates can be trying, can't they.'

It was not a question. Trying to lift the flatness of her tone, she agreed, 'Oh, they certainly can.'

'It sounds as though you had the ones from hell.'

'He—one was not—not congenial.' She put her cup and saucer down, relieved when they arrived on the table without any betraying chinks.

Paul said nothing, and after an awkward moment she went on, 'Gerard found me in the university library one night and realised that I was having a bad time.'

'Ah,' Paul said smoothly, 'he's always found it difficult to cope with tears.'

She fastened down her indignation. 'I wasn't crying,' she told him firmly, and added, 'He's very kind.'

'I'm sure he is,' Paul said, his voice soothing, almost mesmeric. 'Why can't you stay in your flat over the holidays?'

'A friend of the woman who owns it has moved in.'

When Gerard came back in February he'd go into his new house, a house with a flat joined to it, and she'd have a home once more. There was no reason she shouldn't tell Paul McAlpine that, but she fenced the words behind her teeth.

'And now you're waiting for the results of your final exams. Getting your BA has been a long haul. I believe there was a gap between the first two years and the last?'

Had her mother told him that her arthritis had become so bad after her daughter's second year at university that Jacinta had to give up her studies and come home to take care of her? No, she'd been a very private woman, so it had to have been Gerard. Hoping he hadn't coaxed Paul to lend her the bach by implying that she was a deserving case, she said evenly, 'Yes, nine years.'

'What do you intend to do when you've done your Master's? Teach?'

She shook her head. 'I don't think I'd be very good at that.'

Judicially, he observed, 'I shouldn't think there's much call for history masters outside the halls of academe.'

Why was she so—so nervous about her plans, so secretive? Because she didn't yet know whether they were possible—and because she didn't like the prospect of appearing a fool. 'Probably not,' she agreed, feeling ineffectual and foolish.

Goaded by his measuring look, she added, 'Actually, the Master's degree is a promise I made to my mother.'

There, that would show him she wasn't just drifting.

'And you always keep your promises?'

'Yes.'

Without haste her unwilling host surveyed her face, his vivid blue gaze roaming the thick, now untidy mass of her hair, its damp curls clinging to the margins of her high forehead.

Heat burned through her skin. Straight copper brows drawn over her long nose, she met his scrutiny with defiance, knowing that the golden specks in her eyes would be glittering against the green matrix.

Starry Eyes, her mother used to call her when she was a child.

She could read nothing in Paul's scrutiny beyond a cool assessment that prickled her skin and tightened her muscles in a primitive reflex, but when his glance moved to her wide, soft mouth she jutted her chin, fighting back a response in which anger and a forbidden excitement warred.

She didn't want this overwhelming physical attraction. It was something she'd never experienced before, and it was dangerous.

Paul's enigmatic gaze didn't drop any further—and that, she thought angrily, was just as well. Although his scrutiny was too impersonal to be a leer, he'd checked her out beyond the bounds of politeness.

'"Mine honour is my life",' he quoted.

Shakespeare, of course. An equivocal note in his voice scratched at her nerves again. 'Something like that,' she said curtly.

Each word dropped into the tense silence that stretched between them—humming, she thought edgily, with unspoken thoughts, with emotions she didn't intend to examine.

Just when she thought she was going to have to break it, he drawled, 'Very worthy.'

'Hardly.' She wondered why his words should sound like a warning. 'Every child learns the importance of keeping promises.'

'But children often forget as they grow older.'

Too late Jacinta remembered Aura, who had broken her vows to him in the most dramatic way. She opened her mouth to say something—anything—then closed it again when a covert glance at his shuttered expression warned her that nothing she could say would help ease the tension.

He asked her about the new fee structure at the university, and while they discussed the implications Jacinta forgot her reservations, forgot that almost insolent survey of her face. His astute, acerbic sagacity made her think hard and fast, and his understanding of people's motives startled her with its blend of tolerance and cynicism.

'Gerard seems to think you'll get honours when you do your MA,' he said, the blue eyes indolent behind his lashes.

Some obscure note in his voice made the comment ambiguous. 'He's a bit prejudiced,' she said stiffly. She might be Paul's guest, but she didn't owe him any more revelations.

'We're always inclined to be prejudiced about the people we're fond of,' Paul McAlpine said.

She looked sharply up, but those eyes, so transparent she could drown in them, hid his thoughts very effectively.

'Or those people we've taught,' she returned, just as pleasantly. 'I'll unpack now. Shall I take the tray through to the kitchen?'

'I will,' he said, getting to his feet and lifting the tray.

Although Jacinta always noticed hands, it was uncanny that the sight of his sent a tiny shudder of sensation chasing down her spine. Walking back along the hall, she felt an odd weight in her breasts, a kind of tingling fullness that embarrassed and irritated her.

Oh, be sensible, she told herself with self-derisory crispness, trying to be blasé and objective. It was hardly *surprising* that she should be attracted to him. He was magnificent—a splendid figure of a man. There was something about him that made her think of sanity and freedom and enviable, disciplined self-assurance.

Paul McAlpine would probably never find himself in a situation he couldn't control.

Lucky man, she decided crossly, blinking as she stepped from the shaded verandah into the bright light of the sun.

CHAPTER TWO

EVERYTHING Jacinta owned except for some stored furniture was contained in two suitcases. In the back seat of Gerard's car, neatly strapped in by the seatbelts, were a computer and printer, and on the floor several boxes of books.

Not a lot for almost thirty years, she thought wryly as she began to ease a suitcase out of the boot.

'I'll take that,' Paul said from behind.

Jacinta didn't quite stop herself from flinching, but hoped that her swift step away hid her involuntary reaction. 'Oh— thanks,' she said vaguely.

The sun gleamed on his fair hair, gilded his tanned skin. When he picked up the second case in one steady lift, muscles flexed smoothly beneath the fine cotton of his shirt. Oddly breathless, Jacinta reached into the back seat, fumbling with the seatbelt that held the computer in place.

A seagull laughed mockingly, its wings catching the light so that it shone silver, a mythical bow in the sparkling sky. Jacinta hauled the computer out and set off with it after the man who walked so easily up the white path and into the cool shadow of the house.

He put the suitcases onto the floor of the room she'd chosen and said, 'I'll bring in the printer.'

'It's all right,' she said. 'I can do it; you must have work to do.'

'Not today,' he said gravely.

Frankly helpless, she stood in the centre of the room with the computer in her arms and watched him go. Oh, lord, she thought dismally, walking across to the desk. Biting her lip, she turned and settled the computer into place on the desk.

He looked like a white knight, handsome and easygoing,

a golden man—if you could ignore that strong jaw and the hint of hardness in his chiselled mouth. But from behind he looked like a Viking, walking with steady, long-legged, distance-eating strides across a world that trembled before him.

And although imagination was a prime requisite for her next venture, at that moment she wished she didn't possess quite so much of it.

He brought the printer in, and watched while she set it up. She did that because there was no way she'd open her suitcases in front of him. As it was, she was beginning to think that agreeing to stay here had not been a good decision.

While the test pattern ran through she said tentatively, 'I think we should discuss some sort of—of arrangement while I'm here.'

Those intimidating brows lifted again. He didn't say anything.

Jacinta imagined rods of steel going from her head to her heels. 'Money,' she said succinctly.

Eyes the same colour as a winter sky, cold and clear and piercing, moved from the screen to her face. 'You are Gerard's guest,' he said, his voice as unyielding as his expression. 'He asked me to make sure that you were all right while you were here. Money doesn't enter into it.'

She tried again. 'Nevertheless I'll pay for my food.'

He shrugged, his unreadable gaze never leaving her face. 'If it's that important to you, work out some sort of board payment with Fran,' he said negligently. 'As for anything else, just treat this as your home.'

She frowned. 'I don't want to intrude.'

'Oh, you won't,' he said quite gently, and smiled.

God! That smile was as uncompromisingly explosive as Semtex. Jacinta had to draw in a deep, shaken breath before she could even think. Fortunately the printer whirred and chirruped, letting her know it was ready for work. Turning, she stared blindly at it, swallowed, and said, 'Thank you.'

'That looks very like Gerard's set-up,' Paul observed, his voice almost bland.

'It was,' she said shortly. 'When he got a new one he gave me this. They're obsolete as soon as you buy them, unfortunately. Not worth anything.' And she stopped because she'd started to babble, to explain, and she'd made a solemn vow that she was never going to do that again. The experience with Mark Stevens had cured her of ever justifying her actions to any man.

No man was ever again going to believe that he had the right to question what she did or what she thought.

Ever!

One brow drifted upwards. 'Aren't they? Not even as trade-ins?' Paul suggested evenly, and went out across the verandah into the sunlight.

Jacinta glowered after him. Did he think she was sponging off Gerard? Well, she didn't care! Not even if he did look like something chivalrous from a medieval tapestry, she thought sardonically, opening the wardrobe door and surveying the cavernous depths.

First of all she'd unpack, and then she'd go for a short walk—no, first she'd go and see the housekeeper and establish some ground rules.

She was almost in the hall when she realised that Paul was on his way back again, this time carrying a cardboard carton.

'From the weight of this I assume it's books,' he said.

Nodding, Jacinta firmly directed her gaze away as he set the box down on the floor. 'Thank you,' she said.

'I'll get the others.'

She knew how heavy those boxes were; Gerard had helped her carry each one out to the car. Yet the weight didn't seem to affect Paul at all.

Jacinta looked with respect at his shoulders and said again, 'Thank you.'

'It was nothing,' he said, and left her, to reappear before she'd opened the first carton.

Once all the boxes were inside, he showed her the door to the bathroom and said, 'Make yourself at home,' before opening a door that presumably led into his bedroom.

Jacinta stood for a moment staring after him, her stomach gripped by some strong sensation. Hunger, she thought. You didn't have any lunch.

On the floor of the front passenger seat there should have been another carton, packed full of food. She'd brought everything in her pantry, supplementing it with groceries and perishables in the small town twenty minutes away, the town where she'd also taken out a temporary membership in the local library.

It wasn't there.

So Paul must have delivered it to the kitchen. Sure enough, when she'd made her way there, she saw the carton on the bench.

'Oh, he did bring it in here,' she said.

Busy kneading bread, Fran Borthwick smiled. 'Yes.'

'Tell me where to put everything.'

After the housekeeper had done that, and the food was stacked away in a well-stocked pantry, Jacinta explained that she wanted to contribute something to the housekeeping exchequer.

'Have you talked this over with Paul?' Fran asked, sounding surprised.

'Yes.' Jacinta repeated what he'd said.

Pulling off a chunk of dough, the older woman kneaded it expertly into a loaf and placed it into a baking tin. She said, 'Well, you pay whatever you feel is right. As far as meals go, breakfast's at seven. If that's too early—'

'No, no, that's fine,' Jacinta told her hastily.

'OK. Lunch at midday, afternoon tea at four, and dinner at seven-thirty.'

'When P—Mr McAlpine isn't here I'll get my own meals,' Jacinta said.

Fran gave her an approving glance. 'Good. There's always salads and stuff like that in the fridge.'

Back in the bedroom, fortified by a salad sandwich and a banana, Jacinta unpacked her suitcases and set out her books along the back of the desk. Then, obscurely comforted by her familiar things, she changed into shorts and a light shirt and slathered herself in sunscreen. With a wide-brimmed straw hat crammed over her ginger curls, she set off to explore.

About three acres of garden dreamed around the house, sheltered by the hedge on all sides except the seaward one. Even the salt winds couldn't get directly at it; pohutukawa trees leaned over both lawn and sand, forming a wide, informal barrier that would save Paul McAlpine from the indignity of having stray yachties peer into his house.

Seen between the swooping branches and dark, silver-backed leaves, the bay glittered, as blue as his eyes and as compellingly beautiful.

Jacinta wandered across the lawn and found a flight of steps that led out onto the sand, already sizzling under the hot November sun. Some people, she thought, remembering with a shudder the grim little house in which she'd spent most of the past nine years, had all the luck.

She didn't regret giving up her studies to care for her mother. In spite of everything there had been laughter and joy in that farm cottage. Still, she couldn't help thinking wistfully that her mother's long, pain-racked purgatory would have been more bearable in a place like this.

Fishing a handkerchief from her pocket, she blew her nose. The last thing she wanted was for Cynthia Lyttelton to be still enduring that monstrous, unbearable agony and complete loss of autonomy, but her death had left an enormous gap.

For years Jacinta had made all the decisions, done all the

worrying. Grief, and relief that it was all over, and guilt about that relief, and exhaustion, had formed a particularly potent cocktail, one that had rendered her too lethargic to realise that Mark Stevens had begun a campaign to control her life.

Picking up a stone, she straightened and skipped it across the water.

Looking back, her slowness to understand the situation still astonished her. It had taken her three months to realise what was happening and leave the flat.

Another stone followed the first across the water.

With Gerard's help she'd got through that with very little trauma, and doing his housework three days a week had helped her save enough money to see her through the summer holidays without working.

All in all it had been a hard year; she was probably still not wholly recovered from her mother's death, but the crying jags were over, and the stress of trying to find some sort of balance, some firm place to stand, had gone. She'd come a long way in the last six months.

Oh, there were still problems, still decisions to be made. She had to work out what sort of life she wanted, and of course there was always money…

But for the moment she didn't have to worry about any of that. She had another promise to her mother to fulfil, and three months in this perfect place to do it.

Lifting her face and half closing her eyes, she smiled into the sun. Light danced off her lashes, the film of moisture there separating the rays so that they gleamed like diamonds.

Living in the bach would have been perfect. She'd probably only have seen Paul once or twice in the three months, instead of finding herself practically cheek by jowl with him.

Still, she'd manage. She was much stronger than she'd been before, much better able to look after herself. And it didn't really matter that she lusted a bit after Paul McAlpine. So, no doubt, did plenty of women. At least she recognised what she felt as straightforward physical hunger and didn't mistake it for anything more important.

The ringing of small, melodious bells filled the air. Jacinta stopped, watching and remembering. Outside the window of the cottage where she'd lived with her mother was a cherry tree, and each spring her mother had waited for the tuis to come and glut themselves on the nectar.

Just ahead, beside a transparent veil of water that ran over the sand, stood a clump of flax bushes. Strappy leaves supported tall stems with bronze- and wine-coloured flowers, mere tubular twists of petals with dark stamens protruding from the tip.

Yet in those flowers glistened nectar, and a tui, white feathers bobbling at its throat, sat on the stem and sang his spring carillon.

When Paul said her name Jacinta yelped, whirling to say angrily, 'Don't do that, for heaven's sake!'

Paul frowned. 'Your nerves must be shot to pieces.'

'No! I just wasn't— I didn't—'

'It's all right,' he said, his voice deep and sure and strangely soothing.

As the tui broke off its song to indulge in a cacophony of snorts and wheezes, interspersed with the sound of a contented pig, Paul put a hand on her shoulder, grounding her until the sudden surge of panic died away to be replaced by a slow combination of emotions—keen pleasure, and peace, and an oblique foreboding.

Swiftly she stepped away. 'Unusual birds you have here,' she said, snatching at her composure. 'Penguins that bray like donkeys, tuis that mimic pigs...'

'That's normal for both of them. Is it normal for you to jump like that whenever anyone comes up behind you?'

'No, but I didn't hear you and I suppose I am a bit tense. I thought that by now I'd be nicely ensconced in a bach

with just the sea for company. Instead, I've been hijacked.'
She smiled tentatively and his frown disappeared, although
his gaze was still keenly perceptive as it rested on her face.
'Where is the bach, by the way?'

Dropping his hand, he nodded to where a road left the
main one and ran over the headland to the south. 'In the
next bay,' he said.

She nodded too, not quite knowing what to say. The tui
forgot its barnyard imitations and went back to foraging for
nectar. Jacinta enjoyed the iridescent sheen of its plumage
as the thin stem swayed in the sunlight—greens and purples,
blues and bronzes, brighter by far than oil on water.

Every sense she possessed was at full stretch, so that she
heard with keen pleasure the susurration of the waves on
the beach, felt the heat and the wind on her tender skin,
inhaled salty air and tasted her own emotions in her mouth,
a sharp delight edged with wariness.

Paul didn't seem in a hurry to leave, so they watched the
bird until Jacinta was unnerved enough by the silence to
ask, 'What's the name of this bay?'

'Homestead Bay.'

She laughed a little. 'Of course. What a glorious place to
grow up in.'

'I'm sure it would be,' he said calmly, 'but I've only
owned it for five years or so.'

A note in his voice steered her well away from that topic.
Too late she remembered that he'd bought it after he'd been
jilted by the lovely Aura. Stumbling slightly, she asked, 'Is
that the Coromandel Peninsula on the skyline?'

'And Great Barrier Island.'

Gloating, her eyes dreamy, she murmured, 'It's so beautiful.'

'I think so,' he said smoothly.

Jacinta stiffened. However banal and ordinary his words,
there always seemed to be a subtext, some oblique intona-

tion or cool, fleeting amusement adding an extra meaning to what he said.

She couldn't help but feel that in some subtle way Paul McAlpine neither liked nor trusted her.

And that was ridiculous, because she didn't know the man well enough to interpret either his tone of voice or expression. As well, he was a lawyer, trained to keep his features under control.

Although she was prepared to bet that they'd never been exactly open and candid. There was too much self-discipline in that beautiful mouth, and in spite of their vivid colour his blue eyes were surprisingly opaque, hiding Paul McAlpine's emotions very well.

She said abruptly, 'Gerard said you're a lawyer.'

'Most of my work is in international law,' he told her, a hint of reserve flattening his tone.

So he didn't want to talk about it. Neither had Gerard. 'Very high-powered,' he'd said. 'He deals with governments.'

Whatever that meant. As Paul's career seemed to be off-limits, she said, 'And is this a working farm?'

'Certainly. It's a stud; we breed Blonde d'Aquitaines, French beef cattle. We'd better go for a short tour to orient you.'

That not-quite-lazy, assured smile sizzled from the top of her head down to her toes, curling them involuntarily in her sandals. He knew very well the effect he had on women.

She returned his smile, pleased by the slight narrowing of his eyes as she said courteously, 'A good idea. I don't want to end up in the bull paddock.'

'Our bulls are normally placid enough,' he said. 'However, it is a good idea to keep away from them. Any large animal can turn dangerous.'

Like the man who owned them, she thought, startled by the insight. Ignoring a mental image of that easy self-reliance transformed by violent emotion into something much darker and infinitely more hazardous, she asked dulcetly, 'Do you think that pastoral farming has any future in a world that appears to be going green and vegetarian?'

A slight lift of one dark brow recognised the provocation in her question, but he gave a reasoned, restrained reply. This man would scorn an emotional response, an argument based on anything but facts.

Legal training again.

Another thought slipped so stealthily into her mind that it had taken possession before she realised its existence. Had he been hurt by his emotions, hurt so badly that he no longer indulged them?

Not that he looked like someone too wounded by love to risk it again, she thought after a snatched glance at the strong, clear-cut profile. Still, she suspected that his pleasant, approachable attitude was armour. She didn't know what lay beneath it, but she'd be prepared to bet that it would take intense goading to penetrate his shield of self-contained authority.

Gerard, who seemed to still have a mild case of hero-worship for his older cousin, had once told her that Paul never lost his temper.

Not even when Aura had told him she was going to marry his best friend?

As they walked past woolsheds, and an implement shed where brightly coloured monsters lurked, and beneath darkly needled macrocarpa trees along a fenced, metalled race that led to other paddocks, they talked objectively, intelligently, about the world and where it was possibly headed.

Jacinta filed little snippets of information away like hiding treasure. Paul McAlpine moved with a tightly leashed vitality that was at odds with his indolent appearance. He looked at each topic of conversation from both sides; he had a sharp, incisive mind; he enjoyed discussing issues, but when the conversation became personal he blocked.

He needn't worry, she thought when at last they came back to the house. She'd be as detached and dispassionate as he was.

But these next three months would have been a lot simpler if those penguins hadn't decided to take up residence beneath the bach...

If only she had the money to say thanks, but no thanks, and walk away.

Unfortunately, her mother's legacy covered only her tuition fees—although since their rise 'covered' was hardly the word, and if they rose again next year she'd be in trouble. Her student's allowance paid the rent and bought her soap and shampoo and other necessities.

And she was being silly, letting Paul get to her.

She'd certainly make sure she paid her way here. Even if she did look and feel like an unsophisticated hick, she thought ironically as they turned back, she had her pride.

Inside the cool house, Paul said pleasantly, 'Dinner is at seven-thirty. If you'd like a drink first I'll be in the conservatory around seven.'

'Thank you,' she said non-committally, giddily aware of herself, of the way her long limbs moved, of the way her hips swayed, and the fact that her hair had once more slipped free of its clip and was clinging to her hot cheeks.

Back in her bedroom, she switched on the computer, opened a file, typed 'CHAPTER ONE', and then hesitated, before picking up a very old dictionary of quotations she'd bought for fifty cents in a garage sale. She found the lines quickly, from Shakespeare's *Richard the Second*.

Mine honour is my life; both grow in one
Take honour from me, and my life is done.

A hard creed, she thought; a creed for a strong man who held to a spartan belief.

Thoughtfully she closed the book, sat down in front of the computer screen and began to write.

At first the words came easily. She'd told the story so many times to her mother that she almost knew it by heart. *The unicorn snorted, its blue eyes shimmering in the moonlight*, she wrote. *'Very well then,' it said smugly. 'Don't blame me when the Master realises what you've done. I did my best to stop you.'*

But after she'd typed a page she stopped and read it, frowning. It looked—clumsy. And whenever she tried to summon the unicorn's image, its blue eyes had a disconcerting trick of changing to other eyes—quite different ones, cool and distant and enigmatic.

She got to her feet and glowered out of the window. The garden looked very desirable, the lounger eminently appealing.

Doggedly, Jacinta sat down at the desk again. She had promised her mother she'd write this and she was going to do it, even if it did look raw and childish and unformed on paper.

An hour later she got up and walked across to the French windows, trying to recall the look in Paul McAlpine's eyes when she'd told him that the computer equipment had been Gerard's.

Perhaps, she decided, trying to be fair, he had reason to worry about his cousin. She knew and Gerard knew that she wasn't trying to sponge off him, but to an outsider it could look that way. He'd lent her his car, would have lent her money if she hadn't refused it, and out of the kindness of his heart had organised this chance to fulfil one of the promises she'd made to her mother. He didn't know anything about the other promise she'd made, the one she was actually working on now. She owed him a lot.

And, talking of the car, she'd better see where she could garage it, because salt winds were notorious for causing rust.

But before she bearded the lion in whatever den he was ensconced she'd go for a quick walk to the gate and back.

Out in the garden she smiled and clipped a leaf from the lemon verbena. Her mother had loved its citrus perfume, sharp and delightful, and always had a bush of it in the garden. And now she was dead, but the world was still beautiful beyond belief, and it was an insult to her not to enjoy it.

Blinking, Jacinta unlatched the gate and walked through it straight into a pair of hard, masculine arms.

For a moment she thought she'd managed to stumble into Paul McAlpine's grip, but the voice that said, 'Oh, sorry, I didn't know you were there,' was younger than his and lighter, the New Zealand drawl more pronounced.

'No,' she said, stepping backwards, 'I'm sorry, I wasn't looking…'

Dark eyes rested on her face with unmistakable appreciation, and the smile he gave her was open and guileless and very infectious.

'Dean Latrobe,' he said. 'I'm Paul's farm manager.'

Jacinta returned his smile and told him her name, adding after a short pause, 'I'm staying here.'

'Oh, yes, the lady who's supposed to be spending the summer in the bach,' he said, and grinned again. 'Paul was ropable when I told him no one would last a night there.'

'I imagine he would have been,' she said, laughing a little. 'But he very kindly offered me a bed for the holidays just the same.'

'If you've got the keys,' he said, 'I'll put your car in the garage. It is your car, isn't it?'

She said hastily, 'No, it belongs to Paul's cousin. He's in America at the moment.'

'Yeah, thought I recognised it.' He ran a knowledgable glance over it. 'He was up a month or so ago. Got the keys?'

'I'll get them from my room,' she said. 'But there's no

need for you to put it away—if you'll just show me where the garage is…'

'All right,' he said obligingly.

Jacinta hesitated. 'I'd better ask Paul first.'

'Why? There's room in the garage. Trust me, he won't throw his cousin's car out.'

Well, no, he hadn't thrown his cousin's protégée out, but that didn't mean he wanted her there.

'He's a hard man,' Dean Latrobe said cheerfully, 'but he's not unreasonable.'

In other words she was being silly.

'Trust me,' Dean Latrobe said, and winked at her.

He was nice, and there were no undercurrents in his smile or his voice. She laughed back at him and turned to go through the gate.

And there was Paul, the magnificent framework of his face clamped in aloof austerity, eyes slightly narrowed as they went from her smiling face to his manager's.

Startled, Jacinta stopped. 'I thought I should put the car away,' she blurted. 'Is that all right?'

'Yes, of course.'

'I just have to get the keys.'

Courteously he stood aside. Again absurdly self-conscious, she walked swiftly past him and up onto the verandah, found the keys in her bag and ran lightly back.

To find that Dean had gone.

Paul's vivid eyes dwelt on her face with a chilling lack of emotion.

Her smile probably flickered, but she said easily, 'If you'll point me in the direction of the garage, I'll put the car away.'

But Paul said calmly, 'I'll come with you,' and opened the car door for her.

Slowly she climbed in and waited. Because it gave her something to do, she wound the window down and made little fanning motions with one hand, saying as he lowered himself lithely beside her, 'This car really heats up in the sun.'

'Do you use it often?'

Recalled to herself, Jacinta hastily set the engine going and put the car in motion. 'Not often,' she said aloofly. Once a week to pick up groceries from the supermarket, in fact.

'Turn left,' Paul said.

The drive ducked under an archway of Cape honeysuckle and over a cattlestop into a large gravel courtyard at the back of the house. A garage, doors open, formed one wing.

When the house had been first built, the other wing had probably been workshops and the laundry; possibly the pots of flowers at a door indicated a conversion to the house-keeper's flat. Between the two wings stretched the rear wall of the house. In the centre of the courtyard a well-planted herb garden surrounded an arbour where a glorious apricot rose bloomed with prodigal lavishness.

Jacinta concentrated hard on getting the car into the garage, braking with relief as the car slid to a stop beside a substantial continental saloon.

'You drive well,' Paul commented as she unfastened her seatbelt.

'Thank you.' She quelled a sharp pleasure.

'No wonder Gerard trusts you with it.'

'He made sure I could drive properly first,' she said, getting out and putting an end to the conversation as she shut the door a little too heavily.

Walking beside him to the back door, she wondered what on earth was happening to her. Nothing, she thought in profound irritation. She was simply overreacting to a man who attracted her very much on a physical level.

Clearly he felt no such attraction, which was just as well.

It might be more sensible to go back to Auckland and work over the holidays, but why should she run away? She could cope; this inconvenient awareness would die soon, and she'd promised her mother she'd write this book before the year was over, which left her only two months.

One day, Jacinta thought, she was going to earn enough money to give her some control over her life.

'I should perhaps mention that Dean is engaged,' Paul said evenly.

It took her a moment to realise what he was getting at, and when she did her first instinct was to laugh. For heaven's sake, what did he think she was—some sort of *femme fatale*, dangerously attractive to men?

That first response was followed by anger. Far more likely that he thought she was so desperate for a man that she'd flirt with anyone!

'That's nice,' she said agreeably, just managing to keep the note of mockery from her voice.

His swift glance scorched across her profile, bringing her senses to full alert as his mouth curled in a tight parody of a smile that revealed a glimpse of white teeth.

'Very nice,' he said, his voice suspiciously bland. 'Her name is Brenda and she teaches maths at the local high school.'

The colours of the garden sang in violent juxtaposition, and as Jacinta's eyes met his, half-hidden by his lashes, the blue gleaming like the sun on ice, she took a quick, impeded breath.

Beneath that unhurried, confident surface was a primitive streak a mile wide, and she'd do well to stay away from it. This man was every bit as fiercely predatory as a lion.

'Is she local?' she asked, because it was easier, less threatening, to speak than to stay silent.

His smile faded, and she was left shaken, wondering if she had been stupidly romantic when she'd compared him to a lion.

'She's the daughter of one of the oldest families in the district,' he said serenely.

A lion, for heaven's sake! How hackneyed.

Paul McAlpine was no more or less than a clever man, blessed—or cursed—with the sort of good looks and personality that made him automatically attractive to most women. The premonition, the icy breath of danger that had struck through her, was sheer imagination.

All right, she found him intensely attractive, and, yes, that was a nuisance, but it could be dealt with. It would pass, as such things do when ignored.

He held the back door open and Jacinta went through ahead of him, welcoming the room's cool refuge from the heat and the blinding light outside.

'I'll see you at seven,' he said.

It was an unequivocal dismissal, and although she'd been about to say exactly the same words, they stung.

With her shoulders very erect, she went down the hall and into her bedroom.

CHAPTER THREE

ONCE there, Jacinta didn't immediately go back to the computer. Slowly she walked across the room to stop in front of the dressing table and frown into a mirror burnished by that generous, silvery gleam that comes with age.

Perhaps that was why she looked different. Her mouth was fuller, redder, and the green in her eyes was highlighted by golden speckles. Even her skin had some colour in it— a tawny flush that brightened its usual pallor.

'Oh, grow up!' she said crossly, loudly, and turned her back on her reflection and went across to the desk.

Making up the story had been comparatively simple; she and her mother shared a love of fantasy literature, and one day, when Cynthia had been racked with pain and unable to read, Jacinta had tried to take her mind off her agony by soliciting her help with a story she'd had wandering through her mind for weeks.

Her mother had enjoyed the experience so much she'd insisted on an instalment each day, eventually asking Jacinta to write a book from the notes she'd made.

But what had seemed satisfying and complete when she told it was now a chain of words with no interest, no resonance, words that sat flatly on the page and produced no vivid images.

Jacinta was frowning at the screen when Paul McAlpine's voice jerked her head upright. He was outside, speaking to someone in the garden, and although she couldn't discern his words she could hear that he was amused.

And she realised what was wrong with her manuscript. When she'd told the stories to her mother the tone of her voice had provided colour and shading, drama and humour, despair and desperation. She'd have to use words to do the job.

'Thank you, Paul,' she said softly.

So absorbed did she become that when she next looked at her watch it was ten minutes to seven. Hastily she saved, backed up and shut the machine down, then gathered her sponge bag, towel and orange cotton wrap and went down the hall to the bathroom.

After another quick shower she dried herself, pulled her wrap on and hurried back to her room. She was almost at her door when hairs prickled along the back of her neck. Instinctively she flashed a swift glance over her shoulder.

Paul was standing in the door of his bedroom. Jacinta's pulse suddenly hammered in her throat as she registered the impact of his scrutiny right through to the marrow of her bones. He didn't say anything, but she could see dark colour along his cheekbones that both excited and astonished her.

'I won't be long,' she croaked, opening the door and sliding through it as fast as she could.

All right, she commanded her thudding, skipping heart, stop that right this minute! You're just going through delayed adolescence, that's all. You'll get over it.

And probably any man would be interested in a woman—however thin—who was walking about with nothing on underneath her worn cotton dressing gown. That was the way this sex thing worked; it certainly didn't mean that he wanted Jacinta Lyttelton, just that his hormones had been activated.

The wrap unpeeled from her damp body, she got into her bra and pants, then looked through her clothes.

Of course she didn't have anything to wear for a pre-dinner drink with a high-powered international lawyer who lived on a dream farm beside the sea. Something floaty and silken would have done, or casually chic resort wear, but she owned nothing like that.

Her hand hovered over a neat, fitting blouse of vivid orange silk and her teeth sank into her bottom lip. It was her only impulse buy of the past ten years, and she'd not even have considered it if her mother hadn't been with her in that small, spice-scented shop in Fiji, urging her to forget for once their cramped budget.

She'd never worn it, although the hot, bright colour magically transformed her hair and skin and the tight, short-sleeved underblouse and flowing skirt lent her body a grace she didn't really possess, especially when she draped the floating silk veil over the ensemble. The sari was fancy dress, calling far too much attention to its wearer.

Still, she thought, her eyes feasting hungrily on the intense hues, when she could afford clothes again, she'd choose those colours and to hell with basic black!

In the end it came down to a couple of skirts, both of which she'd made several years ago. Shrugging, she got into one, a plain rusty cotton that came to just below her knees. Over the top she wore a tee-shirt the exact green of her eyes, a lucky second-hand bargain from an op shop.

As though it mattered! Paul certainly wouldn't care what she wore.

Dragging her hair from its clip, she brushed it back from her face and folded it into a low knot at the nape of her neck. It was too thick and curly to stay there, but it would look neat enough for an hour or so.

At ten past seven she finally made her way down to the conservatory, despising herself for having to stiffen her knees before she went in.

When he saw her Paul stood up with an automatic courtesy. Although he was only a couple of inches above six feet, no more than four inches taller than she was, he seemed to tower over her as he said pleasantly, 'Good evening. What would you like to drink?'

No sign at all of any extra colour in his face, she told herself. See, it meant nothing.

'Soda water, thanks,' she said, sheer force of character

preventing her from running the tip of her tongue over her lips. Parched as though she'd been lost in sand dunes for a week, she swallowed to ease her arid throat.

He wore a short-sleeved shirt which had almost certainly been made for him, and casual trousers that hugged his hips and revealed the musculature of his thighs. He looked like something from a smart men's magazine, except that he was far more—more *solid*, she thought, groping for the right word. Formidable, that was it. When you looked at Paul McAlpine you knew he was a man to be reckoned with.

He didn't press her to try something alcoholic, for which she was devoutly thankful because she felt drunk enough already. How unfair that she'd plunged into a full-scale crush! At sixteen such situations were accepted, treated with amused sympathy, even taken for granted; blushes and fluttering hearts and starry eyes were almost *de rigueur* while you were growing up.

At twenty-nine you ran the risk of making a total and complete fool of yourself.

She accepted the long, cold glass of soda water with its neat little circle of lime on top, green-skinned and comforting. Bubbles of moisture pearled down the sides as she lifted it gratefully to her lips and drank.

And hiccupped.

Paul gave a sudden grin. 'I always do that,' he said. 'It makes me feel about eight again.'

That smile should be banned.

Returning it as best she could, Jacinta said, 'I should stick to unfizzy drinks.'

'It would be a pity to miss out on champagne,' he said, pouring himself a weak whisky and soda.

'I've never tasted it,' she confessed. The minute the words left her mouth she wanted to recall them. They made her sound so unsophisticated, so deprived, and she was neither.

He didn't look surprised. That irritated her too. Perhaps

he thought she lurked in the background of life like a Victorian poor relation, too spineless to do anything but be grateful for crumbs.

Meeting the enigmatic eyes with a slightly lifted chin, she squelched the urge to explain.

'Don't look so defensive,' he advised odiously. 'Plenty of people don't drink.'

Oh, he knew how to get under her skin. She showed her teeth and said, 'I'm not a teetotaller—I like cider and white wine. It just so happens that I've never tried champagne.'

'Not even on your twenty-first birthday?'

'Not even then,' she said. She'd done her shift in a take-away shop that night, and her mother had cooked a special supper when at last she'd come home.

'In that case,' Paul said calmly, 'we should have some tonight. Sit down while I get a bottle.'

'No—I don't want—' Jacinta stared angrily after him as he strode out of the room; her irritation was very real, but even so her eyes lingered on his wide shoulders.

How smoothly he walked, silently, with a free, lithe grace that melted her bones.

God, she was beginning to be obsessed by him.

After draining half the glass of soda water without a pause or a hiccup, she went to stand at the window.

Almost immediately the colours and contrasts, the quiet hush of the sea and the darkening blue of the sky combined to drag her mind away from the crossfire of recriminations, so that by the time Paul came back she'd regained enough control to turn and say with a composed smile, 'This is very kind of you.'

'It runs in the family,' he said, a thread of irony lacing the comment as he put the bottle down on the drinks tray.

He eased the cork off, startling her into exclaiming, 'I thought it was supposed to pop!'

'Not if it's done correctly and hasn't been shaken,' he said, pouring the honey-gold liquid into two long flutes.

Tiny bubbles ran up the glass to burst with subdued enthusiasm on the surface.

After a pause so slight she almost didn't recognise it, he picked up the glass and proffered it. She took it carefully, concentrating on the glass so that she wasn't looking into his face when their fingers touched and a tingle of electricity sizzled from that brief meeting of skin to some guarded, hitherto inviolate part of her.

Sizzles and tingles are all signs of a crush, she told herself cynically. Perhaps you should enjoy it.

'Congratulations on turning twenty-one,' Paul said, his voice revealing nothing.

'Thank you.' Lifting her gaze, she gave him a set, swift smile before lowering her lashes and cautiously tasting the delicious, frivolous contents of her glass.

It made her hiccup too.

'Oh, dear,' she said, the cool, wonderful taste prickling through her mouth. 'I suppose that's an insult to it.'

'Not if we both do it,' he said, sounding a thousand miles away.

She risked another rapid glance. He *was* a thousand miles away; the moment of communion had passed, and although he was smiling, and his voice was still level and amused, the blue eyes were guarded and remote.

Hurt—so stupid!—she took another sip of champagne and said, 'It's definitely worth waiting for. Thank you.'

With experienced skill he changed the subject, beginning with polite pleasantries that led within a few minutes to a vigorous discussion—so vigorous it almost became an argument—about a political issue. Jacinta enjoyed herself enormously, feeling her mind stretch under his probing, appreciating the keen satisfaction of measuring herself against such intelligence.

Formidable described him exactly.

And very composed; he argued with a singular lack of emotion that had her at a disadvantage several times. Some time later, setting out to refute a statement he'd made, she realised that her cheeks were hot and her voice was rising.

'Hey,' she said, breaking off her impassioned discourse to stare at her now empty glass, 'I'm talking too much. I think I'm drunk!'

'Hardly,' he drawled.

Jacinta put the glass down and pressed the backs of her fingers against her cheeks, hiding the flush. 'If I'm not, I'm getting there,' she said.

He laughed quietly. 'Dinner will fix that. Come on, Fran's just nodded through the door.'

Desperate not to stumble, she got gingerly to her feet, relieved to find that although her head swam a little she didn't sprawl across the floor or lurch into the furniture. Perhaps all it took to control her habitual clumsiness was champagne? She couldn't control a giggle at such an exquisitely amusing idea.

'That's a pretty laugh,' Paul said, holding the door open for her.

Still smiling, she explained, regretting it the instant the words left her mouth, especially when he looked her over thoughtfully. Alcohol and awareness were a powerful combination, releasing too many inhibitions.

'You're not clumsy,' he said as they went through another door. 'You move freely and easily.'

Well, what else could he say?

'You wait until I trip,' she said, hiding her stunned pleasure at the compliment with a tone of dark promise. 'I do it at the worst times.'

'In that case it sounds like self-consciousness, not clumsiness. And the only cure for that is developing some inner esteem.'

'A comment like that,' she parried, startled by his perceptiveness, 'sounds very New-Agey and unlawyerish to me.'

He laughed, but responded with energy, setting the subject for their conversation over dinner. They ate in a room set up as a living and dining area; it opened out onto a wide terrace overlooking the sea and the garden, so that the sound of the waves formed a gentle background.

And Paul was right; after the first course her head cleared completely, but she refused a second glass of champagne, asking anxiously, 'It won't go to waste, will it?'

And could have kicked herself. After all, half a bottle of champagne probably didn't represent any great loss to him.

'No,' he said. 'I have a special stopper that saves the wine from the air and keeps the bubbles in.'

She nodded, and perhaps some of the bubbles were still bursting softly in her bloodstream because she said, 'My mother was very keen on the "waste not, want not" bit.'

'So was mine,' he said. 'I think their generation was encouraged to be thrifty.'

'Unlike ours?'

His brow lifted. 'I don't make generalisations,' he said, teasing her about her inclination to do just that.

Jacinta grinned back. 'I don't make many.'

'Even one is too many.'

He was sitting back in his chair, looking down at the flowers in the middle of the table—satiny golden roses in a translucent white bowl. A long, tanned hand lay loosely on the table in front of him.

He looked, Jacinta thought, profoundly distant, as though the shutters had come down. There was no longer any warmth in his smile; it was merely a movement of his hard mouth, and his eyes were opaque, unreadable. He'd gone away and left her, and she felt cold and isolated and bereft.

'But that,' he said levelly, 'is what the lawyer in me says.'

And again, without seeming to, he changed the subject, leaving Jacinta feeling empty and unsatisfied, as though she'd been promised something and then arbitrarily denied it.

Later that night, wondering whether a walk along the

beach would cure her restlessness, she stood in the dense shade of the pohutukawa trees and listened to the silence. It should have soothed her, sent her serenely to bed, but the steady drumbeat of her heart, the measured, inexorable pulse of excitement through her body, was too insistent to be denied. She stood on the edge of something perilous, something that might colour her life in the hues of summer—or fling her into wintry despair.

The moon, a slender curl in the western sky, silvered the crests of the small waves crisping onto the shore. Its magical light illuminated something else too: Paul McAlpine's head as he walked along the sand.

Jacinta's foolish heart jumped. He was moving slowly, hands in pockets, head slightly bent, and for the few seconds she watched him she thought she saw a vulnerability that wasn't there any other time.

Then he looked up and said in that textured, beautiful voice, 'I didn't realise you were there. Come down and join me.'

Embarrassed, as though she'd been deliberately spying on him, she jumped clumsily onto the sand, landing in its soft depths with an awkwardness that dumped her onto her backside.

Paul held out his hand, asking curtly, 'Are you all right?'

Oh, why had she told him that she tripped at the most inappropriate times? Would that astute mind pick up on her helpless attraction?

Oddly angry, she ignored his offer of support and scrambled to her feet. 'Yes, fine, thanks,' she said, dusting her hands free of sand. 'I forgot that the sand is always deep and dry at the top of the beach. At least it's easy to land on. And I did warn you that I tend to trip over my feet a lot. You might think it's lack of self-esteem but I've always done it, so it's more likely to be a combination of long legs and a bad sense of balance.'

'You could be right,' he said negligently. 'Can't you sleep?'

After two hours of work on the manuscript she was wired, too strung up to even think of going to bed. At least, that was her excuse—she refused to even consider that talking to Paul over the dinner table had affected her so powerfully.

Hoping she didn't sound evasive, she murmured, 'It's such a gorgeous night.'

His smile was a swift, white flash in the darkness. 'Yes. This place seems to specialise in glamorous nights. You'll have to enjoy it without me tomorrow as I'm staying in town.'

'Auckland must be a jolt to the system after Waitapu,' she said prosaically, suppressing a glimmer of nameless emotion.

His shoulders moved in a slight shrug. 'Oh, it has its pleasures.'

The woman in Ponsonby, she thought swiftly, painfully.

He continued, 'I used to live there until I bought Waitapu. While I'm away I'd like you to check with Fran if you decide to further your acquaintance with the property, and of course always tell her where you're going and when you expect to be back.'

Although everything inside her rebelled at the calm suggestion, she nodded. He was right; the last thing his nice farm manager would want was some idiot wandering around getting herself into trouble.

'I'll do that,' she said. 'I don't plan to stray too far from the homestead, but I'm used to living on a farm so I know the protocol.'

'Were you brought up on one?'

'No, we lived in a little one-horse town,' she said. 'We moved to Auckland when I was eighteen so I could go to university. Then my mother was confined to her wheelchair and she longed for the country, so we moved back to a farm cottage on the outskirts of another small town.'

'In Northland?'

'No. A village on the Hauraki Plains.'

It had been a tiny cottage, with two small bedrooms and a big room that was living room, dining room and kitchen. The fence huddled near the house, enclosing a rank, overgrown lawn that the farmer's wife had mown the day they moved in. But it was all on one level, so that as her mother's disease progressed she could get out in her wheelchair, and while she was able she and Jacinta had turned the lawn into a cottage garden, growing their own vegetables and producing flowers from seeds and cuttings and divisions given to them.

Jacinta's eyes blurred as she wondered what had happened to that garden, her mother's last and most loved interest.

'And are you like your mother? Do you prefer living in the country?' Paul asked with idle interest.

Unconsciously she shook her head. 'I don't know—yes, I suppose I do. But I enjoy Auckland.'

'What, particularly?'

'I've loved university, and I like the cultural things—the art galleries especially. And although it's not politically correct, I like Auckland's brashness, that feeling that anything's possible, that the world is a playground and we should all be enjoying it.'

They had reached the end of the beach; he stopped and looked at the low headland crowned with old, sprawling, comfortable pohutukawas. 'That casual attitude would be a lot harder to maintain without the climate and the gulf. New Zealand's other main cities simply don't have the weather to be brash and casual.'

One day, Jacinta told herself, she'd be as familiar with those cities as he so clearly was. Excitement, frothy as the waves, bubbling like champagne, filled her, threatening to reveal itself in her face. Beneath the headland, wave-smoothed rocks rose through the sand; on the pretext of examining one, she moved away.

She could have walked beside him in the beguiling splendour of the moonlight for hours.

Just talking. That would be enough.

But because she understood that soon it wouldn't be enough, she couldn't allow herself to do this again.

The weather, she told herself. Keep talking about the weather; its very banality would temper her emotions.

'We do have a great climate,' she said, 'although some of the students from the south find the humidity unbearable in summer.'

Yes, that was the right touch. Her voice sounded cool and uninvolved, the conversational tone implying that this was not important stuff.

That he was not important.

And how could he be? She didn't know him.

'Ah, Auckland's proverbial steam bath,' he said, an ironic note underpinning the words so that she wondered whether he knew what she was doing. 'You get used to it.'

'You can get used to anything, they say.' Jacinta fervently hoped that this was true.

They walked back along the beach towards the silent house, the light from its windows gleaming through the swooping branches of the trees.

They talked of art and music and their favourite rock bands and sport, only falling to silence as they came up the steps to the lawn. With noiseless footsteps they crossed the grass, dew-damp already, its scent mingling with the soft salt fragrance of the sea.

All Jacinta's responses—to the night-perfumed air, the dim shadows and blurred forms of flowers and foliage, the luminous, light-embossed sky—were heightened by the man who walked beside her. Unbidden anticipation lodged in the pit of her stomach, honed her senses to a keen, subliminal edge.

Four steps up, the verandah surrounded three sides of the house. Beneath its roof lurked a pool of darkness, a still, breathless haven between garden and rooms. Because Jacinta wanted nothing more than to stay outside with Paul, where she wasn't reminded that this man had everything and she had nothing, she took the steps too quickly.

And, of course, she tripped.

Before she had time to fall, hard hands grabbed her by the hips, jerking her back. For fleeting seconds she was held against his strong body, and for the first time in her life she understood the meaning of hunger.

'Thanks,' she muttered, wrenching herself away as though his touch scalded her. Fighting back the urge to scuttle for the safety of her bedroom, she stopped halfway across the wooden boards, grateful for the darkness there.

The words she'd intended to say died. Paul hadn't moved, and beneath his lashes his narrowed eyes gleamed. With eyes attuned to the starlight Jacinta could even see the tiny flicker of a muscle along his jawline.

Her bones deliquesced. She'd barely had time to think exultantly, He feels it too! when he reimposed control and the moment's betrayal was wiped from features now mask-like in their rigidity.

In a voice that revealed only a studied aloofness, he said, 'You'd better watch that step.'

Watch *your* step, he meant.

Swallowing to ease the dryness in her mouth and throat, Jacinta said, 'I will. I did warn you,' adding rapidly, 'although I usually fall down steps, not up them.'

She couldn't bear it if he thought she'd done it deliberately, as a self-seeking, trashy little ploy to attract him.

This was not simple sexual attraction. Whatever it was, it had the power to bring her to total meltdown. How long had she spent in his arms—a couple of seconds? Two seconds to change a life, she thought feverishly.

Terrified by the wild, blind hunger that savaged her, she

retreated a pace towards her bedroom. Her sandals made little scuffing noises, barely audible over the pounding discord of her senses.

'There's the phone,' Paul said. 'Excuse me.'

Inwardly shaking, her eyes dilated and wary, she gazed after him. Breathe, she ordered; just breathe slowly and calmly, and this panic will go away. But before she could summon wits enough to walk into her room, he was back.

'It's Gerard,' he said laconically, expression and voice giving nothing away. 'He wants to say hello.'

'Oh, yes,' she said, stumbling over each word as she skirted him with ridiculous care.

When she picked up the receiver Paul walked out of the room, and she stared at his receding back, saying with an odd, unbidden nervousness, 'Hello, Gerard.'

'Paul said you're staying at the homestead. With him,' Gerard said, his voice unexpectedly close.

'Yes.' Dismayed caution iced her tone. She knew he meant nothing by it, but she refused to make excuses. Frowning, she said levelly, 'Penguins are nesting under the bach.'

There was a moment's silence. Jacinta was about to ask, Are you there? when he said, 'I see. A real nuisance. How are you getting on with the notes for your thesis?'

'I haven't done anything yet,' she said, guiltily resentful of his well-meant interference.

In his generous way, and certainly without realising it, he was trying to force her along the path he'd chosen, dismissing her occasional objections with a tolerant persistence as though she were a small child who needed guidance.

Mark had been sure she needed guidance too.

With a flash of sardonic humour she thought it was strange that although she'd been running her life for years now, in the short space of a year two men had decided she needed their instruction and direction. Perhaps she was giving off vibrations? If so, they were lying ones.

She'd make all her own decisions.

'I see.' Gerard's voice cooled. 'I'd thought I might do some research for you while I'm here.'

'Gerard, I haven't even decided what subject I'm tackling, so it would be wasted effort,' she said, knowing there was no tactful way of saying it. Hastily she added, 'How are you finding Harvard?'

'Cold,' he said stiffly.

'Poor thing. I won't upset you by telling you it's glorious here.'

'No,' he said abstractedly, 'please don't do that.' Again there was a hesitation before he said, 'I hope Paul's being good to you.'

'He's very kind,' she said, her voice flattening.

'He's a decent man, the best. I wish he'd get married, but I don't think he'll ever recover from Aura's betrayal.'

Jacinta's heart clamped in her chest. 'He doesn't look like a modern equivalent of Miss Havisham,' she offered. She didn't want to hear this; with any luck the reference might divert the conversation.

'Who? Oh, Dickens. *Great Expectations.* An overrated writer, in my opinion. Well, Paul's certainly not training up a small child to wreak revenge on all members of the opposite sex, but I think when Aura jilted him it killed something in him. Since then he's had affairs, of course, but he doesn't like women much.'

Was that it? Was the reservation she'd sensed in Paul right from the start so impersonal, a simple mistrust of the whole female world?

Crisply she said, 'Well, that's none of our—'

'Aura was so beautiful,' Gerard interrupted mournfully, refusing to detour. 'The sort of woman you never forget. I don't know how she could do it.'

'It happens.' Jacinta knew she sounded flippant, but she most emphatically didn't want to hear how wonderful the woman who had jilted Paul was.

'I suppose it does. Disloyalty is becoming more common than it used to be, I'm afraid.'

'Careful, Gerard,' she said lightly, 'your years are showing. I don't suppose it was easy for her, either. Decisions like that take some courage. Oh, there was a little rattle in the back of your car on the way up. Do you want me to take it into the garage?'

'No,' he said. 'I know what it is—nothing serious.' His voice altered. 'Well, I'd better go. Missing me?'

'I—yes—yes, of course,' she said, taken aback.

'Take care of yourself, and don't flirt with Paul. He might reciprocate, but he does with every woman he meets. It doesn't mean anything.'

'Flirting never does,' she said. 'That's the essence of the game, surely? To have fun and break no bones? Goodbye, Gerard. Do you want to speak to Paul again?'

'No,' he said. 'Goodbye, Jacinta.'

It was impossible to imagine Paul listening at the door, but as she hung up he came into the room. An eyebrow climbed and he said evenly, 'That didn't take long.'

Perhaps because she'd been discussing him, colour surged upwards from her breasts. 'He just wanted to see how things were going,' she said, carefully banishing the defensive note from her voice.

He nodded, his gaze very shrewd and hard as it rested on her face. 'Would you like a nightcap?'

'No, thanks; I'll go to bed now.'

He stepped aside to let her past. Almost stifled by his size and potent presence, Jacinta hurried through the door and down the hall to her bedroom, closing the door behind her with a shattering relief.

And then, with the curtains safely drawn and the light turned off, she sat in the darkness and shivered while those moments when Paul had held her stormed back into her brain, refusing to cede to any other thoughts.

It was nothing, she told herself. He supported you, that's all, until you got your balance back.

But her pulses were still throbbing through her body with a hypnotic rhythm, and when she closed her eyes she could see the arrogant, chiselled features outlined by the faint glow of the stars, and recall how his sheer, sexual power had consumed her.

Helpless, snared by her primitive, involuntary response, she'd been unable to move.

How could any woman leave him for another man? She simply couldn't believe it. Aura Whoever-she-was must have been a fool.

Jacinta drew a deep breath. It would pay her to remember that he'd retreated behind his armour of self-sufficiency with insulting speed. And it had been antagonism she'd glimpsed in his narrowed eyes.

If she sat here in the dark like a lovelorn teenager, going over and over how his arms had tightened like iron around her, how the heat of his body had enveloped her, she'd be pushing herself deeper and deeper into the murky waters of infatuation.

Setting her jaw, she got to her feet and switched on the light.

As she got ready for bed Gerard's words came back to haunt her. Did Paul dislike all women because one had let him down so spectacularly?

It didn't seem likely; surely he was too sane, too intelligent to generalise so brutally? But if he'd really loved that runaway fiancée the betrayal would have seemed hideous.

Disillusionment did strange things to people.

'Your problem,' she informed her reflection softly as she brushed the long, curling silk of her hair, 'is that you want whatever he feels for you—even if it's only dislike and mistrust—to belong to you alone, not to some unknown woman with more looks than nous.'

This fixation was becoming wretchedly inconvenient. Ah,

well, she'd be able to talk some sense into herself while he was away. Naturally she was a little off balance—she hadn't been expecting to find herself living in the same house as a man with such powerful, incendiary impact.

But as she lay in bed listening to the quiet sound of the sea through the trees, she let her mind drift, and soon became lost in a romantic daydream that merged imperceptibly with sleep, and turned erotic when the constraints of will and self-discipline blurred and vanished.

CHAPTER FOUR

JACINTA woke the next morning with heavy eyes, and a voluptuous exhaustion weighed her down. It was succeeded by a shocked scurry from the bed as memory replayed in vibrant colour the images she'd conjured up from some sensuous, uninhibited, completely unsuspected part of her psyche.

'Oh, lord,' she whispered, uncomfortable and tense as she turned the shower onto cold and stepped determinedly in, 'I've never had that sort of dream before!'

Flicking her hair out of the spray, she scrubbed herself with punishing vigour, and began stubbornly to plan the day's writing. When she finally emerged from her bedroom she'd regained some fragile measure of composure.

She was dressed for the morning in a thin white cotton shirt that hung loosely over her cinnamon three-quarter-length pants. For some inscrutable reason she'd succumbed to a feminine instinct and donned her one good pair of sandals, elderly though they were.

Although for all the glamour they added she might just as well have worn her cheap rubber sandals; they wouldn't have looked much more out of place against the muted opulence of the oriental runner that glowed on the wide, polished boards of the hall. The house was still cool, but it was going to be another unseasonably hot day.

Her hard-won composure fled when she walked into the breakfast room, for there, cup of coffee in front of him, sat Paul, dominant and uncompromisingly masculine, sunlight dancing around him in a golden aura.

'Good morning,' Jacinta said, reining in her reactions with a ruthless hand. 'No, don't get up, please.'

But he did, setting a sheaf of papers down on the table. 'Sleep well?' he enquired.

'Yes, thank you. I thought you'd be gone by now.' And she could have bitten her tongue, for she'd sounded surly and far too aware of him.

'In ten minutes,' he said. 'I gather you don't wake up in the best of moods.'

It was an excuse, but one she couldn't accept. 'Just this morning,' she said, trying to sound casually offhand. 'I think I must have slept too heavily.'

'A headache?' He seemed genuinely concerned.

'No,' she returned gruffly, 'a thick head and a bad temper.'

'Then help yourself to whatever you want,' he said, a note of amusement warming his voice, 'and I won't talk to you.'

His calm, confident good humour banished her surliness instantly. With a rueful smile she turned away to ladle fruit and cereal into a bowl.

If he stayed aloof she'd be all right. Times like this were going to be the problem; when he laughed he was altogether too likeable, the sort of man a woman could lose her heart to.

While he studied his papers Jacinta chewed cereal that tasted like cardboard, and tamarillos with no more flavour. She buttered toast. She drank coffee. Mentally she urged him to get up and leave.

Even though she kept her eyes studiously averted, she *felt* him. His beautifully tailored clothes made her cheap, second-hand ones look shabby and sleazy, and his self-possession was a blow directed at hers.

Finally he got to his feet and Jacinta was forced to look up. His eyes were so blue, she thought mindlessly.

'Enjoy yourself,' he said with laconic pleasantness. 'I'll see you tomorrow night, although I won't be here for dinner.'

Ah, thank God, he'd retreated once more behind the ar-

mour of his pleasantness. 'Have a good day,' Jacinta returned, deliberately banal.

When he left it the room echoed with emptiness. She
heard his car leave, and the house suddenly died. After forcing another cup of coffee down an unwilling throat, she
cleared the table and helped Fran put the dishes away before
walking down to the beach to watch the gulls slowly wheel
overhead.

At length, obscurely soothed by the never-ending, remorseless ebb and flow of the waves, she returned to her
bedroom, tidied it and made the bed, and sat herself down
in front of Gerard's computer.

She'd wondered if her sexual reaction to Paul might in-
hibit her writing, but it was as though someone had pressed
a hidden button and released a barrier in her, the excitement
of her writing somehow seeming to join with the languor
and the febrile passion that lingered like a miasma from her
dreams.

For hours she wrote with complete concentration, ignoring the sounds of the farm around the house, until Fran
tapped on her door and called, 'Jacinta, do you want some
lunch?'

'Hang on,' she answered, and finished the paragraph she
was working on.

'I'm sorry to interrupt,' the housekeeper said when she
emerged, 'but Paul said to make sure you had meals.'

Jacinta came crashing back into real life. 'Oh,' she said.
'Oh, I didn't realise... I thought... Is it lunchtime already?'

'Past one o'clock. Your work must be going well.'

Jacinta nodded, realising that she was both hungry and a
little stiff. 'Very well,' she said cheerfully. 'But I thought
we'd agreed that I'd make my own meals when there's just
us.'

Fran's look was dry and amused. 'In this house what Paul
says goes. He told me to see that you ate decent meals at

the right times, so if you're not out in the kitchen making your meals, I will be.'

She should be angry; after all, she'd hated it when Mark had tried to manage her life, and she resented even Gerard's well-meant suggestions. It was a measure of her infatuation that she felt a tiny warm glow at Paul's thoughtfulness.

Bad response, she thought gloomily, heading towards the kitchen with Fran.

That day set the pattern for the one following—and the one after that, for Paul rang the housekeeper to say that he wouldn't be home that night either, and possibly not for another couple.

I am not disappointed, Jacinta told herself firmly when Fran relayed the news after putting a cup of peppermint tea on one of the verandah tables.

The housekeeper and she had come to an agreement. If Jacinta was typing Fran didn't interrupt, but left food and cups of various interesting drinks on the table outside the bedroom, which Jacinta ate and drank when she emerged.

No, Jacinta thought when the housekeeper had gone, I'm not in the *least* disappointed.

And she went on being not disappointed for the next two days, until she found herself gazing at the page number on the computer screen with something like awe. That was a lot of pages, especially since she was only a two-finger typist.

It was late in the afternoon, the drowsy, slightly ragged end of the day when the sky looked washed out and the earth longed for the refreshing arrival of dusk.

This November was shaping up to be the hottest she'd ever experienced—too hot and dry for farmers. Only the previous evening Dean had told her he was worried about the prospect of a drought. They'd met when she'd gone for a walk before dinner, after being chased from the kitchen by the competent Fran. Dean had stopped his four-wheeled farm bike, and they'd chatted.

He'd noticed her interested look at the quad and offered, 'I'll give you a go on it if you like.'

'With dogs or without?' she asked, eyeing the two black and white collies that perched on the back. 'I might tip it over and they'd get hurt.'

For answer he got off, whistled the dogs onto the grass, and Jacinta spent an enjoyable half hour while he showed her how to drive the bike.

'A natural,' he said eventually. 'I'll hop on the back and you can give me a ride to the homestead.'

Elated at her new accomplishment, Jacinta had done just that, finishing with a flourish in the courtyard outside the back door, laughing as Fran came out to see.

'Thank you,' she said, smiling up at Dean when he got down to help her off. 'I haven't had so much fun for ages!'

He turned to Fran. 'She's a born farm bike rider.'

'Rather her than me,' Fran said, smiling as her glance switched from his face to Jacinta's and back again. 'And you'd better start looking for a born rainmaker, if the long-range weather forecast is right.'

'Are we in for a drought?' Jacinta asked.

'If we don't get rain soon,' he said, squinting at the cloudless sky, 'we'll be in deep and serious trouble.'

But although Jacinta had sympathised, she was enjoying the heat.

Putting down the pages of her manuscript, she wandered out onto the verandah and picked up the mug of peppermint tea, pretending that she wasn't waiting for the sound of a car.

A glance at her watch revealed that it was only five o'clock. Even if Paul did decide to come home tonight he wouldn't be there until after six, unless he got off early.

With determination, she drank the peppermint tea and read the newspaper, then took the cup back to the kitchen.

'You look beat,' Fran said, coming in through the door

with a great handful of salad greens from the herb garden. 'As hot as me.'

'I am.' Jacinta washed and dried the mug, edgy and restless and unable to think of anything she wanted to do to fill in the time.

'Why don't you go for a swim?' Fran asked.

Jacinta asked suspiciously, 'How warm is the water?'

'By November it's as warm as it's ever going to be.'

'I suppose so.' She put the cup and saucer away and said, 'Actually, I'm a wimp about swimming. I have this fantasy that one day I'll be rich enough to afford a heated pool.'

'Join the club,' Fran said cheerfully. 'Paul swims most of the year.'

'Masochist.' But she wasn't surprised.

Back in her room, she unearthed the bathing suit she'd thrust into a bottom drawer. Although an old bikini, it hadn't been used much; while she'd looked after her mother she'd rarely had a chance to swim. Except for Fiji, of course, and then she'd stuck to early in the morning and late at night so that the sun wouldn't burn her skin. Paul hadn't seen her in it.

She got into it, pulled a tee-shirt over the top, and fossicked out a large towel adorned with a pattern of brightly coloured birds.

Fran was right. The water was seductively warm, so she swam for twenty minutes until, limbs languid and weighted with effort, she walked out of the sea, pulling her hair free from the old rubber cap that had kept it dry. It rioted around her head, the thick ginger curls lifting in the slight evening breeze.

At the sound of an engine she looked frantically around for her tee-shirt. But even as she set off towards the towel she heard Dean's voice and relaxed.

'Good swim?' he asked, eyeing her with frank, not unpleasant admiration.

She smiled. 'Wonderful. It's so warm—too warm. I feel as though I've swum a hundred miles.'

He pushed his hat onto the back of his head and grinned at her. 'It does that to you. The blue water's early,' he said. 'The big game sportsmen'll be catching marlin before long.'

'What's the blue water?'

'Oh, tropical currents. Usually it doesn't come inshore until after Christmas, but this year Davy Jones must have known you'd be here and sent it down early.'

Jacinta grinned up into his nice, unhandsome face. She liked Dean, and clearly he liked her; he'd told her all about Brenda, his fiancée, and that they planned to get married in a year's time, and although he looked at Jacinta with candid appreciation there was nothing more subtle in his eyes than a healthy male enjoyment.

When the fairy godmothers had handed out her basic qualities at birth, they'd forgotten to include sex appeal. Boys had liked her, but very few had asked her out. Her mother used to say it was because she was taller than most of them; Jacinta knew she simply didn't have that special quality that made men desperate.

Even Mark hadn't wanted her body; he'd wanted somebody to control, to dominate, someone who'd boost his fragile ego.

'I'd better go on up,' she said. 'It gets a bit chilly out of the water.'

She took a step, tripped, and saved herself with both her hands.

'Here,' Dean said, and hauled her upright. When she winced his grip tightened and he demanded, 'What happened? You all right?'

'I'm clumsy,' she said lightly, 'but I think I must have stood on a broken shell.' She bent her leg at the knee, twisting to peer down at the uplifted sole of her foot.

'It could have been glass. Let's see,' he said, dropping to a crouch beside her and taking her foot in his. 'No, it's not bleeding,' he informed her after a thorough inspection, 'but the skin's marked.'

His thumb rubbed across the sensitive sole, and she gurgled and said, 'You're tickling!'

'Sorry,' he said, laughing and looking up at her with teasing eyes.

The sound of a quiet, 'Good evening,' cut into their shared amusement with the biting, brutal accuracy of a scalpel. Jacinta flinched as though she'd been struck, jerking her foot free from Dean's grip.

He stood up, still smiling, and said, 'G'day, Paul.'

Paul was still in his suit; he should have looked incongruously formal there on the beach, his shiny black city shoes half sunk in the sand, his head smoothly brushed and gold in the sinking sun.

Instead he looked terrifying. And yet there was nothing about the handsome face, nothing about the regular features or the cool blue eyes to set Jacinta's heart thudding sickly, the adrenalin surging through every vein in a swift, warning flood.

Unless it was the splintering moment when his gaze raked the length of her scantily clad body before fixing on Dean's face.

She drew in a ragged breath.

Apparently unaware of anything out of the ordinary, Dean went on cheerfully, 'I need a word whenever you've got time.'

'How about now?' Paul didn't look at Jacinta.

'Yeah, fine.' Dean directed his uncomplicated grin at her. 'Catch you later.'

Jacinta watched them go up under the trees and walk across the lawn towards the back of the house. Slowly, carefully, she expelled the breath that had been imprisoned in her lungs, and bent to pick up the tee-shirt at her feet.

After pulling it on she went back to the house and washed the sand from her legs under the tap beside the back door.

She sat down on the steps and dried her feet, then hung her towel over the clothesline and went back inside, intent on seeking sanctuary in her bedroom.

She had to make herself walk normally past the closed door of the office because her whole instinct was to tiptoe.

As she showered the salt from her body she tried very hard to convince herself that she hadn't sensed an over-whelming blast of antagonism from Paul. There was no rea-son for it, unless he thought that as an engaged man Dean should be a little more circumspect with women.

However, he hadn't seemed angry with Dean.

How long had he been there? He must have seen her trip.

Perhaps he thought she tripped whenever a man came near her. Humiliation oozed through her, but she banished its slimy residue. All right, so she did care what he thought of her.

She was too conscious of Paul, too nervous and tense when he was around, and she was sick of it. She should leave, but—oh, why not admit it?—she wanted to stay.

Her childish infatuation wasn't doing anyone any harm; it wasn't as though she was making a nuisance of herself. And if she got hurt—well, she'd be the only one to know.

She chose her most concealing dress—a short-sleeved thing in soft, tawny cotton that flowed easily—hoping it would wipe from his mind the memory of her body in the scanty bikini.

And she stayed in her room, reading through the day's work, until emerging as close to seven-thirty as she could without seeming to avoid Paul. Relieved to find the conser-vatory empty, she walked out onto the terrace and crouched beside the pond with its resident flotilla of goldfish—large, streamlined creatures of gold and bronze and an orange so intense it was like the heart of the sun.

They were interested in human company, these fish. 'Hello,' she said quietly, and they came swimming up, nos-ing the fingers she put in the water.

She laughed softly. 'No, I haven't got any food. Furthermore, Fran tells me you don't need to be fed.'

'Fran's right,' Paul said from behind, his deep voice toneless.

Jacinta leapt to her feet, turning a flushed, startled face to him. He'd come around the corner of the house, walking through the light of the westering sun.

'Hello,' she said, working hard at a casual smile.

'Fran tells *me* you've been working all hours,' he said, leaning against one of the pergola uprights. Wisteria blossom, white and purple and lilac, cast shadows on his angular features.

She nodded. 'It's coming along rather well,' she said cautiously.

'Are you actually making notes for a thesis?'

After a moment's hesitation she admitted, 'No. I'm fulfilling a promise I made to my mother before she died.'

He nodded, and because he didn't ask she explained, 'I didn't want to tell Gerard because I could well be just wasting my time.'

It sounded both lame and defensive, and she wished she'd kept quiet.

'I see,' Paul said, his voice cool and non-committal. 'Are you planning to go ahead with the Master's degree?'

She should certainly have kept quiet. 'I don't know,' she finally confessed, astounding herself. Taking her MA was the other promise she'd made to her mother, but for the first time she wondered whether she really wanted to do it. It made her feel disloyal and mean.

'What will you do if you decide to give it a miss?'

'I'll find something,' she said, irritated with him for probing.

What she'd like to do was continue writing, but she was a realist—she knew she was unlikely to get her manuscript published. Writing was a highly competitive field and she was a total novice. And even if she was good enough and lucky enough to be published, it could be years before she earned sufficient to be able to do it full-time.

His shaded face gave nothing away, whereas she was in the full glare of the sun; when she realised that she was staring at him she dropped her lashes and pretended to be very interested in the slowly cruising goldfish, feeling hot and foolish and gauche, and resenting both herself for responding so foolishly to him and him for conjuring up that response.

'It's not an enviable position to be in,' he said after a moment, his voice judicial.

She shrugged. 'I'll manage. Did you always know you were going to be a lawyer?'

His mouth twisted. 'I wanted to be an adventurer. At school—a very traditional boarding school—my best friend and I planned a life swashbuckling around the world, but my father was a solicitor who wanted me to follow in his footsteps. And as he was ill that's what I did.'

A promise to a dying parent was hard to break. Smiling, Jacinta asked, 'What happened to your friend? I suppose he turned into an accountant.'

Then she remembered what Gerard had told her about that best friend.

'Oh,' he answered with a chilling lack of emotion, 'he fulfilled his dream. He developed from a tough kid to a dangerous man, who eventually gave everything up to grow grapes and make wine.'

With Aura, the woman Paul had wanted—probably still wanted.

Jacinta said, 'And have you ever regretted making the decision to obey your father?'

His quiet laughter had a cynical note to it. 'No, my father knew me better than I did. I enjoy what I do, and in its less overtly dramatic way it has enough adventure in it for me.'

He moved out from beneath the wisteria, and she was jolted once more by his sheer male beauty—the elemental

golden glory of his colouring, the formation of the bones
beneath his tanned skin that would ensure he made an extraordinarily handsome old man, the powerful male sym-
metry of wide shoulders and lean hips, long legs and muscled forearms—and by his personality that so totally
overshadowed his looks.

Six inches shorter, she thought, with washed-out eyes and
features like Quasimodo, and he'd still stand out in any
crowd. That unforced authority—the indomitable mixture of
intelligence and mastery and focus, of courage and endurance and resolution—rendered him unforgettable.

'You're fortunate in your profession,' she said unevenly,
an unbidden excitement fanning a flame inside her.

'Very.'

When he came towards her she had to stop herself from
stepping backwards, but her fleeing feet carried her sideways, and although she concentrated with ferocious intensity on not stumbling, her wretched sense of balance—or
lack of it—let her down again. It wasn't a dramatic lurch,
but he caught her arm.

'Careful, even if you do like the fish we don't want you
joining them.'

'No,' she said, rendered witless by the touch of his hand.
'I've already had my swim for the day.'

'And enjoyed it, I gather.'

'Yes, it was super.'

Inside the room she moved away from him. When Dean
had touched her she'd felt nothing, yet she'd shivered to the
core of her being at the light pressure of Paul's hand on her
arm.

'How's your foot?' he asked now, glancing down.

Trying to stop her toes from curling, she said, 'What?'

'Your foot.' The words were patient, as though he were
speaking to a child. Or a halfwit. 'You cut it on the beach.'

'No,' she said, 'I just stood on a sharp shell, I think. When
we had a look there was nothing there.'

'Good. Dean was worried in case there was glass on the beach, but it would have broken the skin. You're sure a thin sliver didn't work its way in?'

'Quite sure,' she said fervently.

'In that case, sit down and I'll get you something to drink.'

He chose chilled white wine, but didn't try to persuade her to have any with him, instead giving her the lime and soda she asked for.

There was, she thought as she accepted the cold glass, nothing even vaguely threatening in his attitude. She'd just imagined things down on the beach.

Aloud, she said, 'Did you have a good time in Auckland?'

'I actually flew to America,' he said, smiling at her astonishment. 'To Los Angeles.'

'I didn't know barristers went all around the world.'

'We go wherever we're needed. In this case, I had to organise a meeting with American lawyers to set up a deal for a film production company.' He told her a little about it—no mention of names, nothing she could use to identify any of the people—and made her laugh several times with his ruthless puncturing of a couple of enormous egos.

'Do you have much dealing with film producers?' she asked.

'Quite a lot. New Zealand's becoming very popular for both film and television companies from overseas now, and where there's money there are people determined to protect their investment.'

'It sounds very glamorous,' she said, looking out through the open French windows to the lawn. The late light was sifting down through the clouds of sunset, falling in thick rays across the lawn. Anticipation began to build in her, a slow, heady buzz that was so close to being physical she could almost feel it licking sensuously as fur across her skin.

'It can be.' His lashes fell, half concealing his eyes. 'Would you like to come to a party with me in a couple of days' time? It's a wrap-up for a television series that's just been made here.'

'Oh—no, thank you,' she said after a scant moment of frozen, yearning hesitation. 'It sounds very interesting, but—'

One dark eyebrow lifted and he asked disconcertingly, 'But what?'

Jacinta decided that the truth was the only way to go. 'I don't have the right clothes for it,' she said bluntly, considering the sari for a micro-second before discarding the idea. 'And I don't have the money to buy any new ones.'

'I'm sorry.' He transferred his glance to the glass in his hand, surveying the cool gold liquid with its hints of green.

If he offers to buy me something, she thought furiously, I'll— I'll—

But he went on tightly, 'That was crass of me.'

She didn't refute that. It had been crass—surprisingly so for a man whose courtesy seemed inbred. Pride kept her head high. Poverty was nothing to be ashamed of.

Setting her glass down, she said, 'I don't feel I can spend my mother's legacy on clothes I might never wear again.'

'Is what you wear so important?' he asked with apparent idleness.

She snorted inelegantly. 'Not many people are confident enough to feel good in clothes that don't fit the occasion,' she said, and only when she'd finished realised that she was probably talking to one.

'You're right, of course. I'm sorry you can't come with me; I think you'd have enjoyed it.'

He began to talk about the forthcoming election, and eagerly she followed suit, enjoying that keen, incisive brain until Fran appeared at the door and said, 'Dinner's ready.'

As she went with him into the morning room Jacinta knew she'd never forget that Paul McAlpine had once asked her to go with him to a party.

* * *

After eating the superb dinner without actually tasting it, she went back to work in her room so that Paul didn't feel obliged to entertain her. She wanted too much to stay there and talk to him, and listen to that slow, deep voice, and watch that arrogantly handsome face, and feel little chills of awareness run through her like a summons to heaven.

However, running away didn't work.

She closed the curtains to prevent marauding huhu beetles and moths and mosquitoes from dive-bombing her, and sat in front of the computer and stared at the screen, summoning a variety of images, none of which had anything to do with writing.

Eventually she shook her head and switched off the machine before getting ready for bed. When she'd turned the light out, she opened the curtains again to let the sweet, salty air wash into the room.

Perhaps because she went so early to bed she didn't sleep well, waking with a jolt at one in the morning and spending the next hour tossing and turning and trying to blank out the pictures in her mind. Around two she got up and, thinking ironically that life in New Zealand would be a lot easier without the assorted insects that roamed the night, closed the curtains once more before sitting down to write.

An hour or so later a quiet tap on her door made her jump.

'Just a minute,' she called out, dragging on her dressing gown.

It was Paul, clad in shirt and trousers. 'Are you all right?' he asked, scanning her face with unhurried thoroughness.

She nodded. 'I'm fine. I just couldn't sleep so—am I disturbing you?'

'No,' he said abruptly. 'I couldn't sleep either, so I went for a walk and saw your light on. I thought I'd better investigate.'

'Thank you for checking.' She hesitated, then said, 'Goodnight.'

'I'm going to make some tea,' he said. 'Do you want some? Or do you prefer cocoa at this hour of the night?'

She should say no. She should be firm and aloof and definite—but polite, of course. Instead she yielded to unbearable temptation. 'Tea will be perfect.'

'Would you like me to bring it here?'

'No.' The word came out far too fast and hard. Conscious of her hot cheeks, she said, 'I'll come along to the kitchen,' and stepped back.

He said, 'I'll see you soon,' and went off down the hallway, moving soundlessly.

Five minutes later, respectable in a tee-shirt and a pair of jeans, Jacinta padded quietly down the hall and into the kitchen.

As she came in Paul lifted the electric jug to pour the boiling water into a teapot. When the pot was filled he looked up and smiled.

You should have said no, Jacinta told herself—too late to be of any help. Oh, you should have said never, not at this hour of the night, not if you're going to smile at me...

'Were you working?' he asked.

'Yes.'

'What exactly *are* you doing on Gerard's computer?' He reached to get a couple of mugs down from the cupboard.

Unwillingly Jacinta's eyes followed the slow, purposeful coil and flexion of muscles, the smooth signs of latent energy that marked his every movement. A sweet pang of desire caught her by surprise, demolishing her defences.

She had to force herself to concentrate on what he was saying.

'Fran's dying to know, although she'll never ask—not even me. She's been dropping hints, however. And I must admit to considerable curiosity myself. If it's a secret don't tell me.'

'I think I'm writing a book,' Jacinta confessed, amazed at her surrender.

'Well, yes, I rather gathered that you were. What sort of book?'

Flushing, she said resolutely, 'My mother used to really like reading science fiction, but she found that a lot of it was too technical.'

'The hard stuff,' he said. 'She was a *Star Trek* fan, I'll bet.'

She laughed. 'Of course she was. And she loved the *Star Wars* trilogy too. When she got too sick to be able to read herself, I used to read to her. We got talking about one particular book, and I said that it was all wrong, the characters didn't fit the plot. So she challenged me to give them a plot that fitted them better, and I began to make up a story about a group of people in an alternative universe, where unicorns had always existed, along with dragons and the phoenix.'

She blinked a couple of times and steadied her voice. 'She loved it, and after a while she started to come up with ideas too, and we'd discuss how we could fit them into the book. It gave her something to think about, helped her get through some pretty bad times. When medication clouded her mind so that she began to forget incidents, she suggested I make notes.' Uneasy at the way he was watching her, his eyes remote and yet oddly sympathetic, she looked away briefly.

Gently, he asked, 'Is this another promise?'

'Yes.'

'Have you ever done any writing before?'

Jacinta shrugged. 'I told stories continually throughout my childhood to anyone who'd listen. And when I was an adolescent I wrote obsessively—all about death and destruction and myself. Very gloomy and self-centred.'

'I find that hard to believe,' he said, his eyes amused.

'Aren't all teenagers?'

'I don't recall being gloomy,' he said. 'Self-centred—yes, I'll admit to that. But everyone's self-centred when they're fifteen.'

'I certainly was,' she said with a grimace, wondering just what he'd been like as an adolescent. Always confident, no doubt; that assurance was as much a part of him as the colour of his hair and his brilliant eyes.

'So how is the manuscript getting on?'

'Slowly. It's the oddest thing. I know this story and these people so well, yet I'm having real trouble getting it right.'

'I imagine that in telling a story you use voice and gesture and timing,' he said thoughtfully, reaching into the fridge to get out the milk. 'You have to supply that with words in writing.'

Secretly impressed, Jacinta said, 'That's it exactly. It's far harder than I thought it would be, but I am enjoying it.'

'Fran worries about the long hours.'

'Fran should have been a nanny,' Jacinta said, smiling. 'I told her not to bother getting me meals, but she keeps knocking on my door and insisting I eat regularly. Which, I believe, is your fault.'

'Do you want me to tell her to leave you alone?'

Rather shocked at his cool authority, she shook her head. 'Oh, no, I like structure to my day. I like the food, too.'

'In that case she can continue to knock,' he said dryly, pouring the tea.

They drank it in the morning room. Jacinta chose an armchair, very comfortable and slightly oversized, as everything in the house was. To go with the owner, no doubt.

Paul settled lithely onto the sofa, long legs straight in front of him, broad shoulders against the back, the mug of tea somehow not in the least incongruous in his hands. Jacinta thought—before she realised where her mind was taking her—that his masculine grace overcame the full impact of his size, preventing him from looking clumsy or hulking.

'Gerard certainly wouldn't approve of the use you're making of his computer,' he said thoughtfully, watching her from eyes that should have looked sleepily half closed, but instead revealed the quick, clever mind behind his handsome face.

The name jarred across her contentment. She said quietly, 'I do intend to work on several proposals for the subject of my thesis. I probably should be doing them now, but I don't want to stop writing.'

'I see,' he said, and that smile set her spine tingling. 'You're hooked!'

It was foolish to feel that he'd lightened a burden for her. 'That's it exactly,' she said. 'But Gerard wouldn't understand. His taste in light reading tends to be—'

'Heavy,' Paul supplied laconically. He was silent for several moments, then asked, 'Have you done any walking while you've been here?'

'Oh, yes.' She leaned forward eagerly. 'Dean took me over to the bach yesterday afternoon. How on earth are you going to get rid of that awful smell?'

'We'll dig it out and make sure there's no way they can burrow underneath again,' he said lazily, his lashes drooping.

She frowned. 'Where will the penguins nest then?'

'They've bred perfectly happily in the caves at the base of the headland for thousands of centuries; they're like humans, taking the easy way, the shortcut, whenever they can. I hear you've learned to ride the quad. Fran said you looked as though you'd been on one for years.'

She laughed and told him about it. 'It was great fun, and in the end even the dogs deigned to ride with me.'

'Then you must have impressed them with your skill.' Beneath his heavy lids his eyes gleamed, blue as the bluest sapphires. 'Did Dean tell you that he and Brenda intend to buy their own farm soon?'

'Yes.' And because Paul believed in helping hard work, he'd offered to finance them. Dean and Brenda spent most of their spare time with land agents. 'I think it's a wonderful idea, and very generous of you.'

He frowned. 'He told you a little too much,' he said curtly. 'What else have you been doing?'

There was a slight note of—sarcasm? cynicism?—in his voice. Jacinta drank some of the tea before saying, 'I went into town with Fran and changed my library books. Apart from that, not a lot.'

'Swimming, obviously. How's the water?'

'Lovely.' Hastily, before she could blush like a fifteen-year-old, she added, 'Like swimming in silk.'

'I must come with you tomorrow.'

Which brought even more vivid images to her mind, so vivid that she drank the tea down too quickly and excused herself as soon as she could without being rude.

CHAPTER FIVE

HALF an hour later, back in bed but too tense to sleep, Jacinta relived those words. Her stomach jumped the way it had when he'd said them, at the vision her reckless brain had produced of Paul in swimming togs.

He's not for you, she told herself sternly, turning over to find a cooler place in the sheets. Not for you at all. Just grit your teeth and endure this violent crush because eventually it'll wear out. They always do.

But, oh, how potent it was, this singing in the blood, this untamed hunger that prowled through her days and nights, constantly testing the bars of her will and common sense. Eventually, when the stars were paling in the dawn sky, she managed to drift off into a heavy, dreamless slumber.

Next morning when she sat down and read over what she'd written the day before, she realised that the hero of the book was becoming more and more like Paul McAlpine.

Gritting her teeth, she went through and changed him back into the man she'd originally imagined; if she let Paul infiltrate the pages the characters would be set wildly at odds, because the plot she and her mother had created depended entirely on the interplay of each personality.

And her hero needed nothing of Paul in him.

Well, perhaps a little, she thought, lifting her eyes from the screen to gaze out across the lawn, still wet from heavy dew. Below the verandah the apricot and pink spider flowers of a grevillea bobbed as a tui landed heavily in the bush and proceeded to plunder their nectar. Sunlight burned across iridescent feathers, bathing him in blue and green and purple fire against the crisp white pompom at his throat.

Yes, there were similarities between Paul and Mage; both

were leaders of men, both possessed the authority that came from confidence and success. But Mage was a grimmer, more severe man, and he had a fatal flaw, one he had to overcome. He loved jealously, absolutely, utterly.

A far cry from Paul's serene self-assurance, Jacinta thought with a wry grimace.

Although if Gerard was right—if he'd loved Aura so much that he could never love another woman—that indicated an extravagance of passion very much at odds with the man Jacinta knew.

Moodily she wondered how the unknown Aura, that dark flame of a woman, had captured Paul's heart so completely. And what sort of person was she to leave him like that?

'None of your business,' she told herself robustly, and got back to work—using it, she realised with some shame, to block out her emotions. It seemed a cowardly way to cope with them, but at least she didn't spend all day longing for Paul to return from his office in Auckland, and she certainly finished a lot of pages.

When the sun dipped westwards anticipation began to condense within her, almost physical in its impact, until she was wound as tightly as a spring. In a pathetic attempt to ease it, she went for a walk along the beach, striding strongly while she pretended to be thinking of the next day's work, trying to ignore the need and excitement that strummed a fiery counterpoint inside her.

She'd turned beneath the headland and was walking back in the dense shade of the trees when she saw a tall figure on the beach. Stopping, she feasted her eyes in passionate, eager scrutiny of the sleekly muscled wedge of his torso gleaming above brief black trunks, his lithe grace as he strode across the sand. Like a god, she thought, gilded by the sun, a primeval figure of beauty and power and leadership.

Almost immediately he turned his head and stopped. The air between them sparkled and spun, danced with tension, formed a glittering chain that linked her to him like shackles, like a psychic union.

It lasted only a second. He waved and turned towards the sea. Her heart thudding, Jacinta waved back before fleeing through the garden to the back of the house.

'Aren't you going for a swim?' Fran asked, looking up from the herb bed. 'Paul's just left.'

'How about you?' To hide her face, Jacinta bent to pick a blue borage flower, the exact colour of Paul's eyes.

'Too busy,' Fran said briefly.

Jacinta stood up. 'I'll see you later,' she said vaguely, her pulses still jumping, her body throbbing.

She didn't have to swim. Oh, Fran might think it odd if she didn't—but why should she? Why should she think about you at all? Jacinta asked as she headed for her bedroom. Let's be honest. You're looking for excuses to share an experience with him. You want to swim in the same sea as he is, breath the same air, be warmed by the same sun.

Expectation scorched from nerve-end to nerve-end, hollowing her stomach, tightening her skin.

Closing her door behind her, she said aloud, 'All right then, do it, but at least accept what you're doing. And no more nonsense about quivering air and psychic links!'

Once in her bikini she hesitated for a moment, then pulled on a tee-shirt; she'd keep it on even when she was swimming. If anyone—if Paul—made any comment, she'd say she didn't want to burn.

When she came out onto the beach he was swimming strongly several hundred metres from shore. Her sensible half was relieved; the other—the secret half, the half that longed intolerably for him—was eaten by disappointment. Briskly she strode into the water and struck out away from that gleaming dark gold head, trying to purge herself of the tides that washed through her so darkly, so inevitably, gathering momentum day by day.

Even though she was exhausted when she finally made

her way back across the sand, the cure hadn't worked. She dragged in deep, shuddering breaths, raking a trembling hand through her hair as she pulled the old rubber cap off and shook her hair down past her shoulders.

Behind her, Paul was heading for land. Perhaps, she thought tiredly, he had demons to exorcise too.

Moving slowly, she scooped up her towel and wrapped it around her waist, then made her way through the cool shade of the trees, climbed the steps up the bank and set off across the lawn.

Vibrant whistling warned her that someone was coming from the gate; summoning a smile, she glanced up as Dean strode around the corner of the house.

He finished with a loud, clever variation of a wolf whistle, then as he got closer eyed her with some concern. 'You look as though you've been pushing it,' he commented. 'You're a bit pale.'

She made a comical face. 'I decided I was getting slack, sitting in front of a computer all day, so I swam too long.'

'No,' he said, grinning, 'not a sign of slackness.' His eyes moved and his grin widened as he said to the man coming up behind her, 'No sign of slackness in you, either.'

'I should hope not,' Paul said. He'd swum for longer than she had, but he wasn't even puffing.

As Jacinta turned she felt the casual grip of his hand on her shoulder, burning through the wet material of her tee-shirt, scorching her composure. Startled, her lips parted and she looked into his face.

He didn't return her puzzled glance. His eyes, cool and unyielding between his thick, wet lashes, were fixed on Dean. 'Did you want to see me?' he asked, lifting his hand from Jacinta's far too responsive shoulder.

'I do,' Dean said, his voice oddly formal. 'We need to discuss a staffing problem.'

'I'll see you in the office in ten minutes,' Paul said. 'See if Fran will get us a drink, will you?'

'Sure,' Dean said, smiled at Jacinta with none of his usual cheerful cheek, and left them.

'Are you all right?' Paul asked calmly.

Jacinta nodded. 'Fine. I just went for too long, but I don't want to get unfit. And writing all day is not exactly exercise.'

His brief touch had altered some subtle balance or perception of power, leaving her confused and upset. Every sense was on full alert, avidly soaking in the subtle signs of his masculinity, the vivid, bottomless blue of his eyes, the way the sun gleamed over the burnished slide of wet, golden skin, the masculine pattern of hair scrolled across his chest then arrowing down his flat stomach to disappear beneath the black material of his trunks…

And through the sensory overload came the coldness on her shoulder where his hand had rested.

'I hope,' he said, a bite to his words, 'you don't swim like that when I'm not here.'

'I'm not stupid. I do know my own limitations.'

Thank heavens she was wearing her tee-shirt and her towel! His gaze was intent and utterly disturbing; if she'd had nothing on but her bikini she'd have been enormously embarrassed.

As it was she knew that her nipples were stiffly peaked by a combination of cold and the drag of bra and shirt. Automatically she folded her arms across them and stepped back.

'I hope you do,' he said, and suddenly there was that undercurrent, the note of warning she'd heard when she first arrived at the homestead. 'You're cold. Come on.'

To her astonishment he took her hand and set off for the back door.

Once Jacinta had woken from her dazed grief after her mother's death she'd objected very much to Mark's dominating tactics, but for several moments she went meekly enough with Paul, her pulse jumping under the grip of his long fingers until—almost too late—her instincts shouted a warning. Reflexively she jerked her hand back. His fingers tightened for a second, then he released her.

'Have a warm shower,' he said. 'You still look cold.'

'I'll wash the sand off my feet first.'

Keeping her eyes well averted, she tried to turn the outdoor tap on, but after a moment of her fumbling with it he said, 'Here, let me,' and moved her hand off.

As the water gushed out he straightened up, looked her over with a narrowed, metallic glance, and said, 'Don't stay in the water for so long next time.'

Safely in the bathroom she stared at herself, seeing a woman she didn't know, a woman whose eyes gleamed pure gold beneath sultry lashes, whose mouth was soft and cushioned as though it had just been kissed, whose normally sallow skin was warmed by the lingering delight of those seconds when his hand had closed around hers, strong and warm and safe.

A woman whose breasts strained against the clinging material of the tee-shirt, the nipples prominent and completely at the mercy of the powerful sensations that rushed through her, white-hot and quite unmistakable.

'What am I going to do?' Jacinta asked that unknown woman. 'What on earth am I going to do?'

Angrily she turned the shower to cold and got in under the spray, flinching as needles of water washed away the salt and the heat.

Unfortunately, cold though it was, the water was unable to quench the rising desire that ate into her composure.

For desire was what it was, not the innocent, unformed intensity of a crush; she wanted Paul McAlpine, wanted him so badly she ached with it, and she was perilously close to surrendering to that feverish desperation.

It was just as well he didn't show any signs of reciprocating, because if he did she could well make a complete and utter fool of herself.

Paul could have any woman he wanted; he wasn't likely to want a tall, thin woman entirely lacking in that mysterious quality called allure, because of course the woman who'd gazed with such lazy sensuousness from the mirror was a momentary aberration.

Jacinta wished she'd had more social life when she'd first gone to university eleven years before. Although several men had asked her out, she'd refused them because she'd needed to spend every spare moment working in a local takeaway bar.

But if she'd gone out with some of them she'd have gained some much-needed experience. She might have realised much sooner that Mark was developing an unhealthy attitude towards her, and, more importantly, she might now have some idea of how to deal with her own responses and emotions to a man so different from Mark.

However, she thought mordantly as she towelled herself dry with rather too much vigour, none of the nice men who'd asked her out then would have been able to teach her how to cope with this sudden, inexplicable hunger for a man she could never have.

At dinner that night she was very cool, very restrained, determined to stay aloof, but after half an hour of his pleasant, unthreatening conversation she relaxed, eventually feeling secure enough to watch a television programme with him—an excellent drama with a premise based on the overwhelming passion for each other of two violently disparate people.

When it was over she said, 'Romeo and Juliet I can understand—they were so young. But love at first sight is a hoary old chestnut.'

'One you don't believe in?' he asked, smiling faintly, his hooded gaze resting on her face.

'I certainly don't. Love needs time to grow. The two people in that play were obsessed with each other, but although it was dramatic and overwhelming it's not what I call love.'

Paul leaned back into the big chair that was clearly his. 'You don't believe in soul mates, then?' he said thoughtfully, still watching her.

She shook her head. 'No. It sounds wonderful, doesn't it, someone magically, spiritually linked to you down through the centuries, the one person you can be deliriously happy with, who fulfils every need? But no one can do that; it puts far too heavy a responsibility on the other person in the relationship. I think that anybody can probably fall in love with a whole lot of people—it's just luck as to which one they meet first.'

'So what is love at first sight, then?'

A dangerous delusion, she thought tartly. Aloud she said, 'Attraction. A physical thing.'

Physical definitely, but it had the power to ruin lives. Her mother had never really managed to forget the married man who had seduced her and then abandoned her when he'd got her pregnant.

Paul said, 'You believe that two people can look at each other and want each other—a *coup de foudre*, as my grandmother used to say?'

She restrained the instinct to move uneasily. 'I don't know what that means,' she equivocated.

Irony edged his voice. 'A thunderclap.'

'Oh.' Heat crept through her skin, because that was exactly how she'd felt when she'd seen him that first time in Fiji—as though a thunderclap had robbed her of her wits.

She said swiftly, 'Yes, that happens, but it's dangerous to think it's love.'

'But without it there can be no love. Not the sort of love that leads to marriage, anyway.'

He'd turned the screen off as soon as the drama had finished, so there was no sound but the soft, almost unheard sighing of the waves on the beach.

Hastily, because she wasn't accustomed to discussing desire and passion with men—especially not men like Paul—

she said, 'I agree, but most psychologists seem to feel that there's a lot more to a happy marriage than s-sex.'

God, she was stuttering like an adolescent; the word seared itself into her brain.

'Or love,' Paul said blandly.

She shot him a quick, puzzled look.

He went on, 'People are more likely to form stable, happy relationships if they have the same values, even the same upbringing and social standing.'

'That sounds a bit cold-blooded,' she said. 'I think people can learn to love each other across class and cultural barriers.'

His brows lifted and a mocking smile tilted his mouth. 'Of course you do,' he said, the lightest flick of sarcasm underlining the words.

Greatly daring, Jacinta asked, 'Don't you?'

'I believe that nature does what's necessary to ensure the perpetuation of the species,' he said, his voice as indolent as his smile as he adroitly headed the conversation off into the discovery of a meteorite that suggested there could once have been life on Mars.

Later that night, Jacinta stood in her darkened bedroom and watched the stars wheel with monumental patience across the black sky, their steely light lending an air of mystery and glamour to the gardens.

How long had she known the owner of all this beauty? Not quite a week, because you couldn't count those few days in Fiji.

So according to her own firmly held beliefs she couldn't be falling in love. This complicated, overmastering blend of emotions that assailed her had to be nothing more than straight, unromantic physical attraction, whether you termed it sex, desire, or a hungry concupiscence.

Paul's cynical view of love was probably the correct one; her inner delight, that unfulfilled yearning, was merely the romantic glow Mother Nature flung over the driving need for humankind to reproduce.

If she wasn't careful she could become as obsessed with him as the doomed lovers in the television programme had been with each other.

And that would be stupid.

She should leave Waitapu.

Her heart clenched in her chest, but she knew she was right. It was too dangerous to stay.

Tomorrow she'd scan the ads in the newspaper and see if she could find a place to stay. Many of the flats let during term to university students would be empty now; perhaps she could rent one until the beginning of the new academic year.

She'd have to get a job and think of an excuse to leave.

Running away would complicate things, but if she stayed here she might end up very badly hurt.

She woke with a new and exciting plot twist burning in her brain, and without doing more than washing and dressing sat down in front of the computer, glad that she had an excuse not to go out to breakfast. However, she hadn't been typing for more than a few minutes when someone knocked sharply on her door.

'It's all right, Fran,' she called.

'It's not Fran, and it's not all right.'

She bit her lip, trying to control the sudden racing of her pulse. Reluctantly she got up from the desk.

Paul was dressed for work in a superbly tailored suit that reminded her he lived in an entirely different world from hers.

'What is it?' she said, not attempting to conceal the curtness in her query.

He looked at her with intent, measuring eyes. Then he smiled and her heart turned over. 'Come and have some breakfast,' he commanded pleasantly.

'I'm not really hungry,' she said, masking her uncertainty and exasperation with a crisp briskness. 'And I've just had a brilliant idea—I want to get it down before I forget it.'

His brows drew together. 'How long will it take?'

'Paul, I don't know.'

She'd said his name for the first time. It was like the finest wine on her tongue, complex and tangy and seductive, profoundly fascinating.

He laughed softly. 'All right, I'm sorry. But make sure you have something to eat when the inspiration's waned,' he said, and to her astonishment he picked up the hand clenched at her side and straightened out the tense fingers, running his thumb lightly across the terrified pulse in her narrow wrist.

White-faced, she jerked her hand free.

'I'll see you tonight,' he said evenly.

Jacinta didn't try to write until she heard the car go half an hour later. And only then, it seemed, was she able to breathe again.

'Oh, lord,' she said weakly.

Why had he done that? She cradled the hand he'd touched, looking at the fingers, her brain so utterly bemused she had to shake her head to force herself to move.

Paul's response startled her. If she'd refused to do anything Mark had suggested, he'd have tried to coax her, and if that hadn't worked he'd have insisted, and then sulked and made life uncomfortable for everyone. Paul had simply accepted her decision.

Of course, a cynical part of her brain reminded her, whether or not she ate breakfast with Paul made no real difference to his day. He might be a naturally dominant man, but he wasn't driven by Mark's lust to control.

She drifted into the kitchen and made herself a piece of toast and a cup of coffee, then, ignoring Fran's dark look, wandered back to the bedroom and stood in the French window, eating the toast and drinking the coffee and gazing dreamily at the garden and the sea.

Eventually she forced herself free of the enchanted thraldom of Paul's touch and back into the world she'd created, but the magic stayed with her all day, at once appalling and transporting her, but also reinforcing her decision to leave Waitapu.

When she surfaced again around two, and arrived hungry and thirsty in the kitchen, Fran was coming in through the back door, carrying three large grocery bags.

'Haven't you had any lunch yet?' she asked, easing them down onto the bench. 'You'll get into bad habits if you don't train yourself better.'

'It's not exactly a matter of training,' Jacinta objected mildly, gathering ingredients together for a ham sandwich. 'Ideas come when they're ready.'

'I don't believe that. I think ideas come when you're ready. And erratic meals will ruin your digestion.'

Jacinta grinned. 'I know,' she said, 'and perhaps you're right. I'll try to train my ideas. Have you brought everything in? I'll go out—'

'No, no, that's all.' Fran opened the largest of the bags and hauled out a bag labelled 'couscous'.

'Here, I'll put that away.' Jacinta went to take it from her.

The housekeeper said serenely, 'Jacinta, make that sandwich. It's far quicker for me to stow everything away myself than it is to tell you where it goes.'

Jacinta sighed. 'Oh, all right,' she said. 'You keep all the exciting jobs for yourself.'

She sat down at the table, assembled a large sandwich, and began to demolish it while Fran stored an interesting selection of items in the pantry.

'Paul told me this morning,' Fran said, frowning at a bottle with green detergent in it, 'that he's having a party here this Saturday. As there'll be a couple of guests staying I had to do some preliminary buying.'

The ham and crisp greens from the herb garden turned tasteless as dry rice in Jacinta's mouth. Swallowing, she said, 'That's short notice.'

'Very,' Fran said dryly. 'Still, it's not his fault. Something went wrong with his arrangements, I imagine, because although he does most of his personal entertainment here, Paul's not one for bringing business home.'

'Will you be able to manage? I'm a reasonable plain cook—'

Fran gave her a swift smile. 'Oh, we always use a caterer.'

Naturally. Jacinta laughed and resumed eating, although more slowly. 'So this is the film party,' she said, trying to sound as though she wasn't fishing.

'Yes. Paul had something to do with organising the finances for the joint venture.' She sighed dramatically, rolling her eyes. 'Harry Moore's coming. Fancy having him here! Do you like his acting?'

'He's very good,' said Jacinta, who'd seen him in one film.

'Well, you'll be able to find out if the real man lives up to the man on the screen.'

Jacinta looked up. 'I won't be here,' she said, adding as Fran's eyebrows rose, 'unless I can help with the waiting. I used to be quite good at that.'

The housekeeper shrugged, then said comfortably, 'Oh, well, we'll see. But no, we won't need any extra waitresses.'

Which sent Jacinta into the conservatory to check out the vacancy ads in the day's paper. Most were of the 'Flatmate Wanted' variety, and there weren't many of those, either. After her experience with Mark, who'd persuaded her to join him in a mixed flat—only mixed, she discovered, after she'd arrived to join Mark and another man—she wanted all-female flatmates. And doing it that way she wouldn't have to pay out a month's rent for a deposit.

After taking down the numbers of a couple of the most likely looking, she went out onto the terrace and sat for a long time watching the slow, smooth glide of the fish in the pond.

She should go and ring those numbers.

She wasn't going to.

For once in her life, she thought, dipping her hand into the cool water so that the fish could nibble her fingers, she wasn't going to listen to common sense.

The pond was big enough to take one splendid waterlily, a tropical hybrid that held huge, spiky violet flowers above the still surface. There was nothing sensible about that flower, she thought now, looking at it. It bloomed with defiant, sensuous immediacy.

For years she had put her life on hold. She'd willingly made that sacrifice for her mother, and she didn't regret it at all, but coming to Waitapu had shown her that she'd spent that time deliberately damping down her emotions because it hurt too much to give them free rein. She'd channelled all her energy, all her vitality, into helping her mother.

And because there was nothing she could do about it, she'd ignored that sense of life running past her with little to show for it but inevitable death.

Even finishing her degree had been fulfilling her mother's plan.

Now she wanted to live, to feel with all that was in her, to experience the sharp tang of life, to fall in love...

As she watched the goldfish cruise calmly, serenely, bloodlessly back and forth she accepted that she would be hurt. But before that she would learn to live again.

Oh, she wouldn't embarrass Paul with her emotions; she had too much pride to make herself ridiculous. But she'd enjoy them for what they were, and when the time came to go she'd do it with dignity.

She was lying on the lounger outside her room when the sound of an engine warned her that Paul was home. Delight and a desperate eagerness warred with discretion; in the end she stayed on the lounger, pretending to read the sheets she'd printed that day.

The small sounds of the homestead became suddenly heavy with significance. Listening to the tui singing from its perch on the grevillea and a door that slammed somewhere in the house, Jacinta had to consciously discipline her breathing. Nothing, however, could calm the racing chatter of her heartbeat, or dampen the slow curl of excitement at the base of her spine.

Yet strained though her ears were, she didn't hear him walk along the verandah, so that when he said, 'Good afternoon,' her fingers loosened and a couple of sheets of paper dropped onto the floor.

'I'm sorry,' he said, and stooped to pick them up, handing them to her without looking at them, for which she was extremely grateful.

'I didn't hear you,' she said inanely.

'So I see. Perhaps I should whistle. Although you might mistake me for Dean then.'

Grabbing for her composure, she managed to produce a laugh. 'Yes, I might. I suppose it's all the whistling he does at his dogs.'

'Possibly,' he said, blue eyes limpidly unreadable. 'Do you mind if I join you?'

'No, not at all.' And because she felt defenceless sprawled along the lounger, her faded cotton shorts revealing far too much skin, she swung her legs down and straightened up as he sat in a big rattan chair.

'Have you had a good day?' he asked.

'Fine. And you?'

Just ordinary pleasantries, the small coinage of conversation, yet nothing sounded ordinary or small when Paul spoke.

'Busy,' he said. 'Did Fran tell you about the party this weekend?'

'Yes. I offered to help her, but she didn't think you'd need a waitress or a good plain cook.'

Something glittered beneath his lashes, disappearing so swiftly she couldn't discern it. 'No,' he said blandly. 'The caterer will organise that side of things. I expect you to be a guest.'

No doubt it was kindly meant, although she wondered at the inflexible note in the words. 'Paul,' she said, feeling her way, 'it's very generous and hospitable of you to include me, but I really don't think I'd fit in.'

'If it's clothes—'

'It's not just that,' she said quietly.

'So tell me what it is.'

It was a command, not a suggestion. She said, 'I'd feel that I'd imposed on your hospitality. Would you have asked me if I'd been staying at the bach?'

His smile was hard and sardonic. 'Yes.'

She cast around for another objection. 'Is Dean coming?'

Two lines grooved vertically between his brows, strengthening his subtle air of intimidation. 'Dean will be away this weekend with Brenda. Have you met her yet?'

'No. She's busy with exams, apparently.' It was a sidetrack; she went on, 'I'd rather not, Paul.'

'I'd like you to.'

If he'd been at all arrogant about his request—if he'd said it as though she owed him for his hospitality—she'd have refused him. After all, she could ask Dean for the loan of his cottage while he was away.

But she couldn't resist. Or the smile that accompanied it, oddly sympathetic.

So, perhaps helped by remembering the sari she and her mother had chosen in Fiji—that glittering, beautiful thing of glorious orange-gold that somehow transformed her skin into ivory and her hair into amber, and set the dancing lights gleaming in her eyes—she said, 'All right.'

His smile was ironic, as though he was laughing at both her and himself. 'You'll have fun,' he promised.

Jacinta hadn't been to a party for years. She'd never been to a party with Hollywood film stars; it would be something to tell her children, if she ever had any. 'I'm sure I will,' she agreed.

CHAPTER SIX

PAUL left for Auckland the next morning and didn't return for the rest of the week.

A good thing, Jacinta told herself stubbornly, settling into a calm rhythm of writing and swimming and walking, talking to Dean and Fran—even helping the housekeeper in the garden, although a gardener worked there three days a week.

She might be poised on the brink of falling in love, but she didn't need to go looking for trouble—and that was what she'd do if Paul was there all the time. His absence gave her a breathing space, time to compose herself.

Time to miss him.

The manuscript dawdled along—partly because she often found herself dreaming as she stared at the computer screen, dreams that had nothing to do with the characters she was striving to bring to life. But also because she'd reached an impasse; although she knew what the novel's protagonists had to do, she found to her irritation and indignation that they weren't satisfied with the plot she and her mother had mapped out for them. They sulked and fumed and had to be forced along their preordained paths, and in the process they turned wooden and obstructive and banal.

Jacinta set her chin and struggled on.

Three days before the party she took out the sari from the wardrobe. The short-sleeved blouse in orange silk fitted her well, settling snugly at her waist. She remembered how to get into the soft folds of the skirt, and then draped herself in the silk veil in citrus colours of mandarin and gold and bright, clear orange.

It wasn't her usual style. The Hindu woman in the hot little shop had been an excellent saleswoman, aided as she'd been by Cynthia Lyttelton's cries of delight and pleasure when Jacinta had modelled the sari. Jacinta had only allowed herself to be persuaded because the vivid colours did such amazing things to her skin and eyes and hair.

As she turned away to take it off she remembered with a brittle smile that she'd bought it the day after Paul had danced with her.

Her sandals, of tan leather, had the right oriental air, although to really set the costume off she needed jewellery. She'd have to do without, because apart from a pair of gold hoop earrings she had none. Even her mother's wedding ring had been buried with her, a pathetic reminder of the lengths she'd gone to in order to keep the censorious at bay in the small town where Jacinta had grown up.

Replacing the sari in the wardrobe, she hoped fervently that the guests at Paul's party didn't turn up in shorts and bathing suits!

On Friday the caterers arrived and took over the kitchen. Although Fran complained about the mess, she revelled in the confusion, even bringing Jacinta's lunch to her on a tray so that she wouldn't get in their way.

The caterers drove back to Auckland that night, and Jacinta waited for Paul's car, but at seven the phone rang. Jacinta knew who it was even before she picked up the receiver.

'Has Fran got you on answering duty?' Paul asked.

'No, I was going past when I realised the answering machine hadn't been switched on.'

He said, 'I see. I'm in Sydney at the moment, but I'll be home tomorrow morning.'

'I'll tell Fran,' she said, listening to the slow thud of her heart.

'All well?'

'Yes, everything's fine.'

'Are the caterers under control?'

Jacinta laughed. 'Under Fran's control, certainly. She's enjoying herself very much.'

'She likes bossing people around,' he said dryly. 'And are you enjoying yourself very much?'

'Yes, of course.'

A voice from his background called out: a female voice. 'I have to go now,' he said. 'See you tomorrow.'

Jacinta replaced the receiver, telling herself that the gripping pang in her heart was not jealousy. It couldn't be because she had no reason to be jealous. The woman in the background could easily be a secretary. Sydney was in Australia's eastern time zone, two hours behind New Zealand, so it would be just after five there.

Or she could be a friend's wife. Or a relative—once he'd mentioned cousins in Australia.

Except that the tone of her voice had been seductive rather than businesslike or friendly.

That night the long, wakeful hours dragged by, illuminated by the vivid imaginings of Jacinta's brain as she spun scenarios of Paul with a beautiful woman...

She should have stuck to her original plan and left Waitapu.

When she couldn't bear it any longer she got up and tried to write, but nothing would come, and she wondered whether she was just fooling herself and wasting time with the manuscript.

She began to read it, and it was boring—hackneyed characters in hackneyed situations, clumsily constructed sentences and dull conversation, action sequences that read with all the power and fire of treacle. In disgust she put the sheets back on the desk and went to bed again, and this time she slept.

Only for a short time, however. She woke early, swam until she was exhausted and then, unable even to look at the computer, wandered around the garden to the hammock suspended from the wide branches of a jacaranda tree. It was hung for Paul's long legs, and at the thought of him sleeping in it something clutched her stomach.

After several attempts she managed to climb into it and lay sprawled in its shady embrace, staring up into the feathery dome of the tree.

The sound of her name woke her.

'Oh,' she said feebly, opening her eyes to meet Paul's cobalt gaze.

He'd been frowning, but it faded, so all she saw were the two kinks in his brows as they straightened. Her spine melted.

'You hid yourself well,' he said evenly. He was standing beside the trunk of the tree, and as she lifted herself on her elbow he leaned back against the bark, the small movement emphasising the slight shifting and coiling of his heavily-muscled thighs beneath fine cotton trousers.

Jacinta swallowed. 'What time is it?'

'Just on midday.'

'Good lord!' She sat up, clutching the side of the hammock as it swayed. He reached out a hand and steadied it, regarding her with an enigmatic half-smile. 'I didn't sleep terribly well last night,' she explained.

'Why not?'

'No reason.' She swung her legs over the side and got out, not without some difficulty because the wretched hammock would have thrown her if Paul hadn't held it still. 'Did you have a good trip?' she asked, slightly red-faced when at last she was standing up.

'Excellent, thank you. Come and have some lunch with me. We've been banished to the verandah.'

Just before they reached the table Paul said, 'I saw something in Sydney that might be useful for you,' and detoured into his room.

Keeping her eyes averted, Jacinta waited until he emerged through the French windows with a parcel. It was a book on the techniques of writing novels.

'Oh,' she said, scanning the index eagerly, 'thank you so much! I've read a couple of how-to books from the university library, but this one looks great. I need it too. I'm stuck.'

'I believe it happens all the time,' Paul said, smiling as she flicked through the pages.

Embarrassed, she put the book down on the table and said, 'Thank you, Paul. I'll read it with great interest.'

'I hope it gets you through your block,' he said easily. 'Sit down. We'd better eat before Fran comes to sweep everything away.'

'She's really in her element. I poked my nose in and offered to help, but they all shooed me out and told me to get lost—in the nicest possible manner, of course.'

He laughed. 'They're used to working together,' he said.

Lunch was a salad and quiche, with crusty brown bread and olives and sun-dried tomatoes. Paul drank a beer with it; Jacinta had mineral water, and tea afterwards.

They talked of nothing much. Although Paul was a little remote, happiness hummed through Jacinta, reverberating in every cell, oversetting the common-sense strictures of her mind in a flood of delight. The sea sparkled and scintillated beneath a sky of blazing blue, the small sparrows that waited on the verandah railings for crumbs glowed chestnut and buff in the golden light, and the panicles of lilac-tinted flowers in the cabbage tree—the biggest lily in the world— scented the air with a tropical fervour.

Jacinta asked, 'What time does this party start?'

'We're having a barbecue on the beach at eight. Two people are coming up around five. Laurence Perry is one of the character actors, and Meriam Anderson is the producer's assistant. They'll be staying overnight.'

She nodded. 'If it's a barbecue I suppose they'll be wearing shorts.' It wasn't hard to keep the disappointment from her voice, but he gave her a swift, keen glance.

'I wouldn't like to guess what they'll be wearing,' he said. 'Meriam Anderson dresses in a very understated manner, but I doubt if she'll be in shorts. She's English, and for her shorts are too informal to wear to any party, even a barbecue.'

He knows her very well, Jacinta thought, horrified by the shard of jealousy that pierced her body, so acute that it hurt even when she breathed.

He went on, 'However, Harry Moore's girlfriend, Liane, thinks that dressing formally means putting on another toe ring. I imagine you could wear a nightgown and they'd think nothing of it—beyond the fact that you were making a statement. They understand statements.'

Was her sari a statement? She had no idea, but she certainly wasn't going to wear any of her shorts, all of which showed their age badly.

'I'm wearing casual trousers and a shirt,' he said. 'No tie. Don't worry about them. They're just people.'

She finished the last of her tea and set the cup and saucer down. 'I know, I know, but I don't want to look like an oddity.'

'You won't.' He paused, then said, 'How you treat them will determine how they treat you. Beneath the hype and the beautiful faces and the money they're ordinary people.'

'Surely hype and money and beauty—not to mention power and talent—cut people out from the common herd? Harry Moore, for example, can't even go to a restaurant without being mobbed by fans. A few years of that—and the enormous amount of money he earns—is going to change him, even if he was just a simple farm boy to start with.'

Paul leaned back in his chair and surveyed her with half closed eyes, impenetrable beneath his surface amusement. 'He's intelligent and astute and he knows where he's going, but yes, I was being a bit flippant. Think of them, then, as another species—interesting and worth studying but ultimately not important.'

Because you're never going to meet them again, she thought, hurt—and yet of course he was right.

He added thoughtfully, 'Actually, with hair that colour you've probably had more than your fair share of attention. Do you think it's changed your character?'

'No,' she said. 'I'm a very ordinary person.'

His answering smile lightened her heart.

That night Jacinta dressed with great care. The material of the sari lent its light to her hair, changing unashamed ginger into a molten river of fire. She left her curls to riot and donned the gold earrings, then used a lipgloss she'd had for some years, a peachy-gold colour that made her lips seem fuller and more—interesting, she hoped.

In the grip of a helpless hope, she went out.

The two film people were still in their rooms, so she walked down the hall and into the morning room and across into the conservatory. She was looking down onto the beach, where a sheep was roasting on the spit in the charge of one of the caterer's staff, when some imperceptible alteration in the atmosphere brought her head around.

Paul stood in the open doors between the conservatory and the morning room. He was looking at her, dark brows drawn together, his face set into a rigid cast.

Tension leapt between them, stark, fierce.

I look awful, Jacinta thought, her barely born confidence ebbing into desolation.

And then, as though he'd cut it off, the moment was gone. 'Those colours suit you magnificently,' he said, the words spoken in a tone he might have used to praise a dog.

Rebuffed, she replied stiffly, 'Thank you.' Her smile was set and artificial as she fought to control the pain that slashed through her.

A light, feminine voice, English-accented, said, 'Paul, this is a wonderful place!'

He turned and smiled at the woman who'd followed him

into the room. Jacinta watched Meriam Anderson's response, as involuntary as hers, to the warmth of his smile. In her mid-thirties, and dressed, Jacinta noted, in a soft, navy blue silk dress that managed to look both casual and chic, the woman came across and slid her arm into Paul's, and nodded at Jacinta.

When they'd been introduced earlier that evening Jacinta had been in a blouse and the rusty skirt, and Meriam had been very gracious. But now, although her voice stayed warm and pleasant, her eyes narrowed slightly.

'My dear,' she said, 'what a splendid outfit. You look as though you're going to burst into flames any minute.'

The evening went downhill from there.

At least, Jacinta thought as people began to arrive and be conducted down to the beach, she no longer cared what they thought about her. There was only one man whose opinion meant anything to her, and he'd taken one look at her and switched off. No doubt he thought she was blatant and garish.

However, she was not going to let his rejection—if that was what it was—affect her.

Tilting her chin, she tried to ignore the gnawing ache in her heart. Eventually about sixty guests stood in the last rays of the sun, dressed with the sort of bravura chicness that made them stand out. Her outfit didn't look out of place at all. Not when Liane, Harry Moore's girlfriend, wore a black slip with nothing on underneath, and a fanfare of peacock's feathers in her black hair. Only one toe ring, Jacinta noticed, but that appeared to have a diamond in it.

It was definitely a collection of beautiful people. Amazingly good-looking in a sombre, brooding way, Harry Moore was Jacinta's height, with a mouth that was saved from sulkiness by a humorous quirk. He flirted with Jacinta, but then he flirted with all the other women there except Liane. Her he looked at with a desperate yearning he tried to hide.

I know what it's like, Jacinta thought, and applied herself to the conversation, hoping to help him through whatever private hell he was enduring.

'With that colouring you have to be Irish,' he declared, and when she'd cheerfully disclaimed any Celtic blood, he said, 'I'll bet there's some in your background. You look like a high summer heatwave, sultry and exuberant and lush.'

His moody dark eyes surveyed her with a sensual appreciation that made his career as a screen heart-throb inevitable.

Jacinta smiled as she thanked him, thinking ironically that if you were worried about social graces, wearing a broken heart made evenings like this ridiculously easy because it was impossible to care what people thought of you.

Except for one person, and his opinion had been only too plain. Her eyes searched the crowd, now noisily talking and laughing, and found Paul. He was standing a little apart, talking to two men who, although they wore similar cotton trousers and short-sleeved shirts to every other man there, had 'suits' written all over them.

Against Paul's effortless authority Harry looked somehow unformed, a man in the making. And yet he was her age, almost thirty, not all that much younger than Paul, who had probably been born with that uncompromising aura of dominance. It was something to do with inner strength, a confidence so firmly rooted in character that it was unbreakable.

And a sexual promise that drew her and every other woman there with its subtle, powerful lure. What had happened to turn him off like that? He'd taken one look at her and despised her; she'd seen the swift flash of cold contempt in his eyes before the shutters came down and blocked her out.

She spent the next hour listening to Harry Moore. He drank more than she liked, and although his eyes followed his girlfriend as she flitted from group to group he stayed close to Jacinta, making her laugh with tales of happenings—most funny, but some appalling—on the sets of various films he'd made.

Eventually his girlfriend came back, and Jacinta took the opportunity to move across to Laurence Perry, the pleasantly ugly middle-aged actor who was also staying the night. He gave her a ravaged, intense smile and observed, 'I envy you living in this magnificent place.'

Jacinta's answering smile would probably be engraved on her face for days. 'I'm just visiting, unfortunately. Have you enjoyed your stay in New Zealand?'

His glance moved to the slim woman at Paul's side. 'Very much,' he said. 'You know, when we met this afternoon I thought you reminded me of someone and I couldn't work out who it was until I saw you wrapped in that gauzy golden robe.'

Jacinta fixed an interested look to her face. 'Do I have a double?'

'Not exactly a double, but a hundred or so years ago there was someone who looked very like you,' Laurence said, shrewd eyes studying her. 'My grandmother had a print of a picture painted by a Victorian, one of the Pre-Raphaelites. It's called *Flaming June* and shows a bare-armed girl sleeping; she had your high-bridged nose and soft mouth, and she was your colouring too. As well, she was draped in a cloth the exact orange-gold in your veil.'

Jacinta lifted her brows. 'How intriguing,' she said, her voice steady. Paul and Meriam were making their way towards them, and she'd noted the way the other woman's hand was clinging to his arm. Anguish twisted inside her; she said, 'I must see if I can track down a copy. I wonder if she was teased as much as I was because of her ginger hair.'

'Did they call you Carrots?'

She surprised herself by producing a wry little laugh. 'Oh,

yes. All sorts of variations on the theme of carrots and gin-gerbread.'

'But now you have the last word,' he said, and smiled at her surprise. 'Most of them would probably give their eye-teeth to have green eyes and luminous ivory skin and hair like yours,' he said, embarrassing her.

'I doubt it,' she said. 'Buying sunscreen to stop me burn-ing makes me prohibitively expensive to keep.' And she flushed as she realised how provocative her comment might sound.

Just as Paul and Meriam came up he grinned and said, 'But worth it, surely?'

'Worth what?' Meriam said, looking alertly from one to the other.

'Worth spending an inordinate amount of money on sun-block to protect that glorious skin,' Laurence said promptly.

Jacinta hadn't looked at Paul; his tone came as an un-pleasant surprise. 'Indeed it is,' he drawled, each word like a tiny whip scoring deep into her composure.

Although Meriam Anderson wasn't beautiful, she wore her hair and make-up and clothes with a panache that made up for her lack of looks. 'Thank heavens we live in a time when we have sunblocks,' she said then. 'Paul, you throw a wonderful party. What would you say if I asked to stay an extra couple of days?'

'I'd be delighted. Is there any chance of that?'

'Sadly, no,' she sighed. 'But I'll take a raincheck on the invitation, Paul.'

He smiled at her. Jacinta drew in an uneven breath.

Without trying, she thought, suddenly defenceless against him, he dominated the whole scene. All right, he was clever and handsome, but these people were sophisticated and worldly, and used to the authority and power that money gave, and yet none of them could hold a candle to him.

Even Harry Moore's girlfriend was watching him with an intent, speculative look.

Well, Jacinta was not going to let her own heated yearning and acute awareness of Paul spoil this occasion. It was probably the only time in her life she'd be at a gathering like this, and she was determined to at least appreciate it.

Paul stayed with Meriam. Neither was overt or obvious, unlike Liane, who was now wound around Harry; however, it was perfectly clear that they found each other very interesting.

I am not in love with him, Jacinta told herself as she circulated. *I am not*. Not now, not ever.

But as the evening wore on she found it more and more difficult to keep up the pretence. If it hadn't seemed like an obscure form of surrender she'd have sneaked quietly away after they'd eaten dinner—superb and succulent meat from the spit, fish wrapped in taro leaves and baked in coals, salads that were miracles of taste and freshness, and fruit, cleverly laid out on a table covered with the fronds of New Zealand's native palm and the vivid, incandescent flowers of hibiscuses.

She stuck it out, although later, when she came to sort out her recollections, she found she remembered very little. However, she spoke to everyone there, surprised at how polite and pleasant and interested in her they all seemed.

You didn't know it but you're a snob, she thought when at last she decided that she'd had enough, late enough in the evening for pride to be properly salvaged. You thought they'd all be crass and snobbish and aggressive, like the worst and most newsworthy of Hollywood stars.

Paul and Meriam were talking to a couple of the money men. She'd have liked to leave without anyone noticing, but even as the thought whisked through her mind Paul looked up, his eyes resting on her face with unsettling dispassion. He said something to the others and left them, walking towards her with lithe grace.

An hour or so previously a little wind had sprung up from the sea, and everyone had moved onto the lawn, where the trees sheltered them. In spite of the sea breeze it was still very warm, and the guests had reached that pleasant stage where they were enjoying themselves without tension.

Except for her. And the cause of her tension was walking towards her, his hair gleaming silver in the lights.

'I've had a wonderful party, but if you don't mind I'll slip away now,' she said when he got closer.

'Before anyone else?'

The implied criticism made her stiffen. 'No one's going to miss me,' she said.

'Oh, I think they might. You've been a definite hit. Liane has decided you're a threat to her power over Harry.'

She drew in a swift breath, trying to ignore the soft, cynical drawl. 'She's very insecure,' she said. 'It's been great—fascinating—'

'But you've had enough.'

Jacinta looked up, caught the glitter of his eyes, the hard line of his mouth, a line that gentled into a smile, coaxing, half-rueful, completely compelling. 'No, of course not,' she said, surrendering.

He looked past her. 'Good,' he said, adding, 'It won't be long now anyway. Here comes the coffee.'

He was right. Everyone drank coffee, and soon, amid a flurry of trans-Pacific farewells and best wishes, the convoy of cars left the homestead for Auckland.

'A great evening,' Laurence Perry declared as the last one left. 'Thank you, Paul, for more excellent Kiwi hospitality. I'm turning in.'

'I don't feel like going to bed yet,' Meriam said with a half-laugh. 'I'm wired. It's such a beautiful night, I'd like to go for a walk.'

'Why not?' Paul's deep, beautiful voice was lazily amused.

Jacinta turned away. 'Goodnight,' she said. 'I'll see you in the morning.'

Thank heavens she could retire to her bedroom and close the doors and pull the curtains so that no one could see her.

And thank heavens that even the most shattering emotions eventually gave way to sleep.

A sleep that was disturbed much later by a woman's laughter, and the sound of light footsteps on the verandah. Meriam, she thought; Paul moved noiselessly. But then she heard Paul's voice, and immediately stuffed her head under her pillow.

When she finally emerged from the sanctuary of her pillow all was silent again except for the soft whispering of a wind playing along the wooden fretwork lace above the verandah. For some reason she got up to pull the curtains more tightly, and saw a light glimmering across the floor of the verandah. It came from Paul's room.

It needn't mean anything, she thought desperately, closing her eyes against it. Perhaps he couldn't sleep either. He didn't strike her as promiscuous—but then he could have been conducting an affair with Meriam for months, all the time the film company had been in New Zealand.

Neither he nor the producer's assistant were the sort of person who proclaimed their emotions, but they'd definitely been 'together' the preceding night. Whether that togetherness had extended to the bedroom she had no way of knowing.

And where did that leave the actress Gerard had pointed out to her in Ponsonby?

It's none of your business, she told herself drearily, turning away to crawl back into bed.

She woke late, so late that the house was silent around her, and when she came out the guests were gone, and Paul with them. The caterers had cleaned up and gone the night before, so that all that was left of the party was the darker green of the lawn where it had been crushed by feet.

For the first time Jacinta wondered just how much money Paul had. Such quiet, efficient service was expensive, but more than that, it was difficult to find. Even a housekeeper was hard to get.

Paul could buy such service, apparently without worrying about the cost.

Of course, she thought desolately, he'd been born to this. She had grown up with poverty. And yet in many ways they had a lot in common. New Zealand didn't have much of a class system—

'Oh, for heaven's *sake*!' she said aloud, furious with herself for spinning dreams out of gossamer.

They had nothing in common, and he couldn't have made that plainer the night before.

After she'd eaten toast and fruit for breakfast, she went for a long walk and then settled down in the lounger outside her room to read some of the book he'd bought her. Of course she knew what she was doing; she was waiting.

But after a while the book began to make sense to her. She read and reread a couple of pages and put it down, staring sightlessly out into the sunlight. Ideas began to collect in her mind, too bright to resist. She got to her feet and set off for the computer.

Hours later she came back to herself, thinking exultantly, Yes!

It was good; she knew it was good.

She saved everything, backed it up and stretched, yawning. Suddenly ravenous, she looked at her watch. It was half past two, so for once Fran had forgotten about her.

In the kitchen Jacinta made herself a sandwich—cheese and tomato and cress, with a touch of Fran's pesto. Taking it out across the lawn, she sat down in the gazebo and applied herself to eating it, forcing the food over the lump in her chest.

When she'd finished she drank a glass of the orange juice that Fran squeezed every morning, concentrating ferociously on the thick, delicious freshness, the combination of sweet and tangy flavours, the way it eased across her tongue and down her throat, because that was the only way she could deal with this—this despair that had been lying in wait for her ever since she'd woken.

She wanted to wail and shriek and beat her breast and stamp her feet at the total unfairness of the world, at her own stupidity in falling in love with a man who was not for her.

But, even as she imagined herself losing control so appallingly, a reluctant, unwilling smile tugged at her mouth.

'I seem to remember reading something about how pleasant it is to come upon a woman smiling to herself.' Paul's voice was studied and speculative as he walked around the corner of the gazebo, past the scented, smothering flowers of the rose that draped itself artistically across the white-painted timber.

Jacinta's heart leapt. 'It sounds Victorian,' she said, hoping her voice was as steady as his.

'Sentimental?' The sun gleamed on his hair, caught the vivid depths of his eyes and picked out the arrogant, hard-planed contours of his face.

She smiled again. It was difficult, but she thought she carried it off rather well. 'The Victorians often were sentimental.'

'Agreed.' He scrutinised her with an oddly measuring look, as though he was superimposing another's features on hers, and said, 'Yes, I see what Laurence meant last night. You have the kind of face the Pre-Raphaelites loved to paint.'

It didn't exactly sound like a compliment, and yet his glance lingered a second too long on her mouth. Jacinta's pulse picked up speed.

'I'm flattered,' she returned politely. There followed an unnerving moment of silence, one she broke by asking, 'Have you just come back?'

'About five minutes ago. I took them down to the airport and sent them on their way. What have you been doing?'

'Writing,' she said succinctly, and added, 'And I must thank you again for the book you bought. I read a couple of chapters, and while I was going through a list of dos and don'ts I realised where I was going wrong.'

'Good,' he said, and leaned over to pick a rose from the edge of the gazebo. 'It's the same colour as your hair,' he said, tucking it in behind her ear. Her ear and scalp tingled, and she thought she could feel his touch right to the roots of her hair.

Hair couldn't feel, she reminded herself feverishly, it was dead—but the effects of that moment of closeness rippled down her spine in a shiver of delight.

Eyes half closed, he stepped back and surveyed her. 'Yes, exactly the same colour. So the manuscript is coming along well?'

'I think it is,' she said cautiously, and astonished herself by confiding, 'I've been trying to follow the plot my mother and I worked out, but it was really difficult; when I reread what I'd written it dragged horribly. The book said that if the characters wouldn't do what the writer wanted them to, the writer should give them a chance and see what happened.'

He nodded, blue eyes keen and perceptive. 'And what has happened?'

'Well,' she said ruefully, 'it's heading in a completely different direction from the one Mum and I mapped out.'

'And that worries you?'

She looked down at her hands. 'Yes,' she said quietly, 'I suppose that's why I've resisted it. I feel as though I've cut loose from my mother. Abandoned her, in fact. The book was to be a memorial to her, but if I do follow the characters it won't be the book she loved and helped create.'

'I see,' he said thoughtfully. 'But, you know, you'll never produce anything worthwhile if you don't take it for your own. We can't live other people's lives for them, or produce other people's work.'

Once more surprised at how perceptive he was, she nodded. Although he probably owed his career to his understanding of people's motives and actions.

'I didn't know I had this itch to write,' she said. An itch so powerful that even when her emotional life was in turmoil she was almost able to ignore it while she wrote.

And ease some of the pain by treating it as material for her work.

'How do you go about it?' he asked.

'At first I tried to write each sentence perfectly, but that was impossible, so now I'm getting everything down as quickly as I can, and then I'll go back and tidy it up and cut out the padding and put in the bits I need to expand on.'

'And then?'

She stared at him. 'What do you mean?'

His gaze was a cool blue challenge. 'Where do you plan to send it?'

'I hadn't—'

'Don't tell me you're going to spend three months writing it and then put it in the bottom of your wardrobe for the rest of your life!'

Uncertainly, she said, 'I don't know how good it is.'

'You're not likely to ever find out until you send it off,' he said with matter-of-fact directness. 'I assume that's what your mother wanted you to do?'

Jacinta hesitated. 'I suppose so. We never discussed it.'

'Most writing is done for publication.'

'Do you realise what you've done?' she demanded, half-angry and half-exhilarated at this new idea. 'I'd never really thought of anyone else reading it. Now every time I sit down to write I'll see the public sitting on my shoulder.'

'Inhibiting you?'

'Well—no,' she said. 'At least, I hope not.'

He looked at her for several seconds, his mouth straight and almost grim, before saying calmly, 'I'd certainly give it a go. You're enjoying doing it, aren't you?'

'Mostly,' she admitted. 'When I'm not so frustrated I could jump up and down with rage.'

'I believe that's the way it happens,' he said. 'Let's go for a walk. You probably need it and I certainly do. I'm leaving for Europe tomorrow, and I have a very busy week ahead.'

Loneliness clawed her. Trying to sound normal, she said, 'I'd love to see Europe. Especially France and Italy.'

'You'll get there one day.' He held out his hand and automatically she accepted it; it was strong and warm, not the hand of a man who spent all day indoors. He swam, she knew, but from the calluses on his hands he also did some heavy work.

She stepped away and he relinquished his grip, but not before she caught a glimpse of some fugitive emotion beneath the dark lashes, a coldly calculating gleam that chilled her.

'Tell me,' he said as they started along the beach, 'how you got to know Gerard well enough to accept his offer of help.'

Choosing her words carefully, she said, 'He'd been my tutor since the beginning of the year, so we knew each other. He found me sound asleep in the library one night.'

'Sleeping in the library isn't uncommon,' Paul said, 'especially just before exams.'

'No.'

'So Gerard invited you to live with him.' His voice was amused, almost bland, yet an uneasy little shiver tightened her skin.

'Hardly,' she said dryly. 'He bought me a cup of coffee.'

'And then he asked you to live with him?'

A seagull ran to within a few feet of them, surveying them with greedy, bright eyes. Keeping her eyes on it, Jacinta said, 'Of course he didn't. He offered to drive me home.'

Another silence, heavy with unspoken thoughts, a silence

that compelled her to add, 'I refused, so he insisted on getting me a taxi.'

That was when she'd choked back tears, too exhausted to exert her usual control over her emotions and well aware that Mark was probably waiting for her, ready for another scene like that of the previous evening, when he'd raged at her almost all night. She'd found a temporary place to stay with a friend, but she wasn't able to move until the following week; she had been dreading the intervening days.

'I believe you were having trouble with a relationship,' Paul observed.

'I—how do you know?'

'Gerard,' he said laconically.

'I didn't tell him anything about—about that.'

He paused, then said judicially, 'Presumably he guessed.'

Jacinta bit her lip. 'Yes.'

'And Gerard suggested you move into his spare bedroom.'

Irritation spurred her into a snappy answer. 'Only because his cleaning service had let him down in a big way again. He told me that if I kept house and cooked his meals I could have the spare bedroom for free, but I...' The words trailed away.

One of Paul's greatest assets in his career had to be that warm, almost sympathetic voice; it was too easy to be lulled into confiding things you regretted later.

He said, 'So then he found a flat for you.'

'That was a piece of luck! And as it's not too far from the apartment he was living in I could take up his offer of a job.'

He sent her a heavy-lidded glance. 'Very fortunate,' he said non-committally. 'Gerard seems to be satisfied with the bargain.'

'I hope so. He's been very kind.'

'Not by his reckoning,' he said, his aloof tone unsettling

her. 'Tell me, is this arrangement going to continue at his new house?'

'Yes, but there's a small flat at the back. I'm going to be like Fran and live on the job.' And if there was a hint of defiance in her tone she hoped he noticed it. She objected to being cross-examined ·as though she was a hostile witness.

'And will you enjoy that?'

'It'll be wonderful to have a place to call my own, even if it isn't.'

'Of course, you're helping Gerard too,' he said thoughtfully.

'Well, of course.' Gerard had been a rock at a very stressful time, and she'd always be grateful to him.

CHAPTER SEVEN

PAUL said abruptly, 'It sounds the ideal arrangement.' And waited a second too long before adding, 'Except for one where you wouldn't need to worry about money at all.'

Jacinta stopped herself from shrugging. 'That would be perfect, but it's difficult to arrange nowadays.'

He didn't frown but she felt as though he did. Ridiculous, she thought despairingly.

When he spoke his voice was cool. 'If you don't know what you're going to do with this degree, why did you do it?'

'It seemed the logical thing to do when I left school. I loved history—it was my best subject—and I didn't have the foggiest idea of any sort of career. My mother wanted me to go to university.' She flushed but went on steadily, 'She'd started a degree but wasn't able to finish it, and she blamed herself because she couldn't manage without me after my first two years. It was her ambition to have me capped and gowned, even if it had to be after her death. And—in a way going back to university was convenient; I'd spent years at home and I was—afraid, I suppose—of trying to find a job.'

And that was something she hadn't admitted, even to herself, before.

'Forgive me if this is intrusive, but do you not have a father to call on?'

She said steadily, 'He was killed in a boating accident before I was born, but I have no idea who he was. My mother would never tell me.' It was probably his silence, and the understanding she thought she sensed in him, that emboldened her to continue, 'She just said that he wasn't free.' She'd also said she'd fallen wholly and embarrassingly in love. 'I've always assumed he was married.'

'It certainly sounds like it,' he murmured. 'It must have been tough growing up without a father.'

'It was tougher on her. She brought me up, and worked damned hard to do it.' Startled by the unexpected note of fierceness in her voice, she added lamely, 'She had a difficult life, and it doesn't seem fair that she should die so wretchedly. And don't tell me that life isn't fair.'

'I don't deal in platitudes,' he said, 'especially with someone like you, who's had to face that particular injustice for too many years.'

'I'd like to have been able to repay her for some of her sacrifices. Almost the only pleasure she got out of those last years was thinking of the things I'd be able to do when she died, and quite frankly it stinks!'

She knew she sounded childish, but she couldn't control the sudden, furious outburst. As angry tears started to her eyes she groped in her pocket for a handkerchief.

'It does,' he said gently, holding out a beautifully pressed white one.

Jacinta took it and blew her nose defiantly. 'The worst thing,' she muttered, unable to stop herself from divulging this, 'was that when she died I was relieved.'

'It's all right,' he said, and to her astonishment pulled her into his arms, effortlessly subduing her first resistance until in the end she gave in and leaned against him, desperate to absorb a measure of his calm, quiet strength.

Sheltered in the powerful cage of his embrace, she relaxed, her head coming to rest naturally on his shoulder. His faint, potent scent and the warmth of his skin, the solid bulwark of his body, combined to work an elemental magic. Although Jacinta knew this unspoken compassion was just as dangerous as the wildfire need that consumed her night and day, she couldn't wrest herself away from the hazardous lure of his unfaltering steadiness. Boneless, without volition, she was unable to follow the commands of that tiny part of her brain that could still think.

Eventually common sense returned, and she muttered, 'I'm sorry,' as she steeled herself to pull away.

A lean hand stroked the strands of hair back from her hot cheek and neck. 'Have you really cried for her?' he asked, his voice deep and soothing.

'I— I—'

He couldn't have asked anything more likely to break down the floodgates. How long he supported her while she wept into his cotton shirt she didn't know, but she'd never felt so safe.

Eventually it finished, and this time he let her go.

'I'm sorry,' she mumbled again, refusing to look at him as she tried to tidy away the signs of her grief.

'Why?' He took her arm and turned her around. 'What you need,' he said with cool assurance, 'is a cup of tea. And probably something for a headache.'

'You've done this before,' she said, trying to smile.

'Occasionally. But every Kiwi—even our coffee genera-tion—turns to tea in an emergency.'

He made it for her, drank a cup with her, and followed her lead when she asked him his opinion of the newly an-nounced team for the Commonwealth Games.

That was when she realised that her initial fierce, hopeless attraction, that first violent fervour, was now buttressed by the love growing deep inside her, a love that joined with her sexual awakening, reinforcing it.

Because Paul had to catch an early flight the next morning he left as the stars began to prick holes in the sky; he'd spend the night in his flat. Jacinta wished him luck and waved goodbye, and then trailed into the huge, empty house.

The next week was oddly busy, yet serene and peaceful. The aftermath of her bout of tears was a calm acceptance she'd been lacking before. Her mother was dead; she'd done whatever it was she'd been put on earth to do, and now had left it all behind her.

That recognition renewed a forgotten energy. Jacinta began to plan a future, a future that didn't include Paul. Although she missed him with every cell in her body, longing for him through the endless night hours until shadows darkened the fine skin beneath her eyes, the stark pragmatism she'd inherited from her mother told her that in spite of his kindness he wasn't in love with her.

He'd almost certainly made love to Meriam Anderson the night of the party; if he'd felt anything at all for Jacinta he wouldn't have done that.

No, he was not for her.

That being so, she'd have to organise her life.

What she wanted to do, she admitted, was stay at Waitapu and write. A pretty pipe-dream, but she could write anywhere.

If she gave up university and used the rest of her mother's inheritance, she could rent a small flat in a small town somewhere and buy what furniture she needed as well as a second-hand computer and printer. She couldn't expect Gerard to continue lending her his, and, although the arrangement she had with him would be ideal, he might not want to continue it when she told him she was giving up her MA.

Of course he might, and that would be great.

But if he didn't she'd have to get a job so that she didn't starve, and jobs were notoriously difficult to get in small towns. Especially for people with no commercial qualifications.

Perhaps she should use the money to go to a polytech and qualify in some field that would pay her a living wage. That would be sensible.

Unfortunately, all possible careers filled her with dismay. In spite of the frustrations and moments of utter despair and the unlikeliness of ever making it to publication, she loved sitting down in front of the computer and losing herself in her world.

She wandered out into the soft limpid air of early morning and looked around the garden and the sea, her eyes filling with tears that held something of delight, something of sorrow.

Leaving the man who owned all this beauty would tear her heart to shreds, yet she couldn't wish that things were different; however painful the loss, she could only be grateful that she'd met Paul.

That week, as summer dreamed its way towards Christmas, Jacinta wrote and dreamed with it. She was even cautiously pleased with what she'd written, although by now she was beginning to realise that this book might never be published. This one was her primer; it was teaching her how to weave together all the threads that eventually linked tightly into a novel.

She read and reread the book Paul had bought her, finding something new and useful every time. And each time she picked it up it was with secret delight because he'd been thoughtful enough to think of her. It was a pathetic little flame of pleasure to warm herself at, but she hugged it to her.

The week he'd planned to be away dragged into ten days. Jacinta tried not to think of him. She was reasonably successful while she was awake, but when she slept her unconscious took over, and she was plagued by dreams that ranged perilously close to nightmares, dreams where he turned away from her, dreams where Meriam Anderson threw mud at her sari, and tore the veil…

Dreams that were pitifully simple to understand.

'He's coming back on the weekend,' Fran said one evening. 'His office in Auckland rang—he's on his way back from Europe, but he's decided to stay a couple of days over in Los Angeles.'

Where Meriam Anderson lived.

Jealousy, Jacinta thought, trying hard to be objective, was a strange thing. She had no right to be jealous; Paul had given her no reason to hope. He'd been kind—but then, he was that sort of man. He was kind to Fran, to Dean, he'd been kind to her mother.

And she despised jealousy. Yet there it was, hot and sullen as embers, casting its lurid glow over her life.

'Use it as raw material for Mage in the book,' she told herself, half seriously. It certainly gave her a much better idea of the agony she was putting her hero through, but it made her feel a parasite on her own emotions.

Walking it off with long treks around the coast and across the hills, often accompanied by one of the farm dogs that had grown too old for hard work, did help; she enjoyed Floss's company, and that too was new to her. Her mother had always had cats.

The evening before Paul was due home Fran went out to dinner, so Jacinta made a salad of crisp, frilly red and green lettuce with avocado, cooked some tiny, white-skinned potatoes and the first of the beans, and poached a new-laid egg. She ate it all, but it could just as well have been seaweed for any enjoyment she got from it.

The evenings were drawing out, and in spite of showers that had freshened the garden it was still unseasonably hot. During the afternoon Jacinta had printed out her whole manuscript, and when she'd eaten she took the pages onto the verandah to read.

But after a while she sat motionless as the dusk drifted down around her, appreciating the silent, lush beauty of the garden and the patient, soft murmur of the sea. The light grew thicker, more golden, distilling pure colour from each flower and summoning a loitering sweetness so that the garden glowed with a fragrant, beckoning glamour.

An unknown hunger ached through her bones, filling her with a seeking, rapturous discontent. Anchoring the manuscript with a smooth stone she'd picked up from the beach, she got to her feet and walked out into the radiance; she hadn't bothered to do up her hair after her swim, and she shook it around her shoulders, at once oppressed by its weight and yet enjoying the freedom.

She reached to pull down a rose whose petals blended shades of apricot and gold and pink, burying her nose in the heart to wallow in perfume. Sinful, she thought, breathing it deeply; that scent was both an invitation and a satisfaction, tantalising yet not complete, because it lured another response from deep inside her, a primitive yearning that consumed her.

A movement on the edge of her vision brought her head around; in the pool of darkness beneath the verandah roof stood a darker figure, a figure she'd invoked from the furthest reaches of desire.

And then he walked down the steps, and the last of the sun caught his fair head, turning it suddenly into gold. Jacinta's hand clenched on the stem beneath the rose, and a thorn caught beside her nail, tearing the sensitive flesh. An involuntary whimper broke from her lips.

'What is it?' Paul asked, his stride lengthening.

Mutely she held out her hand.

He took it gently. 'Old Abraham Darby has some fierce thorns,' he said, and lifted her hand and took her finger into his mouth.

Sensation, fierce as wildfire, robbed Jacinta of volition. She felt her eyes dilate as he sucked the little wound before examining it with frowning absorption, and she prayed that he wouldn't notice her quiver when he ran his thumb across her suddenly sensitive palm.

'It should be all right,' he said. 'You smell of the flower.' He leaned across her to snap off the heavy bloom and gave it to her. 'Some small recompense.'

'I didn't think you were coming back until tomorrow,' she said. Her voice was a little thin, but without any noticeable tremors.

'I was, but things changed.'

'Fran's having dinner with friends.'

Dusk was falling swiftly, the dampness of the air intensifying the mingled scents around them—the clean fresh perfume of the grass, the salty tang of the sea, and the erotic perfume of rose and gardenia and bouvardia.

'Is she?' He sounded slightly tense.

Get a grip on yourself, Jacinta commanded. She took what she hoped seemed a casual step away from his suffocating presence and asked, 'Have you had dinner? There's salad—'

'I'm not hungry; they practically force-feed you on planes.' He wasn't curt but she could hear impatience behind the words.

Turned away from the painful pleasure of looking at him, she began to walk back towards the house. He went with her, saying, 'I'm going to make myself a drink. Would you like one?'

Perhaps a cup of tea would calm her down. 'Yes, thank you,' she said. 'I've got some stuff out on the verandah that might get damp so I'll put it away first.'

She was shivering when she got back to the lounger. After staring at the rose in her hand, she thrust it into the buttonhole of her shirt and gathered up the sheaf of paper with no regard for tidiness or order. Her mind drummed with one thought.

Get out of here before it's too late.

But her heart whispered that it was already too late. Out in the sumptuous beauty of the garden, she had taken a step through a forbidden door and into a different world.

Closing her eyes, she took a deep breath and then another, but neither that nor concentration quenched the slow burn of desire. In fact her head spun slightly, and she thought, You're hyperventilating, for heaven's sake!

Cold water would remove that hectic flush from her skin, and might just shock her system back into normality. But when she went out into the hall Paul said from the far end, 'Your drink's ready.'

Oddly intimidated by the way he watched her, by his stillness, she walked towards him. He hadn't made tea; the tray he carried held a decanter and bottles.

'Open the door, will you?' he asked, the deep, cool voice without expression.

She did so, and went ahead of him into the conservatory where the frangipani held its cream and gold flowers up in huge panicles. Behind the hills to the west, the sky glowed scarlet and gold and a glaring orange.

'Red sky at night, shepherd's delight,' Jacinta said, because she couldn't think of anything else and she had to break that silence. 'Dean's going to be disappointed.'

Paul waited until she'd sat down before asking, 'I gather it hasn't rained.'

'Several showers, but not enough. Dean says you haven't enough grass to see the stock through if this turns out to be a dry summer.'

'The long-range forecast says it will be a dry summer.'

She put down untasted the glass of lime and soda he'd given her; she didn't trust herself to carry it to her lips without spilling it. 'What will you do?'

She'd exchange a few meaningless pleasantries with him and then make an excuse and go to bed. She could control the fizzing excitement in her blood for that long. She wouldn't make a fool of herself.

'We've already started to sell stock,' he said. 'And we have dams and springs—we should come through in a reasonably good state unless it doesn't rain until next May. How's your finger?'

He hadn't turned the light on and the burning sky edged his profile with flames.

'It's all right,' she said vaguely, steadying her hand to reach for her glass. She downed half the cold liquid, and hiccuped.

Paul lifted his glass to his lips. He didn't drink much. 'What's been happening while I've been gone?'

'Nothing much,' she said. It sounded a little bleak, so she added, 'Well, not a lot. I found a seagull on the beach with a broken wing, and Fran and I have been looking after it…' Her voice died away. After a moment, she asked, 'Did your trip go well?'

'Very well.' He almost drawled the words.

Had he seen Meriam Anderson in Los Angeles?

'I've got something for you from Laurence Perry,' he said, answering her unspoken question.

Her heart shivered within her. 'Really?' she said politely.

He took an envelope from his pocket and handed it over. Jacinta opened it and looked down at the print, blinking at the woman curled in voluptuous abandon amongst a huddle of gold and orange and rust, arms and neck gleaming in the torrid light of summer, a veil covering hair the same colour as Jacinta's. Essentially naked beneath the orange veiling, the model slept in front of a shimmering sea.

'Good heavens!' Jacinta said.

'What is it?' Paul spoke softly, yet such was the implicit authority in his tone that she handed the print across to him.

'Ah,' he said after a quick survey. 'High Victoriana. One of Lord Leighton's mock-classical affairs, I'd say.'

The sun dipped beneath the horizon and the afterglow—echoing the colours in the print—throbbed for several seconds before beginning to fade into night's serene dimness.

'Laurence thought I looked like her,' Jacinta said, 'but it was just my ginger hair and the colour and draping of the sari.'

'No, there's a definite resemblance.' Paul's gaze moved slowly, deliberately across her face. 'The colouring, of course, and that straight, very English nose. And the innocent mouth. Judging by the pose and the clothing, I imagine the artist intended that innocence to be deceptive.'

Jacinta ignored the cynical note. 'It was sweet of Laurence to track it down for me.'

'He's a nice man. And he thought you were charming.' He spoke without expression, yet when he went on pleasantly, 'But then, most people are kind to you, it seems,' she felt the hairs on the back of her neck lift.

To give herself time to cast about for another, less contentious thing to talk about, she picked up her glass and sipped more of the lime and soda, circumspectly this time.

Setting the print down beside a small parcel on the sidetable, he asked, 'How's the book coming along?'

'I'm writing,' she said cautiously. 'It's more fun now that I'm not sticking so closely to a prescribed storyline, but it's much more scary, and it takes longer. I'll have a better idea of where I'm going with the next one.'

'So there's going to be a next one?'

'I—well, yes, I think so.'

'Where are you planning to send this one?'

'I haven't thought yet. I'll have to do some research.'

He picked up the parcel from the table. 'This might help.'

Although it was wrapped, Jacinta could tell by both look and feel that it was another book. Gripping it in her lap, she stammered, 'You're very kind, but really you shouldn't be buying me books, though I've read the last one so often I just about know it off by heart.'

'This one isn't a how-to—it's a listing of publishers and what they're looking for.'

'Thank you,' she said again, looking down at the packet on her lap. Lamely she added, 'I'm sure it will be very helpful.'

'I hope so,' he said negligently.

The darkness in the room gathered, seemed to thicken. Jacinta's pulses thrummed so loudly she thought he must be able to hear them. She unwrapped the book, very aware of Paul leaning back in the chair, as though the trip had sapped even his vitality, long legs stretched out in front of him, the glass he'd barely touched turning slowly in his fingers.

Mesmerised, she watched the tiny flashes from the heart of the crystal. Her gaze wandered up from the glass to his face, shadowed now, and the pale blur of his hair. Something deep and terrifying blossomed within her, growing to fullness in a second. The door to that different destiny, the world of love, clanged shut behind her, sealing her off from the old familiar life, changing her with inescapable relentlessness.

This, she thought suddenly, is not just love; Paul is the only man I'll ever love like this.

The very banality of the words emphasised them, gave them weight and purpose. Until that moment she'd been playing with the idea of love and passion, skirting it with ambivalence, but between one second and the next she knew that for her there would be no other love.

And even as she shrank back—because if Paul was the only man for her then she'd always be alone—she accepted the bitter knowledge. Her mother had loved her father until she died; his name had been on her lips as she drew her last breath.

For the first time she understood—and understood, too, why her mother had always said that having a daughter had been the one thing that went right in her life. If she could have Paul's child she would love it and care for it...

But for her there would be no child. And that was a burden, a grief she couldn't deal with now, not when the shock of discovery was still piercing her heart.

She waited until she'd regained the control she needed to say with a careful, remote precision, 'You must be tired. I am too, so I'll head for bed now.'

'Goodnight.' He got to his feet as she did, and stood aside courteously, then bent and picked up the print Laurence had found for her. 'You'd better take this,' he said, holding it out.

She took it, but her hand was shaking and their fingers touched.

Paul said between his teeth, 'Damn, damn, *damn*,' and the vivid scrap of paper fell unnoticed to the floor as he pulled Jacinta into his arms.

Yes, she thought exultantly, and with mindless hunger she tilted her face. When he bent his head and took her seeking mouth she met his kiss like a flame.

Heat raged through her, setting her alight until she thought she could feel sparks shooting from her skin. But when his mouth crushed hers the quality of her response altered. Just as intense, just as cataclysmic, sensation ran slow and lazy and languorous through her, melting her bones and seducing open the gates of her will-power.

Lifting his head, he said thickly, 'Jacinta, I've wanted you ever since I saw you. In Fiji I couldn't sleep for wondering what your pretty mouth would feel like under mine...'

Dazzled, she sighed, and he took what he wanted, filling her with his taste, male, dark and mysterious, overwhelming her with expertise, summoning her hidden wildness in response to his passionate mastery.

When at last the kiss ended they were both breathing erratically, and he surveyed her tender mouth with eyes that were narrowed and lit from within, purposeful and determined on conquest.

Desire clutched at her heart; everything inside her deliquesced, to be remade anew by that intent gaze. In a soft, tentative voice she said his name, loving the sound of it on her lips, shaping her mouth to his liking, to her need.

'Paul,' she breathed again, fascinated by the blue fire that ringed the dilating blackness at the centre of his eyes.

Once more she readied her mouth for his erotic plunder, but this time he kissed beneath her ear, and while he showed her how fiercely sensitive that spot was his hands slid up into her hair and he pulled her head back gently, so that he could kiss her jaw, and the corner of her mouth, then down the length of her throat to the throbbing hollow at its base.

Racked by delight, she trembled. An inarticulate murmur broke helplessly from her throat, and he smiled.

God, she thought, appalled for a sane moment by her happiness, what pleasure to feel this man's smile against my skin!

His hands lingered through her hair until she moaned with the pleasure of it, then skimmed her shoulders, and it was no longer happiness she felt, but something thunderous and uncontrollable, a compulsion that demanded satisfaction.

'Jacinta,' he said, his voice impeded and oddly hesitant as he took the crushed rose from her buttonhole and dropped it. 'So sweet and summery and fragrant. What was it Shakespeare asked? ''Shall I compare thee to a summer's day? Thou art more lovely and more temperate.''' His laughter was husky, almost raw. 'Certainly more lovely, but I think he might have got the temperate part wrong, thank God.'

Afterwards she'd think that he'd wielded the instrument of his voice like a weapon, disarming her completely, but at the time she could only respond helplessly to its magnetism.

And then his fingers cupped her breasts. Jacinta shivered, and her head fell back, and the strength seeped from her.

Slowly, murmuring his appreciation, he slipped open the buttons down the front of her shirt, the swift, sure movements of his fingers a delicious torment. Lifting weighted eyelids, she watched the concentration in his face and the pulse flicking in his jaw, and knew that whatever happened she was not going to regret this.

The calm good humour was gone; it had only ever been a mask that hid the hunter, the predator, from the eyes of the world. This man knew what he was doing, held his goal firmly in mind.

And yet she wasn't afraid, for this was Paul and she loved him. Although fierce determination sculpted his face, she knew intuitively that he wouldn't be brutal, or exploit her untutored ardour. He would take, yes, but he would give in equal measure.

So when the front of her shirt fell open and he unclasped her bra and pushed both shirt and bra down her arms, she shrugged free of the cloth and lifted her arms and put them around his neck.

'Not so quickly,' he said, eyes kindling. 'Let me look at you.'

That was harder to deal with; she felt the track of his gaze across pale skin and to her astonishment the apricot centres of her breasts stiffened and sprang forth, and he laughed softly. Before she realised what he was going to do he bent and took one in his mouth while moving a thumb smoothly, persistently over the other.

She knew the mechanics of lovemaking. But no one had ever warned her that such gentle suckling could kindle lightning in her cells. Shuddering, fighting to keep her lashes from drifting down, she looked at the golden head against her breast and felt her womb contract in a fierce, involuntary spasm.

'Paul,' she said soundlessly, but he heard her and straightened, that splintering fire incandescent now around the dark pupils of his eyes.

'Yes,' he said, and this time there was no sweet summer wooing in his words, nothing but a stripped desperation that was infinitely more exciting.

Jacinta gasped when he picked her up. Cradled by iron muscles, made speechless by the sheer primitive force of his actions, she said, 'I'm too heavy!'

'No,' he said harshly, 'just right for me.' And certainly he showed no signs of strain as he carried her down the hallway.

His bedroom door was ajar; he kicked it wide and went through, shouldering it closed behind him, and walked across the shadowy room to put her on her feet beside a big, four-poster bed.

Jacinta stumbled slightly, and wailed, 'I'm so clumsy,' when he grabbed her and supported her.

'You're not,' he said, his voice soothing yet shot through with a turbulent rasp that fired her blood anew. 'Don't worry.'

She stared up into eyes so blue and so blazing she thought they scorched her skin. 'I'm not,' she whispered. 'Worrying, I mean.'

Laughter glinted a moment in the sapphire depths. 'Then would you like to undress me?' he asked gravely. 'I've spent a lot of time imagining how your hands would feel on me.'

Until that moment she'd always assumed that making love was something a man did to a woman. Now, dazzled by the idea of sharing, she nodded, and undid the buttons on his shirt. Tentatively she spread her hands over his heart, feeling the silky abrasion of hair against her palms, the unsteady, driving pulse.

I'm doing that to him, she thought, awed, flexing fingers until he startled her with a muffled groan. Eyes widening, she looked up. Although his mouth was controlled into a straight line, the contours were slightly swollen, and in the severe features she saw a stark hunger that matched hers. It should have frightened her but she wasn't afraid. The secret pathways in her body moistened, heated.

'You're so strong,' she murmured, surprising herself.

'Is that what you like? Strength?'

Her hands slid beneath the fine material of his shirt to find the smooth swell of muscle along his shoulders, the sleekness of his skin only emphasising the male power hidden beneath it.

'I suppose I do.' Her voice was rich and full. 'And beauty.' She laughed a little in her throat. 'And you are beautiful.'

Amazingly, colour patched along the broad sweep of his cheekbones. 'So are you,' he said, shucking off his shirt.

'You don't have to say that.'

He looked at her, his brows drawing together. 'I don't lie,' he said, and kissed the place where her neck joined her shoulder, pulling a strand of hair over so that it curled down to meet the curve of her breast.

'You light the night sky,' he said, and this time she knew he meant it. His voice was implacable, almost fierce, and his hand moved slowly down to cup her breast again, the long fingers dark against the pale ivory of her skin.

'All fire and light and heat, like flames in a dreary world,' he said, and kissed her, his mouth hard and ravenous, as though he couldn't get enough of her.

After that she followed where he led, a novice in the hands of a master, until at last she lay naked before him.

'Flames everywhere,' he said. When she blushed he smiled, the lazy, sexy smile of a man who knew that he was going to get what he wanted, and startled her by kissing her hipbone.

His mouth was warm and persuasive, and she had to remember to breathe, to drag air into parched lungs, because everything she'd taken for granted about her body over the years was now shown to be false.

Paul stood up and shed the rest of his clothes without ceremony, then came down beside her on the bed, slipping an arm under her head.

She lifted a solemn face and met the hard, consuming passion of his gaze. In his throat the pulse hammered rapidly. Jacinta rested her index finger on that small betrayal, then traced down the midline of his chest to one narrow hip and on to the powerful muscles of his thigh.

She didn't touch the thrusting jut of his masculinity, but her body softened, opened, readied itself for him. His hand found her mount of Venus, pressing against nerve-endings that sent their dangerous summons throughout every cell in her body.

One finger gently separated her hidden folds; his mouth was still straight and firmly closed, his eyes masked by dark lashes.

Fire danced through her at the touch of his fingers, soon augmented by a conflagration that overpowered her, a remorseless, building, honeyed sweetness of wanting, an unmeasured compulsion that set the wildness in her free, so that she gasped his name and arced towards him, pulling him down, her hips moving erotically beneath him, her face absorbed and demanding.

Making love with Paul meant surrendering to her own desires so that the focus of her world narrowed to this bed, this man; nothing else mattered. Entirely lost in the sensuous overload, Jacinta spun into a region beyond time and place—a region where she and he were all that existed.

Slowly, skilfully, he brought her to such readiness that her hand on his skin shook, and she shivered and pressed herself against him, eagerly supplicant. Then, at last, he took her, sliding into the passage he'd prepared, both of them so still that the only movement was the tightening muscles in his haunches as he pushed into her.

Jacinta surged suddenly upwards, enclosing him and surrounding him, and the muscles in her legs gripped and held in the same primeval clasp as her secret, inner muscles.

'Yes,' he said, and took her breath away by driving home, and without waiting withdrawing and thrusting again, setting up an erotic rhythm that she soon picked up, meeting each thrust with an answering twist of her hips, her hands clenched across the expanse of his back as the muscles bunched and knotted and she went with him down that long, ravishing path to fulfilment.

At some stage she understood dimly that he was restraining himself, making sure he didn't climax before she reached her peak, and although she loved him for his consideration she didn't want that. She wanted him as lost in this wonderful experience as she was, unable to think of anything other than this miracle.

Excitement began to soar beyond rational thought; sensation, rich and multifarious, flooded her. She grasped his lean hips and held him there while she moved against him, and when his heavy eyelids lifted she smiled and drowned in blueness as wave after wave tossed her higher and higher beyond some impalpable barrier where she was nothing but feeling, so consumed by ecstasy that she cried out as her body shuddered beneath his.

And then he clamped her hips in his callused hands and went with her into that place where nothing else existed but the two of them. For long moments they remained wrapped in each other's arms while the aftershocks of orgasm buffeted through them, leaving them slick with sweat that cooled slowly, yet faster than desire and passion.

When at last he pushed himself up on his elbows she gave an inarticulate murmur of protest and opened sated, drowsy eyes. He looked, she thought with a jolt of the heart, strained, although he smiled and bent to kiss her mouth gently.

'It's all right,' he said, turning onto his side so that she could breathe more easily. He didn't loosen his grip.

After a while she realised that he'd gone to sleep, and outrage warred with amusement.

It somehow made him seem much more—human—and she had to admit that she was tired too.

And more than content to stay where she was.

Oddly enough, just before she drifted off to sleep, her last, barely conscious thought was that she was glad his jilting Aura had never been in this house.

Jacinta woke hours later, to complete bewilderment. A soft light shone through the uncurtained windows, but she wasn't in her own room—and then, as her night-accustomed eyes roamed the room, she remembered.

Fully-clothed, Paul was standing in the window. Suddenly racked by embarrassment at her nudity under the sheet, she said uncertainly, 'Paul?'

'I'm here.'

'I know.' Her fingers plucked nervously at the sheet. 'What—?' The words wouldn't come. She swallowed, and started again. 'What are you doing?'

'Wondering how I'm going to tell my cousin that I've broken his trust and slept with the woman he's engaged to.' He spoke with grim distinctness, every word an arrow directed at himself as well as her.

CHAPTER EIGHT

PAUL'S words hummed and buzzed in her ears, echoing so that she couldn't make sense of them. Secret, inchoate dreams she'd been building in her unconscious mind shrivelled into dust, doomed before she'd even recognised them.

'What?' she asked.

He didn't turn, but the light of dawn caught on his hair. 'You heard me,' he said evenly.

Jacinta forced herself to speak with slow, painstaking care. 'I *thought* I heard you. Where the *hell* did you get that idea?'

'From Gerard, of course,' he said, scorn icing the words. 'He told me when he arranged for you to stay here.'

She drew in a deep, ragged breath and sat up, arms folded across her breasts to hold the sheet in place. Her hair fell across her shoulders, slippery and warm. If she let herself, she'd remember the way his hands had speared through it...

'I don't believe this,' she said, trying to sound reasonable and sensible. 'Gerard wouldn't have told you that because he knows it's not true.'

'He said that you'd kept it secret because universities don't welcome affairs between tutors and students. It makes sense.' His voice was studied and dispassionate, as though they'd never lain together locked in the most intimate embrace of all, breasts crushed against chest, legs intertwined, mouth to mouth, open to each other.

She shook her head, seizing on what seemed to her chaotic mind to be the flaw in his argument. 'I'm not his student now.'

'True, but he's going to be your supervisor next year.'

Although he didn't move, she shivered at the icy condemnation in his tone.

He was serious. Or was this a perverted sort of kiss-off?

She said heavily, 'Do you honestly think that I'd be—here—if I was secretly engaged to Gerard?'

'It depends on why you're engaged to him,' he said almost indifferently. 'If it's because you want security, then, yes, you might well feel that I'm a better bet than he is. I don't blame you for that—your childhood must have been lacking in stability.'

'That's big of you,' she said between her teeth. 'As it happens, you're quite wrong. My mother kept me fed and loved, and that's the sort of stability most children need.' A sudden memory narrowed her eyes. 'I suppose you thought I was eyeing up Dean and Laurence Perry too, seeing which one offered the most *stability.*'

'It seemed possible,' he said stonily.

Pain began to niggle behind her eyes. 'I must be extraordinarily stupid. That's why you kept bringing Dean's Brenda into the conversation.'

'It doesn't matter. What does matter is Gerard.'

'I don't believe this.' Exhaustion numbed her mind, making it impossible to follow her fleeting fragments of thought to a logical conclusion. Ignoring the sheet, she pressed the heels of her hands to her eyes and strove desperately for composure.

Eventually she was able to say woodenly, 'He's never touched me. Never. Not even a kiss.' She paused, but Paul said nothing, didn't move. A wild mixture of emotions clogged her throat. 'If I'd thought he was in love with me I wouldn't have accepted the computer, or worked for him—'

'Or let him subsidise your accommodation?' Paul interpolated smoothly.

Jacinta's head came up. 'What?' she croaked.

In a clipped, metallic voice he said, 'He subsidises your

rent at the flat—the flat he found for you—by fifty dollars a week. He plans to pay out more for your tuition fees next year.'

'He said he knew of a grant,' she said hesitantly. 'For women whose tertiary education has been interrupted by family concerns. It's given out by a trust.'

'Gerard's trust.' He didn't try to hide the scorn that blazed through his words. Inexorably he went on, 'And the flat? Did you really believe his tale of someone who was in Oxford on a scholarship?'

'I had no reason not to,' she cried out, realising for the first time how naïve she'd been.

'It didn't occur to you,' he drawled, 'that to accept the offer of accommodation from a man who was sexually interested in you—'

She leapt out of the bed and flew across to him, hand upraised. 'He wasn't— I didn't—oh!'

For he'd caught her hand and twisted it behind her back, not painfully but with relentless speed, bringing her up against him. He was wearing a cotton robe in some dark material, thin enough to reveal his arousal.

Her breath stopping in her lungs, Jacinta registered the sharp aroma of danger. Her rage ebbed into humiliation as she stared into his implacable eyes, and she shivered, the cool morning air flowing through the open window and over her naked body.

'Don't ever hit me,' Paul said, his voice so soft she barely heard it, yet each word resounded through her head. He was holding onto his control with the thinnest of reins, and for the first time in her life Jacinta was truly afraid of a man.

Gerard had bragged that his cousin never lost his temper, that no one had ever seen him angry. Gerard had been wrong.

That icy, concentrated contempt terrified her.

'Why would he do all that for you if he didn't plan to marry you? He's never been the sort of man who resorts to prostitutes, and he's too intelligent to pay out for a woman with a prostitute's mind. He's been helping the woman he loves, the woman he plans to marry.'

Her hold on reality slipping, she closed her eyes. 'No,' she whispered.

'I've known my cousin for as long as he's lived, and he's not a liar.'

'He lied to both of us,' she shot back on a surge of adrenalin. And because she couldn't surrender to the despair that threatened to exhaust her, she whipped up her anger to add savagely, 'Unless he felt that lying was the only way he could protect me from you.'

His features clamped into an impervious mask. 'If so, it didn't work,' he said, coldly sardonic. 'And if he thought you needed protection from me, that still implies a much closer relationship than you're admitting to. A man is only so protective of the woman he calls his.'

Jacinta jerked her arm, and he released her as though she fouled his hands. Hot denials hovered on her tongue, but she could see from his bleak, uncompromising face that nothing she could say would convince him that Gerard had lied.

Accepting that it was useless, she turned away and drew in a long, agonising breath while she struggled for the strength to get her through the next few minutes.

'For God's sake put some clothes on,' Paul said between his teeth.

Shame and embarrassment roiled over her. She walked quickly back to the small pile of her clothes on the floor and began to get into them.

It didn't help that she understood. Aura had run away with Paul's best friend; he had just spent the night with the woman he believed to be engaged to his cousin. Not only did he despise Jacinta, he despised himself.

Steadily she said, 'Men don't own women.'

He smiled, and a shiver ran down her spine. 'Tell that to a jealous lover.'

'I'm not going to debate that,' she said fiercely, yanking on her shorts. 'You know it's wrong. No one has the right to own anyone else. As for Gerard, he lied.'

'So you say.'

She swallowed, knowing it was hopeless to protest her innocence. He believed his cousin.

And that, she thought painfully, was an even greater betrayal than his physical rejection of her.

Without bothering to put on her bra, she shrugged into the shirt and began to fasten the buttons, concentrating fiercely on the mundane task because it was all she had to keep the demons of despair at bay.

'Unfortunately,' he said, 'I'll have to tell him.'

'It's none of his business,' she said, but without conviction.

The quotation from Shakespeare was burnt in letters of fire across her brain, along with the one he'd murmured to her the preceding evening. She'd never, she thought savagely, be able to read Shakespeare again without having both scenes, last night and this morning, spring to life again.

Mine honour is my life; both grow in one
Take honour from me, and my life is done.

A dangerous honour, she thought bitterly.

A swift glance revealed Paul's austere, ruthless profile against the light of the day outside; she thought of Vikings, of men who held to their conscience in the face of death. Because he hated himself for betraying his cousin's trust, he was putting them both through the rigorous hell he assigned to violators of his code.

He said, 'I can't let him marry you knowing that we—'

'Wanted each other? Slept together?' She scooped up her sandals and headed towards the door. 'Don't spoil your relationship with Gerard over me,' she threw over her shoulder. 'I'm not going to marry him, or sleep with him, ever. Whatever relationship he's implied is a product of his imagination and exists only in his head. He needs a psychiatrist.'

It wasn't a very satisfying parting shot but it was all she could think of. Back in her room she sat down on the bed and tried to reassemble her thoughts, but after a moment her sandals and underwear dropped from limp fingers and she gave in to the luxury of tears, curling up in a ball on the bedcover while she wept.

It was the sudden transition from heaven to hell, she thought drearily, the abrupt and shattering destruction of all her illusions.

Perhaps she'd deserved to have them destroyed. She'd been utterly credulous.

Shame dried the tears. Why had Gerard lied? Why, when she wouldn't accept money from him, had he come up with this elaborate deception—helped, of course, by her gullibility?

Simple kindness was no answer. Had he truly fantasised that her acceptance of his help meant that she was falling in love with him? Surely he didn't plan to reveal the amount she owed him and suggest the oldest way in the world to repay it?

Jacinta got up and walked across to the window. Several blackbirds immediately shrieked a warning from the lawn and flew low and straight into the garden border.

He was sick, or he was like Mark, who fed a shaky ego on women's vulnerability. And she'd fallen for it. Was there something in her that signalled to men that she was a fool?

She owed Gerard money she wasn't going to be able to repay. Unless she used her mother's money.

'Oh, Mum,' she whispered thickly, resting her head against the cool glass.

She stayed like that until the sun bounded up over the

edge of the sea. Then, exhausted and aching, she collected clean clothes together and went to the bathroom.

As she dried herself in front of the big mirror she looked gravely at the soft red marks on her breasts with a heavy-lidded, sated gaze that the morning's events hadn't been able to banish.

Paul had tempered his great strength until his control had snapped. And even then he hadn't hurt her; her skin was fine and easily bruised.

A wave of erotic longing gathered in the pit of her stomach. As an initiation into the delights of making love—sex, she corrected—hers had been wonderful. Perhaps Paul had been born knowing how to bring a woman to the heights of ecstasy, but experience had refined that initial understanding to a skilled, passionate mastery that overwhelmed her.

Yet in some basic way he mistrusted all women.

Because of the woman who'd left him to run away with his best friend? It was too easy, too pat. Other men had endured similar experiences yet learned to trust again.

Her mother used to say 'Look to the child' when they discussed the foibles of friends and neighbours. Probably the root cause of Paul's mistrust, of his rigid insistence on honour, lay buried deep in his childhood.

While she'd showered her unconscious had made her decision for her. She'd give up her university studies and find a job, using her mother's legacy to reimburse Gerard.

Back in her room she began to pack, biting her lip to hold in the tears until she managed to achieve a measure of self-control.

A knock on the door made her freeze, her breath solidifying in a hard lump at the centre of her chest.

Don't be silly, she told herself as she went across to open it. He won't hurt you.

Paul stood outside, his expression remote and guarded. 'We have to talk,' he said. His eyes, their blueness leached of emotion and warmth, focused on the suitcase at the side of the bed. 'But not now. Jacinta, there's an emergency at sea—a boat's on fire—and I'm going out with Dean in a spotter plane from the Aero Club. Wait here until I get back. And don't make any arrangements until you hear what I have to say.'

A hidden, fugitive hope persuaded her to say, 'All right.'

He nodded. 'Thank you,' he said, meticulously polite as ever, and turned and strode down the hall towards his room.

It was a long morning. After Jacinta had finished packing she went into the kitchen and forced down toast and coffee.

Fran said, 'That's not going to keep you going for long.'

'It's enough. Why are Dean and Paul searching for a boat that's on fire?'

'Because the idiot has no idea where he is,' Fran said shortly. 'He radioed in to the coastguard, but he's out of sight of land so he's lost.'

Aren't we all? Jacinta thought cynically.

Still cocooned in a merciful numbness, she cleared everything from the computer so that no one would be able to read her manuscript, and put the two sets of diskettes into her suitcase.

At morning tea Jacinta surrendered to her driving curiosity and asked Fran as casually as she could, 'How long have you worked for Paul?'

'Five years; since my marriage broke up,' the housekeeper told her readily. 'But my dad used to work for his parents, so I've known him all my life. He was a lovely boy: a bit serious and always very responsible, and that smile of his—well, you know what it's like.'

Once she'd left Waitapu she'd never see that smile again. Jacinta said, 'His parents are both dead, aren't they?'

'Yes. His father was a hard man and you didn't cross him—everyone liked him as well as respected him, though. He was a good man. A bit like Paul, really, without the charm. Paul got that from his mother. She was lovely, but she was sort of distant, as though she didn't really live in this world. I don't think she knew how to deal with children.' Fran glanced out of the window. 'Yes,' she said, 'I thought we might have rain today. Look at that front coming up.'

By lunchtime it was raining properly. Jacinta couldn't eat anything, and she couldn't settle either. Was that distant mother the clue to Paul's character? A hard father and a distant, charming mother...

Fran, who'd apparently been keeping an eye on her, came into the morning room as she put down a book, and said, 'Why don't you watch a video?'

'I suppose I could.' Perhaps a video would help keep the gnawing agony at bay. She might be able to lose herself in a good story.

'There's a stack of them in the bottom left-hand cupboard there, underneath the bookshelves,' Fran said.

The books in the morning room were the sort kept to entertain visitors—local history and geology, books by New Zealanders. Paul's main collection was kept in his office, into which Jacinta had never even looked, let alone stepped. He also read magazines of all sorts: literary, science, farming, and manufacturing and business. Jacinta had enjoyed herself with the contents of the morning room bookshelves, but she'd never bothered with the videos.

They turned out to be an interesting selection. Several classics, some very good dramas, a few comedies, and items that had been taped from the television, most labelled in a strong hand.

Fascinated, because these were programmes Paul had wanted to watch, Jacinta sat through a hard-hitting political discussion recorded a few months previously, a programme on a small New Zealand town she remembered seeing some years ago with her mother, and what appeared to be an amateur video of a pastoral show.

Halfway through that it switched to a few minutes of a

party that someone had filmed on a camcorder. Jacinta didn't know anyone until the camera swivelled, and there was Paul. A younger Paul, somehow more—more lightweight than the man she knew. As the camera fixed onto him he smiled, and that smile was heartbreakingly familiar, warm and lazy and sweet.

He was smiling at the woman beside him. Jacinta drew in an anguished breath as she scrutinised the beautiful, passionate face beneath hair that glowed like burgundy. 'A dark flame', Gerard had called her.

This was Aura, who'd run away with Paul's best friend.

Jacinta sat very still while the man who'd been taking the video called out, 'Smile for me, Aura,' and, sure enough, the woman smiled.

Something tore inside Jacinta. How could she even think of comparing herself to such beauty?

Scarcely knowing what she did, she stopped the video, rewound it to play those fleeting moments over in excruciating detail.

Aura looked at Paul with loving affection, with pleasure and friendliness, but there was nothing in those wonderful eyes that came close to the feelings Jacinta had for him.

She was watching the couple turn away from the camera to talk to an elderly woman when a lethal voice said behind her, 'Turn that bloody thing off.'

Terror kicking in her stomach, Jacinta twisted. Paul stood just inside the door, his eyes the searing blue at the heart of a diamond, a white line around his mouth.

The hubbub of the party was cut abruptly short, replaced by the unctuous voice of a television front-man announcing another documentary.

'Turn it off,' Paul repeated, his voice as cold and violent as an Arctic storm.

Jacinta had to force herself to press the switch on the remote so that the picture was swallowed up in blackness.

Self-protection drove her stiffly to her feet. 'Did you find the boat?'

At first she thought he wasn't going to answer, but after a taut couple of seconds he said, 'Yes. Where the hell did you get that video?'

Refusing to let her hands clench at her side, she said, 'It's just a fragment. I was watching a documentary you'd taped, and it appeared between it and the next thing you taped.' She bit her lip to stop the babbling words.

'I see.' Leashed by superhuman control, his anger was replaced by a frigid detachment that was even more forbidding. Apparently thinking she needed some sort of explanation, he said, 'It's old—over five years old.'

And he turned. He was, she realised, going to leave it at that.

She said, 'It still hurts, doesn't it?'

'No.'

'Then why did you react so aggressively?'

'Jacinta, stop it.' He sounded tired.

Oh, God, she wanted to. If she could wipe the impressions of the last ten minutes from her brain she'd do it—and even as the thought was born she knew she lied. There could be no peace for her without the truth. She waited, her eyes fixed on his handsome face.

'I loved her once,' he said impatiently, frowning. 'It's over now—has been for years.'

'If you no longer love her why do you keep up the feud?'

His eyes narrowed. With silky, unpleasant emphasis he said, 'Gerard's been gossiping, has he? There is no feud. Never has been.'

'So you see them regularly? Aura and her husband.'

Through thin lips he said, 'No.'

'Because you can't bear to.'

'Not at all,' he said with calm, snubbing courtesy. 'I have as little taste as most people for being made to look a fool, so I suppose it's pride that prevents us from being a cosy, friendly trio.'

Jacinta looked at him. Not only the intervening five years had made the difference between the man who stood in front of her now and the Paul McAlpine who'd smiled at Aura with such love and confidence. That man had been—softer? No, that was the wrong word.

Losing the woman had hardened Paul, put an edge to his personality that hadn't been there before. That inborn strength and assurance had been honed by anger and determination into compelling power and authority. Aura's betrayal had turned him into a dominating, almost disturbingly formidable man, intensely attractive to women.

Would Aura have run away with her Flint if she'd truly known this man?

Jacinta said quietly, 'I think you're still in love with her.'

He took a step towards her, but halted when she braced herself. He swore beneath his breath, a curse she couldn't quite hear, then she saw him reimpose control, all emotion transmuted by his iron self-discipline into harsh inflexibility.

'That's quite an assumption to make after seeing a minute of old film,' he said aloofly, watching her with eyes opaque as blue stones.

'It was your reaction that gave you away.' Jacinta tested her courage, found it wanting, yet persisted. 'If you don't love her then you must hate her.'

His handsome features were as unrevealing as granite. 'Far from it,' he said, his calculated politeness hurting Jacinta more than open anger ever could have. 'I wish her every happiness.'

That was when Jacinta accepted that the only thing she could do was leave the homestead and go away and hope that she never saw him again. Even if he told her that he loved her she'd have to go, but he was not, she thought with a trace of bitterness, going to lie to her.

He couldn't love another woman because his heart was buried in Aura's shrine.

'It's none of my business,' she said, scarcely knowing what the words were, falling back on conventional phrases because she could never say what she really felt.

'You're right, it's not. It's long over. What are your plans?'

'I'll go back to Auckland.'

His gaze flicked past her to the window. 'Not in this downpour,' he said.

Shrugging, she said, 'I'll go on the bus. I rang to see if they had a spare seat for this afternoon, and they have. I'll have to ask someone to take me in to the village, if that's all right.'

Speaking slowly, he said, 'If you stay the night here I'll take you back tomorrow morning.'

'It will be much easier if I go tonight.'

'Where are you going?'

Oddly enough, she hadn't thought of that. She stared at her hands, laced tightly together in front of her, and tried to think, but the thoughts were lost in a woolly fog. 'The YWCA,' she finally blurted when the silence had stretched on too long.

'Have you got everything you own packed into those two suitcases?'

Pity she could definitely do without. In a tone that matched his for evenness, she said, 'No, and don't worry about me, Paul, I'll be all right. I may have been very naïve with Gerard, but I'm actually quite competent at managing my life. I'll cope.'

With a twist of his lips, he said brutally, 'How? You've no job—'

'I'll find one.'

'—and very little money. I will worry about you.' He paused, then added stiffly, 'And so will Gerard.'

Anger kindled in her, fast and lethal as a backblast. Lifting her head, she demanded fiercely, 'Do you still believe that I'm engaged to him?'

His expression revealed nothing. 'I don't know,' he said after a prolonged pause. 'One of you is lying. If Gerard lied it would make him psychologically unstable, and I've never seen any evidence of that in him. Whereas I've seen a lot of women who consciously or unconsciously look for security in the man they plan to marry. It's probably inbred in us; men go for beauty, women go for money and status, and I'm sure it's all for the better perpetuation of the species.'

She had no answer to the cynical observation, no defences against him.

He added in a different voice, 'But I'm not going to just drop you at the YWCA and leave you, so you'd better come up with some sort of address to go to.'

Rain drove at the windows, and with the sudden intensity of a summer storm overflowed the gutterings, so that the rest of the world was walled off by a shimmering, liquid tent. To her horror Jacinta's eyes began to fill; hastily she grabbed her handkerchief from her pocket and blew her nose.

I will not cry, she vowed. I will *not*...

Stiffly Paul said, 'Jacinta, you don't have to flee to the YWCA as though you've been thrown out. I'll move back to town until you can find a permanent place to go to. I usually spend this time in Auckland anyway; it's the busiest time of the year because everyone wants every deal settled by Christmas Eve.'

She shook her head. 'It'll be easier on everyone if I go now. This afternoon.'

Unerringly, he chose the one thing that might change her mind. 'It won't be easier on me,' he said coolly. 'Be sensible. Shall we make it a week? You should be able to find somewhere to live in that time, and I'll know you're safe.'

'I'd be perfectly safe at the YWCA,' she pointed out desperately.

'They might not have a room,' he said.

Clearly he was prepared to argue all day until she gave in. She could just go, but she didn't want to use Gerard's car—the thought of driving it down to Auckland made her feel unclean. Someone from Waitapu was going to have to drive her in to catch the bus, and one look at Paul's implacable face told her she wasn't going to get any co-operation from him.

Jacinta gave in. 'All right,' she said, because she was exhausted and he was right; a week would give her a chance to find a new home.

'Of course,' he said, 'I want your promise that you won't run away the moment I get out of the gate.'

She flushed and kept her eyes averted. 'Why should you believe my promise?' she asked. 'You won't believe anything else I tell you.'

'Ah, but you keep promises,' he said smoothly. 'You told me so once.'

She flinched. 'I'm supposed to be engaged to Gerard,' she retorted snidely. 'That's a promise too.'

'If you don't give me your word I'll just have to immobilise his car and let everyone here know that you are not to be let out of the gate until I get back,' he said.

It was so outrageous a statement that she stared at him. The blue eyes were darkly shadowed by his lashes, but there was no amusement in his voice or the grim line of his mouth. He looked like someone about to go into battle—a warrior determined to win, steel-honed with implacable purpose.

He meant it.

'Make me a prisoner?' she asked, tight-lipped.

'If I have to.' His tone gave no quarter.

Jacinta loved him. She had just spent the night making love with him. She would remember him all her life.

But at that moment she could have happily strangled him. Very steadily she said, 'Threats have a way of rebounding on the people who issue them. However, you don't need to make any more. I'll stay here until I find a place to go to.'

'Thank you.' He turned, then stopped. Tonelessly he said, 'I'm sorry.'

'Why?'

'For last night.'

Jacinta had always thought herself placid and even-tempered, but before he could say any more she interrupted rapidly, 'I'm not. I enjoyed it immensely. And although you don't believe me, there was no reason why we shouldn't have made love. We both wanted it, and neither of us is responsible for any plans Gerard may have made, or his attempts to manipulate us.'

He didn't answer directly. Instead he said, 'I'm away for the afternoon and won't be back until late, so unless you're up when I leave tomorrow morning, I'll see you in a week's time.'

She refused to watch him go out of the room, refused to think of anything but the necessity of getting a place to live in. Outside the rain stopped and the sun came out, summoning steam from the paths as it set about drying up the downpour.

When she heard the car leave she went down the hall and into her bedroom. Thank God they had slept together in his bed. This one held no memories.

After a while she fought back the debilitating listlessness she recognised as grief and forced herself into the morning room, where once more she scanned the classified advertisements in the newspaper. This time there would be no decision to stay at Waitapu, no stupid conviction that she could deal easily with the results of her actions.

First she needed somewhere to stay for the next few nights while she found a place to live. A friend in a flat in Grey Lynn wouldn't mind if she dossed down there for a week or so. Then she had to find a job, otherwise she'd soon use up the small amount of money she'd have in the bank after she'd repaid Gerard. She looked on the calendar and worked out just how much she owed him.

All right, she told her skipping, racing heart, don't have a panic attack. Calm down. Do this thing in logical steps.

A bed, then a job. That shouldn't be too difficult; she was a good waitress, she could serve behind a fast food counter, or she could work in an old people's home.

Fear kicked her in the stomach. She didn't want to spend the rest of her life working in takeaway shops or waitressing, but what on earth was she to do? A history degree was utterly useless on the job market.

Logic, she reminded herself.

Until she got settled she wouldn't think about the lies Gerard had told, or his reason for telling them.

At least the need to leave Waitapu, the necessity of organising that departure, gave her something to think about and stopped her from giving in to the intense desolation that lay behind the barriers of her will like a howling wasteland.

After a couple of deep breaths she read slowly and carefully through the 'Flatmates Wanted' section. Her heart lifted slightly when she saw that there were still plenty. Having scribbled likely looking numbers down, she turned to the 'Situations Vacant' columns.

Ten minutes later she set the newspaper aside and got up. So close to Christmas very few firms wanted new employees. And what there was wasn't exactly interesting.

'To hell with *interesting*,' she muttered. 'I need to earn a living. Interest can come later.'

She went across to the telephone and began to dial.

CHAPTER NINE

AFTER she'd written down ads and phone numbers to contact in Auckland, Jacinta went back to her room, took out her bank statement and worked out exactly how much money she'd have after she'd repaid Gerard every cent she owed him. It wasn't much, but she'd be able to manage.

She'd have to manage.

Then she wrote a cheque and put it in an envelope on which she wrote his name in big black letters. She'd leave it in her room when she left—Paul would make sure that his cousin got it.

Filled with a desperate need to escape, she told Fran she'd be on the beach, and set off to walk as far and as fast as she could.

Just before dinner, hot and tired, she came back towards the house, watching dotterels bob up and down in avian courtesy, then flow across the sand like silk. These ones were in breeding plumage; no doubt—like the penguins who'd taken over the bach, thereby exposing Jacinta to greater danger than she'd ever envisaged—they had nests nearby.

Warned by some instinct, she looked away from the shiny expanse of sand and saw Paul walk through the barrier of the pohutukawas, his head gleaming like red gold in the sun.

Her heart jumped; she'd never believed that making love could join people in any way other than the purely temporary, but for the rest of her life she'd be living on the memory of the previous night. Oh, she'd get over him, she might even fall in love again, but it would be vastly different from this incandescent emotion.

It was cruel of him to come back while she was still awake, she thought while her treacherous heart rejoiced.

159

'You're back early,' she said quietly.

'I'm sorry.'

'Why be sorry? This is your home.' The dotterels bowed, and bowed again, then continued their swift gliding across the beach, smooth as skaters. 'Anyway, you won't have to stay in Auckland now if you don't want to. I've found a place to live.'

'Where?'

Surprised at the note of aggression in his voice, she returned coolly, 'In Grey Lynn. It's a mixed flat—two men and three women. It sounds very nice.'

'I see. You haven't met them?'

Her brain spun. Finally she said, 'As it happens, yes. One of the women took the same papers as I did, and during the year we got quite friendly.' Nadia was in Southland for the holidays, but one of her flatmates had rung her and she'd given Jacinta permission to use her bed for as long as she liked.

'When are you going?' he asked flatly.

'I'll catch the bus tomorrow morning.'

He shook his head. 'I'm going down so you might as well come with me.' And before she had time to object he looked past her to the expanse of shining beach, and the small birds going about their age-old ritual. 'I'll have to tell Gerard what happened.'

'Why?'

She could hear his shrug in his voice. 'He should know.'

'So that he can hate you?' she said quietly, knowing she wouldn't make any difference. 'You haven't betrayed him.'

There was silence before he said, 'That's a simplistic attitude. Even if what you say is true, and there is nothing between you, he told me there was because he wanted me to keep away from you. I didn't.'

'So you'll purge a guilt that isn't necessary by ruining your relationship with your cousin.'

He said nothing. Austere, self-sufficient, he looked out to sea, the stark lines of his profile set in iron.

Maddened by her total lack of influence over him, by her

helplessness, Jacinta went on, 'I don't understand why he told such lies. Especially as he must know that sooner or later I'd find out. And if he thought that putting me into debt would make me sleep with him—well, he's a throwback to the nineteenth century.' Each word had a bitter, jagged bite to it; she took a moment to compose herself before adding curtly, 'The days are long gone when women could be blackmailed into marriage.'

Paul asked impersonally, 'What are your plans?'

'I've found a job and a place to stay, so neither you nor Gerard need to concern yourselves about me.' She couldn't hold back a savage corollary. 'I've had it up to my teeth with men trying to manipulate me.'

'I'm not trying to manipulate you,' he returned with silky quietness. 'However, I can't help worrying about you.'

'Because I've been so naïve about men?' Infuriatingly, her voice cracked halfway through the sentence. Steadying it, she went on, 'I learn quickly. I'll be all right.'

'And if you're pregnant?' he demanded.

She shook her head. 'It's not likely, is it? We used protection.'

'It has been known to fail,' he said roughly. 'In ten per cent of cases, I understand.'

Her shoulders lifted slightly. Staring ahead with eyes that saw nothing, she said, 'I'll face that if it happens.'

'We'll face it,' he said, a hard note warning her that he wouldn't give way.

'All right,' she said quickly.

She lied, of course. If she had his child he would want to look after her, but she could think of nothing more painful than to be forced to endure constant contact with him. However, she'd deal with that if and when it happened.

The conversation had exhausted her small store of composure; she said, 'I'll go back now. I'll eat in my room.'

Something predatory and coldly reckless splintered in the crystalline eyes. 'Don't hide away because of me,' he said caustically, standing aside to let her past. 'I'm going out tonight.'

How foolish to hope that he'd come back because of her!

He stayed on the beach while she walked away from him into the house, leaving her heart and her innocence behind.

They met at breakfast the next morning. Exhausted after a sleepless night, Jacinta knew that her eyes had dark rings around them, and after a keen glance from Paul wished that she used cosmetics. Good armour, she thought wretchedly. It would have been much better to stick to her guns and leave on the bus; this long-drawn-out farewell was an endurance test, as was eating. Jacinta had to force the food down a throat almost blocked by a knot of grief.

They set off through another brilliant morning, radiant with the promise of heat and humidity. After taping the envelope containing Gerard's cheque to the computer, Jacinta thanked Fran and in spite of Paul's presence asked her to say goodbye to Dean for her.

'Oh,' she said, after Fran had promised to do that, 'I've left a pile of library books beside the bed. Can you take them back?'

'Yes, of course.' Fran looked from Paul's impassive face to Jacinta's, then commanded, 'Take care now, and look after yourself. Make sure you eat your meals on time!'

Jacinta gave her a swift hug and went out to the car. In silence Paul drove towards Auckland; she looked out of the side window until her stomach began to feel queasy, and then she sat staring at the road ahead, noticing nothing.

'What's the address?' he asked halfway across the harbour bridge.

'Drop me in town and I'll get a bus.'

'With two suitcases and those boxes of books? What's the address?'

It would have been a lot easier if he'd let her go, but she hadn't really expected him to. 'Don't you have to be at your office at nine?'

'They can wait.'

It wouldn't be much out of his way because Grey Lynn was one of the inner city suburbs. When the car slid to a stop outside the run-down house Paul asked harshly, 'Is this the best you can do?'

'Students live like this,' she returned with an acid undernote to the words. 'It's quite comfortable inside.'

He got out of the car and opened the boot. Grim-faced, he lifted out her two suitcases and the boxes of books. Jacinta snatched up both suitcases and, panting but determined, carried them through the gate and deposited them at the bottom of the steps before going up the three steps onto the verandah.

She didn't need to knock. The door opened to reveal a tall, thin young man clad only in a villainous overnight shadow and a pair of shorts, who yawned and said, 'Oh, hi, Jacinta.' His gaze went past her to where Paul was bringing the boxes up the path and he straightened up. 'Leave your gear here,' he said. 'I'll bring it inside.'

'Thank you,' Jacinta said again, donning an armour forged of desperation as she swivelled to meet Paul's eyes. 'Goodbye.'

Frowning, he set the boxes down. From the car came the insistent summons of his telephone, and he said brusquely, 'I'll be in contact.'

She watched him go, then turned to the curious gaze of the man in the doorway.

'Thanks,' she said again.

'Think nothing of it, although why you should want to lose a dude like that, heaven knows,' he said, grinning. 'Get a load of that car, will you? He didn't find that in his breakfast cereal.'

From behind her, Jacinta heard the car engine start. Paul acknowledged her wave with a toot, and then the car moved quietly away from the kerb and down the narrow street.

When it was out of sight she gave the man at the door a pale smile and said, 'Nadia said it would be all right if I stayed here until I found board, but with any luck I'll be out of here by tonight.'

'Doesn't matter,' he said cheerfully. 'You can stay as long as you like.'

'And I don't want him to find out where I go.'

'Don't tell me, then,' he said promptly. 'He looks as though he'd know how to get information, that guy—not a good man to cross. But, hey, if I don't know I can't tell him, can I?'

'And don't tell him where Nadia is, either.' It was unlikely, but if Paul really wanted to find out where she was he'd turn on the charm and Nadia, notoriously susceptible, would tell him everything.

He shrugged. 'Don't know that, either. Yesterday when I rang for you she was talking about going to Sydney to work.'

He helped her take the cases and boxes inside and stack them in the hallway. She'd done her best to cover her tracks, because it was just Paul's sense of responsibility that would make him want her address.

And she had no intention of telling Carl, he of the shorts and unshaven chin, where she was going. She didn't know herself yet.

'Can I use your phone? And have you got a bus timetable?' she asked.

At four-thirty that afternoon she was unpacking in a room on the other side of town. Of the same vintage as Nadia's, the house was charming and sunny, surrounded by a somewhat overgrown cottage garden in which the white trumpet flowers of a datura hung dramatically against a hedge, their heavy scent almost banishing the persistent petrol fumes.

A cheerful woman about her own age owned the place. 'There's another woman living here—it's a flat situation, although you're both helping me pay the mortgage,' she'd said, when they'd met in her lunch hour. 'Shall we say a month to see if we all get on well?'

'Sounds fine to me,' Jacinta had agreed.

She sat down on the single bed. It would help, she thought wearily, if she could cry, but although she was locked into an aching, desolate grief, no tears came.

Just as well, because the next day she had to find a job.

*   *   *

It took her a week, but by the end of it she was behind the counter in a bookshop, a small, busy affair in the next suburb which sold mostly paperbacks. Although she was on a month's trial, at least it removed her immediate financial worry. At the end of the first day she rested her aching feet and legs in her room and made a list of goals.

She would work two hours a day on the manuscript, because now that was the only promise she could keep to her mother. Writing by hand was going to be slow, but she'd get there.

She would not think of Paul more than five times a day.

This one she couldn't keep, but she became adept at turning her mind away from him.

She would think seriously about her future—a future empty of Paul.

That became less frightening when she realised that she enjoyed working in the bookshop, and that she had a talent for helping people find what they wanted to read. Although the money wasn't too good she managed to survive on it, and when, just before Christmas, the owner of the store asked her if she'd like to work there permanently she was delighted.

So now she had two goals. She'd finish the manuscript and one day she'd own her own bookshop.

Three goals. One day she'd say the word 'Paul' and feel no more than a mildly regretful reminiscence.

It surprised her that her grief was so different from that she'd endured after her mother's death, which had been tempered by relief that Cynthia no longer suffered. This was bone-deep and bitter, with the added edge of physical loss. During the hot nights she'd dream of Paul, then wake, eager and expectant, her body singing with anticipation and memories.

That was bad, but what was worse was the small things she remembered—the way his mouth had quirked when she'd said something he considered funny, the gilt of his hair beneath the sun, the tanned strength of his hands, his elusive male scent, faint yet so powerful that it still clung to the recesses of her brain.

And the way he walked, lithe, unconsciously predatory, with the smooth power of perfect health and strong, masculine grace.

This must have been how her mother felt. But Jacinta was not to have a permanent reminder of the man she loved; there would be no baby. It was a profound relief, yet the arrival of her period added another layer to the burden of her days.

Striving to deal with the memories, she got on with her life. As the summer days heated and the humidity intensified she discovered that she had passed all of her examinations, so was now able to put the letters BA after her name. With the knowledge came a sense of closure, of finality.

Christmas was every bit as agonising as she'd imagined it would be. Both of her flatmates invited her to spend the day itself with them and their families, but for some reason—masochism, she decided—she wanted to be alone. So she stayed in the house and wrote.

Afterwards she thought, Nothing is ever going to be as bad as that again. Next year will be better.

One weekend at the beginning of a hot and sticky January she opened the door to an insistent ring. Oddly enough she wasn't surprised when her eyes met hard, bright blue ones. Deep inside she'd known that Paul would find her.

She was alone, so she said, 'Come on in,' and fell back as he came through the door like a force of nature, silently, his bearing proclaiming an implacable purposefulness that should have intimidated her.

Instead she felt rejuvenated.

'How are you?' she asked, leading him into the sitting room.

'Do you care?'

Taking a deep breath, she steadied her voice and lifted her chin. 'Of course I care.'

'So much so that you deliberately lied to me. And don't

tell me you didn't say a word—you didn't have to. Losing me was a clever piece of work.'

The cold condemnation in his tone cut her composure to shreds, but she managed to say, 'Sit down. How did you find me?'

'I put a private detective onto you,' he told her, watching her as though even then he expected her to try and run. 'He targeted libraries. But you didn't join any library until three days ago.'

Because she'd been reading her way through the stock in the shop. The owner felt it was important she know what her customers were buying.

'It seems an awful lot of trouble,' she said carefully.

'I went to see Gerard,' he astounded her by saying, his hooded gaze fixed onto her face.

'Why? No, don't tell me. I don't want to hear anything about it.'

'Tough,' he said. 'Sit down.'

She defied him a moment with jutted chin, then sank into a chair. His eyes were polished brighter than lapis lazuli—completely opaque—and she could see he wasn't going until she'd heard him out.

Before he could say anything she said, 'I'm not in love with him. I've never been in love with him; it's utterly incredible that he claimed to be in love with me.' Her voice was level and emotionless; her heart was shattering.

'Oh, he wanted you,' Paul said between his teeth.

'I feel now as though he was stalking me.'

'I don't blame you.' He frowned, and she knew that the interview with Gerard hadn't been easy for him, or pleasant.

After a moment he said evenly, 'He was afraid to try his luck.'

'I don't understand,' she said, fighting the feeling of helplessness that still assailed her when she thought of Gerard's stealthy pursuit. 'Why didn't he come out into the open?'

'It's no excuse, but he lacks confidence. His mother is one of those people who are experts at snide put-downs. His father didn't even bother to be snide. He wanted a big,

strong, athletic son who'd make the All Blacks and follow
him into the family business. Instead Gerard became an academic. I suspect he found the idea of actually opening himself up to rejection terrifying.'

'Even so,' Jacinta said stonily, 'he must have known that
what he was doing was—'

'Sinister? He doesn't see it that way. He wanted to help
you but he knew you'd never take money from him, so he
did what he could for you.' He paused, then said, 'He said
you were desperate to get away from the flat you were living
in.'

'I—' Jacinta drew in a deep breath. 'Yes,' she said, looking down at her hands. 'Yes, I was. But I had organised a
place to go to—the house in Grey Lynn where you dropped
me off. I knew I'd be able to doss down with Nadia for as
long as it took me to find somewhere else to stay. Unfortunately she was away on a field trip, and I had to wait a
week before she came back.'

'Did he—the man you were living with—beat you?' He
spoke with a chilling lack of emotion that pulled the hairs
on the back of her neck upright.

'No! Not so long ago I read a book about psychological
abusers, and Mark fits all the signs. I met him just after my
mother died, when I was moving out of the house we rented;
he was staying with the family who owned it. He was Mrs
Atkinson's nephew; anyway, I suppose I trusted him because they could vouch for him. He was very kind and sympathetic, and I was—'

'Vulnerable.'

She closed her eyes for a second. 'Oh, yes, very vulnerable,' she admitted. 'And swept away. He organised the flat
for me—until I moved in I didn't know that he lived there
too. I wasn't able to even conceive of any sort of romantic
relationship then. I was just too tired.'

'So you weren't lovers?' He spoke austerely.

'No.' She frowned, trying to recall those miserable
months. 'I thought he was wonderful because he could make
me laugh,' she said at length. 'But when I moved in he

changed. At first I didn't see it; he did everything for me—ran errands, made it so that I had no responsibilities, took me to the campus and picked me up—cosseted me in every way. I couldn't work out why, instead of wallowing in it after all those years when I'd had to be strong, I was so—so uneasy. And he manipulated me by putting on a sad face if I did anything he didn't want so that I felt I was hurting him. He didn't exactly sulk—although that's what it was, really. It all came to a head when I went to a party with Nadia—'

She stopped and he said curtly, 'Go on.'

'Mark didn't want me to go, and when I did he made me feel that I'd done something terrible—wounded him to the quick. After that I noticed that he resented anything I did that he hadn't organised. And then I found out that he'd been reading my mail and monitoring my phone calls, deciding who should talk to me and who shouldn't. That was when I realised I had to get out.'

'And Gerard offered you board.' He spoke without expression.

'I wasn't going to jump from the frying pan into the fire, so I turned him down. Then he mentioned the flat.' Jacinta sent him a swift glance, then let her gaze fall. 'The night before Gerard found me asleep in the library I'd told Mark I was leaving. He horrified me and astounded me by insisting that I couldn't go, that he was in love with me and he was nothing without me. I—I didn't know what to say. He kept me up all night pleading with me. That was why I was exhausted. But I didn't tell Gerard anything about Mark,' she finished. 'I was ashamed that I'd let myself get into such a situation.'

'He knew, nevertheless.'

'Apparently.' Her hands lay tense in her lap, still dusted with gold by Waitapu sun. She said slowly, 'But nothing gave Gerard the right to think that he had—bought me. Why did he tell you we were engaged?'

A thin wash of colour appeared over Paul's angular cheekbones. 'He's always been envious of me. In spite of my break-up with Aura he pretends to believe that I have no difficulty with women,' he said unsparingly.

Jacinta narrowed her eyes. 'Possibly,' she said dulcetly, 'because you don't.'

'That's ridiculous, and you, of all women, should know it. Gerard understands how important loyalty is to me, so he was reasonably sure I wouldn't try to seduce the woman he was engaged to. And whether he believed it or not—I think he did—he told me you were looking for security. I assumed you were using him, which is why I was so rude to you when you arrived.'

She said bleakly, 'You were distant, but not rude.'

'I wanted you the minute I saw you in Fiji,' he said with a savage smile. 'And when I danced with you I thought you weren't indifferent to me. But I could see that the last thing you needed was any emotional involvement—you were wrapped up with your mother. I wanted to help you both, but you and Cynthia were so linked that in some odd way I felt I'd be intruding. However, I had your address. I rang about six weeks after you'd come back, and the wife of the man who owned the house you rented told me that your mother had died and you'd moved into a flat with a man in Auckland.'

Astonished, Jacinta stared at him. His mouth shaped a cynical smile. 'So I wrote you off as just another woman who preferred another man. And then you turned up as Gerard's fiancée. I could have broken his neck when he told me your name.'

Jacinta said shakily, 'I don't believe this.'

'Why? You must know the effect you have on men.'

Stunned, she shook her head, and he said, 'When I reminded you that Dean was engaged, I wasn't thinking of Brenda. It was far more primitive than that. I was eaten up with jealousy. I had no reason to disbelieve Gerard, and to me it seemed that you were flirting with Dean, with Harry Moore, even with Laurence.'

She stared at him. 'I was being friendly,' she retorted scathingly.

A mocking smile—humourless, hard—twisted his mouth. 'And I wasn't being reasonable,' he said, his amusement directed at himself. 'I thought—Damn it, she flirts with everyone else, why not with me? You let Dean touch you— you laughed when he tickled your foot—but every time I laid a finger on you you leapt away as though I was poison.'

In a quiet, uneven voice Jacinta said, 'I was afraid. Of myself. Of the way I felt.'

'So,' he said grimly, 'was I. I realised very early after you came to Waitapu that I was in too deep; the only honourable thing to do was to pull away, and I tried. I travelled—God, I left the country every chance I could—but I couldn't stay away from Waitapu. And that first physical attraction was supported and strengthened when I found that you were intelligent and funny and easy to talk to, that I liked just being with you, that I longed for the end of the day when I could come home and talk to you.'

Jacinta's hands tightened into knots in her lap. His voice was steady, almost thoughtful, but although she understood the words and sentences, she couldn't believe them.

'And then,' he said, rawness roughening his tone, 'I made love to you, and it was the most wonderful thing that has ever happened to me. Were you a virgin, Jacinta?'

Her knuckles ached as her grip tightened. 'Yes,' she said almost inaudibly.

He made a smothered sound and she looked up, to see the strong features compressed in what looked suspiciously like pain. 'I didn't know,' he said, mastering his expression so swiftly she thought she must be mistaken. 'Afterwards I realised that you were so surprised—so—so innocent—and I wondered. But you ran away and I couldn't find you. Do you know what you did to me?'

She refused to meet his eyes. 'I had to go.'

'Because I drove you away? Because I didn't believe you when you told me Gerard had lied?'

'Partly.' Her throat was dry and parched, as though she'd been without water for days.

Paul walked across to the window and looked out at the

roses on the edge of the terrace. The sun streamed in, gilding his profile. Blinking as she stole a swift glance, Jacinta's heart tightened within her chest. He looked tired, she thought anxiously, that dynamic power dimmed.

'When I turned up at Gerard's temporary lodgings in Massachusetts the week after you left—and the gods must be laughing at this—he was not particularly glad to see me. I'd arrived at an awkward time.'

Jacinta shivered.

'He was in bed with a woman,' Paul finished, swinging to look at her, sitting there with the merciless light of the sun illuminating her every feature.

She said in a bewildered voice, 'Who?'

'An American. When she'd gone he admitted—very reluctantly—that he'd lied when he'd claimed to be engaged to you. He thought he was in love with you, and he was certain that if I thought so too I'd keep well away from you. He was wrong on both counts. Apparently he's really fallen in love this time, and he wants to marry her.'

Explosively, Jacinta said, 'I'll *kill* him—does he have any idea of what he did?'

Just caused weeks of misery and pain!

Grimly, Paul said, 'If he didn't before, he does now, believe me. I was not tactful.' He came and sat down beside her, taking her cold hands in his warm clasp. 'Jacinta,' he said, his voice deep and caressing, his eyes bluer than the sky at midday, 'come back to Waitapu with me. I've missed you so much that I can't even eat without remembering you. You took all the colour from my life when you fled. Bring it back.'

He meant it, she could tell, and he was totally confident that she would come.

'I can't,' she said quietly.

His head came up. For a terrifying moment she saw the Viking in his eyes, determined, possessive, ruthless. With lips that barely moved, in a voice so silkily soft she had to strain to hear it, he asked, 'Why?'

'I can't live with you when you're still in love with another woman.'

Sheer male satisfaction gleamed in his eyes. 'So you do love me,' he said, his smile tight and feral.

Wrenching her hands free, she folded them again in her lap and said in a dead voice, 'Yes, I love you. I wouldn't have slept with you if I hadn't loved you. But it's no use. You might not think you're still in love with Aura, but since she left you no woman's ever got close to you.'

'You have,' he said curtly, his eyes watchful, almost calculating.

Colour fired her skin. Almost she wavered, but a gritty, uncompromising stubbornness urged her on. 'Am I the first woman you've made love to since she left you?'

His brows drew together. 'No. I am not, however, still in love with Aura.'

She wanted to believe him so much that the wanting ate into her heart. Her determination almost wavered, almost let her take the easy path. But she couldn't rid herself of the memory of his face when he'd seen the woman he'd once been engaged to on that scrap of video film.

Whatever emotions he still felt for Aura had not been resolved. Jacinta had lived, she thought with sudden blinding clarity, a second-hand life. Instead of striking out on her own she'd fulfilled her mother's thwarted ambitions, and although she didn't regret that, she was not going to take second-best for love. She wanted Paul intensely, but she wanted all of him, not the hand-me-down love he offered.

If she surrendered to her own driving needs without that commitment from him, her love would eventually degenerate into an angry passion diluted by resentful yearning.

The stark moment of insight gave her the strength to continue. 'Do you ever talk to her when you see her at parties and social occasions?'

'No.'

She thought that was going to be his sole answer, but he got up and walked across the room, his shoulders set, his spine straight as a steel rod. At the window he swung around and looked at her. His voice was cool, detached, glacial. 'I haven't spoken to either of them since the day Aura told me she wasn't marrying me.'

Jacinta waited. He remained silent, so eventually she said huskily, 'Her husband was your best friend, yet you haven't said a word to him for five years. Even if you aren't in love with her—and I think you are—she still controls your life.'

'What the hell do you mean by that?' he asked, each word falling distinctly into the still air.

She wouldn't retreat. 'Would you be happy if she walked into this room right now?'

As the rigidity of his expression gave her the answer a hope—so fragile she hadn't been aware of its existence—died.

To have heaven offered to her and be forced to turn it down...

Stiffly he said, 'No.'

At least he didn't try to explain or excuse his response. 'Paul, it won't work.'

Fury glittered, dangerous as lightning, in the blue of his eyes. 'What do you want?' he demanded. 'I love you, but I'm not going to—'

She had to interrupt before he broke her heart. 'It won't work,' she repeated, unable to think of anything else to say. 'I'm sorry.'

He didn't beg, but then she didn't expect him to. 'In that case,' he said with dangerous calmness, 'there's nothing I can do.'

Jacinta sat still, her urgent heart shouting, Give in, give in.

With a cold-blooded calculation, Paul said, 'I assume you're not pregnant.'

'I'm not.'

'Good. And you don't need to run away from me; I won't be bothering you again.'

Surprisingly enough, she coped.

Work helped. She lost more weight, but she forced herself

to make friends, to go out, to ignore the ravening physical hunger that tore at her, and the even more insidious need to hold Paul close, to hear his voice, to see him.

But she never managed to banish him entirely from her mind, and several times she almost gave up and went back to Waitapu to see if he still wanted her. Each time an instinct stronger than need warned her that she wasn't able to compromise so drastically. For her, it seemed, it had to be all or nothing.

Summer dragged wearily on; she still enjoyed the shop, liked the two women she shared the house with, stoically endured the slow process of making some sort of life for herself. As autumn swept in, with mellow days and cooler nights and a blessed reduction of humidity, she finished her manuscript and began to doggedly edit and rewrite.

Once she saw an article in the newspaper raving over the introduction of a new wine; it was not normally something that would have interested her, but the name 'Aura' sprang out and snared her attention. Angry with herself for wilfully adding to her pain, she read about the superb red which was already a classic, grown some forty miles north of Auckland. It had been released with an enormous amount of fanfare—orchestrated by the vintner's wife, Aura Jansen. The wine writer was obviously in love with the woman as well as the wine.

'Join the gang,' Jacinta said viciously.

There was a photograph. Even in the newspaper shot the woman's beauty shone forth, warm and ripe and—loved, Jacinta thought as her gaze went from Aura Jansen to the man beside her.

She sucked in a deep breath. This fiercely dominating man had been Paul's best friend. Not handsome, no, far from it, yet Flint Jansen's starkly hewn buccaneer's face drew the eye.

As she threw the newspaper out she thought that it said a lot about Paul's personality. He looked a golden man, one of fortune's darlings, yet beneath that handsome exterior was a wild streak, buttressed by force of personality and a formidable will that could break bones.

And hearts, she thought.

Oh, it would be so easy to take what he offered.

And her will was every bit as strong as his, because she couldn't do it, couldn't surrender herself and her life to a man who valued her only as second-best.

A couple of days later a sudden foretaste of winter whipped a cold southerly wind through the city, accompanied by swift showers that brought with them the acrid scent of long-dry roads and pavements. As it was Jacinta's turn to buy the groceries, she was carrying two large bags from the bus when she tripped in a puddle and skidded onto her knee, dropping one bag.

Muttering maledictions, she dragged herself up and stumbled on her way. With the malice of fate the plastic bag, weakened by its collision with the wet pavement, waited until she was halfway up the front steps before it burst.

Furious, she raced up and dumped what she'd been able to save by the door, then set off to pick up the cauliflower that had bounced all the way down. It didn't surprise her in the least when she slipped on the last step and landed in a puddle put there expressly for that purpose.

The cauliflower was there before her, lying in the muddy water with its florets buried. She'd probably have to disinfect it before it was fit to eat.

'Oh, hell!' Jacinta spluttered.

Two hard hands grabbed her shoulders and with a swift, smooth movement hauled her upright. Confounded, she stared into eyes the clear, fierce blue of a summer sky.

And realised just how much she'd been lying to herself since she'd last seen him. To her horror and astonishment, she began to cry.

'You've hurt yourself,' Paul said harshly. 'Where? Your ankle? Your knee? Jacinta, stop that and tell me where it hurts!'

'I'm not hurt,' she sobbed. 'Not physically, damn you! How dare you come here and—'

'We have to talk. Do you want me to carry you up the steps?'

'No!' She pushed him away.

Instantly she felt bereft, her addiction fed and intensified by the few moments spent hugged against his hard body. She turned, but remembered the cauliflower and stooped to retrieve it. With jangling nerves and an odd emptiness in her stomach, she led the way into the house, walking straight past the rest of the groceries.

Paul scooped them up, and followed her down the chilly hall and into the kitchen. As soon as he'd dumped the bags onto the bench he turned and surveyed her.

'Good,' he said, 'I'm not the only one who's suffered. Will you come back with me to Waitapu?'

Tears ached in her throat and behind her eyes. Swallowing, she shook her head.

His smile was sharp and brutal as a bayonet. 'Yet you love me.'

It was useless trying to deny it. She nodded and went to put the cauliflower, still dripping with water from the puddle and probably inedible, into the sink.

'I went to see Aura and Flint,' Paul said casually.

The vegetable fell from her nerveless fingers and thudded onto stainless steel. Jacinta stared at it without seeing it, her whole attention on the man who stood behind her. 'Why?' she asked in a thin voice.

'Because I decided you could be right.'

God, she was an idiot. 'I know I am,' she muttered.

'In one thing only,' he amended swiftly. 'I proved that I'm certainly no longer in love with Aura, but you were right in that I needed to see her.'

Hope blew faintly on Jacinta's dreams, warming the embers. Jumpy, her pulses racing, she turned and began to pick up the groceries from the faded bench that had been someone's idea of high kitchen fashion in the seventies and stack them into the pantry.

'Leave those alone, for heaven's sake.'

A voice from the door enquired, 'Jacinta, is everything all right?'

'Yes, no problems,' Jacinta said swiftly.

'Oh. OK.' The owner of the house retreated down the hall.

Paul said curtly, 'I have to see you alone. Come for a drive with me.'

She couldn't think, could barely breathe—so completely focused on the man behind her that she sensed his movements and stiffened even before his hand fastened onto her arm and he swung her to face him.

'You look like a ghost,' he said, his voice deepening into concern.

Ignoring her resistance, he pulled her into his arms, surrounding her with warmth and strength and the wonderful male scent of him.

'Darling,' he muttered, a note she'd never heard before in his voice. 'What have I done to you? How can I convince you that I love you more than I ever loved Aura, who has turned out to be a very nice woman—'

It was that last comment that fanned the embers of hope into a small flame. Startled, she lifted her face and asked incredulously, 'A nice woman?'

His eyes were blue and fierce, lit by a tiny glint of humour. 'Yes,' he said seriously, his mouth ironic. 'A very nice woman. Oh, marriage and happiness has made her even more beautiful, but that sultry glamour that ensnared me before no longer has any power over me. I looked at her, and although I enjoyed her beauty I felt nothing but interest and a wry sort of friendship. You were right. I'd managed to convince myself that I'd buried my heart along with our engagement. Oh, not consciously, and in a way I'm glad it happened—'

'Why?' she repeated, back on the roller-coaster again.

'Because I might have given in earlier to my desire for a settled family life and children, and got married.'

Her heart lurched. He was looking at her with naked intensity, the good humour and confidence stripped from him to reveal the man beneath, a man consumed by his emotions.

At that moment she believed. 'Then I'm glad too,' she whispered, losing herself in the vivid clarity of his gaze. He bent his head, but from down the hallway came the sound of more footsteps. Paul said something curt and crisp beneath his breath and let Jacinta go.

'Let's go,' he said grimly. 'We can't talk here.'

Jacinta nodded, and went with him. The showers had stopped coming, and to the west the sky was a clear, sparkling blue beneath an arch of cloud. Jacinta looked at the neighbour's dahlias, glowing in colours so hot they almost hurt the eyes, set bravely against the dark hedge.

Once in the car Paul said, 'We can go back to my flat.'

For some reason she didn't want to. She said, 'No, let's go up One Tree Hill.'

He gave her an ironic glance, but drove there, winding up the side of the small extinct volcano until they reached the car park at the summit. Neither said anything on the way, nor did they speak until Paul had switched off the ignition and they'd both gazed for a short time at the panorama below, city and seascape, small volcanic domes and parks. Up on the grassy hill, they were separated from the everyday bustle and hurry.

Paul said, 'I began to fall in love with you the first time I saw you at Waitapu.'

'You despised me,' she said indignantly.

'Not as much as I despised myself for wanting the woman who was using Gerard.'

She flinched, and he said swiftly, 'I couldn't keep on believing that.'

'But you accused me of it after we'd spent the night together.'

Paul turned his head to look at her. She glowered back. His handsome face was taut, his eyes very bright and piercing as they held hers.

'I was running away,' he said, choosing his words carefully, 'behaving like a coward. By then I couldn't believe

Gerard, but I knew that whatever I felt for you wasn't something I could control. Right from the start I was in a fight I couldn't win; half of me was trying to convince myself that you were just looking for security, the other, clearer-eyed, half insisted that the honesty I saw in your eyes was the truth. But that I was falling in love—so much that I no longer cared whether you were engaged to him—no, I wouldn't face that.'

Jacinta thought she understood. 'And that's why you fought it, because you hated losing control. I suppose that's how you felt with Aura.'

He shook his head. 'No, that's what frightened me,' he admitted. 'I thought I loved her, yet there was simply no comparison. I couldn't analyse the emotions you caused— they were too bloody fresh and painful and overwhelming, and they scared the hell out of me.'

She blinked. 'I kept telling myself that attraction wasn't the same as falling in love,' she confessed shakily. 'I didn't believe in love at first sight, therefore it had to be sex.'

'Idiots, both of us. I knew I had no right to make love to you; I'd done to Gerard exactly what Aura did to me.' He smiled without humour, self-condemning. 'My cowardice and refusal to accept that I'd actually fallen in love with you persuaded me to drive you away. But I had no intention of losing sight of you.'

She looked out across the harbour. A small plane newly escaped from the pull of gravity soared into the east and headed away. 'I know,' she said.

'I learned,' he said in a clipped, tight voice, 'that the small amount of honour I'd salvaged was no recompense for the agony of not knowing where you were, of sleeping each night in an empty bed that seemed scented by your body. So I set my bloodhound on your track, and went to see Gerard. And when I found you again, you turned me down.'

'I love you too much to be second-best,' she said quietly. 'But, oh, it was the most enormous temptation, and I don't know how long I'd have held out.'

'Good,' he said with a satisfaction that swung perilously

close to arrogance. 'And you were right, of course. I needed to see Aura again.'

Jacinta understood. She said, 'And now you're sure.'

'Not about you. I need to know,' he said, his voice thickened and uneven, 'whether you'll marry me.' His smile twisted. 'My life isn't worth much without you. I go through the motions but I don't seem to be actually alive. When you left me, Jacinta, you took the sun with you.'

And then the smile vanished, to be replaced by a hard line. 'Oh, what the hell?' he said unsteadily. 'I can't even fool myself any longer. I need you so intensely, so passionately, that I have no defences. That's what infuriated me and scared me when I saw you in Fiji. I'd been burnt once—I had no intention of letting myself fall in thraldom to another *belle dame sans merci.*'

'Is that what Aura is? A beautiful, merciless woman?'

'No,' he said on a harsh breath. 'And neither are you. It was a shoddy little piece of self-deception on my part. Jacinta—'

With troubled eyes she interrupted. 'What about the woman who was in Fiji with you?'

'She's a good friend who needed time off to get over a situation she'd found herself in. We weren't lovers.'

Jacinta believed him, but she had to probe further. 'Gerard pointed out a woman in Ponsonby one day—'

'We broke up after I came back from that trip,' he said, his gaze holding hers. 'We'd been lovers for over a year, but I was never in love with her, nor she with me. After Fiji I knew it had come to an end. I hated leaving you there—I wanted to snatch you up and somehow make everything right for you, but I couldn't.'

'Nobody could,' she said soberly. 'We had to get through it together, Mum and I. In the end she died a lot sooner than we thought she would.'

'I didn't see the death notice. I was going to write.'

'I only put it in the local paper.'

He gave a short, unamused laugh. 'And then you turned up as Gerard's fiancée, and from that first night at Waitapu

I knew just how much trouble I was in. You said you'd never tasted champagne, and I wanted to be the one who introduced you to all the things you'd never known.'

Jacinta said, 'You hid it very well!'

His smile was sardonic and self-derisory. 'Did I? I thought I was very easy to read. What really got me worried was that for days at a time it was perilously easy to forget all about Gerard.'

'But sometimes you remembered,' she said softly, recalling the times when he'd 'gone away', changing from the Paul she'd been falling in love with to a distant, grimmer man.

'Then I'd look at you and think, She's nothing like Aura.' His mouth hardened into a straight line. 'In fact, that's one of the reasons I first fell in love with you. You are her exact opposite.'

It hurt, but she couldn't let him see that. As the beautiful face of the woman he'd loved and lost flashed into her mind she said, 'Very much so.'

He laughed, a cynical sound with no humour. 'Don't put yourself down, Jacinta. On the night of the party I realised that you had the same passionate allure as Aura, and I thought, I've done it again.'

'I'm not—'

'You looked just like that picture Laurence Perry said you reminded him of—Leighton's *Flaming June*. When I saw the print I understood exactly what he saw—a luscious, totally, splendidly over-the-top woman reeking with lazy, seductive sensuousness. I wanted to drag you off to bed away from everyone else—and I despised myself for wanting you so much.'

'Paul, I know those colours look good on me, but—'

'Every man at that party was slavering at the jaws,' he said. Blue fire heated his eyes. 'Although I'm possessive I can control it, but that night I was eaten up with jealousy and desire and disgusted anger with myself.'

'So that's why you were so cold.'

'Yes.'

'Did you make love to Meriam Anderson?' she demanded fiercely.

He lifted his head. 'No. I didn't want to, and even if I had, I don't use women to appease a meaningless hunger.'

Jacinta was ashamed, but she said, 'She gave the impression that you were together, and you did nothing to change it.'

'I was running scared. I wanted you out of my life and as far away from me as possible, but I knew I couldn't throw you out because I'd promised bloody Gerard.' His voice hardened. 'I didn't know what to do, so I used Meriam in that way.'

She laughed softly. 'I thought you were so rational, so level-headed.'

'I used to think so too, but cowardice makes fools of us all. I didn't want to make love to you—I knew it would only complicate things—but when you touched me that night nothing could have stopped me. I'd starved for you, become obsessed with you, and at that moment I'd have killed to get you into my bed.'

Chills ran down her spine, pulled her skin taut. 'I know,' she said slowly. 'I knew it was dangerous, but—I was like you.'

'Then I drove you away.' His fingers drummed a few seconds on the steering wheel, fell still. In silence they watched a huge plane swoop low over the city before landing at the airport some miles away.

Without looking at her, Paul said roughly, 'And when I found you again I thought that everything would be all right, that you'd fall into my arms and we'd be happy together. But you refused to have anything to do with me, and I walked out in a monumental temper. I had to go overseas for ten days, and when I came back I hoped you'd be at Waitapu, waiting for me. It took me quite a while to realise that you weren't going to give in. So I wangled an invitation to the launching of Flint and Aura's new wine.'

'Were they pleased to see you?' she asked.

'I think so.'

He leaned over and took her hands in his big, warm clasp, pulling them up to lie over his heart. 'We might become friends again,' he said with a calm detachment that was belied by the thundering pulse beneath her palm. 'And if we do I'll be glad, because I've missed them both. But you—I more than miss you. I ache for you at night and I get up and walk the beach, remembering the night we made love, and the way you tasted, sweet and tempting and mysterious, and the ache turns into a hard, hot hunger that drives me insane.'

'Oh, yes,' she said, and was drawn into the warm security of his arms. 'Like losing half of myself, like dying slowly by inches, like walking alone through a world of grey emptiness…'

'Never again,' he said, and the words were a vow. 'Never again, my heart, my glorious, summer girl, I swear.'

CHAPTER TEN

JACINTA MCALPINE slid into the slip dress of gold satin and surveyed herself in the mirror. Her hair, caught up into a demure knot at the back of her head, glowed in the light of the lamp.

She looked good, she thought, allowing herself a slightly immodest satisfaction. A year ago she'd never have worn a dress like this. It revealed an awful lot of skin.

But then a year ago she'd only been married for six months and she'd still found it difficult to see herself through Paul's eyes. Now she knew she looked good in the vivid, tawny sunset hues that made the most of her hair and eyes and colouring. And the happiness of being loved had given her grace at last; it was quite some time since the last time she'd tripped.

She grinned wickedly at the framed print tucked behind the door. *Flaming June*, indeed!

'Ready, darling?' Paul came through from the bedroom, stopping just inside the door. 'You look like high summer,' he said, eyes kindling.

'We both look very glamorous,' she told him, adjusting his black bow tie with a languorous finger. 'Evening clothes do something electric to your hair and eyes,' she said softly, tracing very lightly the contours of his mouth. 'And yes, I'm ready.'

He laughed deeply, catching her hand and kissing the palm before his other hand emerged from behind his back, a ribbon of fire running through his fingers. 'Not quite ready, not yet. Turn around,' he said.

The stones were gorgeous, in a modern setting of gold that enhanced their magnificent colour. Paul put the necklace around her throat and did up the clasp.

'Paul, you spoil me. They're so beautiful—thank you. What are they?' Jacinta leaned back into the warm solidity of him as she surveyed their images in the mirror. Strong and lithe and safe, she thought dreamily; he was the rock-solid base for her life, because the dynamic power and intensity, the spice of danger, were leashed firmly by his mastery of himself and his emotions.

'Padparadscha sapphires,' he said, his hands coming to rest on her shoulders. 'It's a Singhalese word meaning lotus blossom. Did you know that ''jacinth'' was the word used for the colour orange until oranges came on the scene in the Middle Ages?'

'No,' she said, shivering as he slid his hands beneath her breasts. They tingled, subtly expanding, and through the gold silk she saw the nipples bud.

'That's what your name means. It's the Spanish form of the Greek word for hyacinth.'

'Hyacinth?' She turned her head. 'Really? I've never seen an orange hyacinth. I have seen hyacinths the colour of your eyes, though.'

'Perhaps there used to be orange hyacinths in ancient Greece,' he murmured, his serene expression belying the glitter of his eyes. 'The stones suit you—they look like flames around that elegant throat.'

Because she needed to think, she pulled his hands down to her waist and held them still. 'I got a phone call from America today.'

'America?' He'd bent to kiss the pale skin of her shoulder, but now his head came up.

'Yes.' She met his eyes in the mirror, hers shimmering with gold. 'It was the editor I sent the manuscript to. Paul, they want to publish it!'

'I knew it,' he said triumphantly. 'I knew you'd get there one day. When?'

'Some months after the baby's born, I imagine,' she said sweetly.

He went very still. 'I didn't know we were pregnant,' he said eventually in a neutral voice.

'Neither did I until today. Do you mind?'

His arms tightened around her. In a voice she'd never heard him use before, he said, 'When I look at you I see everything there is—in this world and the next—for me to love. Even delighted doesn't exactly describe how I feel. Thrilled—ecstatic—no, exalted probably describes it best.'

He turned her and kissed her, gently and then with increasing ardour, so that she gasped and yielded, some dim part of her brain remembering to be grateful that she hadn't yet put on lipstick.

And then she didn't think for a long time. Eighteen months of marriage had proved entirely wrong the old adage that familiarity bred contempt. Jacinta still shivered with anticipation whenever she saw her husband, and their love-making was sweet and fiercely tender and heated, a wild, rapturous joining of bodies and souls.

'How do you feel?' he asked later, when she was stroking colour onto her slightly tender lips.

'Great. Shall we tell anyone or keep it a secret?'

He laughed. 'Darling, we'll do whatever you want to, although isn't there some female Mafia that knows exactly when a woman is pregnant?'

She put the lipstick down and gave him a saucy grin. 'Let's see if Aura realises.'

He dropped a kiss on her head. 'I love you so much,' he said, his voice steady and sure and vibrant. 'You've gathered all the sunlight in the world into yourself and surrounded me with it.'

Jacinta sighed and whispered, 'If Aura and Flint weren't celebrating their gold medal wine I'd suggest we stay home. But one day soon we'll want their help to celebrate a book, so we'd better go. Afterwards…'

Hand in hand, they went out and into their future.

Anne Weale was still at school when a women's magazine published some of her stories. At twenty-five she had her first novel accepted by Mills & Boon®. Now, with a grown-up son and still happily married to her first love, Anne divides her life between her winter home, a Spanish village ringed by mountains and vineyards, and a summer place in Guernsey, one of the many islands around the world she has used as backgrounds for her books. Visit her at:-
anne@anneweale.com

Look out for
A Spanish Honeymoon by Anne Weale
In Tender Romance™, March 2002

A Night to Remember

by
Anne Weale

CHAPTER ONE

THEY arrived at a quiet time of day, when everyone staying at the hotel was either up on the ski-slopes of the Sierra Nevada or out on a sightseeing excursion.

Sitting behind the reception desk in her neat black dress, with her long mane of light brown hair brushed smoothly back from her face and fastened with pins and a black bow attached to a comb, Cassia was reading a French novel left behind by one of the guests and given to her by their room maid who had found it in the waste-paper basket.

The book was propped on the shelf beneath the counter, and as soon as Cassia heard a car drawing up to the entrance she raised her head and returned to the real world.

The car was a Mercedes sports coupé. Its driver, visible through the hotel's glass doors which would slide apart when he came near them, was a tall, dark man, casually dressed in a sweater and jeans.

She watched him walk round the front of the car to open the passenger door for a girl with long, sexy legs revealed by a very short skirt. It rode even higher up her thighs as she twisted round to reach for something on the back seat. The something proved to be a fur jacket. When she was on her feet, standing almost as tall as the man, she slung the fur round her shoulders, over the red cashmere sweater defining her voluptuous breasts.

They were a spectacular couple, whose looks suggested that they might be show business personalities. But they wouldn't be adding their names to the long list of stars and

5

directors who had stayed at Granada's most expensive hotel.

Tonight the Castillo del Sultán was fully booked. Only one suite was unoccupied, but that was reserved for the Marqués de Mondragón, who was driving down from Madrid and wasn't expected to arrive until shortly before dinner.

When he did, he would be welcomed by the manager, Señor Alvarez, and conducted upstairs with the ceremony befitting a grandee of Spain whose high rank had been conferred on an ancestor by Queen Isabella I, whose statue, on a high plinth with fountains playing round its base, was one of the most photographed monuments in the historic city of Granada.

As the newcomers entered the lobby the girl's eyes focused on the windows of the small shop, closed until four p.m., offering a selection of expensive souvenirs and gifts. She made a beeline for the enticing displays, leaving the man to approach the desk on his own.

Speaking Spanish with almost no trace of her native language, Cassia said pleasantly, 'Good afternoon, sir.'

'Good afternoon.' His voice was deeper and quieter than the opulent car and the ostentatiously glamorous girl had led her to expect.

Before she could tell him that unfortunately they were fully booked, and offer to ring up one of the other hotels for him, he said, 'My secretary booked the Mirador for us two or three weeks ago.'

His Spanish was pure *castellano*, like that of the aged professor who, to supplement his pension, had taught Cassia to speak as he did, not with the more guttural accent of the *granadinos*.

'You weren't expecting us till later,' he went on. 'But I changed my plans and left Madrid this morning.'

The Mirador was the name of the hotel's most beautiful suite. But it was seldom occupied by beautiful people. Most of those who could afford to enjoy its luxury were middle-aged, if not elderly. Cassia had assumed that the Marqués would be many years older than this man, who looked to be in his early thirties, with thick dark hair and an aura of health and vigour, not to say animal magnetism.

She was not often disconcerted. Her life, with its many upheavals and fluctuations of fortune, had made her unusually self-possessed. But something about the way he was looking down at her from the other side of the counter threw her into confusion.

However, she tried not to show it, saying politely, 'Would you sign the register, please?' and offering him a gold-nibbed fountain pen filled with black ink, one of the many small touches of style which combined to give the Castillo its reputation as one of Spain's finest hotels.

Given the opportunity to live at the level of the Castillo's guests, Cassia would have chosen to stay at a smaller and quieter establishment, once a monastery and now a State-run *parador*, inside the walls of the Alhambra. But the Parador San Francisco was always booked up for months ahead, especially as its charges were not high in relation to the exorbitant rates charged by the Castillo del Sultán.

Even though the cost of living in Spain was no longer as low as when she and her father had first come here, on what this man would be paying for his week here she could have lived well for months.

The Marqués took the pen in his long brown fingers and signed his name—or part of it—below the previous entry in the leather-bound, gold-stamped register. She knew that written in full his name would occupy two or three lines. Acquired over many generations, his family's subsidiary titles had become almost as numerous as those of Spain's best known grandee, the Duchess of Alba.

But all he wrote was one word—Mondragón. Like 'Alba', it was enough to identify him to anyone with the smallest interest in Spanish history.

As he signed Cassia pressed two bells—one to summon a baggage porter, the other to alert one of the attendants responsible for parking the guests' cars in the hotel's underground garage and bringing them to the entrance when they were needed again.

It was a measure of the efficiency with which the Castillo was run that, although it was a slack time of day, there was very little delay before both men came through the staff door behind the imposing marble staircase, their uniforms immaculate, their expressions friendly but respectful.

Although she knew it wasn't the first time that the Marqués had stayed at the hotel, Cassia was surprised when he greeted José, the senior car valet, by his name, and even shook hands with him before handing over his keys.

As she opened the gate of the area behind the reception desk Manolo, the oldest of the hall porters, returned to his desk on the opposite side of the lobby. He had worked at the hotel for years and had many tales to tell of gala occasions, scandals discreetly hushed up and outrageous behaviour by people who should have known better.

He also received a cordial greeting from the Marqués, who enquired after Manolo's wife and family but did not present the porter to his own companion, Cassia noticed. Whoever she was, she was obviously not the Marquesa. Perhaps he wasn't married yet. In which case there was no reason why he shouldn't amuse himself with whoever was willing to partner him on a temporary basis.

Although she worked in a milieu where such liaisons were commonplace, Cassia herself marched to a different drummer. She was a romantic, with high ideals and probably hopeless expectations. The man who captured *her* heart would not be one who regarded women as playthings.

She waited until the two men had finished talking before stepping forward to say, 'Unfortunately Señor Alvarez isn't here at the moment. May I show you to your suite, Excellency?'

'Thank you, but that's unnecessary, *señorita*. I've been staying here since I was so high.' The Marqués indicated the height of a small boy. As he spoke he gave Cassia's figure a brief but comprehensive appraisal.

Although she wasn't as tall as his long-stemmed girlfriend, in proportion to her own medium height her legs were equally long and slender. But, while some of the maids wore short skirts under their uniform overalls, Señor Alvarez wouldn't have approved of one of his receptionists showing her knees. It was Cassia's willingness to conform to his somewhat old-fashioned standards, as well as her fluency in several languages, which had made him promote her from her first lowly job as one of the early-morning cleaners.

Holding out his hand for the key to the suite, the Marqués glanced over his shoulder. 'Come along, Isa.'

As Isa turned from her inspection of the wares in the shop Cassia asked him, 'Shall I send up a valet and maid to unpack for you?'

'A valet, no. But Señorita Sanchez has more luggage than I have.' As she joined him he said, 'Do you want your gear unpacked for you, Isa?'

'Of course…and I shall need some clothes pressed.' She slipped her hand into his and gave him an intimate smile.

The smile he gave her had a predatory gleam, making Cassia think that it wouldn't be long before the glamorous

Isa was called upon to justify her existence in his scheme of things.

It might have been that they had only recently met, and this was his first opportunity to take her to bed. Cassia wished them joy of each other. The idea of having sex—one couldn't call it making love—with a partner for whom one had no tender feelings disgusted her. She knew lots of people did it, but that didn't make it a good or wise way to behave.

The strength of her intuition—that before Isa had had time to admire the panoramic view of Granada from the windows of the Mirador suite she would find herself gazing at the ceiling above the vast double bed—brought a slight flush to her cheeks as she handed the Marqués the key with its *taracea* tag—an example of the fine marquetry crafted in the city for centuries.

To her discomfiture, he noticed. She had read what was in his mind, and now he was reading hers. She was almost certain of it.

'I hope you enjoy your stay with us,' she said stiltedly.

Normally when she said that to guests she was sincerely hopeful that they would enjoy their time in Granada. This time the words were mechanical, and not accompanied by her usual warm smile. There was something about this couple that made her uncomfortable with them.

'Thank you, I'm sure we shall. Señorita Sanchez will let you know when she's ready for the maid.'

Confirming Cassia's hunch that between the arrival of their luggage and the arrangement of its contents the Marqués had another priority, he steered his *amiguita* towards the waiting lift.

'*Ay, ay*…what it is to be young and handsome.' As the lift was taking its passengers to the top floor, where the best suites were located, Manolo was crossing the lobby to join Cassia at the reception desk. 'Every time he comes here he has a different girl—each one more beautiful than the last.'

'But only interested in what they can get out of him,' she said caustically, turning the register round to look at the swift but easily decipherable signature 'Mondragón'.

'No, no. There you're wrong,' said Manolo. 'Maybe that will be true in thirty years' time, when he's an old rake like his grandfather. I was here when the old Marqués brought his last mistress to stay with us. A lovely little creature, she was, but May to his December. On their third day here, she killed him.'

'I'm not surprised,' said Cassia. She was about to add that she couldn't imagine anything more horrible than going to bed with an old man in his sixties when she realised it might offend Manolo, who was himself nearing retirement. 'Did she stab him or shoot him?'

Either way, it must have caused the hotel a lot of bother and expense to keep the scandal out of the newspapers and refurbish the scene of the crime.

Manolo's face crinkled into a network of laughter lines and his chest heaved with the wheezy mirth of a heavy off-duty smoker. 'She killed him with kindness, *chica*. Not a bad way to go, if you ask me…in the arms of a beautiful girl. I should be so lucky!'

His chuckles were infectious, and Cassia couldn't help smiling. Besides, he was only joking. She had met his plump, loving wife, and knew that they were deeply devoted to each other and to the progeny of their teenage marriage—five children and numerous grandchildren.

'Did you also know the Marqués's father?' she asked.

The porter shook his head. 'He never came to Granada. The family has many estates all over Spain but no property here. The *papá* of the present Marqués was thrown from a

horse soon after this one was born. He struck his head on
a rock and his brain was damaged. They say his wife had
him packed off to one of their smaller *palacios* with a couple of nurses to look after him. After that she kicked up
her heels until this young fellow was almost grown up.
Then she divorced his father and married a rich American.'

At this point a florist's messenger entered the lobby with
a lavish basket of flowers for one of the German guests.
After that answering the telephone and attending to other
duties prevented Manolo and Cassia from continuing their
conversation.

During her father's last months, at the end of every work-
shift she had hurried back to their studio apartment in the
Albaicín, the old Moorish quarter of the city, to spend all
her free time with him.

Now she was on her own she did as much overtime as
possible, partly because the apartment was full of painful
memories, and partly to earn enough money to return to
the country of which, having been born there, she was officially a citizen but where she had never lived.

Cassia's father had been English, her mother French.
Without any effort on her part she had grown up speaking
both languages and, until she was seven, absorbing both
cultures. Then her parents had split up, her mother running
away with a lover who hadn't wanted to be encumbered
with another man's child. The arrangement had suited
Cassia, who had always adored her father and had found
her mother disturbingly volatile—sometimes extravagantly
affectionate and then, without reason or warning, impatient
and even unkind.

Now, fifteen years later, she understood the wisdom of
the French adage—*Tout comprendre est tout pardonner*.
Understanding *did* bring forgiveness. In some of his moods
her father would have tried the patience of a saint. With

hindsight, it wasn't surprising that he had driven his much younger and equally mercurial wife to leave him.

The only surprising thing was that Cassia was so unlike either of them in temperament. She was forced to conclude that her own more phlegmatic and practical nature must be an inheritance from her grandparents. But if they were still alive she had no idea where they lived, so that was a conjecture which would remain unproven.

In order to add to her savings, she was still on duty in the now crowded lobby when, at nine o'clock that evening, Isa Sanchez stepped out of the lift and drew the eyes of every man there to her beautiful, lissom body, only partly concealed by a sliver of thin silk velvet, hand-painted with jewel colours.

Tonight her arresting legs were hosed to tone with the dress and her matching slippers. Her black hair, earlier hidden by a Hermès silk scarf, was now a cloud of silky curls round her exquisitely made-up face.

No wonder they're all gawping at her. Physically, she's a knock-out, thought Cassia. Whether she has any brains in that beautiful head...*quién sabe*? But, looking like that, does it matter? Except that she won't always. Beauty fades. Intelligence lasts.

The lift was full, and it wasn't until two other women had emerged that Isa's escort stepped out. He too caught and held attention, not because he was also dressed to kill, but because of his height and physique.

Nearly all the young men in Spain were taller and better built than their fathers and grandfathers, whose growth had often been stunted by the inadequate nutrition of earlier decades when Spain had been a poor country. Even now the average height of the Spanish was still below that of more prosperous parts of the European Community. Heightwise, the Marqués had more in common with the tall

Scandinavians than with his own countrymen, and few men in any country carried themselves with that proudly upright bearing.

Tonight, as it had been earlier, his style of dress was casual—designer jeans and a blazer over a dark blue shirt, the button-down collar unbuttoned at the neck. From the open collar of his shirt down to his polished black loafers he could have been an Ivy League American, a member of the French *gratin* or of almost any élite social group the world over.

From the neck up he could only be Spanish. Those fiery black eyes, the aquiline nose and haughty cheek-bones had their origins in the time when the great red-walled fortress overlooking Granada had encapsulated what had been then the world's most advanced civilisation.

The Moors, who had built the Alhambra and the ancient part of the city where Cassia lived, had eventually been driven out. But they had bequeathed to the Spanish not only some of their knowledge of science, philosophy and art, but also their exotic dark looks.

Somewhere, far back in the lineage of the tall man now crossing the lobby in the direction of the bar, there had to be a link with the Moors who had dominated Spain for hundreds of years.

Half an hour later the Marqués and Isa emerged from the bar, and she went to the ladies' cloakroom, crossing the lobby with an arrogant, hip-swinging walk copied from the catwalk strut of the supermodels.

It was early January, and although the day had been sunny and warm, at this time of year the nights were cold. The Marqués was carrying his girlfriend's fur jacket for her. Cassia recognised it as wolf fur, presumably made from the pelts of animals bred in the wild. The thought of their suffering after they had been trapped would have stopped her buying and wearing such a coat, even if she could have afforded it.

But in Spain furs were much in evidence during the winter months, when parts of the country were under snow and the wind blowing over the high sierras was often bitterly cold. Guests passing through the lobby were frequently swathed in luxurious, ankle-length mink coats.

She was waiting for Isa Sanchez to re-emerge from the cloakroom when the Marqués suddenly swung round and walked towards her.

'Still on duty, *señorita*? You work long hours. Do you live in the hotel?'

Surprised that he should take the trouble to speak to her, she shook her head. 'But I don't have far to go home, *señor*.'

Switching to English, he said, 'I think you're British, aren't you?' Before she could reply, he went on, 'It's your beautiful skin and your eyes which give the game away. Your Spanish is very nearly perfect. You can even roll your Rs to the manner born…an astonishing accomplishment for a Brit.' He smiled at her. 'If you don't mind my saying so, most of your compatriots are hopelessly bad linguists.'

'I'm afraid so,' she agreed, trying not to show her amazement, not only at his compliments but at his command of English. If her Spanish was nearly perfect, his English *was* perfect.

She had heard that in Jerez de la Frontera, the home of sherry, the children of families whose wealth derived from the wine had always had English nannies and, in times gone by, English governesses. But she couldn't believe that a nanny could have taught him the flawless and idiomatic English he spoke now. Perhaps his amorous conquests had included an English girl.

'How long have you lived in Spain?' he asked.

Isa appeared at his elbow. 'Come on, Simón...I'm hungry.'

He turned to her, holding out the jacket. As the Spanish girl put her evening bag on the counter, and turned her back in order to slip her bare arms into the satin-lined sleeves, they were both given a view of her beautiful bra-less bosom inside the low *décolletage* of the velvet dress. For the Marqués, being taller and closer to her, it must have been even more revealing than Cassia's glimpse of his *amiguita*'s ripe golden breasts.

As Isa picked up her bag she flashed a brief glance at Cassia, in which the English girl read the arrogant condescension of a glamorous playgirl with a ten-out-of-ten escort for one of the world's little people.

'Let's go!' Smiling gaily at the Marqués, the Spanish girl flashed her teeth, snapped her fingers and did a brief, sexy shimmy. 'I want to eat and dance.'

'Just as long as you remember that tomorrow, at eight, no later, we leave for the ski-slopes. If you aren't up, I'll leave you behind.'

Although the Spaniard spoke lightly, there could be no doubting that he meant it.

'Why must we start so early?' Her tone was faintly petulant.

'Because that's why we're here...to ski. Not for the discos.' Turning to Cassia, he said, 'Goodnight, *señorita*.'

Watching them walk away, she was surprised that he had remembered to wrap up their conversation with a courteous goodnight.

Then she heard Isa ask, 'What were you talking to her about?'

Whatever the Marqués replied was drowned by the conversation of a group of people descending the staircase.

* * *

Many foreigners who came to Granada were nervous of venturing into the Albaicín district unescorted. They felt safer going there with a tour group, or on a minibus excursion which would take them to selected vantage points without the risk of having their pockets picked or their bags snatched.

In fact, the modern part of Granada was no more dangerous than any big city anywhere, and the Albaicín was safe enough during the day. At night it was not advisable for lone tourists to wander there. After working late, even Cassia went home by taxi rather than on foot. As she had her main meals at the hotel, the apartment was now a place where she only slept and had breakfast.

The following morning, wrapped in a warm wool dressing-gown and wearing a pair of gaudy, plaid-patterned carpet slippers bought at the Saturday market in the Plaza Larga, she took her breakfast onto the little roof terrace from which her father John Browning had painted dozens of pictures of the Alhambra's towers and battlements silhouetted against the snowy peaks of the Sierra Nevada.

It had to be one of the world's most magical views, especially at sunrise and sunset, or on a hot summer night with a full moon riding the sky. Sometimes Cassia thought that she must be crazy to be planning to leave this beautiful place for the cloudy skies and long, cold winters of northern Europe.

But her father's lease on the apartment was running out, and the owner wouldn't renew it. Nor could she find another apartment nearby. To live amid the noise and air pollution of the modern city was not an attractive prospect. The alternative was to go to England and find out if that was where she really belonged.

After breakfast she had a quick shower. Then, wearing a Turkish bathrobe which had belonged to John Browning,

she started to make up her face. It didn't take long. Apart
from using a sunblock to shield her fine, creamy skin from
sun damage, and spending five minutes on her eyelids and
lips, she didn't go in for the sort of complicated *maquillage*
she had seen on Isa Sanchez the night before. *Her* eyes had
been works of art, and her mouth outlined, rouged and
glossed to look like the petals of some rare and exquisite
orchid.

'It's your beautiful skin and your eyes which give the
game away. Your Spanish is very nearly perfect.'

The Marqués's startling compliment echoed in Cassia's
mind as she dabbed blobs of sunblock on her forehead and
cheeks. Did her skin deserve such an accolade? Being fair,
it was finer in texture than the olive skins of most Spanish
women, but it wouldn't necessarily wear as well as their
oilier complexions. And surely grey eyes were a common
feature among all the Western nations?

She was forced to conclude that the Spanish lord's compliments carried as little weight as the term *guapa*, applied
to girl babies regardless of whether they really were pretty
infants.

She was due on duty at eight, but arrived a quarter of an
hour early. The lobby was full of people in colourful ski-
suits, some with the ski-passes called *taquillas* clipped to
their jackets or on wristbands, many with goggles round
their necks and carrying heavy ski-boots. Perhaps the
Marqués and Isa had already left for Pradollano, the complex serving the *pistas*.

Annoyed with herself, Cassia realised that the reason she
was here ahead of time was that she had hoped to catch
sight of them before they went off for the day.

She was on the telephone, taking down the name and
address of someone who wanted to book a room for the
following month, when she saw the Marqués coming down

the staircase. He was wearing a black salopette—the close-fitting, chest-high trousers held up by shoulder straps favoured by the most active skiers. He was carrying a discreet black and grey ski-jacket, and at present the upper part of his body was clad only in a bright, coral-coloured T-shirt, with a cotton scarf of the same colour knotted round his throat. His brown arms were bare to the point where the swell of powerful muscles was visible between elbow and shoulder.

Without glancing towards the reception desk he crossed the lobby to the newspaper kiosk. Moments later Isa appeared on the staircase, stifling a yawn. She was wearing a shimmery pale yellow all-in-one ski-suit with a deeper yellow peaked cap, and yellow hoops in her ears.

The Marqués came away from the kiosk with several women's magazines which he handed over to Isa, presumably for her to read on the drive to Pradollano. Perhaps he didn't find her conversational abilities matched her talents in other directions.

Watching them leaving the hotel, Cassia suppressed a sigh. She had always longed to try skiing. But, even though they lived within an hour's bus ride of the slopes, the cost of hiring the necessary equipment had been beyond their means. Besides, her father hadn't been interested and would never have allowed her to try the sport on her own.

In the middle of the afternoon the switchboard operator rang through to Reception.

'Cassia, the Marqués de Mondragón is on the line. He's asking for Señor Alvarez, but I know he's having a family party for his wife's birthday today. I don't want to disturb them unless it's essential. Can I put him through to you?'

'Of course.' As she waited to be connected Cassia was

aware of an involuntary quiver of excitement. 'You have a problem, Excellency?'

'Señorita Sanchez has hurt herself,' the deep voice said in her ear. 'Nothing serious. Another novice cannoned into her on the nursery slopes. They both fell over and got their skis in a tangle. I think it's merely a sprain, but rather than taking her to the first-aid clinic up here I'd like the hotel doctor to look at her. Can you arrange for him to be there when we get back to the hotel in about forty-five minutes?'

'Certainly, *señor*. We have an excellent doctor on call. He has a lot of experience in dealing with skiing injuries.'

'Good.' Instead of ringing off, he said, 'You're the British girl I spoke to last night. What's your name?'

'Cassia Browning, *señor*.'

'Any relation to Robert Browning, the poet?'

'I shouldn't think so.'

'But you know his work?'

'Of course.'

'Unusual!' was his reply. 'Most girls of your age have only heard of pop stars.' And then he did ring off.

After she had alerted the hotel's doctor Cassia returned to the novel she had been reading when the Marqués arrived the day before. But it didn't hold her attention, which kept switching to Isa Sanchez's accident.

Such mishaps were common on the nursery slopes, before the beginners learnt control. According to Señor Alvarez, now that skiing was the sport of the masses all ski-resorts everywhere were too crowded for comfort and safety. He always advised guests at the Castillo not to go skiing on Saturdays and Sundays, when the *granadinos* were out in force. A few years ago even the king, Don Juan Carlos, himself an expert skier, had been in collision with a schoolboy learner.

The week before, a Swedish guest at the hotel had

chipped a bone in her shoulder, and had had to spend the rest of her holiday with her arm in a sling. It might be that Isa Sanchez had also been put out of action. If she had, Cassia wondered if the Marqués would change his plans and keep her company, or leave her behind while he went skiing on his own. If she was a beginner and he an experienced skier, they wouldn't have seen much of each other anyway. Most of the difficult red and black *pistas* used by the experts were a long way from the nursery slopes. Perhaps today, being the first day, he had returned to have lunch with her.

The doctor was waiting in the lobby when the sleek car with the Madrid registration glided up to the entrance, and a porter pushed a wheelchair down the ramp provided for disabled guests. When Señorita Sanchez was wheeled into the lobby, her smeared mascara showed that she had been crying. Cassia wondered if she was in great pain, or if the Marqués had been unsympathetic, even impatient with her. He didn't look as if he would have much time for weaker beings, especially if their shortcomings interfered with his enjoyment.

About fifteen minutes later the doctor returned to the lobby. Normally in Señor Alvarez's absence he would have dealt with the assistant manager. But as he was away on his honeymoon the doctor spoke to Cassia.

'The young lady has wrenched the muscles of her inner thigh. A few days' rest is the cure. I'll look in on her tomorrow.'

Presently Cassia wrote a brief report of the incident to give to the other receptionist, who today was replacing her at four. In spite of his family party, it was likely that during the evening the manager would ring up and expect to be informed of any untoward events. It was his obsessive at-

tention to every aspect of the running of the Castillo that
had put it ahead of its rivals.

Just before she went off duty she was summoned to the
housekeeper's room.

'As tomorrow's your morning off, I thought you might
like these flowers to take to the cemetery,' Señora Ortiz
said kindly, indicating the florist's basket on her desk.
'They were only delivered the day before yesterday, but the
lady they were sent to didn't want to take them with her.'

All the flowers in the public rooms were supplied and
refreshed by Granada's best florist, but those left over from
special occasions or discarded by guests were one of the
housekeeper's perks, sometimes shared with her minions.

'That's very kind of you, *señora*. They're lovely.'

'It gets dark early at this time of year. Why not take
them home and enjoy them yourself tonight? You can take
them to your father in the morning.'

The quickest way from the hotel to the Albaicín quarter
was by the wooded road passing the Alhambra. Restfully
shady in the heat of high summer, this afternoon the tall
trees cast gloomy shadows. An elderly vagrant who fre-
quented the area, muttering to himself, glowered at Cassia
as she passed him, and she felt very conscious of the abyss
separating him from the hotel guest from whom she had
inherited the flowers she was carrying.

She was halfway down the hill when she heard a whistle
of the kind meant to call attention. Turning, she was astonished to see the Marqués loping towards her.

'I thought it was you by the bow in your hair,' he said,
catching up with her. 'I'm going down to find a pharmacy.
The doctor has prescribed a gel for my friend to rub on her
sprained leg.'

'We could have sent someone to fetch it for you,' she said.

'I needed some more air and exercise. Let me carry that for you?' He took over the basket of flowers. 'You said you hadn't far to go home, but isn't there a bus you could catch? This is a dismal walk, and I just passed a drunk who gave me a mouthful of abuse.'

'He doesn't swear if you say good afternoon to him. He must be very unhappy, poor old fellow.'

'No doubt his troubles are of his own making,' the Marqués said drily.

Coming from someone born with a silver spoon in his mouth as well as exceptionally good looks, Cassia found his reply deeply irritating.

'Not necessarily. Life can be hard for the strong…for the weak, impossible,' she answered. 'You don't know what pressures have brought that man to his present state…and you obviously don't care either,' she added impulsively.

Matching his stride to her shorter steps, he looked down at her, one eyebrow raised.

Suddenly switching to English, as he had the day before, he said, 'Do you care, Miss Browning?'

'Yes, I do. I feel very sorry for people like that. It may sometimes be their own fault that they've hit bottom, but not always.'

'And what, if anything, do you do about it?'

'Not very much,' she admitted. 'But at least I don't dismiss them as garbage.'

'Is that what you think I do?'

The truthful answer was yes, but her spurt of anger had died down, and she was becoming aware that she shouldn't have let it flare up. He was accustomed to deference. He wouldn't like being criticised, not even by an equal, and much less by an inferior.

'For all I know, you may be exceedingly generous to the poor and the misfits,' she said quietly. 'How is Miss Sanchez feeling? What bad luck for her to be hurt on her first day here.'

'She would have done better to spend the days shopping,' he said. 'But she was keen to learn…or at least to have a reason to dress up in the last word in designer ski-kit. I left her in the care of an instructor and came back at lunchtime to find her a casualty. Do you ski, Miss Browning?'

'No, I don't.'

If her reply surprised him, in view of the nearness of the Sierra Nevada, he didn't query the reason for it, but repeated his question of the night before. 'How long have you lived here?'

'In Granada—four years. In Spain—since I was fifteen.'

'How long ago is that?'

'I'm twenty-two. Before we came here we lived on the seaward side of the Sierra. Then my father became ill and needed complicated hospital treatment so we moved here. Unfortunately he died. I'll be leaving Spain soon. There are many things I shall miss. Which is your favourite part of Spain?'

'It depends on my mood. Sometimes I like Madrid. Sometimes I like Galicia…even though it rains a lot there. Even Extramadura, so arid and parched in the summer, can be beautiful in the spring. I like most parts of my country…but sometimes I want to get out of it and enjoy other places. Where are you going when you leave here?'

'To England.'

'To relations?'

'No, both my parents were only children. I'm on my own now.'

'That can be an advantage. Families aren't always the

support they're supposed to be. I have no brothers or sisters, but I do have numerous more distant relations and they're mostly a pain in the…neck.'

By now they had passed the souvenir shops near the bottom of the hill and were in the Plaza Nueva, not far from a chemist's shop. Cassia showed him where it was, and would have retrieved the basket and taken her leave.

The Marqués had other ideas. Keeping a firm hold on it, he said, 'If you don't mind waiting while I buy this stuff for Isa, I'll walk you home.'

Why he should wish to do so was a puzzle she couldn't fathom. Then a wild possibility occurred, which made her heart lurch with apprehension.

CHAPTER TWO

COULD it possibly be that with Isa put out of action by her wrenched thigh muscle the Marqués had it in mind to make a pass at herself?

Cassia had read about men with insatiable sexual appetites. If Simón de Mondragón's grandfather had died because of that predilection, perhaps it was a family trait.

The chemist's shop was an old-fashioned establishment, its walls lined with mahogany lockers topped by ceramic jars painted with the names of the physics they had once contained. Having recently reopened after the afternoon closure it was crowded, mainly with elderly people who knew the chemist and his assistant and liked to have a chat while they made their purchases.

Standing at the side of the shop while the Marqués waited his turn, Cassia expected to see signs of impatience on his face. But in fact he appeared to be interested in the conversations going on at the counter. More than once the grooves down his lean cheeks deepened with amusement as he listened to forthright opinions on the government and the city fathers from people whose lives were at the opposite end of the social spectrum from his own.

Among Cassia's neighbours in the Albaicín, many of the older ones could remember the civil war in the thirties. It was probable that, being aristocrats, the Marqués's family had supported the Nationalists led by General Franco. Acts of heroism as well as many terrible atrocities had taken place on both sides. In the public cemetery near the Alhambra, where her father was buried, more than two thousand *granadinos* had been executed, most of them long forgotten. Only the brutal execution by Nationalist partisans of Granada's young but already famous poet, Federico García Lorca, was a war crime still widely remembered.

Thinking about the poet, Cassia wasn't aware that the Marqués had finished being served until he said, 'Sorry to keep you waiting so long.'

She came down to earth with a start. 'It doesn't matter.'

Outside the shop he said. 'You were looking very sad in there. Were you thinking about your father? Tell me about him.'

'He was an artist. Not a very successful one. The things he wanted to paint didn't sell. To keep us housed and fed he had to paint what would sell—picturesque views of the Alhambra and the Generalife gardens. I liked them, but he despised them and the people who bought them. It's a difficult life, being an artist. I'm glad I haven't inherited his gift. I can't draw for peanuts,' she said lightly.

'Nor can I, but I'm interested in art. I've inherited some fine paintings and I'm adding to the collection. Do you have any of the paintings your father did to please himself?'

'A few.'

'I'd like to see them, if I may.'

'They're not for sale,' said Cassia, in case he had hopes of buying the works of an undiscovered genius for bargain prices. 'I shall never part with them.'

'I'd still like to see them.'

A woman from the gypsy community in the cave-houses on Sacromonte, the hilltop above the Albaicín, approached them, offering a sprig of heather.

'To bring luck to you and your pretty young lady, *señor*,' she wheedled.

Cassia expected him to ignore her, or to wave her away with a gesture. To her surprise, he took some coins from his pocket. 'People make their own luck, *señora*,' he said, putting them into her hand and taking the already wilted sprig.

'But they aren't all born with your looks, handsome,' she quipped, with a flash of gold teeth. She turned to Cassia. 'You've picked yourself a fine fellow, *señorita*. But when they're as fine as this one they have many opportunities. Don't give him all he wants. Keep him guessing. Remember, the fruit on the tree inside the locked patio always looks more delicious than oranges growing in a roadside orchard where anyone can pick them.'

'You should be writing poetry, not selling heather,' said the Marqués. With a bow he presented her with a flower removed from the basket he was carrying.

'She'll need a strong will to resist *you*!' Laughing, the gypsy touched the rose to his cheek before going on her way.

'I hope you don't mind my giving away one of your flowers,' he said, reverting to English. 'I've always liked the gypsies. They're part of the Spain of my childhood, which is rapidly disappearing. Every year we become more like the rest of Europe. A homogenised world may have some advantages, but it isn't as colourful and interesting.'

He handed the heather to her. 'Do you believe in luck and fortune-telling and all those gypsy stock-in-trades?'

Cassia shook her head. But she did believe that gypsies were shrewd judges of characters, able to gauge at a glance a great deal about the people they accosted. Clearly the gypsy had recognised that the Marqués was a practised charmer, and also that she, Cassia, lacked the experience to handle him.

They were now at the point where the New Square merged with the old Plaza Santa Ana. A few yards further Cassia would be turning off into the labyrinth of narrow streets and steep alleys, where the churches had once been mosques and many of the little squares still had the public wells known by the Moorish name *agilbes*.

She said, in a businesslike tone, 'It's a long trudge up to my place. I doubt if you'd find my father's pictures worth the effort…and the sooner Señorita Sanchez rubs that stuff on her leg the better, don't you think?'

'In my experience of minor skiing injuries it's rest not ointment that cures them.' After giving her a thoughtful look he added, 'And I think the gypsy's warning rather than concern for Isa is your main reason for trying to put me off, Miss Browning. Let me relieve your mind. At this stage of our acquaintance I have no intention of…' he paused for a moment, his black eyes glinting with amusement '…trespassing in the locked patio.'

'I never supposed that you had,' she said untruthfully, unable to stop herself blushing under that mocking regard.

'Yes, you did. Why deny it? There's been a strong hint of disapproval in your manner since we arrived. It interests me. I should have thought in your job you'd be used to unmarried people taking holidays together. There's nothing unusual about it. But you seem to have me tabbed as an incorrigible stud who might even make a pass at you, given the smallest encouragement.'

It was disconcertingly close to what she had been thinking about him earlier.

She decided to speak her mind. 'Hotel receptionists—like air stewardesses—do get quite a lot of passes made at them. More on the Everest principle—because they are there—than because of their personal attributes. I don't flatter myself I'm the sort of girl who would normally attract your attention. But you might flatter yourself that, being a *marqués* as well as good-looking, you have only to crook your finger and…' She left the conclusion unspoken.

He laughed. 'Do I really strike you like that? An arrogant rooster who thinks he has only to crow and all the hens will…? Well, as the chickens you eat come to supermarkets via broiler houses, you won't know what hens do when the rooster puffs up his feathers and signals his virility.'

In fact, Cassia had lived in places where domestic fowls scratched the earth for things to eat, laid their eggs where they wished and abased themselves in readiness when the rooster wanted to tread them. But it wasn't an analogy she had ever expected to hear in conversation with a man who was almost a stranger.

Momentarily forgetting that she ought not to reveal staff gossip concerning the guests, she said incautiously, 'I gather Señorita Sanchez isn't the first girlfriend you've brought to the Castillo. There seems to have been quite a string of them…and your grandfather was the same.'

'But he had a wife and I don't. That makes a difference. Or do you belong to a sect which believes all sexual relationships are wrong unless their object is procreation?' he asked.

'No, I don't believe that…but nor do I believe in promiscuity,' she added. 'Anyway, how you behave is none of my business. I'm sorry if I've been impertinent, but it was you who raised the subject.'

'Actually it was the gypsy who brought it up. They're great judges of character. She recognised you as a lamb consorting with a wolf. Has your father been the only man in your life?'

It was a shrewd guess that she would have liked to contradict. In the face of his wide experience she didn't want to admit that her own was negligible. Her father had frightened men off. A jealous and suspicious husband—not without reason, as matters had turned out—he had been a possessive father. In his eyes she had never grown up. He had seen all young men as a threat to his little girl's purity.

It was only after he had been told that his illness was incurable that he had consented to her taking evening classes in secretarial skills, financed by her job as a cleaner. She had never had any real freedom until the day John Browning had died.

'My life has been rather a strange one. But I've liked it that way. What I see of other people's lives doesn't make me feel I've missed out,' she answered. 'Probably you don't have much time for reading. But for me books are better companions than people.'

Yet again he surprised her by saying, 'Up to a point I'd agree with that. But it doesn't do to spend *all* one's time in imaginary worlds, or even in worlds that were real but are now part of history. Books are only one of life's pleasures. There are many others—skiing, for example. Living so near a ski-resort, it's a pity you haven't tried it. Was that a question of expense, or wasn't your father ever well enough to ski?'

'He wasn't always an invalid, but he wasn't interested in sports. Only in art. Have you been in the Albaicín before?'

'Only once, but that was at night and by taxi. We were trying out a recommended restaurant. I come to Granada for the skiing, not for the other attractions.'

'But you have been inside the Alhambra?'

'Yes, and envied my ancestor who saw it as it was when Boabdil, the last sultan, surrendered it to Isabella and Ferdinand five hundred years ago. What the tourists see today is only a pale shadow of the way it was then.'

'But it's still a magical place, especially at night when it's floodlit. Do you know that definition of heaven as eating *pâté de foie gras* to the sound of trumpets? For me, the

summit of bliss would be having the Alhambra all to myself
for a whole day, early in May.'

Her face lit up at the thought of it. Then with a laugh
she added, 'An eventuality as unlikely as...as buying a
share in the ticket which wins the big prize in the national
lottery. But at least by living in Granada I can get into the
Alhambra for less than the tourists pay.'

Speaking of tourists reminded her that many of them
found the cobbled lanes and long flights of uneven steps in
this ancient neighbourhood a tax on their stamina. But, as
she led the way up a succession of ascents which left unfit
sightseers red-faced and breathless, the Marqués followed
at her heels with the ease of a man conditioned to strenuous
exercise.

The house where she lived had nothing about its façde
to suggest what lay behind its tall, heavy door and shuttered
windows. Unlocked by a heavy, old-fashioned key weighing half a kilo, the door gave into a dark hall with a wide
stone staircase which narrowed on the next flight and narrowed again on the third.

'Who else lives here?' asked the Marqués.

'No one at this time of year. In the summer the owner
and his family move up from their apartment in the city
centre. When the temperature down there hits thirty it's
cooler and quieter up here.'

'But as cold as a vault in January,' was his comment.

'On the staircase—yes. But I have a gas heater and I
wear woolly tights in the evening. You may find it hard to
believe, but one can survive without central heating,' she
said, glancing over her shoulder.

'You don't need to tell me that,' he said drily. 'The house
where I spent a lot of my early life was heated by *braseros*
under the tables. Our shins scorched while our backsides
froze.'

She had seen the large shallow containers he was talking about. They fetched high prices in street markets and antiques shops, being used now as decorative objects, not for their original purpose—burning charcoal. But she hadn't expected him to be familiar with their shortcomings as heaters.

'If you heat by *estufa*, how do you get the gas bottles up to this floor?' he asked.

The question was another surprise. Stoves fuelled by butane gas in heavy metal canisters were the heaters in common use among ordinary people. Lorries delivering the brightly painted canisters were a frequent sight. But why should a rich man know that handling them was a problem for women living alone and old people?

'The lorry drops them off at the top of the street and I have a trolley,' she said, unlocking the door to the studio. 'I couldn't carry a full bottle upstairs, but pulling it up isn't difficult.'

'Not for a man, or even a big, beefy woman, but you don't come into that category,' he said as she took off her coat.

His appraisal reminded Cassia that shortly after her father's death a plumber had come to the flat. He had been about the same age as the Marqués. After repairing the washing machine he had continued talking, watching her in a way which had made her increasingly nervous. She had felt seriously at risk and, although nothing had happened, had afterwards vowed that never again would she be alone with anyone she couldn't be certain was trustworthy.

Now she was in that situation again: alone, at the top of an empty house, with a man who had insisted on coming home with her for no better reason than to carry a basket of flowers which weighed less than the average bag of groceries, and to look at paintings she had told him were not for sale.

'I see you have a roof terrace…and a spectacular view,' he said, moving towards the wall of glass installed, with the owner's permission, by an earlier tenant who had also been an artist.

'Yes, the view makes the flat. If it looked out on a blank wall it wouldn't be anything special.'

Cassia opened the door to the terrace and gestured for him to precede her. Not only did the flat have the breathtaking view of the Alhambra and the snowy peaks beyond, it also had, looking down, a bird's-eye view of the many walled gardens called *cármenes* for which the Albaicín was famous.

After admiring both views her visitor turned his attention to the terrace itself. 'Were all these plants here when you moved in?'

'No, they're ours…mine—the nearest I've come to a garden.'

'You obviously have green fingers,' he said, strolling round. 'To have so many flowers out in January is quite an achievement.'

'Some of them are really weeds. This creeper with the yellow flowers wouldn't be allowed in most people's gardens, but I like it and it grows anywhere…as this does.' She touched the glossy dark leaves of the ivy growing up the wall of the house next door which, being higher up the steep street, had its top floor above where they were standing. 'It's hard to believe that as the pigeon flies we're not far from the Gran Vía, isn't it?'

The Marqués nodded. 'If I were your landlord I'd live up here all year round.'

'But where would you put your car? None of the houses in this street has a garage or even a parking space.'

'I should have to walk, as you do.' He returned to the studio and began to study the paintings arrayed on its walls.

In the final months of his life John Browning had destroyed more than half his canvases, leaving only what he considered his finest works. He had also weeded out many of the drawings and sketches in his portfolios. Another artist living in the Albaicín had offered to buy his easels and other painting equipment. They had now gone from the working end of the studio, leaving only the boards on trestles which, with the few bits of furniture, had been there when they'd arrived.

She had done what she could to make the place homely, but it must have seemed a stark and comfortless habitation to anyone accustomed to the luxurious elegance of Simón de Mondragón's various homes. She wondered what he was thinking as he moved slowly from picture to picture.

'Do you like your father's work?' he asked suddenly.

She didn't, but had never said so, and wasn't about to disclose her private reactions now. Her taste was for figurative paintings, not these wild abstracts, the strong, often clashing colours applied with a palette knife or with strokes of her father's thumb, the impression they gave being one of violence and anger.

'I'm not qualified to judge it, but, anyway, time is the only true test of an artist's worth, so I've read.'

From his glance at her Cassia saw that he knew she was being evasive, but he didn't press her for a more definite answer. Nor did he express his own reaction except to say, 'There's a lot of luck involved in an artist being successful in his lifetime. Where did you and your father live before you came to Spain?'

'Lots of places. France…Italy…Greece…Morocco. I liked Greece the best, because we lived on an island and I did a lot of swimming. In the summer Señor Alvarez lets me use the hotel pool, very early in the morning before the guests are up, but it's not like the sea.'

'Did you learn to speak Greek as well as you speak Spanish?'

'No, we didn't stay there long enough. How do you come to have such idiomatic English?'

'My mother was brought up in England. She has friends there whose children are now friends of mine. I have plenty of opportunities to keep my English updated.'

As he spoke the Spaniard's dark eyes were ranging over the rest of the room. 'You don't have a TV or a telephone?'

'We used to have a rented television. I've given it up. It was company for Father when he hadn't the energy to paint, but there wasn't much I wanted to watch. We didn't need a telephone.'

'When is your day off?'

'I don't have a regular day off now. If I need time off I can have it, but I enjoy my job and I'd rather be working than not working.'

'Don't you have any friends?'

'Only among the hotel staff. My father wasn't very sociable. Creative people often prefer their own company.'

'So they may, but their children need friends.'

'*Your* friend will be wondering where you've got to,' Cassia pointed out.

'Unlike you, Isa laps up TV. She won't notice how long I'm gone if she's watching the latest crisis in one of her favourite soaps. But I can take a hint. You'd rather I pushed off.'

Cassia didn't contradict him. It was growing dusk now, and as they left the studio the stairs and landings were almost in darkness. She switched on the lights, although there were not enough of them to illuminate the staircase properly.

The Marqués went down ahead of her, and again she was struck by the fluid grace of his movements. When they passed under one of the light bulbs, dangling from a long flex, she noticed the healthy gloss of his thick dark hair. She couldn't remember ever being more strongly aware of someone's physical attributes.

At the doorway he turned to shake hands—a normal politeness in all walks of Spanish society, but one often mocked by her father, an undemonstrative man who had never gone in for the kissing, hugging and handshaking indulged in by *granadino* families.

'Goodnight, Cassia.'

She could feel the latent strength in the fingers enclosing hers.

'Goodnight, *señor*. Thank you for carrying the flowers for me.'

'My pleasure. Until tomorrow…'

The following morning, after taking the flowers to the cemetery, Cassia was tempted to call in at the hotel on her way back. She was curious to find out if the Marqués had gone skiing or was keeping Isa company until she recovered. However, she resisted the impulse and spent the rest of her free time window-shopping.

She enjoyed looking at fashionable clothes and shoes, even if she couldn't afford them. But this morning she was more than usually aware that most of the other women doing the same thing were in pairs—mothers and daughters, or sisters, or friends, often walking with arms linked. She felt strangely lonely and restless.

When she returned to the Castillo to take over from her colleague, she found that a drama had taken place in her absence. Apparently Simón de Mondragón had waited for the doctor's second visit, soon after nine o'clock. Shortly after the doctor's departure, the Marqués had come down-stairs and asked for a maid to help Señorita Sanchez re-pack her cases. He had also arranged for a car to take her to the station in time to catch the midday train for Madrid.

'You could see she was in a raging temper when she left,' Rosita told Cassia. 'But whether she broke the mirror while the Marqués was with her or in a tantrum after he walked out on her, we can't be certain. It could be that he sent her packing *because* she threw an onyx ashtray at him, which, being fast on his feet, he dodged. Or she could have hurled it at the mirror afterwards, because she was furious at being left on her own.

'Luckily for him it's insured, or he'd have had to pay. It's a valuable antique, with its original glass. Señor Alvarez is very annoyed about it. He won't say so, of course. You know how he bends over backwards for any-one important. But he didn't mince words about Señorita Sanchez when his wife rang up. I was quite surprised at the way he described her. She'd have thrown an ashtray at him if she'd heard him.'

'She was probably spoilt as a child…and we don't know what the Marqués said to provoke her to throw it,' said Cassia. 'I wouldn't mind betting it was aimed at him, not the mirror. They were well matched, if you ask me. She was only interested in having a good time at his expense, and his only interest in her was for sex. Not very nice people, either of them.'

Yet even as she said it she knew that she was being a hypocrite. Somewhere deep down inside her a part of her envied Isa Sanchez. Both for her panache and her escort.

Since Cassia had been on her own, she had often been woken at night by noises peculiar to old buildings, which hadn't disturbed her while her father had been there. Last night, unable to get back to sleep after a loud creak had woken her, she had imagined herself in Isa's place.

But in the scenario she had visualised the Marqués had come to Granada alone, and Cassia had first set eyes on him in the *rápido*—the fast gondola from Pradollano up to Borreguiles, where chair-lifts and ski-lifts took skiers to the start of the *pistas* suited to their abilities.

In her imagination she had been skiing every weekend since their arrival in Granada. She and the Marqués had been the only two people going almost to the top of Veleta, the peak which, at 3,470 metres, was only a few metres lower than the sierra's highest pinnacle.

They had skied down the Olimpica, a long difficult *pista* eventually connecting with a very difficult stretch on the way back to Borreguiles. There the Marqués had admired her prowess, offered her a lift back to the city and, on the way, invited her to dine with him.

At what point she had fallen asleep, her conscious imaginings causing her subconscious mind to invent a long, vivid dream, Cassia wasn't sure. But she could remember very clearly how, over a candlelit dinner in his suite, the Marqués had invited her to become his mistress, and she had accepted.

The memory of how easily she had succumbed to the inducements he'd offered—a jet-set lifestyle, an unlimited dress allowance, her own car—had shocked her when she'd woken up. Of course it had been only a dream. But, if it was true that under hypnosis people could not be made to perform acts unacceptable to their conscious minds, why had her subconscious allowed her to say yes to him? At the end of the dream she had been in his arms, about to be kissed, soon to be taken to bed.

The kiss had been averted by the ringing of a telephone...actually Cassia's alarm clock. Her reaction on waking up had been disappointment that now she would never know what it would be like to feel his firm lips on hers.

Rosita took a more tolerant view of the Marqués and his *amiguita*. 'I don't see any harm in guys and girls getting together, as long as they're not doing it behind other people's backs,' she said. 'If he had a wife or she had a husband I wouldn't hold with it. But Manolo says the Marqués is still single, and I'd be surprised if Sanchez had ever trotted up the aisle and promised to spend the rest of her life having babies and washing dishes.

'You can bet she had an eye to the main chance from the day she started to sprout those spectacular bosoms. If I had her looks I wouldn't be doing this job. I'd be swanning around with a boyfriend like the Marqués…but not chucking ashtrays at him. You only live once. If you've got what it takes to catch the eye of a guy like that, you're a fool not to make the most of it.'

'You say that, but I don't think you mean it, Rosita. If the Marqués came back this evening and invited you to have dinner with him in the Mirador, you wouldn't stand up Tomás. You know you wouldn't.'

Cassia had met Rosita's boyfriend. He worked in a bank and they were planning to marry as soon as he got his next pay rise.

'Sometimes I think I ought to break it off with Tomás,' the other receptionist said worriedly. 'I was in love with him—or thought I was—at the beginning, but now…he's beginning to bore me, Cassia. All he ever talks about is sport, and he's not the world's greatest lover either.'

Lowering her voice to a confidential undertone, she said, 'He never makes me feel the way you're supposed to. He doesn't switch me on at all. He did at first, before I let him go the whole way. But now he doesn't bother with the things I used to enjoy. He only does what he likes.'

To Cassia's relief these unexpected revelations were cut short as Rosita caught sight of the time and realised she would have to run or miss her regular bus. She had only been gone a few minutes when a party of four Americans checked in. They had been to Sevilla and Córdoba, and now wished to make the most of a two-night stay in Granada.

When all the other guests who were skiing had returned from their day on the snowy shoulders of Veleta, with the exception of Simón de Mondragón, Cassia began to wonder if he might have had an accident.

According to Rosita, *he* had not looked in a temper when he'd left the hotel, but he might have been raging inwardly. When people were angry it impaired their concentration, and skiing down *pistas* which were graded 'difficult', and driving a powerful sports car on a busy mountain road, were both activities calling for care and attention.

She was on the point of speaking to the manager about him and suggesting a call to the clinic up at Borreguiles when the Marqués strode in, picking up his key from the porter's desk before turning towards the lifts. The indicators showed that one lift was travelling upwards and the other was on the top floor. Rather than pressing the button to call it to ground level, he chose to go up the stairs, taking them two at a time with a long, lithe stride which suggested that he wasn't as tired as the other skiers had looked when they'd returned.

Cassia was still on duty when, a couple of hours later, he stepped out of the lift and headed for the dining room. He had a book in his hand but she couldn't see its title. He didn't look in her direction. He had probably forgotten her existence.

Next morning she was working the early shift when he came down the stairs in his black salopette with an apricot-coloured T-shirt—another colour which complemented his tawny skin and black hair and eyebrows.

'Good morning, Cassia.'

On his way out he gave her a friendly smile. For no sensible reason, being noticed lifted her spirits.

She went off duty before he came back, and spent the evening washing her hair, doing her nails and pressing two white blouses left out to dry on the roof terrace. As she mended the start of a run in one foot of a pair of black tights she wondered if the Marqués was dining alone and would remain on his own for the rest of his time here, or if he would find a substitute for Isa Sanchez.

There were plenty of beautiful girls in Granada who would be glad to keep him company—not only the top-level call-girls, but young women of good family and more discriminating habits.

At nine o'clock the next day she was inserting tariffs on separate slips into the Castillo's stylish brochures, before replenishing the perspex stand that displayed them, when he came to the desk.

'Good morning, Cassia. How are you this morning?'

'I'm fine, thank you. And you, *señor*? Did you have a good day yesterday?'

'Very good. Better in the morning than in the afternoon, when the sun makes the snow rather slushy. If you're free this evening, will you have dinner with me?'

She couldn't believe her ears. Why should he want *her*, of all people, to dine with him? She wasn't beautiful. Her figure was nothing outstanding. She wasn't witty and amusing. She certainly wasn't available.

'You did say you could take time off when you wanted it, and I have a proposition to put to you,' he went on. 'The dining room can be noisy when the hotel is full. Let's eat in my suite, where we can talk in peace. I'll expect you at seven-thirty. There's no need to change. Come as you are.'

Before Cassia could recover her wits and her voice, someone else came to the desk. The Marqués stepped politely aside. Taking her acceptance as read, he gave her a smiling, '*Adiós*,' before turning away to give his key to Manolo.

character would be so wide of the mark that he'd think she would succumb to his blandishments. Not to give the devil his due, did she feel that he was the kind of man who would attempt to seduce—

It would have been, in a sense, quite a thing to do and some

CHAPTER THREE

FOR the rest of the morning Cassia found it an effort to keep her mind on her job and not let her thoughts wander off in futile speculation about what the Marqués might have meant by 'a proposition to put to you'.

When her lunch break came, instead of eating a hot meal in the staff room she asked the assistant chef to make her up a snack to take up the hill to the Generalife gardens.

After paying for a ticket at the gate, she walked up the cypress-lined drive leading to the open-air theatre. A young man with a rucksack beside him was sitting there, writing postcards. He looked up and smiled at her. Cassia smiled back, giving him a friendly '*Hola!*' before walking on to find a secluded seat with a closer view of the Alhambra's towers than the one she saw from her terrace.

It was a peaceful spot in which to ponder why Simón de Mondragón wanted to 'talk in peace' with her. Unwrapping her lunch—a crusty loaf slit lengthwise and filled with lettuce-heart leaves, asparagus and slices of mountain ham—she bit off a mouthful and sat thoughtfully munching.

She knew what Rosita would say if asked to give an opinion on the motive for his behest. She could hear her colleague's response as clearly as if she *had* consulted her. 'There's only one sort of proposition a man like the Marqués makes to girls like us,' Rosita would have answered, with a cynical shrug.

But Rosita, with her full breasts and merry dark eyes, was far more propositionable than Cassia felt herself to be.

She couldn't believe that the Marqués's reading of her

character would be so wide of the mark that he'd think she would succumb to his blandishments. Nor, to give the devil his due, did she feel that he was the kind of man who would attempt to seduce an inexperienced girl.

It would have been such a mean thing to do, and somehow she didn't want him to turn out to be an ignoble nobleman. There were many worse vices than being a womaniser, provided that he only made love to women who knew the rules and that no one else was hurt.

But supposing he was less scrupulous? Supposing he *did* make a pass? What was the best way to handle it?

'Do you speak any English?'

In the act of pouring herself a beaker of mineral water, she looked up to find the young man with the rucksack standing near her.

He introduced himself: an American from a small town in New England who was touring Spain on a rented bicycle, at present chained to the entrance gates.

Cassia returned to the Castillo with her dilemma unresolved. Even if she hadn't had to talk to the American, she doubted if she would have decided how to react if the worst came to the worst. She could only hope and pray that it wouldn't.

Most girls of her age would have known how to tackle the situation, because they would have experienced it before. But her father's possessive vigilance during her teens, followed by his dependence while he was ill, had meant that most of her knowledge was theoretical, gleaned from books.

First by choice, and later by circumstance, John Browning had kept her as cloistered as a nun. Only by running away could she have freed herself from his controlling influence. But where could she have run to?

Besides, she had loved him, and love was as inescapable as the web a spider bound round a captive fly. Loving someone, you couldn't deliberately hurt them—not even if their way of loving was unintentionally hurting you.

All afternoon she was on a mental treadmill, her thoughts in continuous motion but only going round and round, never reaching a conclusion.

When the skiers began to return she became increasingly tense. Those who had been at the hotel for a few days or longer were sporting deep golden tans, except one or two who had neglected to take the necessary precautions and were now lobster-pink and peeling.

The Marqués had the type of skin which would never burn unless he was lost in a desert. By the end of the week he would be even more deeply bronzed—as dark as the Moorish invaders of long ago, and in some ways as exotic and fearsome as they must have seemed to the indigenous population.

When she saw him entering the lobby, carrying his ski-boots, his thick hair still in some disorder from the hours on the long, fast runs, her heart began to pump uncomfortably fast.

He collected his key and an envelope the porter on duty had already taken from the Mirador suite's pigeon-hole. Cassia knew that the envelope contained a long facsimile transmission to the machine in Señor Alvarez's office. She had been talking to his secretary when it came through and had watched her clip the pages together. Evidently it was something the Marqués had been waiting for. Pocketing his key and slinging his boots, already linked together, over one shoulder, he slit the envelope and started to read the contents.

She watched him crossing the lobby, a slight frown contracting his eyebrows. It seemed that he was too preoccupied to remember his invitation and verify her acceptance.

As he entered the open lift, still reading, she felt angry with herself for spending all day in a state of conjecture while doubtlessly he had dismissed her from his mind when he'd left, and now that he was back was too intent on his fax even to notice and acknowledge her.

The lift did not go to the top floor as she'd expected. It stopped at the first floor. Seconds later the Marqués appeared at the top of the stairs and came down them, looking at her, smiling.

Reaching the desk, he said, 'Some news from Madrid made me forget for a moment that we have a dinner date. Is the time I suggested all right for you? What time are you off duty?'

She found herself saying, 'I finish at seven.'

'In that case, why not come up as soon as you're free? Until seven.'

In fact it was a quarter past seven when she arrived at the door of the Mirador suite, after spending ten minutes in the women's staff washroom, redoing her hair and repairing her make-up.

Today she was wearing a black skirt with an inexpensive white blouse found on the racks at Tienda Corty, the new supermarket-style store which had replaced the city-centre branch of El Corte Inglés, one of Spain's two best known department-store chains. The blouse, an import from India, had cost less than Isa Sanchez probably spent on her tights, and it was no longer as crisp as it had been when the day had started. But there wasn't time to rush back to the Albaicín and put on something more appropriate for dinner in the hotel's most expensive suite.

Not that she owned anything to match the luxurious elegance of the suite.

As she waited for the Marqués to answer the door she wondered what Señor Alvarez and the others would think about her having dinner with Simón de Mondragón. They would soon find out. The waiter who served the meal would be sure to report her presence, and in no time at all the news would be buzzing round the staff grapevine.

The door opened. The Marqués stood looking down at her, his hair freshly washed and smoothly brushed. He was wearing a dark brown linen open-necked shirt and pale grey trousers, with a dark brown braided leather belt slotted through the loops. He wore no jewellery, nor did he smell of the strong cologne favoured by most Spanish men. But his cheeks and chin were a lighter shade than they had been when he'd returned to the hotel, indicating that he had shaved.

He stepped back for her to enter the spacious sitting room. This was the first time that she had been inside one of the top-floor suites, although she had had them described to her by the maids responsible for keeping them immaculate.

Even so, she was unprepared for the exuberant colour and richness of the room, with its three massive sofas grouped round a huge coffee-table made from a slab of darkly veined, rose-coloured marble, on which were stacked old and new books about the history of Spain as well as the current issues of all the Spanish glossies.

'What would you like to drink?' her host asked. 'Shall we share this champagne?' he went on, with a gesture to the bottle in the ice-bucket which must have arrived shortly before she had. 'Or would you prefer a soft drink?'

If his object was seduction, it seemed odd that he should offer the alternative.

'Champagne would be lovely,' she said. 'What a beautiful room. I've never been in here before.'

'It has more character than many hotel rooms,' he agreed. 'Most of my friends who ski here prefer to stay at the *parador* on the Sierra Nevada, to save driving up and down every day. But if I were staying up there I wouldn't have met you—a meeting which could prove opportune for both of us.'

Wondering what he meant by that, Cassia continued to survey her surroundings while he dealt with the champagne. Above a carved and gilded side-table was a painting she had seen being carried through the lobby at mid-morning. It was a temporary replacement, on loan from a local art gallery, for the valuable mirror that Isa Sanchez had broken.

Perhaps, having sent her packing, the Marqués considered it opportune that he had already made the acquaintance of another girl who took his fugitive fancy.

'Was the skiing good today?' she asked, hoping that he couldn't tell how nervous she was.

'Excellent this morning. As usual, less good after lunch. Today I was skiing on the longest *pista*, the Aguila. Here you are.' He came to where she was standing and put a glass in her hand. '*Salud.*'

'*Salud,*' she echoed, before sipping the wine.

'First things first. Come and sit down and decide what you'd like to eat,' he said, with a gesture giving her the choice of the three huge sofas piled with cushions covered in antique velvets and pieces of needlework.

She was far too strung-up to feel like eating anything. She hoped that the champagne would act as a tranquiliser. Seating herself at one end of the sofa facing the massive fireplace in which a clever simulation of a log fire was creating an illusion of leaping flames, she took the folder he handed her before seating himself in the centre of the adjoining sofa.

In the angles formed by the arms, the end-tables held large, silk-shaded lamps and arrangements of flowers. Each sofa had a fine oriental rug in front of it, laid over a floor of huge terracotta tiles, polished to a soft sheen. The room's real heat came from electric elements embedded in the floor—a form of heating used throughout the hotel during the winter months.

The folder contained details in four languages of all the à la carte dishes that the kitchens offered, preceded by the statement that if what a guest desired was not included in the menu the chef would exert himself to satisfy their wishes.

Eager to learn everything she could about the hotel business, Cassia had long since familiarised herself with everything on the menu. Some dishes she had tried. Some had been explained to her.

She said, 'You must be ravenous after skiing for five or six hours, but I normally have a big lunch and eat lightly in the evening. If you don't mind, I'll just have soup and a salad.'

'As you wish.'

He ordered the meal for eight o'clock, which was when the dining room opened for the benefit of short-stay foreigners accustomed to eating at earlier times than the Spanish. Cassia couldn't help wondering if tonight he was eating early to precipitate the main purpose of the evening—seducing her.

But then, in a businesslike tone, he said, 'Before we dine I want to explain the proposition I mentioned to you. Is your mind fixed on going to England? Or would you be interested in seeing another part of Spain?'

'I might. It depends…' she said cautiously.

He rose to top up her glass. She wondered if he was going to sit down beside her.

To her relief he returned to the other sofa. 'A long time ago, when resorts like Marbella and Benidorm were still undiscovered fishing villages, one of my aunts married a man whose family had a beach house near a small seaport called Jávea. It's midway between Valencia and Alicante on what, since tourism started, has been called the Costa Blanca. As a small boy I often stayed there with my cousins. There was also a house in the mountains behind the coast, belonging to my family. It hadn't been used for years but there was an ancient caretaker living in the servants' quarters. Sometimes we picnicked in the garden.'

He paused, his expression abstracted. She wondered what he had looked like when he was a child. Tall for his age, no doubt, and perhaps rather thin and gangly, as big men often were in early childhood.

'I went back there recently,' he continued. 'The whole coast is scarcely recognisable. It's been colonised by retired expats from northern Europe and North America. Even inland it's changed. The mules have gone, replaced by tractors and cultivators. In the villages a few old women still use the communal wash-house, mainly to have a gossip, but the younger ones all have washing machines. Only my house and garden are still in a time-warp. The caretaker I remember was succeeded by his son. Now he wants to give up and live with his married daughter at Callosa de Ensarriá. I have to decide what to do with the place.'

'How large is the house?' asked Cassia.

Surely he couldn't see her as a replacement caretaker? It was so far removed from what she had thought he might have in mind that she had to suppress an upsurge of slightly hysterical amusement.

'It has eight bedrooms, but only one primitive bathroom.

It needs drastic modernisation to make it habitable and comfortable, but I don't envisage ever living there myself. On the other hand, it's ideally situated for a project I'm organising. What, if anything, do you know about the so-called Mozarabic trails?'

'Not much. Only that they were a network of tracks and stairways used by mule-trains in previous centuries.'

'Not very much more *is* known,' said the Marqués. 'Their origins are lost in the past. Now that they're no longer the main routes between remote mountain villages and over the passes between valleys, the trails themselves are in danger of being destroyed by neglect. It was actually an American professor who brought them to my attention.'

Having crossed his long legs a few moments earlier, he now drew the ankle of one onto the knee of the other—a relaxed posture which reminded her of her father, who had often sat in the same position.

'The professor and his wife are amateur botanists who spend their holidays mountain-walking,' the Marqués continued. 'While they were staying with his brother—an ex-Navy yachtsman who's chosen the Costa Blanca as his base for sailing the Mediterranean—they discovered and walked some of the old trails. They were concerned to see them in danger of disappearing.'

'But if they're not used any more how can they be preserved? In the past, presumably, the people who used them did running repairs as and when they were necessary.'

'I imagine so. Clearly, now times have changed, they can't all be maintained in good order. But if only a few are kept up it'll be better than letting part of our national heritage be lost. One of Spain's problems is that advances which have taken centuries to evolve in other parts of Europe have happened to us in a few decades. As recently

as thirty years ago great tracts of this country were still in
the Middle Ages. Some parts are still fairly backward.'

'Even Granada lags behind the times in some ways,' said
Cassia. 'Only the other day I heard two Americans discussing the fact that the street sweepers use brooms made
of twigs, and that they'd seen a man with three panniered
donkeys stopping the traffic in the Gran Vía while he led
them across it.'

'That's one of Spain's charms—that it isn't all of a piece.
I don't think the next generation will see donkeys in city
streets, but we can keep some of the ancient trails and, I
hope, combine their preservation with another rescue operation.'

The Marqués's expression was different from any of his
that she had seen before as he leaned towards her, saying
seriously, 'Our most valuable resource is the youth of this
country. At present thousands of teenagers are unemployed.
Even those who aren't out of work are exposed to damaging influences, notably drugs. I want to set up a hostel
where youths and girls from the cities can spend a few
weeks in a totally different environment from the poor *barrios* they come from. It won't be a holiday for them. They'll
be expected to work…work very hard.'

'Clearing the trails?'

'Exactly. Doing something useful for the community and
in the process, I hope, achieving a self-esteem they may
never have experienced before.'

This was so totally at variance with what she had been
expecting, and threw such an unexpected and different light
on Simón de Mondragón's character, that she was lost for
words.

'By a lucky chance, the last time I was in England I
happened to hear of a man who seems the ideal person to
be an instructor-cum-taskmaster,' he continued. 'Like you,

he's British by birth, but has knocked about the world and picked up several languages, including fluent if ungrammatical Spanish. Although he isn't Scottish, the Scots word ''dour'' is a good description of Jack Locke.

'He grew up in circumstances as tough and disadvantaged as those of the youngsters he'll be dealing with. I suspect it was touch-and-go whether he turned to crime or lived on the right side of the law. So he'll be on their wavelength. I doubt if you'll like him, but you needn't have much to do with him. Your role, if you take the job, will be administration.'

'But I have no experience of that sort of thing.'

'That can be an advantage. Any intelligent person, given a project to tackle, can quickly pick up the necessary expertise. The whole thing is an experiment, which may or may not come off. We'll start small and, I hope, build up.

'Have some more champagne. If you'll excuse me, I have a couple of telephone calls to make. While I'm making them, you can be thinking it over…making a note of questions you want to ask.'

Having replenished her glass and handed her the pad and pencil provided for the sitting-room extension, he then opened a marquetry cabinet containing a large television and cassette player. A few seconds later, orchestral music began. The Marqués closed the cabinet and disappeared into the next room.

He was gone for nearly twenty minutes. In his absence Cassia relaxed for the first time since he had summoned her here.

It was a huge relief to have her misgivings allayed. Now it seemed foolishly alarmist ever to have imagined that he would look lustfully at her.

And with this thought came another, quickly suppressed—a faint flicker of regret that she wasn't the sort of girl for whom he would feel desire.

When he came back, he switched off the music. 'I expect your first question is what salary am I offering. What do you earn at the moment?'

She told him, explaining the hours required for her basic pay, and the overtime rate.

'Right. I'll raise that by fifty per cent, with bed and board provided, and we'll review the situation in six months' time. At this stage it's hard to say what your hours will be. Fairly long, but not always very taxing, I should imagine. Next question.'

'You mentioned administration. Can you be more explicit?'

'You'll be responsible for paying the bills, organising and supervising the cleaners, controlling all household supplies, liaising with contractors. Anything which isn't the cook's responsibility, or the instructor's, will fall on your shoulders.'

'When are you planning to start this operation? I can't leave without giving Señor Alvarez adequate notice.'

'I'll be coming to Granada for more skiing next month. If you've accepted the job and finalised your affairs here, I'll drive you to the village, Castell de los Torres. If you have a lot of belongings you want to take with you, some may have to be sent by carrier. My car has limited luggage space.'

'Perhaps it might be better if I went there by coach. How far is Castell de los Torres from the nearest bus station?'

'About fifteen miles, and the coach trip will take you all day. With me you'll be there in a few hours. But first you must make up your mind if you want the job. You won't see any jet-set people, only peasants and uncouth teenagers.'

'Some jet-set people can be surprisingly uncouth,' she said drily.

'No doubt, but you know what I mean. Life in a mountain village of four hundred people is very different from life in a five-star hotel. When the fish van comes it's a major event.'

'I wonder if your peasants will mind having city teenagers inflicted on them by an absentee aristocrat.'

A gleam of sardonic mockery came into his shrewd dark eyes.

'You don't like my calling them peasants?'

'Possibly they might not like it.'

'It's not a derogatory description. A peasant is someone who makes his living by agricultural labour. I respect such a man. The people of Castell de los Torres aren't "my" peasants. If they were ever exploited by a large landowner it was a long time ago, and not by one of my forebears. I inherited the house and its garden. Nothing else. The surrounding vineyards and almond groves are smallholdings. I expect you're right—at first they'll be watchful and wary. That's where the skills you've learned here will come in useful. Instead of being charming to hotel guests, you can calm and reassure the village people.'

'Don't they view all outsiders with some suspicion?'

'We aren't an insular race like the British,' he said, with a teasing gleam. 'Spaniards are naturally hospitable. You have till the morning I leave to make up your mind. In the meantime, if there's anything you want to know you have only to ask.'

Soon after they finished dining he drove her home, leaving his car at the top of the street for a few minutes while he saw her to her door.

Already there was no doubt in Cassia's mind that she would take the job. The money was good. She would have more responsibility. It would be interesting to live and work in a different part of Spain. She could go to England next year. A reference from a Spanish *marqués* would be an impressive addition to her CV.

Not unexpectedly, after his morning tour of the hotel the next day the manager called her into his office and told her to close the door.

'What's this I hear about you having dinner in the Mirador suite last night, Cassia?'

'The Marqués has offered me a job, Señor Alvarez.' Anticipating his next question, she explained the nature of the post.

The manager gestured for her to sit down. 'As you have no family to guide you, I regard myself in some measure as *in loco parentis*. What I'm about to say to you is strictly confidential. It's not our place to judge the manners and morals of the guests, but I should have thought your own powers of observation would have told you the Marqués is not—how shall I put it?—a pillar of rectitude.'

'I realise that, but I'm quite sure he hasn't any designs of that nature on me. Once he's set up this project, I don't expect we'll see much of him.'

After questioning her more closely, the manager said, 'In my opinion, you're too young for the job. It needs someone more mature. You're a sensible, conscientious girl, but not old enough to impose discipline on youths and girls who have no respect for authority.'

'They'll be kept in order by the Englishman. He's a tough nut who won't stand any nonsense.'

'Not a congenial companion for someone as refined as yourself,' Señor Alvarez said disapprovingly. 'I advise you to stay here. If you feel some embarrassment about turning down the Marqués's offer, would you like me to speak to him for you?'

'He's given me until he leaves to make up my mind. I haven't done that yet. I appreciate your advice, and your offer, but I shan't be afraid to tell him if I decide to turn the job down,' Cassia said, politely but firmly.

For the rest of his stay the Marqués acknowledged her presence with friendly courtesy whenever she was in the lobby when he passed through it. But they had no conversation, and the curiosity aroused by her visit to his suite soon died down when it was seen that he was spending his evenings alone or with other skiing guests.

As she had feared, the manager was very put out when, the night before Simón de Mondragón's departure, Cassia gave in her notice.

'I shall have to replace you. You can't expect to come back if things go badly,' he warned her.

'I realise that. If it doesn't work out I'll go to England.'

'A beautiful country with an impossible climate,' said Señor Alvarez. 'As a young man I spent a year in London. I couldn't wait to get back to our better weather. You're throwing away a promising career at the Castillo, Cassia. But young people nowadays will never listen to advice. They think they know it all.'

She spent a restless night, wondering if he was right. A key factor in her decision was the imminent end of her lease of the studio. But for that, she might have played safe and put off leaving Granada. But if she had to leave the Albaicín she might as well leave the city altogether.

The Marqués was leaving earlier than other guests on the list of those checking out the next day. Cassia had scrutinised his bill to make sure that it was in order when he came downstairs after breakfasting in his suite. His luggage and skis would be taken directly to the garage and stowed in his car for him before it was brought to the entrance.

'Good morning, Cassia.'

'Good morning, *señor*. I hope you've enjoyed your stay with us.'

'Very much, thank you.' He took a wallet from the back pocket of his trousers, extracted a card and placed it on the counter while he cast an eye down the bill.

While Cassia placed his card in the machine he said, 'What have you decided?'

She looked up. Taking a deep breath, she said, 'I'd like to join your project.'

'Good. In that case I'll expect you to be ready to leave at the end of my next visit. In the meantime, if you have any queries you can fax them to this number.' He produced a business card.

It wasn't until after he had gone that she looked at it and found it wasn't his own card but that of his secretary.

The following month was not an easy one. The hotel manager wasn't the only person who thought that she was mad to throw in a good job with prospects for an insecure position somewhere in the backwoods of País Valencia, once the kingdom of Valencia but now, to judge by the way her *granadino* colleagues referred to it, a backward part of the country fit only for *campesinos*—a term they used with a much more scornful inflexion than the Marqués speaking of peasants.

It was not her first experience of the disdain that Spaniards from one part of the country felt for people of other regions, all of them wanting autonomy for their own region. But instead of undermining her confidence their attitude made her more resolute.

She had let her father rule her life, but from now on she was going to make her own decisions, be her own woman.

CHAPTER FOUR

AT FIVE minutes to nine on a sunny February morning, Cassia carried her suitcase to the top of the street to await the arrival of the Marqués at the place where he had left his car after driving her home a month earlier.

She had finished working at the hotel the day before yesterday, spending the previous day leaving the studio far cleaner than it had been when she and her father had moved in. His paintings and a trunk containing some of their other belongings were now in storage. All she had with her were her clothes and a few personal treasures to make her feel at home in her room at Casa Mondragón in Castell de los Torres.

Contrary to the belief that Spaniards had little regard for punctuality, the Marqués arrived as various church clocks in the area were chiming the hour. She had seen little of him during the past few days. This time he had come to Granada alone.

'Good morning,' he said through the open window as he pulled up beside her. 'All ready for your adventure?'

'Good morning. Yes, I'm looking forward to it.'

Before springing out he touched a button inside the car which caused the boot to open. Before she could lift her case he was looming over her, picking it up as easily as if it were empty. Having stowed her cheap case on top of his own expensive one, he opened the passenger door for her.

Apart from the night he had run her home, Cassia had never driven in a luxurious car before. Nor could she herself drive. She bent to sit down and then straightened again, saying anxiously, 'I've just realised that you may be assuming I can drive. Shall I need to? Does the fact that I can't rule me out?'

'It's a disadvantage, but not an insuperable one. You'll have to take driving lessons. If I'd realised you couldn't drive, I would have suggested that you start to learn right away. But it's not essential…not at the outset anyway.'

The Albaicín being on the north side of the city, the road to Murcia—the next city on their route—ran close by. Within five minutes of Cassia fastening her seatbelt Granada was lost to view, and they were gliding smoothly up a serpentine hill road, leaving everything familiar behind.

A few kilometres on the Marqués stopped for *gasolina*. While the tank was filling he talked in his easy way to the pump attendant. She wondered if he would chat to her on the way along, or if he would play one of the tapes filling a special storage compartment under the dashboard.

The night they had dined together their conversation had ranged over various topics, and she hadn't found it a strain or felt that he might be bored by someone whose horizons were more limited than his own.

As they were leaving the service area he said, 'Your previous boss isn't pleased with me for filching you from him. This morning, as I was leaving, he dropped the unctuous manner of all hoteliers to tell me, almost severely, that you are a girl of the highest character, deserving scrupulous kindness and consideration.'

'He's a very kind man himself. He takes a paternal interest in all his employees.'

'I am not kind,' said the Marqués. 'Nor have I ever felt fatherly. But Alvarez seemed relieved when I told him the personnel on our project would include a middle-aged cook. No doubt that will ease your mind too,' he added, with an amused sideways glance.

'My mind was never uneasy. Is the cook a local person?'

'No. Her husband was French and she's lived in France for twenty years. She is now a widow and wants to return to Spain. Her name is Laura Boisson. Until she arrives in a few days' time we shall have to manage as best we can.'

She wondered who 'we' referred to, and if it included himself. But instead of asking she said, 'When do you expect the project to become operational?'

'If things go to plan—which in any small village is highly unlikely—we could be ready for action in six weeks.' He selected a tape and slotted it into the player. 'I hope you won't dislike this. My musical taste is the result of early brainwashing by my mother, who might have become a professional pianist if she hadn't married young.'

Cassia said, 'I liked the music you played the night I had dinner with you.'

'I can't remember what it was. This is Rachmaninov.'

Her first glimpse of their journey's end was six hours later when they came to the crest of a hill and, the road being deserted, the Marqués stopped the car to let her take in the vista directly ahead of them—a long, shallow valley sheltered on three sides by mountains and encompassing several small villages, the most distant being their destination.

In the afternoon light of a warm day the long valley presented a pleasant picture of vineyards interspersed with orchards of almond trees, and in places some orange groves.

The modern world had encroached to the extent that one of the villages they passed had a large petrol station on its outskirts, but the valley had so far escaped the incursions of tourism. Here, instead of the colonies of villas to be seen nearer the coast, the lower slopes of the mountains were still either bare or terraced with dry-stone walls, some crumbling from long neglect, others supporting land still in use.

A roadside sign—'Castell de los Torres'—announced that they had arrived at the next addition to the many places where she had lived—so many she had lost count. She wondered how long she would stay here, and if it would be a happy experience or one she would later regret having embarked on.

There were not many people about, and those they saw stared curiously at the car and its occupants. Only one old man raised his hand, but perhaps from habit rather than recognition that although the car had a Madrid registration number its driver was not altogether a stranger here.

'That's the Plaza Mayor—the hub of the village,' said the Marqués, with a gesture at a square with the Spanish flag flying from one of its buildings, and a couple of small dark bars. Even here there were few signs of life.

The Casa Mondragón stood in a smaller square, occupying the whole of one side and towering over its neighbours although they were substantial houses. While they were well kept, with no dust on the wrought-iron *rejas* guarding the windows, and brightly burnished knockers and knobs on their doors, the larger house looked neglected, if not deserted.

'Don't be put off. It won't look like this for much longer,' said the Marqués as he parked the car. 'Luckily this isn't the only way in,' he went on, unlocking the Judas-door in one of the two huge double doors. 'There's a road at the rear, and the builders use that way in.'

Cassia had lived in Spain long enough to know that the fronts of apparently modest Spanish houses often concealed surprisingly roomy interiors. As soon as she stepped inside the Casa Mondragón, she realised that it was even more palatial than its façde suggested. Beyond the wide hall with its stately stairway was a window wall, and beyond it a large patio.

After she had followed the Marqués on his tour of the building to see how the builders were progressing, he said to her, 'We shan't be spending the night here. I've arranged for you to stay at the pharmacist's house, and I'll be at a *hostal* a few miles away where they cater to botanists and walkers. Manners and mores in Castell are some way behind the times. We don't want to raise any eyebrows by sleeping here on our own, without Laura to make it respectable.'

This announcement was a relief to her. With its thick walls and shuttered windows, except where the builders were working, the house was both cold and spooky, and would be more so at night. She wouldn't have fancied sleeping here on her own, but would have been equally uneasy at being alone with him—not because she thought that he might take advantage of the situation, but because she knew how the villagers would view it. It was a point in his favour that although unconventional himself he did sometimes respect other people's sense of propriety.

Madame Boisson returned to her homeland by coach, in the company of a French friend who had an apartment in Benidorm, once a quiet fishing village but now a resort whose skyscraping profile Cassia had glimpsed from the *autopista* on their way to the valley.

Simón had arranged to drive to Benidorm and collect the cook after she had spent a couple of nights with her friend, helping her to put the flat in order for a winter holiday.

As the daily bus service from the valley to and from the city of Alicante passed through Benidorm, many employers would have expected the housekeeper to come to Castell by public transport. It threw an unexpected light on Simón's character that he was prepared to put himself out to fetch her.

'That's Continente, one of the big supermarkets where you'll be buying some supplies,' he said, indicating a large, modern structure flying the flags of many nations on the outskirts of Benidorm. 'Which reminds me—we must fix up some driving lessons for you. Perhaps I'll give you the basic lessons myself.'

'Oh, no…please don't,' she said hurriedly. 'It's kind of you to suggest it, but it would make me nervous to learn in a car like this. I'd hate to damage it.'

'I shouldn't let you,' he said, smiling at her. 'But maybe you're right… Teaching women to drive is notoriously difficult for anyone but a qualified instructor. Perhaps women can teach each other, but when a man attempts it usually it ends with his blood pressure going up ten points and his pupil in tears.'

Suspecting him of teasing her, Cassia said, 'So they say. I'd certainly feel a lot happier learning to drive in a small car belonging to an auto school.' The environs of Benidorm offering an easy change of subject, she went on, 'Did you ever see this place before they put up the high-rise hotels?'

'No, we never used to come here. But these are only baby skyscrapers compared with the ones in New York and Hong Kong and Rio.'

To find the address that Madame Boisson had given him, he had to ask a policeman for directions. The town was teeming with foreigners, most of them grey-haired but with healthy tans and happy faces.

'I wonder if they realise how much nicer it is only a few miles inland,' said Cassia as they drove along a wide bou-

levard lined with hotels and cafés and shops full of tourist
tat.

'They probably wouldn't agree with you. Life in Castell
isn't to everyone's taste. You may get bored with it yourself
when you've been there a bit longer.'

Two days after Laura's arrival Simón returned to Madrid,
saying that he would come and go as his other commitments permitted.

No doubt he was bored with them, thought Cassia after
his departure. In spite of his obvious enthusiasm for the
project he was setting up, Castell was a very different environment from his natural milieu, and she and Laura were
not the sort of women he was accustomed to spending time
with.

Small, overweight and vivacious, Laura was a natural
chatterbox who had begun the story of her life on the drive
back from Benidorm and every day, at every meal, related
some more of the details. Cassia didn't mind this. She was
interested in other people's lives. What she found mildly
tiresome were Laura's frequent criticisms of the way things
were done in Spain compared with the superior methods in
force in her adopted country. But perhaps the attitude
would wear off as she settled down.

One morning, after Cassia had been to the Plaza Mayor to
post some letters to Granada, she was on her way back to
the house when a vehicle pulled up and the man in it spoke
to her.

'I'm looking for the house of Mondragón,' he said, in
Spanish.

He was on the other side of the road, leaning out of the
offside window of a right-hand-drive, travel-dusty Range

Rover. That and his accent told her he was the man they were expecting.

She crossed the street and said in English, 'You must be Jack Locke?'

If he was surprised he didn't show it. 'That's right. Who are you?'

'Cassia Browning...another member of the team. I'm the dogsbody,' she added, smiling.

She got no smile in response, although he did take the hand she offered in a large paw with oil-stained nails and calluses on the palm. Unlike the Marqués he hadn't learned to moderate his grip when shaking hands with women, but she managed not to wince as he ground her knuckles together.

'You'd better hop in,' he said, opening the door for her.

'Turn left at the end of the street, and then first right and second left,' she said as she settled herself beside him. 'How was your journey?'

'OK. When did you get here?'

'Two weeks ago. When the Marqués recruited me I was working in a hotel in Granada. I don't know this part of Spain, but already I'm getting to like it. Where did you stop last night?'

'Dossed down in the back,' he said, jerking a thumb at the space behind them.

'You'll be glad to have a shower and stretch your legs.'

He made no comment, perhaps because he was steering his large, high vehicle between a parked car and a moped propped on the opposite kerb, making the narrow street almost impassable.

While his attention was engaged Cassia made a quick study of him. She had seen at first glance that his hair was cut close to his scalp, giving him the look of a Victorian gaolbird. Usually earrings and even noserings went with that brutal crop, but the man beside her wore no adornment; nor did the sleeves of his shirt, rolled high above his biceps, reveal any tattoos.

All the same, he looked a tough, rough type, who could pass the night by the roadside or in a motorway lorry park without fear of being molested by the pirates-on-wheels who had made random camping unsafe for more vulnerable travellers.

A scruff he was not. The pugnacious jaw had been shaved before he'd set out and his clothes, though cheap and well-worn, were clean. Even his heavy-soled, cross-laced rough-country boots had been polished recently. At the moment she couldn't tell what colour his eyes were. They were hidden by dark glasses with wide side-pieces.

'Left, right and second left…correct?' he said, checking her directions.

'Correct,' she said, equally briskly. Was he always so laconic? She wondered how he would get on with the garrulous Laura.

'Is the *jefe* here?'

It was a term with many meanings, ranging from boss to commanding officer. Concluding that he meant the Marqués, she said, 'He's gone to Madrid for a few days. We're expecting him back tonight or tomorrow.'

'Where's your base in the UK?' he asked.

'I've never lived in the UK. My father was an artist…a nomad. We moved round the Mediterranean as the fancy took him. Where are you from?'

'London…the East End. The wrong end of town,' he said tersely.

Was this the first sign of a chip on his shoulder? she wondered. Chippy people could be a bore, always sniping at those they considered to have unfair advantages.

Moments later they turned the last corner into the street

behind their employer's house. After Jack had parked the
Range Rover in a corner of the back patio—at present look-
ing more like a builders' yard—Cassia explained about
Laura.

'Come and meet her. Then I'll show you your room and
leave you to freshen up before lunch.'

Laura, when her plump hand was compressed by his
large, rough paw, gave a stifled squeak.

'What a brute!' she said, with a grimace, when Cassia
returned to the kitchen after taking him upstairs. 'I hope
his table manners are not going to put us off our lunch.'

However, although the new arrival seemed unaware of
such niceties as drawing out the women's chairs for them,
or waiting until they had everything they needed before
starting to eat, at least he didn't do it noisily or with his
mouth open.

After he had answered four or five questions with curt
monosyllables, Laura gave up trying to draw him out and
ignored him, except to offer second helpings.

At the end of the meal he surprised and mollified her by
complimenting her on her cooking, albeit in less gracious
terms than the Marqués would have used. The
Englishman's Spanish, while fluent, was the crude speech
of the mean streets rather than the cultured Castilian spoken
by Simón.

When he had left them, to unload the equipment he had
brought with him, Laura said, 'At least he won't have any
trouble keeping the young ones in order. That's something
to be thankful for. But as company for us...' She finished
the sentence with a negative gesture.

Presently, from the kitchen window, as Laura washed
and Cassia wiped the dishes, they saw Jack unloading and
then, stripped to the waist, hosing down the Range Rover.

'Such muscles!' Laura exclaimed. 'He's built like that creature Rambo.'

She sounded half repelled, half excited by the sight of Jack's brawny torso. Although several inches shorter in the leg than the Marqués, he was equally broad of shoulder, and obviously tuned to a high degree of fitness.

'You'll have to take care of that one,' Laura went on in a warning tone. 'You saw the way he devoured his lunch. He'll be the same with women. You'd better lock your door tonight.'

Cassia couldn't help laughing. 'I don't think he's going to pounce on me without some encouragement, Laura.'

'You don't know as much about men as I do,' said the older woman. 'I can tell you're not as experienced as many girls of your age. Men are not like us, my dear. They have appetites which must be satisfied. When they're in that mood they forget all finer feelings. It's not altogether their fault. It's the way nature made them.'

The statement cast an unflattering light on her late husband, thought Cassia. Aloud she said, 'I expect when Jack's in that mood he'll drive to the coast and find himself a pretty tourist who's looking for a holiday romance. I'm sure there are plenty around.'

'Very likely…but I still wouldn't put it past him to try his luck with you,' said Laura. 'You're very attractive, and to some men every girl they meet is a challenge to their virility.'

'Jack hasn't indicated any interest in me so far,' she said. 'The way he's sprucing the Range Rover, I should think that means more to him than any woman ever could. It wouldn't surprise me if he were a misogynist.'

'Even they feel the lusts of the flesh,' was Laura's comment. 'Sometimes all the more powerful for being repressed,' she added darkly, her eyes on the strapping figure in the courtyard.

Cassia was on the roof, enjoying a magnificent sunset over the mountains to the west, when she heard the toot-toot of a horn and looked over the parapet to see Simón's car gliding into the rear courtyard.

She watched him climb out, stretch himself, and then go to close the tall gates, left open for him after the builders had finished for the day. In the heat of summer they probably took a longer lunch break and would have been working later. At this time of year they spent an hour at the village bar before resuming operations.

While the Marqués was locking the gates Jack came out of the house. As they shook hands she was struck by the contrast between them—the tall, elegant, self-assured Spanish aristocrat and the stockier, plebeian Englishman, with his own brand of assurance but very few social graces.

It was he who, while they were talking, suddenly seemed to sense that they were being observed and, looking up, saw her peering down.

She had noticed at lunch that his eyes were a good shade of grey. What colour his hair might be if grown to a normal length was hard to guess, except that around his ears the stubble was noticeably silvery.

When Simón also looked up she waved to them both and withdrew. She had come to the roof to retrieve some underwear hung out to dry on a line strung between the chimney stacks. There was also a weather-bleached cane chair and table on the roof, suggesting that the last caretaker had sometimes sat up here.

Provided the timbers would stand the additional weight of plant pots, it could be made into a roof garden, Cassia thought. One which, unless a helicopter or a microlight passed overhead, was as private as the main patio. There were many flat roofs in the village, but all on a lower level. Even the bell tower of the church didn't overlook the roof of the Casa Mondragón.

At supper that evening, discussing the project which had brought him to Castell de los Torres, Jack showed that he could be talkative on a subject of interest to him. In spite of their disparate lives and backgrounds, he and Simón seemed to have more in common than Cassia had expected.

It turned out that the Marqués was not only a skier but a climber and scuba-diver. He had also tried paragliding and free-fall parachute jumping—a sport which made Laura shudder with horror at the thought of it.

After declining coffee, saying that he never drank it, Jack leaned back in his chair and gave a hippopotamus-sized yawn, only remembering to hide a healthy set of teeth with his hand when he noticed the housekeeper's disapproving expression.

'Why don't you turn in, my friend?' said the Marqués in Spanish—the language they had been speaking throughout the meal. 'Tomorrow I'll show you some of the terrain around here. We'll take a packed lunch and spend the day "on the hill" as the Scots say.'

The remark reminded Cassia of his description of Jack the first time he'd mentioned him to her. She was beginning to feel that Jack might not be dour by nature. It could be merely a façade he put up in the company of people with whom he wasn't at ease, such as women like Laura and herself.

'I'll do that.' The feet of his chair scraped on the worn clay tiles as he rose to his feet. 'Goodnight all.'

'Perhaps you'd be good enough to prepare substantial packed lunches for us, Laura,' said the Marqués as Jack was leaving the room. 'The bakery here makes excellent *barras negras* which I prefer to their white bread, especially for picnics.'

'I'll fetch them for you, Laura,' Cassia offered. 'I love the smell of new bread in the bakery when they take the first batch of loaves out of the oven.' She turned to the Marqués. 'But I find it very frustrating to listen to people talking in the shops and not understand what they're saying. They speak Castilian to me, but only Valenciano among themselves. It's like being in another country.'

'I'm sure you'll soon pick it up, but whether you'll find their conversations worth listening to is another matter,' he said drily. 'Most of the locals have very narrow horizons. Television could open their minds…if they watched the better programmes and there were more of them. Mostly they watch the soaps, imported and home-grown.'

This prompted Laura, who was missing the French soap operas, to ask if he'd mind if she had an aerial erected for a TV in her room.

'Not as long as you don't allow any of our guests to watch it. While they're here the emphasis will be on active rather than passive entertainments.'

'I shall keep my room locked once they arrive,' she assured him.

After drinking his coffee, Simón said, 'I'm going to stroll up to the *mirador* by the cemetery. Will you join me, Cassia?'

Although expressed as a suggestion, she had a feeling the question might be a directive.

'I'll get my jacket.'

The days since her arrival had been mild and, at midday in the sun, warm. But once darkness fell the temperature took a sharp drop.

They left the house by the imposing main door, the

Marqués wearing a quilted gilet over his sweater with a canary-yellow scarf wound round his neck, and Cassia in her old anorak.

They walked in silence as far as the *plaza* in front of the church. As they began to climb the steep, sloping way to the cemetery, bordered on one side by tall cypresses and the whitewashed pillars representing the first stations of the Cross, he said, 'Would you like to come with us tomorrow? We shan't be doing any serious climbing. I'm sure you can cope with some easy rock scrambling.'

Although she suspected that Jack wouldn't be pleased to have her with them, she said, 'I'd like to come.'

'Now you've met him, what do you make of Jack Locke?'

'It's too soon to say. He was much less forthcoming at lunch than he was at supper. I don't think he's too keen on Laura, or she on him.'

'They're opposite poles,' he agreed. 'How are you getting on with her?'

'From my point of view, very well. I hope from hers too.'

'Her outlook could be more flexible. I hope she's going to be good with the youngsters. From what I've read, most of the teenagers we'll be dealing with have very little sense of self-worth. They won't respond to disapproval. What they need is encouragement to develop their best qualities…and praise when they succeed.'

'I'm sure when Laura actually meets them they'll appeal to her motherly instincts. She's been very nice to me,' said Cassia.

'Being nice to you isn't difficult. Are you warm enough?' He surprised her by taking her hand. Finding her fingers cold, he said, 'No, you aren't. Here, have this. I don't need it.'

Pulling off his scarf, he curled it into a loose roll and tucked her hands inside it, as if it were a muff. It was very soft—perhaps cashmere—and warm from being round his neck.

At the top of the slope, where a hairpin bend led up to a hilltop Calvary, they came to the wrought-iron gates of the enclosure where the village dead were interred in rows of vaults which were built into the white walls and sealed with slabs of marble engraved with the occupants' names, and in most cases accompanied by a photograph.

'Perhaps I shouldn't have brought you here. It must remind you of your father,' Simón said quietly.

'Yes, but I like this place. I've been up here before,' she answered. 'I don't find it sad or depressing. It seems part of the natural cycle of birth, life and death. I think this is the way people are meant to live—in small communities where everyone knows each other and their forebears' graves are close by.'

'You wouldn't think that if you'd lived here since you were born. You'd be itching to spread your wings and escape all the watchful eyes and the tattling tongues. It's because you've never had a permanent home that you envy these people their more restricted existence. We all tend to want something different from whatever life has assigned to us.'

They were standing beside the low wall surrounding the *mirador*, looking out at the moonlit valley, ringed by the mountains whose names she had yet to learn.

'I shouldn't think you do...do you?' she asked, glancing up at him.

Behind him the high lime-washed wall of the cemetery made his dark hair look even darker. The moonlight accentuated the forceful structure of his face.

'I used to when I was your age. I wanted to be free to go where I pleased and do as I chose.'

'But surely you *are* free…far more than most people. You're rich, you're educated, you're a grandee of Spain, you're—'

She had been about to add 'very good-looking' but stopped short, substituting, 'You have it all, as they say.'

'You may not realise it, but being a *marqués* has its downside,' he told her drily. 'When I was twenty it felt like a strait-jacket. The price of privilege is responsibility, and young men don't want to be lumbered with a load of baggage handed down from their ancestors. My inheritance was a burden—half a dozen houses, some of them falling apart, numerous dependent relations and even more numerous retainers…'

The broad shoulders shrugged, the hard mouth twisted sardonically. 'I wanted to pack a rollbag and get the hell out of all that. Sometimes I did…and do. But only for short spells—like my visits to Granada.'

Something impelled her to say, 'How is Señorita Sanchez? Completely recovered, I hope?'

'I believe so. I saw her dancing at a party in Madrid last week. We are not on close terms any more. She has found other fish to fry.'

'Only because you ditched her, I should imagine.' As soon as the words were out Cassia regretted speaking her thought aloud.

Tensely, her eyes on the moonlit rooftops below them, she waited for his reaction.

CHAPTER FIVE

'AM I to conclude from that combative statement that you think I treat women badly?' Simón asked, with an edge in his voice.

'I spoke out of turn,' said Cassia. 'Your relationships with other people are none of my business. I'm sorry I said that. It was impertinent of me.'

'Having said it, you can't retrieve it. I'd like to know your reasoning. Is it based on something you heard from other members of the staff?'

As he wasn't going to let her off the hook, she said, 'The thing which caused talk was the damage to the antique mirror. Naturally everyone thought you and Señorita Sanchez had a major row before she walked out or you sent her packing. What other conclusion would they draw? The staff at the hotel are very discreet. It would cost them their jobs if they weren't. But you can't expect them not to gossip among themselves when something unusual happens.'

'What was the consensus?'

'I don't think there was one. Everyone saw it differently.'

'*Your* sympathies being with Isa?'

'I'm not in sympathy with anyone damaging other people's property—particularly something irreplaceable—in a fit of temper. But some people aren't brought up to control their emotions, and I don't know what provoked her to hurl something at you. You may have driven her to it. I should think you could, if you felt like it,' she added, with impulsive candour.

In a *corral* somewhere below them three or four Spanish

hunting dogs began barking in unison, perhaps because one of the village cats had walked along the wall of their enclosure. A lot of the men in Castell kept a pair or a pack of the large ginger dogs. Friendly enough when not hunting, they were as lean as greyhounds but with larger ears, like the dogs of the ancient Egyptians. In her first few nights in the village Cassia had found their occasional outbursts—and the half-hourly chiming from the bell-tower—disturbing. But already she was used to both noises and no longer woke up.

Simón waited for the barks to subside before he said, 'Could I provoke you into letting your emotions off the leash? Or are they so tightly controlled that you never lose your temper?'

'I don't know. I never have so far. But I suppose everyone has a breaking-point. I can imagine getting pretty angry if someone ill-treated a child or an animal in front of me.'

'What about if someone kissed you—someone you didn't approve of?'

A long time ago with her father Cassia had flown on a cheap flight to the Canary Islands, where John Browning had thought that he might settle in preference to mainland Spain. Part of the flight had been alarmingly bumpy.

The sensations she was feeling now—expecting that at any moment the man beside her would kiss her—were remarkably similar to the inner turmoil experienced in those scary moments at thirty-nine thousand feet.

But instead of doing what she expected, Simón answered the question for her.

'No, I don't think that would be enough provocation,' he said reflectively. 'My guess is that you'd handle the situation with outward hauteur but be inwardly seething…even if you had liked it.'

While the aircraft had been bouncing its way through ten

minutes of strong air turbulence, and other passengers had shown varying degrees of alarm, Cassia had managed to continue reading her book, while inwardly longing for a reassuring smile and pat on the hand from her father.

Now, although her heart was behaving like a yo-yo and she was aware of other disturbing reactions, she said with assumed self-possession, 'I think I'll be able to cope if any of the boys who come here try getting out of line. But why should they bother with me when they'll have girls of their own age to make passes at?'

'Under the macho posturing, teenage boys are often a lot less confident than they appear, and teenage girls can dish out some nasty put-downs. The skills you used to keep the hotel guests happy could be balm to these boys' fragile egos—an aphrodisiac balm,' he added, in an amused tone. 'If you haven't had much to do with adolescent males, I should warn you they live in an almost permanent state of arousal. It doesn't take a lot to start them snorting and pawing as excitably as young bulls.'

Seeing a chance to change the subject, she seized it. 'Are you an aficionado of bullfighting?'

'I admire the courage of the matadors. I don't go to the corrida. I'm not keen on any spectator sports. Have you been to a bullfight?'

She shook her head. 'I know I shouldn't enjoy it. I've seen bits of fights on television at the hotel, but watching a man risk his life doesn't excite me, and I felt the horses must be terrified, even with protective padding.' The church clock chimed the half-hour. 'I think it's time I turned in.'

'As you wish.'

Near the house she returned his scarf. 'Thank you.'

'My pleasure. I'm not used to country hours so I'll go for a walk. I'll see you at breakfast tomorrow. Sleep well.'

Taking her by surprise, he took one of her hands and brushed a kiss on the knuckles before turning to cross the *plaza* and disappear round the corner.

Cassia was almost at the door of her room when she changed her mind and went up to the roof. Simón had turned in a direction which led to the lanes through the vineyards. A few minutes later, as she stood in the shadow of the chimmey-stack, she saw him come into view, and would have recognised him even if she hadn't been expecting to see him.

She could still feel the fleeting pressure of his lips on her knuckles, and her thoughts and emotions were in a confusion induced by their conversation up at the *mirador* as well as by the unexpected caress.

A kiss on the hand at meeting or parting was a courtesy normally reserved for married women. On one or two occasions she had seen Señor Alvarez greet the wives of regular guests with the old-fashioned salutation, 'At your feet, *señora*.'

It seemed a shame that the expression had fallen into disuse. From what she had seen at the hotel, young Spaniards rarely kissed women's hands—not even those of girls they appeared to be in love with.

What had prompted Simón to kiss hers she couldn't imagine. Unless, in the absence of any better entertainment, it amused him to see how she would respond to his flirting with her.

She watched him until he was lost to view, envying him the freedom to go where he pleased at night. Not that the lanes through the vineyards held the hazards of city streets, but it wouldn't have occurred to her to go for a walk at this hour.

Jack looked displeased when, next morning, he learned that Cassia was going with them.

'Have you got boots?' he asked.

She shook her head. 'Won't trainers do?'

'Not in the mountains.'

'She can buy some boots on the way,' said the Marqués. 'Not as good as yours and mine, but adequate for the easy terrain we'll be covering.'

Both men had come down to breakfast in sweatshirts with shorts and wool socks but the Spaniard's long legs were tanned and Jack's thicker legs were white under a heavy furring of curly hair.

Cassia was wearing jeans and one of her father's shirts, with a patchwork waistcoat bought from an arts and crafts shop in an alley at the foot of the Albaicín.

'You'll need a sweater and a waterproof,' Jack told her.

'But it's going to be another hot day. There isn't a cloud in sight.'

'Not now. There could be later. No one who knows what they're doing ever goes mountain-walking without the gear they'll need if the weather changes. If you haven't got a cagoule, I'll lend you one.'

He also lent her a knapsack in which to carry her lunch and a litre of water.

'One would think you were going to walk to the other side of Spain. What do you have in there?' asked Laura, voicing Cassia's curiosity about the contents of Jack's much larger pack.

'First-aid stuff, flares, emergency rations, a survival bag. People who go off the beaten track can get lost or have an accident which might involve staying out overnight,' he told her. 'It isn't likely that will happen today, but I never take chances. If you're always prepared you never get caught out.'

The Marqués also had a pack, although not as large as Jack's. After they had stowed their gear in the back of the

Range Rover, he opened the front passenger door but, instead of climbing in, waited for Cassia to take the seat next to the driver's.

'She can go in the back. I'll need you in front to direct me,' Jack said abruptly.

With a slight movement of one eyebrow, Simón opened the rear door for her.

The small town where they stopped *en route* had a shop selling all the equipment used by hunters, from shotguns to cartridge jackets. The proprietor produced a pair of boots in a boy's size which Cassia found comfortable and Jack considered adequate if not ideal. They were not expensive, and she had brought some money with her, but the Marqués insisted on paying.

'They're not something you'd have bought if you hadn't come to work for me,' he said. 'I'll cover any expenses to do with the job.'

'I didn't realise you spoke Valenciano,' she said as they left the shop.

'The gift of tongues is a family characteristic. One of my uncles was a diplomat, and I also spent a few years in our foreign service.'

'How many languages do you speak?'

'Half a dozen,' he said casually. 'If those boots start to feel uncomfortable you must tell us. Ideally they need to be used for several short periods before being worn on a long walk.'

'At the moment they feel very comfortable.'

'They're to light for serious walking,' Jack said critically.

She felt that he was still annoyed at having her with them.

The village where they left the Range Rover to continue on foot was even smaller than Castell de los Torres. Only one old woman was using the *lavadero*—a long, waist-high tank of running water, roofed but open on three sides— when they passed it. She gave them a friendly greeting, her small, black-clad figure making Cassia aware of the vast gulf between her own life and opportunities and those of the Spanish widow—the growth of her generation stunted by malnutrition, the pattern of her life determined by lack of education.

The Marqués was leading the way, with Jack behind him and Cassia at the rear. As the path wound downhill between plots of vegetables and small orchards of fruit trees with their blossom season approaching, she noticed how differently the two ahead of her moved, and wondered if a man's gait was a reflection of his character.

The Marqués was light on his feet, even in thick-soled boots. Jack walked with a heavier tread. In summer, when snakes might be sunning themselves on the less used parts of the mountain tracks, they would feel the reverberations of those clumping footsteps in plenty of time to glide out of sight.

Jack's smile at the granny in the washhouse had been the first sign that he could smile. For a moment it had changed him into someone different from the man whose manner so far had been anything but friendly.

Presently they came to a spot where Simón stopped to point out a zigzag line on the hillside on the far side of the valley below them.

'That's one of the ancient trails.'

He had a small pair of field-glasses hanging from a strap round his neck. Lifting it over his head, he handed the glasses to her. As their fingers touched she felt the same unnerving tingle induced by his caress last night—like a very slight electric shock.

They walked for an hour, then stopped for a five-minute break and a drink from their water bottles.

'In April this will be a botanist's paradise,' said Simón, with a gesture at the scrubby vegetation around them.

Cassia took the opportunity to apply some more sun-cream to her nose, eyelids and hairline. She debated offering the tube to Jack, but decided that he had probably applied some protection of his own before coming out.

When they set off again he took the lead, setting a pace which presently made Simón glance round to ask her, 'Are you OK with this?'

'I'm fine, thanks.'

Even if she had not been happy with their present rate of knots, she wouldn't have admitted it. She was determined to keep up, not to confirm Jack's evident feeling that her presence was a liability.

All morning the temperature rose. This still being wintertime, it wasn't hard to understand why only the hardiest plants survived the scorching heat of the summer months on these almost treeless mountainsides.

They had lunch where an overhanging rock created a patch of shade. The backs of the men's shirts when they took off their packs were soaked with sweat where the packs had rested. Both stripped to the waist, spreading their shirts in the sun to dry. Cassia had already removed her waistcoat, and wished that she had had the forethought to put on a bathing top instead of a bra. The one she was wearing was too transparent for her to sit shirtless.

'Where did you come by your tan?' Jack asked Simón as they unwrapped their food.

His own torso was pale, like his legs, but Simón's shoulders and chest were as brown as his face and legs.

'I spent Christmas in the Seychelles. A friend of mine lives there. His island, Praslin, is a great place for sailing and fishing, but there isn't much else to do there unless you're a painter, as my friend is.'

'I don't go for the Tropics myself. I don't like the humidity,' said Jack. 'I was in Canada at Christmas. A pal of mine in the Legion asked me over. He's in security now…a married man with a family. It was nice and warm in his house, but outside it was cold enough to freeze the—'

'Jack served in the French Foreign Legion,' Simón cut in. 'For how long? Five years, wasn't it?'

'Ten,' the other man said tersely, and bit off a mouthful of roll.

'Spain also has a legion, but it no longer accepts foreign recruits,' Simón continued smoothly. 'There were never as many foreigners in our Legión Extranjera as in the French one.'

Cassia wondered if he had intervened to prevent her hearing an expression he thought would embarrass her, or to spare Jack embarrassment. In her view, the Englishman was much too plain-spoken to care if his barrack-room language offended people like Laura and herself.

She could see that Simón's upbringing would make him aware that women of Laura's age and older were put off by coarseness, but she doubted if his own girlfriends would have minded the expression Jack would have used if he hadn't been interrupted. Her impression of Isa Sanchez had been that plenty of four-letter words would have been screeched at Simón before he'd dodged the ashtray that Isa had hurled at the mirror.

'Your friend was a French Canadian, presumably?' said the Marqués.

The other man nodded. 'He spoke the lingo from day one. I had to pick it up. I reckon now I speak it better than the teachers who thought I hadn't the brains to learn it at school.'

It was after the lunch stop, when they had set off again, that Cassia became aware that her right boot was starting to rub the back of her heel. She was wondering whether to ask Jack if his first-aid equipment included a plaster which, applied now, would prevent the slight soreness from becoming a blister, when Simón called, 'Hold it, Jack!'

The Englishman stopped and looked round. 'What's up?'

'I thought I heard bells.'

As they listened a muffled tinkling could be heard from somewhere nearby.

'There must be sheep grazing near here,' said Jack.

'I doubt it. Not at this height. The shepherds stay lower down. I think we're about to meet some much larger animals.'

'Bulls, do you mean?' asked Cassia rather apprehensively.

'Either bulls or their mothers and sisters…who also need to be treated respectfully. Don't worry—they'll be with a herdsman. I'll go ahead and have a word with him.'

Passing Jack, Simón went ahead towards a gap between two large crags forming a gateway into the adjoining valley.

'Rather him than me,' Jack remarked to Cassia as she closed the gap between them. 'The cows can be more dangerous than the bulls from what I've heard.'

She had heard the same thing, but in Jack's place would have held her tongue. She had a feeling that he wasn't worried himself but expected her to be afraid and was testing her nerve.

'I've never heard of any walkers being attacked by Spanish cattle,' she said calmly.

'You wouldn't, would you? They keep that sort of news out of the papers. Gorings aren't good for the tourist trade,' he said, with a wicked grin.

He was obviously trying to alarm her. She felt the best way to handle him was with a succinct comment used by her father to dismiss something as nonsense.

Having said it, she didn't pause to see his reaction but moved quickly past him to follow Simón between the crags.

The valley through which they had to pass as part of a circular route back to their starting point presented a peaceful scene—except that the beasts grazing in it were not dairy cattle but the fighting bulls bred not only for the *corrida* but also for running through the streets and being challenged in small rings by youths during the many town and village fiestas.

Only one animal was belled—a large cow who stood out from the others, not only because her movements caused the bell on her leather collar to make a clanking sound, but also because she was a brown and white piebald, while the rest, apart from a couple of brown cows and calves, were black.

They were spread out across the valley. There was no way of avoiding them. Among them, clearly their leader, was one very large bull who seemed to be gazing directly at her. At the thought of walking past him, expecting at every moment that massive head to swing low before a charge, Cassia felt her stomach clench.

But Simón had been right. There *was* a herdsman, and he and Simón were walking towards each other, the bulls' guardian with the assurance that his charges wouldn't harm him, and Simón with an air of confidence which Cassia wouldn't have felt had she been in his place.

After some conversation the two Spaniards came over to where she and Jack were waiting and Simón introduced the herdsman.

'He's going to escort us through,' he told them. 'These cattle aren't usually aggressive when they're grazing, but they're not used to seeing anyone but him when they're up here.'

Even in the herdsman's charge, and with a stalwart man on either side of her, passing through the herd was not an experience that Cassia wished to repeat. Every step of the way she was conscious of the large bull turning his head to follow their progress. It made her respect more than ever the courage of men who duelled with such formidable animals.

The herdsman seemed pleased to have someone to chat to, and they were delayed for some time while he and Simón talked. Then, with thanks and more handshakes, they resumed their walk.

By half a mile further on, the chafing inside Cassia's boot was becoming increasingly uncomfortable. But she thought that they would probably stop to drink water again before long, and then, on the pretext of going behind a bush, she could take a quick look at her heel. It might be that a wad of tissue would serve better than a plaster. If she could avoid it she didn't want to let on that she had a problem.

Unfortunately her plan was thwarted, because neither of the men seemed to want another stop. Instead of keeping an eye on her, as he had during the morning, Simón now took it for granted that at least on this route anything they could do, she could do.

With Jack in the lead and Simón close on his heels they were talking about cars, and, on the downhill sections, moving very fast, their thick soles designed for these rocky tracks.

Cassia found that she had to concentrate hard to avoid losing her balance on pockets of loose stone or rocks worn and weathered to a slippery smoothness. As well as the pain in her heel, the fronts of her thighs were beginning to ache from several hours' unaccustomed exercise. But she gritted her teeth and pressed on, determined not to let them know that, for her, the day's outing was turning into an ordeal.

By the time they got back to the village the pain was intense, like a red-hot wire lancing her heel at every step. Somehow she managed neither to limp nor to wince. But when Jack suggested having coffee in the bar she almost groaned aloud at the thought of having to walk past the Range Rover in search of some smoky bar full of men with loud voices and a television going full-blast.

'I think Cassia might prefer a long, iced drink in the patio at home,' said Simón. 'You look tired,' he told her.

'I enjoyed it,' she said, half-truthfully. 'But I am looking forward to a shower and taking these boots off. They feel much heavier than the loafers and sandals I mainly wear.'

'I wear boots most of the time. I'm more comfortable in them,' said Jack, unlocking his vehicle.

Simón said, 'You have the front seat on the way back, Cassia.'

It was bliss to sit down. Her blistered heel was still painful, but less agonising than when she had been walking on it.

An hour later, in the privacy of her room, Cassia took off her left boot and then, with gritted teeth, the right one. On Jack's advice she was wearing two pairs of socks—an inner pair of white cotton and an outer pair of brown wool. Both were sticking to the back of her foot, and what the white sock revealed as she peeled it away from her heel made her grimace with dismay. She had had small blisters before but never one this big. It had blown up and burst, and now the raw flesh was bleeding.

Hours too late, she regretted not asking Jack for a plaster as soon as it had started to hurt. Now it was long past the stage when a plaster would cover the damage and protect it from infection.

After a few moments' thought she decided that the first thing to do was to have a refreshing shower. Then, wearing her flip-flops, she would slip out to the pharmacy and hope to buy dressings large enough to cover the site of the blister while it healed.

After the day's exertions it was good to stand in the shower and feel her energy reviving as the hot water streamed down her body. Probably Simón and Jack had already had their showers and would soon be having a beer together in the patio. She would have to sneak out the back way, and cut through the alley connecting the road at the rear with the street leading to the chemist's shop with its distinctive green cross.

As far back as she could remember, her father had always sought advice from chemists rather than doctors. In his view they knew as much as many GPs, and their advice was free. Thinking of her father, she sighed. He had been a difficult man, but there were times when she missed him with an almost physical ache, and this was one of them. The painful smarting of her heel reminded her of all the times in her childhood when he had patched her up after some minor injury.

There was still a small scar on her wrist where another child had accidentally jabbed her with one blade of a pair of scissors. The mother of the child had panicked and wanted to rush Cassia to hospital, but John Browning had told her to calm down. He had pressed the lips of the cut together and fastened them with a butterfly suture made from a strip of plaster. A week later it had healed, leaving only the small pearly mark now hidden by her watch strap.

There being no one about when she left the first-floor shower room a few doors away from her bedroom, she allowed herself to limp. Simón and Jack had rooms on the floor above and, the main staircase being on the other side of the building, had no reason to come past her room whether going down or up.

So it was a shock when a voice behind her said, 'What the hell have you done to your heel, girl?'

Cassia gasped and whirled round. 'What are you doing— sneaking up on me?'

'I was coming to get your boots. New boots need going over with dubbin.' Jack had on a clean white T-shirt and a pair of black jeans. The reason she hadn't heard him coming was that he was barefoot.

'What's dubbin?'

'It's a leather dressing. Makes boots waterproof and softens them. How long were you walking on that bloody great blister?'

'It looks worse than it is. It's nothing to make a fuss about.'

'Are you kidding? It looks like raw steak. If that isn't dealt with properly it could go septic on you. You'd better come up to my room and let me sort it out for you.'

'If you'll lend me your first-aid stuff, I can do it myself.'

'I'll do it better. I've had some training in first aid. Have you?'

'No, but it's just common sense.'

'If you had any of that you wouldn't have walked all the skin off your heel,' he informed her. 'But you've plenty of guts, I'll say that for you. Most girls would have been in tears long before it had got that bad.'

Again taking her by surprise, he stepped forward and scooped her off her feet.

'I don't need to be carried!' she protested.

'The way you were walking, you do.' He settled her against his chest. 'Put your arm round my neck.'

She was wearing a clean pair of briefs under her thin cotton robe, but her clean bra was in her room, where the underwear she had put on that morning was soaking in the hand basin. Fortunately her toilet bag had a wrist-loop at one end of the zipper. She was able to put her left arm round Jack's solid shoulders while holding the front of her robe securely together with her other hand.

'If you'd been in my company in the Legion, I'd have put you on a charge,' said Jack.

'Do they have women soldiers even in the French Legion now?' she asked incredulously. 'I'd have thought it was the last bastion of masculine solidarity.'

'It is…and it always will be,' Jack said with grim satisfaction. 'Women are useless as soldiers. The army's a man's world.'

'There are quite a few armies which do recruit women,' she said.

'You wouldn't catch me serving in them. Fighting is a man's life. Women should stick to nursing and jobs like that.'

Cassia had already decided that among male chauvinists Jack was a fundamentalist. She wasn't planning to try to open his mind to less reactionary ideas. There might be some committed feminists among the girls coming in who would attempt to convert him. She doubted if they would succeed. It was a waste of breath to reason with people like him. They had a fixed view of the world, and no amount of argument would budge them from their beliefs.

'I thought in the Legion a soldier would be expected to ignore a minor flesh-wound,' she said as they reached the stairs to the floor above.

'Depends on the circumstances. In action he might have to. What you did was plain bloody stupid.'

She said in French, 'Watch your language, please,

Captain. I'm not one of your soldiers. You can't have it both ways. If you want us to be ladylike, you have to remember to behave like gentlemen towards us.'

He took the reproof in good part. 'I didn't know you spoke French. Where did you learn it—at school?'

'Like you, I picked it up out of necessity. My father was an artist. We spent a few years in France, mostly at Collioure near the border with Spain.'

Taking the stairs two at a time, Jack reached the top of the flight with no obvious sign of exertion. Considering she weighed a hundred and twenty-five pounds, it was not something any man could do. But she had the feeling that he had been showing off a little. She wondered who, if he and Simón had to fight each other, would win the contest. Jack was more heavily built, and presumably trained in all forms of hand-to-hand combat, but Simón was a powerful man with a more subtle mind. At least, that was her impression. He would think faster than Jack and perhaps beat him that way.

At the door of his room Jack said, 'Open it, will you?'

Cassia let go of her robe and reached down to turn the doorknob.

He set her down by his bed. 'Lie on your face so I can get at you heel.'

She stepped out of her flip-flops and, after a moment's hesitation, did as he told her, raising herself on her elbows to watch him going to the cupboard for a large plastic box of the kind sold in DIY stores for storing nails and screws.

He put this on the foot of the bed and then crossed the room to the washbasin. On the way there he swung the door closed.

This made Cassia slightly uneasy. Why did the door need to be closed if all he had in mind was to attend to her heel?

CHAPTER SIX

TELLING herself not to be foolish, while being at the same time aware that they were a long way away from the two other people in the house, or any workmen who might still be about, Cassia noticed that this room of Jack's was much the same as hers in size and appointments.

But while she had tried to personalise her room—draping a Spanish shawl over the bed and tucking picture postcards and snapshots under the frame of the large mirror over the writing-cum-dressing table—this room had no individual touches. Only his toothbrush and shaving kit on the glass shelf over the washbasin, and a magazine, a book and a rubber-clad torch on the bedside table showed that someone was sleeping here. All his other possessions were in the cupboards and drawers.

She angled her head to read the title of the book—*Climbing in Patagonia*. The magazine underneath was called *High* and subtitled *Mountain Sports*.

Jack finished washing his hands, which must have been clean already. While he had been carrying her she had smelt the aroma of soap or shower gel on him. If his hair had been longer it would still have been damp, as hers was.

Jack grasped the back of the upright chair at the table and moved it to the foot of the bed.

'Move further down, will you? So your foot's sticking over the edge.'

She obeyed, rucking up her robe above the backs of her knees. She was not showing any more leg than if she had been wearing a short skirt, but somehow, in these circumstances, she felt over-exposed. But to try to pull her robe down would only draw attention to it.

'I'm going to swab this with antiseptic,' he told her.

'OK. Whatever you say.'

Considering the size of his hands, he was surprisingly deft and gentle. Presently he said, 'You could do with a pair of clogs to wear until this has healed. D'you know the things I mean? Thick soles and no backs to 'em.'

'Mules,' said Cassia. 'Hospital nurses wear them, but I don't know where I'd get a pair around here. Anyway, it wouldn't be worth buying them for the short time my heel will be sore.'

'You were stupid to get in this state...but I'll give you credit for pluck. Stamina too. You kept up with us better than I expected. You don't look what I'd call sturdy, but I reckon you are.' For the first time he sounded friendly.

'My word, that *is* a compliment,' she said, with a teasing glance over her shoulder.

Jack gave her one of his rare smiles. 'Don't let it go to your head, kid.'

Suddenly she felt certain that he wasn't the type to try anything unwelcome.

At that moment someone knocked on the door.

'Come in,' Jack called.

The door opened and Simón stood on the threshold, one black eyebrow shooting up when he saw Cassia lying on the bed.

'Would you look at what this silly girl's done to herself?' said Jack.

He seemed oblivious of a change in the atmosphere, but she was instantly aware that although it wasn't apparent in his manner their employer was seriously displeased at finding her there. To her, the glacial vibes were so strong that they were almost palpable.

Simón moved forward to inspect the damage. 'You don't get a blister this size in five minutes, Cassia. Why didn't you say you were in trouble?'

'I didn't realise it was as bad as it is.'

'An air-head, but she gets ten for grit,' said Jack.

'Not from me,' Simón said curtly. 'I've no sympathy for self-inflicted injuries. It's going to take at least a week for that to heal.'

Apparently forgetting the reason he had come to Jack's room, he walked out, leaving the door open behind him.

Jack said nothing, and neither did Cassia. He gave her a pat on the back of her calf. 'You can get up now. I'll take another look tomorrow.'

'Thanks very much.' Being careful not to let her robe gape open, she rolled over and swung her feet to the floor. The whole of her heel was now neatly sealed by a large, ventilated dressing.

'Any time.' Jack was replacing the things he had used in the well-stocked box. 'We'd better find out what the facilities are, in case the kids need professional medical attention. I'll check that out in the morning.'

Cassia returned to her room. Before dressing, she blow-dried her hair. She had a feeling that Simón's terse comment in Jack's bedroom wouldn't be his last word on the subject.

When she went downstairs to help Laura with the supper, the housekeeper said it had been put back an hour because 'Excellency' had had to go out. Referring to Simón in the official style seemed to give her a buzz. She didn't approve of the others using his first name. She herself always called him Don Simón.

While all Spain's *duques* were grandees, she had explained to Cassia, not all the *marquéses* were. Because he was so informal himself, it was easy to forget that Excellency's title was very old and illustrious, she had added, glancing at Jack, whose manner towards their employer she didn't consider sufficiently respectful.

The first part of the house to be modernised had been the old-fashioned kitchen and the adjoining refectory. This didn't yet have its tables and benches installed but did have some easy chairs grouped round the corner fireplace. Jack had fetched in some logs cut from an old olive tree from the woodstack left by the caretaker, and had a cheerful blaze going by the time Simón returned.

The others were sitting round it having a glass of wine, and there was a savoury smell emanating from a large pan on top of the kitchen stove when Excellency returned.

'You look very cosy,' he said. 'It's much colder out now. I'm told there's often a spell of bad weather at this time of year. But it doesn't usually last more than three or four days.'

'A glass of wine for you, *jefe*?' Jack asked him. 'Or something stronger?'

'Wine will be fine.'

After taking off his leather jacket Simón opened a carrier and took out what looked like a shoe box. He handed it to Cassia.

'What's this?' she asked, puzzled.

'If you open it, you'll see.' There was an edge in his tone which might not have been audible to the others but was to her. She knew that he was still annoyed with her.

She opened the box, turned back a fold of coarse tissue and uncovered a pair of dark blue leather mules of the kind suitable for street wear.

'You can't go about in those flimsy rubber things at this time of year.' Evidently he had noticed her flip-flops on the floor by Jack's bed.

'You didn't go out specially to get these, did you?' she asked.

He shrugged. 'I also needed some stationery. You told the man at the boot shop you normally wore size thirty-seven, so those ought to fit you. Try them on.'

This evening Cassia was wearing a pair of red and pink carpet slippers with the backs folded down. She slipped them off and replaced them with the cork-soled mules.

'They fit perfectly. It was very good of you to go out and get them for me.' She didn't ask him what she owed him. The price would be on the box. She would put the money in an envelope and slip it under his door.

He dismissed her thanks with the customary '*De nada*' and turned away to talk to Jack.

Laura had bought *cocas* from the village baker. They resembled small pizzas, usually topped with slices of tomato and red pepper, or perhaps snippets of tinned anchovy or whatever else the baker had to hand. Laura had embellished them with some additions of her own, and the discs of hot dough with their savoury toppings made an appetising start to the meal.

The *cocas* were followed by a French dish of pork with potatoes and mushrooms in a rich garlicky gravy.

While they ate Simón made pleasant conversation, but addressing himself to the others, never to Cassia. His behaviour baffled her. To make a special trip to the nearest town to buy footwear which would enable her to move about comfortably while her heel healed, and yet now to ignore her seemed strangely inconsistent.

During the afternoon two dishwashers had been delivered and plumbed in. When the meal was over Simón said, 'If you'd help Laura load the machine, Jack, I want to speak to Cassia in private. We'll talk in the office, Cassia.'

She followed him from the room, telling herself that it

was absurd to feel like a miscreant schoolgirl about to be given a carpeting by a severe headmaster. She had done nothing wrong.

It was cold in the rest of the house. In the office Simón switched on an electric radiator before waving her to a chair and lifting one long, hard thigh onto the front edge of the desk, with his other leg stretched out straight.

It was a characteristic posture. When he was talking to the workmen, she had noticed, he often stood with his fingers thrust into the back pockets of his jeans. Unlike most Spaniards, he didn't usually gesticulate when he was talking. Only rarely did he illustrate a point with a graphic gesture. Now he sat with one hand in his pocket and the other resting on his thigh.

'The day I brought you away from Granada I told you that Señor Alvarez had charged me with being responsible for your welfare,' he began. 'He said you had been more sheltered than most of your peers and had no experience of discos or boyfriends. You knew the theory of sex, he said, from reading and listening to your colleagues. But he didn't think you had any practical knowledge. After finding you in Jack's bedroom this evening, I wonder if you know the theory as well as you should.'

Sitting very straight, with her chin up, Cassia said, 'Jack took me to his room to attend to my heel. Perhaps *you* can't envisage having a girl in *your* room without making a pass at her. I don't think it occurred to him.'

'It occurred to him,' Simón said sardonically. 'That he did nothing about it only shows he has more sense than you have. But if I hadn't come in he might have done something about it. When a girl lies down on a bed, in a flimsy dressing-gown, she's putting a lot of strain on a man's self-control—especially a guy like Jack who's in peak condition and may not have had a roll in the hay for some time.'

Cassia sprang to her feet. 'That's how you think of us, isn't it? Rolls in the hay…on a par with a meal or a drink. If the world was run to suit you, we'd all be slaves and concubines.'

Simón said coldly, 'You're losing your temper over nothing. I didn't set out to provoke a tirade on equality and all the rest of that claptrap. I was merely explaining what you appear not to know—that most single men spend a lot of time starving for sex. Therefore it's neither fair nor sensible to excite needs you aren't going to satisfy. Your mother would have explained that to you. Perhaps your father didn't discuss such matters.'

'My father set an example of how decent men treat women…with respect and consideration…not as playthings,' Cassia retorted.

'In general men give women the treatment they invite,' he answered. 'If they walk down the street showing their cleavage and wearing a tight miniskirt, they get whistles and lewd remarks. If they dress in a more modest style but have very good figures, they may still get the whistles without the coarse commentary. Going to Jack's room in your dressing-gown was giving a misleading signal. You should have got dressed first.'

'I didn't *go* to his room. As a matter of fact I was going to consult the chemist. Jack saw me leaving the shower. I was limping and he insisted on carrying me. I didn't have a lot of option.'

Simón's dark eyes narrowed slightly. 'Was that exciting?' he asked her.

'It saved me a lot of discomfort climbing the stairs.'

'That doesn't answer my question. Did it excite you?'

'The question doesn't make sense to me. Where does excitement come in when someone has a painful foot?'

'You didn't have a broken leg. I wouldn't have thought your heel was sufficiently painful to make you indifferent to being swept off your feet by Jack in caveman mode,' Simón said drily.

'He wasn't. He was just being kind...as you were when you went into town to get me those mules,' she added, suddenly remembering that he was her employer and she shouldn't have flared at him.

If the hotel manager had read her a homily, she wouldn't have answered back. She had momentarily forgotten that Simón was paying her wages.

'Sit down and listen to me,' he said quietly. 'Jack has changed his mind about you. This morning you were an encumbrance. He would have preferred to leave you behind. Perhaps you knew that.'

She nodded.

'Today, although you behaved like what he calls "an air-head",' he went on, 'you also showed you had grit— the quality he admires above everything else. That could create problems.'

'Surely it's better for your staff to be on good terms with each other?'

'Good terms—yes. But not too close. I know more about Jack than you do. Nothing to his discredit, but he was brought up in a children's home and he's led a tough, lonely life. I'm telling you this to make you realise that under his rugged exterior he may be extremely vulnerable. I don't want him falling in love with you, which he might very easily do.'

Cassia was taken aback. After a pause, she said, 'I think that's most unlikely. I'm not his type.'

'What is his type?'

'I don't know, but certainly not me.'

'I agree…but that won't stop it happening. Men frequently fall in love with women who aren't right for them. Women do the same. If you haven't experienced it yet, love is like a squall at sea. It sweeps people off their right course and can do a lot of damage.'

'Are you speaking from experience?'

'No, from observation only. I have friends who are happily married and other friends with a trail of disasters behind them. There's one big difference between them. The ones who—' He was interrupted by the telephone. 'Excuse me a moment.' He picked up the receiver. '*Diga!*'

After a pause he asked the caller to wait and, putting his hand over the mouthpiece, said to Cassia, 'This call will take some time. We'll continue our talk tomorrow. You've had a long, stressful day. Go to bed now. Goodnight.'

As she was leaving the room he started speaking Italian. It was a language with many similarities to Spanish, and she thought what he said was, 'No, you're not interrupting anything important. You know I am always delighted to hear your voice.'

'What did Don Simón have to say to you last night?' Laura enquired when Cassia went down to the breakfast.

As she didn't want to take Laura into her confidence, Cassia said, 'He gave me a ticking off for not saying I had a blister as soon as it started.'

'Yes, it was very silly of you,' the housekeeper agreed. 'But you've come out of it with a nice new pair of shoes.'

'They weren't a present. I've paid him for them.'

'Did he ask you to pay?'

'No. I put the money in an envelope and slipped it under his door before I went to bed.'

'If he didn't ask, I should have taken them as a gift. He

can afford a few *mil* better than we can,' said Laura. 'He's rolling in money. If you ask me, this set-up here is probably some kind of tax dodge. Do you believe he's really interested in young drop-outs and delinquents? I don't. Why should he be? If I had been born in a fine cradle like he was—' she was using the Spanish equivalent of a silver spoon in the mouth '—I wouldn't worry about the rest of the world. I'd concentrate on enjoying myself.'

'Why did you take this job if the project doesn't interest you?'

'I didn't say *I* wasn't interested. But is he?' Laura shrugged her plump shoulders. 'Perhaps…for a while. Then he'll lose interest. When rich people take up causes, it's usually to suit themselves. There's a lot of corruption in high places in this country,' she added darkly.

Later, thinking over her remarks, Cassia had to admit that her own first impression of Simón as a playboy and womaniser didn't tie in with the role of a caring philanthropist. But had he arrived at the hotel without Isa Sanchez in tow, she would not have had that impression.

She remembered what he had said to her in the office the night before. 'Most single men spend a lot of time starving for sex.' Perhaps he was speaking from experience. He, like Jack, was in peak condition. Perhaps his libido drove him to have affairs with girls like Isa, apparently prepared to sleep with anyone who gave them a good time in luxurious surroundings. Cassia's father hadn't been a philandering man, but from time to time his libido had driven him into relationships which had differed from Simón's affairs only in being longer-lasting.

She found her thoughts about Simón deeply puzzling and unsettling. Also, she was intensely curious to know what he had been going to say about the difference between the happy and unhappy marriages of his friends. When the right moment arose she would remind him.

But the right moment didn't arise that day, or the next, and the day after that the Marqués announced at breakfast that he was off to Madrid.

Before he left they did have a few moments together. 'Remember what I told you. Don't get too friendly with Jack. Don't let your curiosity lead you down the wrong road. That's all it would be if you let him start something with you. That's the irresistible urge which gets most girls into bed the first time. Not because they need or want sex. Not even because they're in love. But because they can't wait to find out what it's all about.'

He had written out lists of tasks he expected them each to accomplish in his absence. She had not expected advice on her personal conduct.

'And a big disappointment it is, in most cases,' he added. 'So don't be tempted to let Jack initiate you.'

Retaining her self-possession with difficulty, she said, 'I don't need this lecture…Excellency. I'm not just out of a convent, although you seem to think so. Compared with other people of my age, I've been around more than most.'

'Geographically, yes. Not emotionally. It wouldn't surprise me if you've never been kissed,' he said, smiling.

'Of course I've been kissed!' she exploded indignantly.

'Like this?' He cupped her chin and her cheek in the warm curve of his palm and, tilting her face up, put his lips lightly on hers. For a moment, while her heart bungee jumped, his mouth remained on hers, motionless. Then, softly and slowly, it moved in a kiss so gentle yet so subtly arousing that her response astonished and horrified her.

Simón raised his head and looked down at her, knowing—she could see it in his eyes—precisely how she was feeling—how he had made her feel.

'Not like that,' he said mockingly. '*Adiós, chica.*'

The effect of his kiss stayed with her all the time he was gone. She went to sleep thinking about it, dreamed about him, and woke up wondering if today he would come back.

She knew that she had fallen in love with him. Madly, deeply, foolishly. Unutterably foolishly. For the chance of his loving her was infinitesimal.

In his absence, her heel made good progress. Every morning Jack brought his first-aid case down to breakfast and replaced the dressing with a fresh one. Within a week of the walk the place didn't need to be covered, although it was still somewhat tender and he felt a plaster would protect it from an accidental knock.

The following Saturday night Jack went out for the evening. Before he left he said that if the weather stayed fine the next day he might have a swim.

'At this time of year! You must be mad,' exclaimed Laura.

'I met an old guy—a German—in the village this morning who swims all year round. He's seventy-something. If he can do it, I reckon I can. Would you like to come, Cass?'

The thought of a day by the sea was very tempting. It was a long time since she'd seen it. She couldn't resist saying, 'Yes, please. But I don't promise to swim if the water's cold.'

'No use asking you to join us, I suppose?' he said to Laura.

With a vehement shake of the head, she said, 'My friend from Benidorm is coming to spend the day with me. She rents a little car while she's here. We may go out for a drive. Do you wish to take a packed lunch, or will you eat out?'

'We'll find somewhere to eat—if that's all right with you, Cassia?'

She took this as a hint that they would be going Dutch. 'Fine,' she agreed.

They set out just before nine the next morning, by which time the misty vapour lying over the vineyards had cleared and it promised to be a hot day.

'Brought your swimsuit?' Jack asked as they left the village behind.

'Yes, but it's falling to bits. I shall have to buy another for the summer. I used to love swimming when we lived on a boat. But that was a long time ago. Did you grow up near the sea?'

He shook his head. 'Never saw it when I was a kid. I learnt to swim in a big indoor pool with the water stinking of chlorine, making your eyes sting. But with us lot all peeing in it I reckon it would have smelt worse without the chemicals.'

Cassia laughed. 'Children aren't the only ones who do that. I've seen grown-ups get up from their beach chairs, wander into the sea for a few minutes and then come out again. It was perfectly obvious what they were doing.'

'That doesn't bother me,' said Jack. 'It's the bad pollution I watch out for. But I've heard the beaches on this coast are cleaner than most. Anyway, the old fellow who recommended the one we're going to says he's swum there for years, and he looks as fit as a flea.'

Their route took them over a pass into the neighbouring valley and then by the bed of a river which, although dry at the moment—perhaps because its main source had been dammed higher up—had at some time swept its way through the rocky terrain, scouring away the red earth which around it nurtured *almendros*, their branches now bursting with blossom.

Some groves were pink, others white. Soon, Cassia knew, the ephemeral beauty of the blossom would be replaced by green leaves and furry cases already almost as large as when the embryos inside had grown to full-size almonds. But today, as they would for a week or two more, the trees gave the arid landscape its most beautiful aspect— long before spring would break in more northerly Europe.

'Where did you learn to swim?' asked Jack.

'I can't remember. Probably somewhere in Greece. My father said I could swim before I could walk. Babies living on boats have to be drownproofed as soon as possible.'

'You're on your own now, is that right?'

'If my grandparents are alive, I don't know where they are.'

Jack said, 'I suppose I've got grandparents somewhere. It's not likely they'll all be dead yet. Me, I don't even know who my parents were.' After a pause he added, 'I used not to like having no family when I was a kid. Now it doesn't bother me. Families aren't always that close. Sometimes they hate each other.'

'Families in Spain seem closer than families in some other countries,' said Cassia. 'I always feel envious when I see them on Sunday picnics—the grannies dandling the babies and all the sons and sons-in-law attending to the paella while their wives have a rest and a gossip and the older children run about.'

Jack didn't answer, perhaps because there was a blind bend ahead and the road there was barely wide enough for two vehicles to pass each other. After a winding stretch the view opened out, traversed by the east-coast *autopista*—a broad ribbon of speeding traffic supported, where the land dipped, on massive pillars of concrete. Far from being an eyesore, its sweeping curves were beautiful.

It reminded Cassia of the journey from Granada. She wondered if Simón would disapprove of her accepting Jack's invitation. But if she hadn't she would have been at a loose end today. Laura and her French friend wouldn't have wanted her with them.

The beach that Jack had been told about was a small, stony cove at the foot of rust-coloured cliffs. It was at one end of a large bay near the town called Jávea, which stood a kilometre inland but had spread to form a resort of a quieter type than Benidorm. At the back of the cove was a terrace belonging to a café-bar, but at present the bar wasn't open and they had the cove to themselves.

'I expect most people are having a lie-in,' said Jack. 'It's early yet. Give it an hour. The sea looks pretty good, don't you think?'

'It *looks* most inviting,' she agreed, admiring the sparkling blue-green water lapping the sea-shiny cobbles.

'I'll check it out,' said Jack.

This morning, in place of boots, he was wearing thick rubber soles attached to his feet by Velcro-fastened straps. He walked down to the water's edge, bending to roll up his trouser legs before letting the sea wash over his sandalled feet.

'It's not too bad,' he reported. 'I won't say it's warm, but it should feel pretty good...once you're in.'

'Maybe I'll go in later. We're going to be here all morning, aren't we?'

'I thought we'd have lunch here,' said Jack, returning to where he had dumped his knapsack. 'In summer, so the old guy says, there's a place at the other end of the bay where they serve *paella* out of doors under a split-cane awning. But it isn't open at this time of year.'

As he spoke he unzipped his trousers. He was already wearing a brief black slip. In a matter of moments he was ready to bathe.

'Right…here we go, then!' Still wearing the sandals, he strode into the sea, and when it was up to his thighs flung up his arms for a plunge dive.

He was under the water for some seconds, surfacing with a characteristically masculine shake of the head—a reflex, perhaps, from the days when he had had longer hair.

His scalp, almost bald when she'd first met him, was looking a little less shorn, she noticed as he started an energetic crawl in the direction of some red floats lying on the surface two or three hundred yards out.

Predictably Jack was a powerful swimmer, but he made a lot of splash. Cassia had the feeling that Simón would also swim well, but in a more stylish manner.

Suddenly changing her mind, she unzipped her holdall and pulled out a towel and a black Lycra one-piece dating back to her mid-teens. Since the last time she had worn it, her vital statistics had changed, her waist now being slimmer than at sixteen, her bust and hips fuller.

She was wearing a white T-shirt under a loose blue denim pinafore with a dropped waist and side-seam pockets. There still being no one about, she pulled off her briefs and stepped into the swimsuit, drawing it over her hips before stripping down to her bra and reaching behind her to unfasten the clip.

As she did so Jack stopped swimming. He rolled over and, treading water, waved to her at the same moment as Cassia removed her bra and felt the warmth of the sun caressing her bare breasts.

Although she had never exposed her breasts in public, as many women did at the beach, he was too far away for her to feel any embarrassment. She waved back and pulled up her swimsuit, then applied a waterproof suncream to her shoulders and back. Her face and arms she had sunproofed before coming out.

Having no plastic beach shoes, she found the stony beach made walking very uncomfortable. Nor was getting in painless. Unable to stride in and plunge, she had to endure the ordeal of the water creeping up her legs as she felt her way forward on slippery footholds. When she did throw herself forward the shock of immersing her warm flesh in the cold sea made her stifle a howl of agony.

'It's great…once you're in, isn't it?' said Jack when they met a hundred yards out. 'I'm told there's a nice little beach over there.' He jerked a thumb at the cliffs between the cove and the end of the headland. 'Let's go and investigate, shall we?'

The beach, hidden from the cove, was sandy. As they landed on it Jack said, 'Old Fritz—or whatever his name is—comes out here to strip off and tan his backside. Don't worry, I'm not going to do that,' he added with a grin, sitting down and leaning back on his elbows.

Cassia sat down beside him and surveyed the view from this different perspective. Halfway across the bay, on a low promontory, was a grove of palm trees.

Pointing them out to Jack, she said, 'I wonder what they're doing there. It seems a funny place for palm trees to be growing.'

'That's where the main beach is. The palms were brought in for the garden of a modern *parador*. Fritz said we can drive back that way, cutting across those low hills at the back,' he said, pointing to a wooded hinterland dotted with white villas. 'You're not cold now, are you?' Jerking into a sitting position, he laid the flat of his hand on the bare skin between her shoulder blades.

She had an intuitive feeling that he wanted to kiss her.

CHAPTER SEVEN

EITHER Cassia's instinct was wrong or Jack chose not to act on the impulse.

Answering the question himself, he said, 'No, you feel warm as toast.' Then, taking his palm away to lock both hands behind his head and stretch himself at full length, he went on, 'I should have brought a mask and fins. Have you done any snorkelling?'

Relieved that she'd been mistaken, Cassia said, 'As a child, yes. Not for a long time.' She was struck by a worrying thought. 'Do you think it's all right to leave our gear unattended? When I followed you in I didn't think I'd be coming out of sight. Maybe I should go back in case someone grabs the chance to make off with our valuables.'

'By God…you're right!' he exclaimed, jackknifing to his feet. 'My credit card's in my wallet. If that gets nicked I'll have to ring the UK, and I don't know the bloody number. It'll mean going back to the house.'

Seconds later he was in the water, thrashing up foam as he tore back the way they had come.

Swimming flat out, Cassia was not far behind him when a shout made her pause.

'Panic over,' Jack called.

Treading water, she saw that the bar had opened and now an elderly couple were sitting at a table on the terrace. But the beach was still empty.

They swam the rest of the way breast-stroking alongside each other. Where the water came up to his chest, Jack stood up. 'I've got sea shoes. You haven't. I'll give you a lift over the stones.'

This time being picked up and carried was less surprising, but in a way more disturbing. It was her first close contact with a naked male torso.

Beside their things, he set her on her feet.

'Thanks,' she said casually, bending to pluck her towel from the rock where she'd left it after unintentionally catching sight of the evidence that he too had been affected by the intimate contact.

Jack wrapped his towel round his hips and sat down. 'Have you ever smoked?' he asked.

Starting to towel her hair, Cassia paused to shake her head. 'I tried one once. I didn't like it.'

'People don't…not the first few. Then they get hooked. I gave it up five years ago. Sometimes—like after a swim— I feel the old urge to light up. But I never will. I've more respect for my body than I had then. Most soldiers smoke and drink. You'll find the odd one who doesn't, but not many.'

'Tell me about your time in the French Foreign Legion.'

'Légion Étrangère,' he corrected her. 'Well, I served two five-year contracts. It's a great outfit. I went in a bumptious kid with a chip on my shoulder, and they made a man of me.'

'If you liked it, why did you leave?'

'I liked it and I miss it,' he said, staring at the horizon. 'But there's more to life than being a fighter, which is what the Légion is about. They're crack fighting men—France's best—but it's like being a monk—except that a *légionnaire* doesn't swear to give up women,' he added, with a fleeting grin.

'Are they allowed to marry?' Cassia asked.

'They're allowed to, and some do. But they can be away

from their families for months on end. It's better for a *légionnaire* to be single and screw around,' he went on bluntly. 'There's no shortage of willing birds for any guy wearing the *képi blanc*.' Suddenly turning his head to look directly at her, he said quietly, 'That's OK in your early twenties, but after a while it's not what you want any more. You want a woman of your own. Someone to love...to love you.'

Cassia found this statement, coming from such a tough-looking man, profoundly touching. It brought a lump to her throat.

'Everyone wants that, I guess,' she said, hunting for a comb to sort out her tangled hair. 'How old were you when you joined the Légion, Jack?'

'Seventeen, but I looked older. I've been out four years. I'm thirty-one. How old are you?'

'Twenty-two.'

'At times you seem younger...other times older,' he told her. 'I guess that's because you're quiet. Most young girls make a lot of noise. I don't like all that giggling and chattering. Shall we go up and have a coffee?'

It was late afternoon when they returned to the village. Laura and her friend were still out.

'Would you like a cup of tea?' Cassia asked.

'Good thinking. While you're making it I'll rinse the salt out of our beach stuff and hang it out to dry.'

Handing over her rolled-up towel, she cautioned, 'My swimsuit won't stand a lot of vigorous wringing. It needs to drip dry.'

While they were drinking tea, and Jack was eating a wedge of Manchego cheese in a chunk of *barra negra* to keep him going until suppertime, he said, 'Would you like to see my photo gallery of the guys I was with in *sauteurs ops*?'

Thinking he meant to bring down a photograph album, she said, 'Yes, please.'

'They're taped to the door of my cupboard. Let's take a refill up with us,' he said, reaching for the teapot.

Mindful of Simón's warning, she searched for a tactful pretext for changing her mind, but couldn't think of one. Anyway, she was sure that Jack had no ulterior motive for inviting her up to his room. Or was she being foolishly naïve? They were alone in the house.

'What does *sauteurs ops* mean?' she asked on the way upstairs. 'Something to do with parachuting?'

'It's a special operations force—the equivalent of the Special Air Service in the UK. At the end of my basic training I went on to do parachute training.'

In his room he opened the wardrobe, revealing that both doors were covered with mementoes of his service life.

'That's a picture of Capitaine Danjou's wooden hand,' he explained, pointing to a photograph of an articulated hand lying on top of an elaborate, glass-sided casket. 'It's the Légion's most revered relic.'

While she peered at the finely carved and polished hand, Jack brought a chair for her to sit on and named and described some of his brothers-in-arms. As he talked she began to understand the strength of their camaraderie and to sense how much he missed it.

She was about to ask him if he could re-enlist if he wished, when they heard a sound from below.

'That'll be Laura coming back.' Jack swallowed a mouthful of cooling tea.

'Was that your everyday headgear?' Cassia asked, looking at the green beret hanging near the top of the door.

He took it down from its hook. 'Yes, the *képi blanc* is

for walking out and parades. We wear these pulled down to the left, not to the right like the British.' Suddenly he put it on, moulding it to his head, his expression remote, as if the feel of it took him back to the world he had left and still missed.

'You've been swimming, I see,' said a voice from the doorway, making Cassia jump. It wasn't Laura who had come up to join them.

It was Simón.

Jack whipped off the beret, as if he felt foolish to have been caught wearing it. Cassia rose to her feet, also feeling uncomfortable. Suddenly the atmosphere was full of tension.

'Ah, Capitaine Danjou's famous hand,' Simón said, his eyes on the photograph.

'You know about him?' Jack sounded surprised.

'Of course,' said Simón. 'The stand at Camerone is one of the most famous incidents in modern military history. Sixty men against two thousand…and, when the Mexican commander demanded the last three *légionnaires* surrender to him, although they were wounded they would only give up on condition that they kept their arms and were allowed to look after their comrades with worse wounds. He's on record as saying, "One can refuse nothing to men like you".'

As he spoke Cassia saw the reason they hadn't heard him coming was that he was wearing tennis clothes and rubber-soled shoes, suggesting the decision to return to Castell today had been an impulse.

'We weren't expecting you,' she said. 'Laura's still out with her friend. As we've all had lunch out today, it's going to be a cold supper…if that's all right with you?'

She was thinking that if he hadn't had his main meal at lunchtime she had better start preparing something hot for him. It was possible that Laura might not get back until late if, after their drive, the two women had gone to Benidorm.

'Fine with me,' he answered, giving her the briefest of glances before returning his attention to the array of mementoes.

'The founder and hero of Spain's Foreign Legion was Colonel Millan Astray,' he told Jack. 'He was wounded five times and lost a leg and an eye. His battle cry was "*Viva la muerte*!" Long live death. He borrowed a lot of ideas from the French Legion.'

Cassia knew that he was angry with her. It would not be apparent to Jack, but she knew it was so—even though it must be clear to Simón that nothing had been going on except a demonstration of the other man's on-going allegiance to the army which had, in his own words, made a man of him.

In a gap in the men's conversation she excused herself and slipped away. It had not needed Simón's return to remind her of his parting kiss. It had been at the back of her mind every hour of every day since he'd left. Why he had kissed her goodbye she was still not sure. To tease her, seemed the most likely answer.

In her room, tidying herself for the evening, she remembered the feel of his palm against her cheek and the pressure of his lips on hers. Not technically her first kiss, because when she was fourteen a boy of fifteen had planted an inexpert kiss on her startled mouth while they'd gathered shellfish together. And there had been a couple of one-off kisses since then. But Simón's kiss had been the first to make her long for more.

She had changed her T-shirt for a butter-coloured cotton sweater, replacing the pinafore over it and adding a twisted scarf to the neck of the sweater, when there was a knock on her door.

Unless Laura had returned, it could be Jack or it could be Simón. She couldn't see any reason for Jack to come to her room, which meant that it was probably Simón. She debated calling out that she wasn't decent at the moment, but she knew that would only postpone the reprimand she was expecting. She went to the door and opened it.

Simón was still in his tennis kit, but the cable-knit sweater which earlier had been thrown over his shoulders with the sleeves loosely tied at the front was now pulled on over his white shirt.

His expression unrevealing, he said, 'How have things been going?'

'Pretty well.' She took a step back. 'Come in.'

He walked into her room, looking round it, taking in the changes she'd made—the shawl and cushions on the bed, the books on the chest of drawers, the other personal touches.

'Won't you sit down?' She gestured towards the basket chair by the window, seating herself on the upright chair by the table. 'I think I know what you're going to say.'

The other chair creaked as he settled himself, crossing his long brown legs, their colour emphasised by the whiteness of his shorts and socks.

'What am I going to say?'

'My guess is you're going to repeat what you said before…about my being in Jack's room.'

'Actually, no…it would be wasting my breath. I told you what I thought. You chose to ignore it. That's that,' he said astringently.

'I didn't *ignore* what you said. I did think about it. When Jack offered to show me his Legion photos I didn't realise where he kept them. I thought they'd be in an album he meant to bring down to the kitchen. When I found out they weren't, how could I refuse to go upstairs with him? It would have been hurtful and insulting.'

'If Jack were half as au fait with the outcome of recent battles in the sex war as he is with successful actions carried out by the Légion Étrangère, he might have been wary of asking you to his room,' he said coldly. 'These days a woman has only to claim sexual harassment and a man is in serious trouble.'

'Jack knows I wouldn't do that.'

'You might, if something happened you couldn't cope with and you panicked. According to my mother, a lot of the things defined as "harassment" now were, in her day, considered the natural hazards of being an attractive female.'

'I thought Spanish girls of your mother's generation always had a duenna keeping an eye on them.'

'Most of them did, but my mother happens to be English. She had to cope on her own…and, judging by what she's told me, did it with great aplomb.'

'You mentioned that your mother was brought up in England, but I didn't realise she *was* English,' said Cassia. 'You look totally Spanish.'

'The de Mondragóns are mongrels. We have Moorish genes, Genoese genes—all kinds of genes in our bloodline. Fifty-seven varieties. Being mostly diplomats or soldiers, the majority of my ancestors found their wives outside Spain, although my grandfather married a girl who gave us a transfusion of undiluted Spanish blood.'

His eye fell on the photographs on her dressing table. 'Are those your parents?'

'Yes.'

Simón rose, crossed the room and picked up the picture

of her father—a snap she had taken herself while John Browning had been at work on a painting.

'A very distinguished-looking man,' he said as he replaced it.

The photograph of her mother was a print of a studio portrait that Cassia had found between the pages of a book. Fearing that her father might order her to destroy it, she had said nothing about it, and had not bought a frame for it until after his death.

'Very pretty,' observed Simón, studying the oval face and then turning his head to compare it with Cassia's. 'Much prettier than her daughter,' he said, with deflating frankness. 'But you, as your father could have told you but probably didn't, have the makings of a beauty.'

'Me…a beauty?' she said, staggered.

'Certainly…in a few years. Even now you're…very taking.' He replaced the photo beside that of her father and cast his eye over the other things on the dressing table, which luckily she had dusted and tidied that morning. They included the silver hoop earrings that she had been going to put on when his rap on the door had deflected her. He picked them up. 'Are you wearing these tonight?'

She nodded, intensely aware of his nearness. Being close to him like this disturbed her more, she discovered, than lying against Jack's bare chest.

Simón removed the butterfly fastener from the pin of one of the hoops. Holding it between his finger and thumb, he put the tip of his longest finger behind the lobe of her ear and inserted the pin in the hole, then made it secure with the butterfly. The touch of his hand against her cheek, and the intimacy of the service he was performing, made her heart lose its normal rhythm and beat in palpitating thumps. He did the same with the other hoop.

'Spanish girls have their ears pierced as babies. When were yours done?'

'When I was sixteen.'

'Was it very painful?'

'Only for a few seconds.' She had fixed her eyes on the V of the neck of his tennis sweater, unable to meet his gaze at such close quarters. 'The jeweller did something to deaden the pain. He was very quick and expert.'

'Take care to choose someone equally expert to perform that other, not dissimilar rite of passage in a woman's life,' he said, resting his hands on her shoulders.

As she grasped what he meant she flashed a quick, upward glance and saw his dark eyes glinting with wicked amusement.

On an uneven breath, she said, 'What makes you think someone already hasn't?'

'If they had, you wouldn't be blushing so deliciously. You may have been kissed before, but you haven't had a lover, have you?'

'No, I haven't,' she admitted. 'I suppose in your world that makes me some kind of freak.'

'It makes you a rarity,' he said drily. 'Do you understand the term "sport" in its botanical sense?'

She shook her head.

'I picked it up from my mother, an enthusiastic gardener. A sport is a plant that differs from others of the same species in some significant way. That can make it very desirable.' His hands shifted slightly, his forefingers gently caressing the sides of her neck.

She knew that he was making love to her and she didn't know how to deal with it, so she did nothing, submitting in pulse-racing silence to his touch and his look, waiting for what he would do next, which she was almost certain would be to kiss her again.

It was one of those moments in life when time seemed to come to a stop.

'Cassia…Cassia…telephone…'

Laura's urgent voice, coming up from somewhere below, made the world start spinning again.

Simón took his hands from her shoulders and Cassia pulled herself together. 'It can't be for me. I don't know anyone who would telephone me. It must be for you.'

'Perhaps it's Alvarez, calling to find out how you're getting on,' he suggested.

'I did write to him last week, but he wouldn't ring me on a Sunday. He'll be at home with his family,' she said as, with Simón moving more leisurely at her heels, she hurried downstairs.

'Ah, there you are!' exclaimed Laura, starting to come up the stairs as they came quickly down.

'Who is it, Laura? Did they say?'

'A girl…she didn't give her name. I had only come in a few moments before the telephone started ringing. When did you get back, Don Simón? I didn't see your car outside.'

On her way to the telephone, Cassia heard him say, 'I came in a friend's private plane and he dropped me off in his car.'

The call was from Rosita, wanting to know how Cassia was getting on. 'Señor Alvarez said he'd heard from you, but he didn't pass on any details. How's it working out?'

'Very well up to now. We haven't really got going yet. How are things with you?'

'The same as they were when you left. I could do with some excitement in my life, I can tell you,' Rosita said, with a loud sigh. 'So how are things going with your new boss? Has he made a pass at you yet?'

Cassia said firmly, '*Absolutamente*!' in the negative sense of 'Absolutely not!'

But even as she said it she was wondering if what had happened upstairs had been the beginning of a pass that Simón would have followed through if her ex-colleague hadn't chosen this moment to call.

Whether he would do that later was the thought paramount in her mind while she helped Laura prepare some tapas, and listened to the housekeeper describing her lunch out with her French friend.

When the men joined them conversation became general. Jack had heard that the king of Spain, Don Juan Carlos, was the owner of a Harley-Davidson motorbike on which, his identity concealed by his crash helmet, he had been known occasionally to give a lift to one of his subjects.

Simón confirmed that this was so, and was then asked by Laura if he had met the king and Doña Sophia, the popular queen of Spain.

'Only in formal circumstances—receptions and so on,' he told her, clearly not as interested in the life of his country's royal family as Laura.

Cassia was still digesting the surprising fact that his mother was an Englishwoman.

After supper Jack said that he was going to stroll down to the bar for a *tercio*, which she knew was a third of a litre of beer, and Simón said that he would join him.

'There's no side about him, is there?' said Laura when they had gone. 'I know people much lower down the scale than Excellency, who would turn up their noses at that scruffy little bar.'

Cassia suspected that going to the bar was a deliberate PR exercise on Simón's part. In small doses he might find the company of the men of the village interesting. But she doubted if he liked the noise level in the bar.

The two men were still out when she and Laura retired to their rooms. Cassia spent ten minutes resewing a couple of buttons which had been coming adrift on the shirt she would be wearing tomorrow.

As she stitched them on more securely she wondered what would have happened if Rosita hadn't rung up. Had Simón been toying with the idea of initiating her so far non-existent love-life? He certainly had the expertise, if indeed a long list of experienced ex-girlfriends was a qualification for teaching a girl with no experience.

She had always hoped that when, at long last, her curiosity was satisfied it would be with someone she loved, who loved her. Perhaps, if she hadn't met Simón, she could have fallen in love with Jack. They had a lot in common. With Simón she had nothing in common, except that he seemed to fancy her and she was irresistibly drawn to him.

The next day, her heel having healed, she accompanied the men on another day in the mountains.

They were looking for a place where Jack could teach abseiling and climbing on a bluff of sound rock. There were many spectacular bluffs within a few miles' radius of the village, but not all were stable. They looked at one where several huge chunks of rock, each weighing many tons, had fallen away from the face. It looked as if it might jettison others before long.

After some more exploring they arrived at a cliff which looked more promising. This was half an hour before their planned lunch break. Leaving Cassia to relax after the strenuous walk from where they had left the Range Rover, the two men set out to climb the cliff and, if successful, to abseil down it.

To her it looked unclimbable. But, starting in different places, each man found his own route up it, and she couldn't help wondering if there was a competitive element in the way they tackled the ascent, perhaps both hoping to reach the top first. Or perhaps not, for although his relations with women might suggest the reverse she didn't think Simón was an irresponsible man in the other areas of his life. He didn't drive recklessly, and she didn't think he would take chances on a rockface in order to beat Jack to the top.

Shading her eyes to watch their slow but steady upward progress, she wondered if she could do it. Perhaps when Simón had gone back to Madrid she would ask Jack to give her a lesson. With him, she wouldn't mind finding out that she had no aptitude or even a poor head for heights.

Women did climb, and climb well. She remembered reading a feature in a French magazine left behind by one of the guests at the Castillo about the woman who was one of France's most daring and expert rock climbers. Cassia didn't aspire to reach that level, but suddenly, watching the technique the men were using to climb the escarpment above her, she wished she were up there with them instead of being left behind.

But the first time she tried it she didn't want Simón to be there, in case she chickened out. Not that she thought he would despise her or mock her—he wasn't that sort of person—it was just that she wanted him to respect and admire her, to take her more seriously than any of his other women. Not that she was in that category, and she had no intention of joining it.

But it was one thing to tell herself that while she was down here, with her feet firmly on the ground, and he was up there with his mind focused on scaling a rockface. Later today he might find an opportunity to focus his attention on *her*. If and when he did, she knew it would be much harder to stick to her resolution not to succumb to the almost overwhelming magnetism he could exert—had exerted on her last night.

She hadn't forgotten the feel of his hands on her shoulders, his fingers moving against her neck. She had no illusions about her own vulnerability if he was determined to have her.

CHAPTER EIGHT

AFTER spending some time out of sight, presumably admiring the views from their higher vantage point, the men came down the escarpment in a fraction of the time it had taken them to haul themselves arduously up it.

Abseiling also looked fun, thought Cassia, watching Jack descend in a series of swoops, on a line attached to a harness round his hips, his feet keeping him clear of the rockface.

During lunch, as they discussed other climbs that they had done in other places, their conversation was peppered with words—arête, traverse, slabby rake, flake—which had little meaning for her. She felt that in some way the climb had put them on a new footing, their shared enthusiasm for the sport making other differences irrelevant.

'This must be boring for Cassia,' said Simón, suddenly turning to her.

'She might like to try it,' said Jack. 'I've met some first-rate women climbers.'

'Have you?' Her eyes lit up with interest. 'Where did you meet them?'

Before he could answer, Simón said, 'Some women do climb well, but the ones I've met have been very tough and not very feminine. Would you agree with that, Jack? I'm not saying they looked aggressively masculine—except for having more muscle to call on than most women—but they had different mind-sets from other women.'

'I couldn't say about that. I've seen them climbing but I haven't had a lot of direct contact.' Jack turned to Cassia.

'Climbing goes on everywhere, but the public don't see much of it because they're not usually near the places where it happens. You don't see it on TV often, because of the technical problems and because it's either a loner's sport or co-operative, not competitive. I've climbed in France and Corsica, where I was based as a para. I've also—' He broke off to look through binoculars at something which had caught his eye on a shoulder of hillside further along the valley.

A few moments later he said, 'Seems like someone's in trouble.'

Simón put aside his bread roll to have a look through his glasses. With the naked eye Cassia could only see a number of people moving slowly downhill.

'A party of walkers…one of them injured by the look of it. Perhaps we'd better get down there and see if they need any help,' he said, scrambling to his feet and beginning to gather his belongings together.

Jack followed suit. 'At the rate they're going down, it'll take them a month of Sundays to get up that steeper track on the other side of the valley…assuming they set out where we did.'

'There's nowhere else they could have started from in the area,' said Simón. 'Ready, Cassia? Right—let's get going.'

With him setting a cracking pace, it took them about twenty minutes to catch up with the four elderly people who had stopped for a rest when his party joined them.

The others turned out to be Belgians. One of the two women had tripped and fallen off the path, which at that point had skirted a drop of two or three feet. She was not only badly shaken but had a gash on her forehead and couldn't walk on her right foot. The two men—one tall, but overweight and unhealthily florid, and the other much shorter—had been carrying her down, but with difficulty. She was now in tears, being fussed over by the other wife.

'Would you look at their shoes, for heaven's sake?' Jack murmured to Cassia. 'This lot belong on the esplanade at Benidorm. What the hell are they doing out here, got up like that?'

She gave a nod of agreement. It seemed an act of madness for two women, both in open-toed town shoes and tights, to be where they were. Looking at the two men, both of whom had been sweating heavily in the midday heat, she thought it wouldn't be long before they became dehydrated.

Between them, Simón and Jack attended to the hurt woman's cut and the worst of her scratches and gave her a painkiller. Then they took turns to carry her on their backs, the one who wasn't transporting her carrying both their packs.

Cassia, left in charge of escorting the other three up, found it an anxious assignment. They went up the steep track like snails on what at the outset, she learned, had begun as a leisurely ramble before lunching on leg of lamb at a restaurant in the village.

As she gave her hand to the second woman and heaved her up the steepest sections while keeping an eye on the two men, she was worried that one of them might collapse before reaching the top.

Earlier, Jack had been saying how quickly mishaps could escalate into disasters when people were badly equipped or mentally unequal to coping with the unexpected. What had befallen these four townies seemed a good example of that.

Presently Simón reappeared. 'We assumed they had come by car,' he said to her. 'Unfortunately not. They came in a taxi which is coming back to pick them up—but not until four.'

By this time Cassia had discovered that both couples lived on one of the many *urbanizaciónes* near the coast—enclaves of holiday and retirement houses built to accommodate the droves of sun-seeking foreigners who had been colonising Spain since before she was born.

'They can't hang about until then,' she said. 'Can't we contact the taxi driver and get him to come back immediately?'

'Jack has a better idea. He can squeeze them into the Range Rover and take them to the nearest hospital for the other old girl to have her foot X-rayed. You and I can either wait for the taxi or try to hitch a lift back.'

'Before they go anywhere these three need something to drink, or they're going to flake out with heat exhaustion.'

'Yes, they're all in bad shape,' he agreed. 'Couch potatoes trying, in a moment of madness, to be mountain goats.' His smiling glance lingered on her slimmer contours.

The look took her back to the evening before, in her bedroom.

Half an hour later, rehydrated with water supplied by the village bar, and with ham rolls to eat on the way, Jack's charges left for the coast—the injured woman in front with him, the other three squeezed in the back.

'Better expect me when you see me,' he said, leaning out of the window. 'As they don't have a word of Spanish, I can't dump them at the hospital and leave them to it. I'll have to hang around. *Dios*!'

With a wave of the hand, he drove off.

'Let's have some coffee, shall we?' said Simón as the vehicle disappeared round a bend in the narrow village street. 'I'll bring it out.' He went back inside the bar, leaving Cassia to sink gratefully into a chair at one of the two metal tables on the pavement outside.

The morning's brisk walking hadn't tired her. It was the laggardly drag up the hill with the elderly Belgians which had been fatiguing. She felt hot and sticky, and longed for a cooling wash, but a brief visit to the bar's loo had discouraged her from attempting to freshen up there. In her experience it was unusual in Spain for the washrooms in bars to be squalid. But they were at this establishment.

When Simón came out with the coffee he said, 'I'm told there's a path we can take that cuts across country, connecting with a road going in the general direction of Castell. If you feel equal to walking a few more kilometres, we stand more chance of picking up a lift from there.'

'It sounds a better idea than hanging about for nearly an hour and a half for the Belgians' taxi to come back.'

'That's what I think.' He stretched his long legs. 'The driver won't be pleased when he finds he's come back for nothing and has to chase up his fare.'

'It's a long way to come by taxi from where they live. It seems strange they don't have their own cars.'

'Perhaps they don't often leave their urbanisation,' he suggested. 'It has its own supermarket and shopping arcade, so our piggy-back passenger was telling us. Most of the residents have their own pools, so they don't need to go to the beach. It's a world of its own. *In* Spain, but not *of* Spain.'

'You've certainly done your good deed for the day, lugging the one who hurt herself up that steep bit. She'd be where we found them still if you and Jack hadn't turned up.'

'I'd rather have carried you the day you blistered your heel. Are you sure it's not hurting today?'

'No, no…it's fine,' she assured him.

After they'd left the bar their way led them past a *la-*

vadero similar to the one they had passed on the first walk, except that this wasn't in use.

'I'd like to wash my face and hands,' said Cassia.

'A good idea,' he agreed. 'I could do with a clean-up myself.'

To her surprise, while she washed her face and hands with a small piece of soap from her pack, and dried them with a cotton kerchief, Simón stripped off his shirt to sluice his chest and arms as well as his face and neck. Then, after drying himself with his discarded shirt, he produced a clean white T-shirt.

'That feels better.' He raked back his wetted hair which, being thick, clean and well cut, seemed not to need a comb to make it look presentable.

They moved on, their pace more leisurely than earlier in the day. Where the path was too narrow for them to walk abreast, Simón drew back to let her go ahead of him.

That morning they had passed a mountain which took its name from a legend going back to Moorish times. Now they talked again about the Moors—a subject on which he was unexpectedly well-informed, although she was less surprised by that now than she would have been in the early days of their acquaintance. Then it had seemed unlikely that he would have any seriously intellectual interests.

Talking, they reached the road much sooner than she expected. She felt a twinge of regret that this enjoyable interlude—the easy path with its peaceful views, an interesting conversation free from personal undercurrents—had ended so quickly.

'Shall we wait, or continue walking until something comes along?' Simón asked.

'Which would you rather do?'

He glanced up and down the road. 'In the absence of anywhere to sit, I think we may as well stroll on. Unless you've had enough of St Ferdinand's car, as my nurse used to call going on foot.'

'No, I don't mind walking,' said Cassia. 'Did you see much of your parents when you were small? Or were you mostly with your nurse?'

'Unfortunately my father was an invalid. A riding accident had damaged his brain. It was very hard on my mother and says a great deal for her character that she stayed with him and never allowed herself to become over-possessive with me. She's remarried now, and lives in America, but we see quite a lot of each other. She's an extraordinarily strong, fine person.'

This was a different version of the story that Cassia had heard, and she would have liked to hear more about his mother. But Simón changed the subject. Perhaps he felt that the conversation had become too personal.

The first car to come along was a large Mercedes. Although the back seat was empty it swept past them, with the driver and his passenger averting their eyes from the two would-be hitchhikers.

'As they've probably both got gold watches and wallets stuffed with five *mil* notes, maybe they're right not to pick up strangers,' said Simón, watching the opulent car glide round the bend ahead of them.

'Here comes another,' said Cassia, a few minutes later.

This time the car was a small blue saloon. As they saw when it pulled up in response to his signal, it had only one seat to spare, the back being occupied by the elderly mother of either the portly Spanish driver or his buxom wife.

'Where are you going, my friend?' the driver enquired.

'To Castell de los Torres. But I can see you haven't room for us. It was good of you to stop,' said Simón.

'We're going near Castell. We can fit you in, if you don't

mind a bit of a squeeze. You're a big fellow, but the young lady isn't. She can sit between you and my mother.'

The invitation was seconded by the driver's wife and parent with smiles and beckoning gestures.

In view of Simón's height, it would have made sense for him to sit in front with the three women sharing the back seat. However, as this wasn't suggested, after Cassia climbed in, making polite remarks about their kindness, he followed her.

Instructed by her husband, the driver's wife did adjust her seat to give Simón a few more inches to accommodate his long legs. But, as her mother-in-law weighed at least a stone more than she did, there was very little room for Cassia, squashed between the billows of female flesh on her left and the less yielding male physique on her right.

As the driver let in his clutch Simón lifted the arm pressing against hers and, shifting sideways, laid it along the shelf behind the backrest, a manoeuvre that made better use of the space available but left her less comfortable inwardly, because now she was tucked against him in a far more intimate way than merely shoulder to shoulder.

The Spaniards were curious to know who their passengers were, where they had come from and why they were going to Castell. Cassia left it to Simón to answer their questions, and to fire back several of his own, so that soon the others were telling him their life stories without gleaning more than the bare essentials from him.

Presently they came to a succession of bends which made the driver's mother grasp the handgrip above the window and caused Cassia, with nothing to hold, to sway from side to side until Simón again moved his arm, this time to hold her against him.

Turning her face towards the offside window, in the hope

that he wouldn't see her heightened colour, she met a beady look from the old lady.

'You are *novios*—yes?' she asked.

Cassia shook her head.

The old lady clicked her tongue. 'It's different from my young days. I wouldn't have been allowed to go for a walk in the country with a man, not even if we were engaged to be married.'

'That was fifty-five years ago, Madre. The world has changed,' said the driver.

'You're telling me! And not for the better,' his mother said tartly. She laid her hand on Cassia's arm. 'I was younger than you when I married his father, and we stayed married until his heart attack, two years ago. Life was never easy for us, but we managed. I still miss him. He was a good husband and father.' With her other hand, she fumbled in the pocket of her grey and black print dress for a handkerchief and mopped her eyes.

Cassia patted the hand still resting on her arm. 'I'm sure you were a very good wife to him, *señora*.'

Unembarrassed by her tears, the old lady said, 'What part of the country do you come from? Not from round here, by your accent.'

'I'm a foreigner.'

'You're not an American, are you? My eldest brother Alfonso went to America. He liked it there and did well for himself.'

By this time the road was running fairly straight again, but Simón didn't take his arm away. All the time that the old lady was talking about her brother's decision to try his luck on the other side of the Atlantic, his fingers were moving lightly over Cassia's outer arm, several fingers slipping gently under her rolled-up shirt sleeve—not far, but far enough to send a slow quiver through her.

She tried to pay attention to Alfonso's experiences, to ignore the sensations engendered by having her back heat-sealed to Simón's chest.

The driver's wife rolled down her window, increasing the current of air fanning the interior of the car and ruffling Cassia's hair. A strand must have blown across Simón's face. He removed it and tucked it behind her ear, his fingertips lingering on her neck.

She wondered how much further they had to go—how much further *he* would go before they were dropped off. There wasn't much more that he could do without the old lady noticing. But what he was doing now was enough to stir dangerous longings in her.

It wasn't solely out of gratitude to these kind people that, when they were back in the familiar landscape of the valley surrounding Castell de los Torres, Cassia said in English, 'Would they like to be invited in for a drink or coffee, do you think?'

She couldn't see Simón's expression without twisting her neck to look up at him, but the pause before he replied made her wonder if he'd guessed that she had an ulterior motive for the suggestion—to put off being alone with him. It was doubtful if Jack would be back yet, and Laura had an appointment with the hairdresser in the next village immediately after the afternoon closing hours.

His response, when it came, was to ask the driver if he and the two ladies had the time to take some refreshment before continuing their journey.

The outcome was that the Lopez family were still at Casa Mondragón when Laura returned with her hair done in a style which, she told Cassia later, was not at all to her liking.

'Next time I shall go to Babette's hairdresser in

Benidorm. The girl who did my hair today is useless,' she said crossly.

In Cassia's private opinion, the softer style was actually more becoming than the way Laura's hair had been before. But she kept that thought to herself, saying only, 'The pharmacist has her hair nicely done. I wonder where she goes. Why not ask her? It would be more convenient to have yours done locally than go all the way to Benidorm.'

Preparations for supper were under way when Jack returned. There had been a long wait at the hospital, and after the X-ray the Belgian woman's foot had had to be put in plaster.

'I should think you could do with a stiff drink,' said Simón, when Jack had finished explaining why he had been so long.

'Several!' Jack said, with feeling. 'But I guess it was useful to locate the hospital's casualty department in case I ever have to take one of our lot there. How did you two get on, getting back here?'

'No problems…apart from the fact that the people who gave us a lift outstayed their welcome when we invited them in,' Simón told him, glancing at Cassia with a look suggesting that he knew she had been glad they had.

'Although they didn't find out that their host was a *marqués*, they were very impressed by the house. They'd never been in such a large one,' she told Jack.

'Who did they think he was, then?' he asked her when, a few minutes later, Simón was answering the telephone.

'I don't know. He told them his first name but glossed over his identity. I suppose they assumed he was an employee, like me. Did you tell the Belgians who he was?'

Jack shook his head. 'Those four weren't the sort to be interested in anyone except TV personalities.'

Simón came back with the news that the friend on whose

plane he had come had had an unexpected change of plan and was returning to Madrid the following day instead of next weekend.

'I'll have to go back with him, if you wouldn't mind running me to the airstrip early tomorrow, Jack?'

'Sure. What time d'you want to leave?'

'He wants to take off at nine, so we'd better leave here at eight.'

Disappointed that he wasn't going to be with them for the rest of the week, Cassia wondered when they would see him again.

After supper, at Jack's suggestion, the men went out to the bar. Laura, complaining that the tightness of the rollers and the excessive heat of the drier at the hairdresser's had given her a headache, retired to her room.

Left on her own, Cassia put on a jacket and went up to the roof. It was a mild, clear night, and she stood with her elbows resting on the parapet and her head tilted back to gaze at the starry sky. She had often done this on the terrace of the house in the Albaicín. In some ways she longed to be back there, still working as a receptionist, her senses undisturbed by the turmoil aroused by being pressed close to Simón in the car this afternoon.

She had not been there long when she heard the door to the staircase creak on its hinges, and the next moment saw him stepping onto the roof.

She tensed. 'You're back soon.'

'I wasn't in the mood for the noise down there.' He came towards her, his expression unreadable in the pale half-light of a crescent moon and innumerable stars. 'I kept thinking about you—how you felt against me in the car...the scent of your hair...the enticing glimpse of your breasts...'

He put both arms round her and drew her against him and kissed her.

When the long kiss ended, it was like coming up for air after her first deep dive into the amazing world under the surface of the sea.

This too was a revelation of wonders that she had read about, seen at the cinema and elsewhere, but had never fully understood. Like diving, it had to be experienced. Reading about it, even watching other people do it wasn't the same as living it, feeling the strength of his arms, the compelling warmth of his mouth.

'It's a nuisance I have to leave tomorrow,' he murmured against her cheek. 'But anyway not having my car here is an inconvenience. I'll be back very soon. Meanwhile...'

He kissed her again, sending a long shudder through her. She found herself pressing against him, sliding her arms around his neck, touching the thick black hair with its own distinctive texture—crisper than cats' fur, springier than her own hair.

When he kissed her eyelids, she felt the slight roughness of his chin rasping her cheek. But his lips were gentle on the delicate skin of her closed eyes.

A few moments later he swung her up in his arms, carrying her to the old chair, sitting down with her on his lap, kissing her again, less gently.

For Cassia this belated experience of passion, until now only imagined, was even more exciting and wonderful than she had thought it would be. Intoxicated by it, she returned his kisses with all the pent-up longing of her innermost nature.

As he cradled her close to him, each kiss a little more demanding, she felt herself coming alive in a completely new way. Her responses were instinctive—as involuntary as laughter or a lump in the throat. There was no other way she could react except with this wordless expression of love and tenderness.

When his hand slid under her jacket, and she felt him unbuttoning her shirt, desire overwhelmed her. It was like being swept off her feet by a powerful wave, but in a warm summer sea so that she felt no alarm, only a willing surrender to an imperative force.

His exploring hand was gentle. She was scarcely aware of the strap being slipped off her shoulder and the cup of her bra being peeled away, replaced by the warmth of his palm. It felt as if all her life she had been waiting to experience these delicious sensations, and now, at long last, they were happening with the man she had always known would materialise some day—the only man she would ever want as a lover.

'You feel as soft as a dove,' he murmured, stroking her.

When he kissed her neck, it made her gasp with pleasure. If she felt like this now, at the beginning…

A few minutes later he said, 'The air's turning cold. Let's go down.'

Replacing her bra, closing the front of her shirt, he rose and set her on her feet. With her hand in his, he led her towards the staircase.

They were on the way to his room when, from below, the reverberating bang of the main outer door being closed broke the stillness of the huge house. It was Jack coming back from the bar.

The sound didn't cause Simón to pause. Leading her swiftly along the glassed-in gallery between the main stairs and his room, he appeared not to notice it.

But for Cassia the muffled thump brought an abrupt awakening from the daze of sensual delight induced by his caresses.

What am I doing? she asked herself. How am I going to feel about this in the morning?

Simón felt her hanging back and misread the reason for

it. 'He's gone to the kitchen,' he said quietly. 'He isn't coming up here.'

'I know, but...' She slipped her hand free, her thoughts in a whirl of confusion. It was another deep instinct which made her say awkwardly, 'I'm sorry...I know I led you on...but...this isn't what I want.'

She expected him to be angry. To her surprise, he smiled. Taking her face in his hands, he said, 'I think I was doing the leading, not you, my sweet girl. Don't worry, I'll take care of you.'

The light kiss he dropped on her mouth was irresistibly tender and seductive. But somehow she did resist it, pushing him away and forcing herself to say firmly, 'I'm sorry, Simón...truly sorry...but I can't go to bed with you.'

And then, because she couldn't trust herself to go on resisting him, or to fight down the traitorous feelings undermining that resistance, she turned and fled.

The following morning, Cassia was tempted to stay in her room until after Simón and Jack had left from the airstrip where Simón's friend kept his plane. But, apart from the fact that Laura and Jack would think she had overslept, and Laura would bustle upstairs to bang on her door, not to go down would be cowardly. It would also leave her not knowing how Simón was going to react to her chickening out last night.

Unaccustomed to being rejected, would he now be in a rage with her? What man wouldn't? From what she had heard and read, the one thing calculated to exasperate the entire male sex was being turned on and then turned down. Especially now, when it didn't happen as often as it had in the past. Now, if women were going to say no, they took care not to get to the stage where yes or no became an issue.

Looking at her reflection as she brushed her teeth, wondering if the others would notice the signs that she hadn't slept much, Cassia wondered if it wasn't only men but also most of her own sex who would think her last-moment panic incredibly stupid.

It hadn't been the fear of getting pregnant which had made her back off. Nor had she any doubt that a night in Simón's bed would have been a gloriously sensual experience.

But not the best experience. That was the one she wanted. And for that you had to have love—on both sides. Anything less was bound to be a let-down—something she would have regretted had she woken in his room instead of her own.

The men were already at the table when she entered the kitchen. As he always did, Simón half rose from his chair. Jack stayed seated. Both said 'Good morning'.

'Good morning.' With the briefest of glances in their direction, she went to the hotplate to pour herself a cup of coffee. Then Laura came out from the pantry with a bag of sugar in her hand.

'Is your headache better?' Cassia asked.

'Much better, thank you, dear. But you look a bit heavy-eyed. I suppose you were reading till all hours? Ruins your eyes, reading in bed.'

Cassia said nothing. Many of Laura's ideas had no basis in fact, but it was pointless to argue. She believed them, and her mind was set.

'So when d'you think you'll be back?' Jack asked, spreading butter on a hunk of bread.

The men were eating French omelettes with grilled tomatoes.

'I'm not sure. I have other commitments as well as this

project. If, for some reason, I couldn't come back for several weeks, you could manage without me,' said Simón. 'All the basic arrangements are set up. From here on, it's up to you.'

As he spoke he looked down the table at Cassia. It was impossible to tell what he was thinking. The possibility that it might be weeks before she saw him again made her spirits sink. How could she live with the uncertainty of not knowing what he thought about her, if he had written her off as an uptight puritan whom he wouldn't waste any more time on?

She wondered if he would find a way to speak to her privately before he left the house. Or if he would go without even shaking her hand.

CHAPTER NINE

JACK looked at his watch. 'If you've nothing more urgent to do this morning, Cass, how about coming to the airfield with us? On the way back I'll give you a driving lesson.'

'All right...if Simón doesn't mind?'

Without looking up from his breakfast, he said, 'Whatever suits you.'

A few minutes later both men rose from the table, leaving Cassia to finish her coffee. She had her sunglasses with her, and was ready to go without returning to her room.

'He's not in a good mood this morning,' Laura murmured, looking sage.

'Who? Jack or Simón?'

'Don Simón. I'm very sensitive to atmosphere. I knew he wasn't pleased about something as soon as he said good morning to me. Perhaps he's annoyed at having to go back sooner than he intended. He's a man who doesn't like having his arrangements altered, except by his own wish. It's important to him always to be in control. I'm a student of human nature. I can sum people up very quickly.'

In Cassia's opinion Laura's judgement of character was elementary compared with Señor Alvarez's penetrating assessments. But even he would have been unlikely to attribute the Marqués's mood to its true cause—the failure of an attempted conquest. One which, on the face of it, should have been easier than most.

She was waiting beside the Range Rover when the two men came out of the house.

Simón slung his grip in the back and then, with his usual courtesy, opened the front passenger door for her.

'No, no…you sit with Jack. I'll go in the back.'

As she moved to open the rear door he did the same. Their hands reached the handle simultaneously. Her reaction—to recoil as if from an accidental contact with a razor-sharp blade—made Simón raise his eyebrows and give her a sardonic look.

'There's no need to be nervous,' he said quietly, so that Jack, who had opened the bonnet, wouldn't hear. 'You made yourself clear last night. We'll go back to square one…and stay there.'

During the half-hour drive to the airfield the men discussed Jack's vehicle and various cars that Simón and his forebears had owned. Jack had bought his third-hand, his dream being to own a new model.

Cassia would have preferred to learn to drive on one of the small runabouts used by the driving schools, but enquiries had revealed long waiting-lists. While the grandparent generation still thought nothing of walking to neighbouring villages and distant parcels of land, all her contemporaries—of both sexes—wanted wheels.

While the men were discussing emission controls and automotive gas turbines, she was preoccupied with Simón's last remark to her. How could they go back to square one after the passionate embrace on the roof last night? To put back the clock was impossible. Perhaps he, having slept with so many girls, could forget what had happened quite easily. She never could.

Looking at the broad shoulders rising from the seat in front of her, remembering how strong and solid they had felt against her hands, she knew that she would have total recall of every moment in his arms for the rest of her life.

And would always be plagued by doubts about her decision not to trust herself to him.

'Don't worry, I'll take care of you.'

If only that statement had meant 'for ever'. But she knew it hadn't. All he had meant was that she needn't be afraid of getting pregnant.

No doubt with most of his girlfriends there was no risk of that happening. They were too experienced and worldly-wise not to be armed against such eventualities.

Playgirls like Isa didn't have accidental babies. It was girls like herself who did that—unwise virgins, usually much younger than she, who let themselves be swept away on a tide of reckless emotions, only to be left high and dry when their lovers opted out of the consequences.

At least she wasn't going to find herself in *that* situation. The most marvellous night of love in the history of the world couldn't be worth the ordeal of having a baby on one's own—especially in her circumstances, with no family to help her. Even with a supportive family it couldn't be easy to be a single parent. And children needed two parents. She knew that better than most.

She wondered how Simón would react in the unlikely circumstance that someone he made love to did become pregnant. Somehow she couldn't see him walking away from the responsibility. If he were that sort of man, he wouldn't have bothered to set up this project. His only concern would be to enjoy life, and to hell with everyone else.

On the other hand it wasn't responsible to make love to a girl with no sexual track record, who might easily take the affair far too seriously.

At the entrance to the airfield, Simón said to Jack, 'If any problems come up, my secretary always knows where to contact me. In any case, keep me informed. I'd like a situation report twice a week.'

They dropped him off near the building topped by a small control tower. Jack got out to unlock the tailgate and when Simón had retrieved his grip the two men exchanged powerful handshakes.

Out of politeness Cassia had turned sideways to respond to Simón's goodbye. His good manners were too deeply ingrained for him to ignore her, even if he might feel like it.

For a moment he looked straight at her, his expression at its most unreadable, except that the shape of his face and the tautness of his brown skin made it easy to see the sudden tightening of his jaw.

But his voice, when he spoke, didn't confirm the impression that inwardly he was displeased. 'Goodbye, Cassia. The next time I come down you may be able to drive this thing.' Turning to Jack, he added, 'When she makes a mistake, remember she's a girl—not one of your paras.'

Jack grinned. 'I'll go easy on her.'

Simón clapped him on the shoulder. '*Hasta luego.*'

Then he walked away, Jack closed the tailgate and Cassia turned to face forward, blinking back foolish tears.

'You're picking it up a lot faster than I expected. We'd better find out how soon you can take a test,' said Jack, at the end of Cassia's third driving lesson.

They had found a stretch of a new, wide road through the mountains, which eventually would carry a lot of traffic from the coast to the inland part of the province. At present virtually deserted, it was an ideal place for her to become thoroughly familiar with gear changes, three-point turns and the other basics of driving before attempting to drive in traffic.

Under Spanish law, novice drivers had not only to prove

their capabilities at the wheel, they also had to have some knowledge of how a vehicle functioned. Jack taught her about the Range Rover's internal workings in what he called 'the backyard'—actually a large, walled garden where, next year, if the project proved successful, Simón was considering building a swimming pool.

'You're a very good teacher, Jack,' she said, after the latest of his mechanical tutorials. 'I thought you might be impatient if I didn't get the hang of it right away.'

'I like showing people how to do things…if they're interested. It's the bolshie, couldn't-care-less attitude that gets up my nose. You may hear some blasts of barrack-room language if I see any signs of that among the riff-raff,' he said in a grim tone.

He had taken to using this term to refer to the young people that they were expecting. Sometimes he called them 'the rabble'. Cassia suspected that this was partly to annoy Laura. She also thought that at rock bottom it was the housekeeper, with her deeply embedded, genteel middle-class values, who would view the teenagers with suspicion and distrust while Jack, outwardly a ruthless disciplinarian, would be the one who understood and cared for them.

'Time I had a haircut,' he said, passing a hand over his head. They were sitting on an old stone bench, he drinking beer, Cassia eating a *mandarina*.

'Must you? You look much nicer with it as it is now.'

In the time she had known him the original convict-crop had grown to a GI crew cut, and now was beginning to show signs that, left to itself, it might be luxuriantly curly. Even at its present length it made him look much less brutal than her initial impression of him. He would never be a handsome man, but neither was he as *bruto* as he had seemed at first sight. In a sisterly way, she was becoming very fond of him.

'Why not let it grow a bit more?' she suggested. 'One day you may go bald, and then you'll wish you'd enjoyed your hair while you had it.'

'Maybe I should have a perm like Manuel,' Jack said sarcastically.

The builders had only a few minor jobs left to do. Manuel was the youngest and least skilled, his heart set on becoming a pop star like the idol whose long, tangled hairstyle he had copied. In a few days the men would be gone, and the house would no longer resound with shouted exchanges in Valenciano, and bursts of heavy metal from Manuel's ghetto-blaster.

Cassia laughed. 'I can't see you with a perm or a ponytail, but in a different way a shaved head is just as wayout. It makes you look threatening.'

'That could be a good way to look when the riff-raff arrive,' was Jack's comment. 'That reminds me—we'd better fax another sit. rep. tonight. We haven't done one since Monday, and we'll have the *jefe* on our backs if we don't keep him up to date. Don't let his friendliness fool you. He may not stand on ceremony, but when that guy says do something, he means it. I've met officers like him in the Légion. They don't throw their weight about. They don't have to. They're tough on themselves and even tougher on anyone who doesn't match their standards.'

'I wouldn't describe the Marqués as tough on himself,' said Cassia.

Since his departure, she had taken to referring to Simón by his title rather than by his first name. Probably there was some fancy psychological term for her reason for this, but she wasn't into self-analysis at present. She felt that the cure for her condition—if there was a cure—was keeping busy, not thinking.

However, as Jack had raised the subject, she couldn't

help saying, 'Some people would consider his lifestyle was the acme of self-indulgence.'

Jack shook his head. 'No way. OK, he's got plenty of loot, and a title as long as your arm. But if you forget what you know about him, and look at the guy himself, what do you see?'

In her mind's eye Cassia saw various images. The Marqués coming down the stairs at the hotel in his black salopette and coral-coloured T-shirt, his arms as brown as a gypsy's. At the wheel of his car on the drive from Granada. Vigorously washing himself in the cold spring water flowing through the *lavadero* a few hours before he had changed the world for her.

'I don't know. What do you see?'

'Someone who in a rough-house I'd sooner have with me than against me.' Jack drained his bottle of beer. 'He may go to glitzy parties and know lots of VIPs, but he wouldn't be in good shape if his life was all wine and women. Come on—let's get that fax done. This time next week we won't be taking it easy. We'll have the first batch of rabble here.'

The first intake of teenage 'rabble' arrived on a coach from Madrid. Watching them disembark, Cassia was torn between foreboding and pity. Some looked troublemakers. Others looked apprehensive. But, having not always had it easy in her own life, she guessed that even the most loutish were inwardly somewhat nervous at being taken far from their sleazy but familiar *barrios* and dumped down in an alien environment.

'*Gracias a Dios por Juanito!*' was Laura's heartfelt exclamation as she looked at a youth with tattoos on the backs of his hands and a safety pin in his ear.

Jack didn't like it when she called him by the Spanish

equivalent of his name, and it was a measure of her reaction to the coachload that she should thank God for his presence. Their mutual antipathy was, if anything, growing more pronounced.

Although he had not yet had his head shorn, this afternoon he was wearing military-green combat·clothes, with a strip of Velcro over the right breast pocket where the tape with his name had been worn when he was in the Légion. As he checked off the youngsters' identities on the list on his clipboard, and gave them each a fierce stare, he looked more than capable of keeping them in order.

Although Jack had made several caustic remarks about social workers *en masse*, the two people in charge of the coach party looked a sensible pair. The man introduced himself as Roberto and his colleague as Maria-José. He looked to be about forty, she in her middle thirties. Their friendly but no-nonsense manner towards their charges led Cassia to hope that they would turn out to be very different from Jack's estimation of the profession as a whole. Having never come into contact with social workers before, she was reserving judgement.

While Jack took Roberto and the boys to their quarters, Cassia showed Maria-José and the girls to theirs. The girls would be sleeping in a dormitory, their supervisor in a room nearby.

'This is very nice,' said Maria-José as she looked round her accommodation.

By the standards of the Castillo del Sultán, its appointments were adequate but basic. But, compared with those in lower-rated hotels, the bed was probably more comfortable, the furnishings in better taste. All it lacked were some personal touches, and Cassia had done what she could to remedy this by hanging a chart of Spanish wild flowers on the wall, putting some second-hand paperbacks from a swap-shop on the bedside table and buying a pottery vase at a car-boot sale. This, filled with pale carnations, stood on the window ledge with a hand-written card—'Welcome to Casa Mondragón. We hope you'll enjoy your stay here'—propped against it.

'The meal times, the fire drill and so on are pinned up inside the wardrobe door,' Cassia explained. 'If you haven't enough hangers, or if there's anything else you need, please let me know.'

'Thank you. I'm sure we're all going to have a wonderful time. I've never been to this part of the country before. This is a beautiful valley,' said the older woman, looking out of the window at the mountains.

'I'm a newcomer here too. I came from Granada.'

They exchanged the basic facts of their lives before Cassia said, 'I'll leave you to settle in.'

On her way downstairs she was astonished to hear a distinctive male voice speaking to someone below. Her heart turned over. Simón was back.

He had finished his conversation and was on his way up the staircase when they met.

'I…we weren't expecting you today,' she said, suddenly breathless.

He gave her a sweeping appraisal. 'Am I a pleasant surprise?'

'Of course.' For something to say, she added, 'I—I've just been chatting to Maria-José—Señorita Moreno, the girls' supervisor. Have you met her?'

'Many times. She was once a social butterfly. Then her *novio* was killed in a microlight accident. It made her rethink her life. She's now committed to helping other people. Considering her background, she has an extraordinary rapport with girls from the roughest *barrios* in the city…and Madrid has some very bad quarters, where many girls see prostitution as their only option.'

He moved on up the stairs and Cassia continued down, wondering what Maria-José would say about him, if questioned. It would be interesting to know how someone who had her origins in his milieu but was now dedicated to helping the underprivileged would see him.

Of course, from Maria-José's point of view he was a benefactor. But how would she reconcile that aspect of his character with the downside? If she had been a butterfly in the upper echelons of Madrid society, she would be bound to know about Simón's reputation. She might even have attracted his attention. Ten years ago, fashionably dressed and coiffed, she must have been strikingly attractive. Even now, in a sweatshirt and jeans, with her hair cut close to her head and no make-up, she might not turn heads but she wouldn't be ignored.

Maria-José sat next to the Marqués during the evening meal. On his other side was a girl whose make-up and clothes suggested that she might already have taken the option he had referred to. None of the girls was more than sixteen, but this one appeared to be eighteen or nineteen, until one looked closely and saw the signs of adolescence lurking under the veneer of mean-street sophistication.

Later that evening, the six adults met for a drink and discussion in a room reserved for them to relax in.

Warned that they would be called very early the following morning, most of the girls had already gone to their dormitory. The boys were still in the games room, playing pool and table tennis. Most of them were accustomed to staying up, watching TV or hanging about in the streets until midnight or later.

'But this time tomorrow night I'll have them all so flaked

out they'll be hitting the sack as soon as they've swallowed supper,' Jack said with grim humour.

'There was a lot of waste after tonight's meal,' Laura said crossly. 'They hardly touched the salads.'

'These young people aren't used to good food, *señora*,' said Maria-José. 'In general we eat a healthy diet in this country. But now, in the cities, the junk-food culture of other countries is taking hold. I'm sure, after a few days here, in this wonderful fresh air and with plenty of physical activity, they'll be eating their meals with as much enjoyment as Roberto and I did tonight.'

Her tact earned her an approving look from Simón, Cassia noticed. For supper the girls' supervisor had changed into a white shirt and black skirt. Even in flat-heeled black shoes, gun-metal-coloured tights and a conservative mid-calf-length skirt, her legs were noticeably good. Except that her head was uncovered, she could have belonged to a religious order.

Cassia wondered if it might be her presence which had brought Simón back, and if he found Maria-José's nun-like appearance a challenge.

The next day when, except for Laura, they all went out on the first trail-clearing exercise, it became clear to Cassia that whether or not the Marqués was challenged by Maria-José, he would be wasting his time. She was interested in her colleague, and he in her. The warmth of their feelings for each other might not have been obvious to anyone else, but Cassia, in love herself, was more than ordinarily attuned to the nuances of other people's behaviour. She quickly picked up the small but significant signs of a more than professional rapport between the two supervisors.

By mid-afternoon most of the youngsters were as tired as Jack had predicted they would be. Their day had begun with a pre-breakfast march along the lanes through the vineyards. He wouldn't tolerate lagging on the return to the village at the end of the first day's work. He had taught them a simple marching song and moved back and forth along the double line, making them pick up their feet, straighten their backs and swing their arms. No one rebelled. In the combat fatigues he was wearing he looked awesomely tough. Even the youth with the pin in his ear didn't have the nerve to test Jack's authority.

A kilometre from the village, Simón fell into step with Cassia.

'Tired?' he asked, in English.

'Do I look it?'

'No, but you're good at hiding your feelings and may feel it's incumbent on you to set the girls an example. Maria-José tells me there were flowers and a welcome note in her room and in the girls' dormitory. Was that your idea or Laura's?'

'Mine, but I expect Laura would have suggested it if I hadn't.'

'I doubt it. I'm not sure Laura fits in as well as I'd hoped. What do you think?'

It surprised her that he should discuss the housekeeper with her. 'She seems very capable to me, and she gets on well with the cleaners.'

'Yes, but she disapproves of this lot…and is also nervous of them,' he said, indicating the double file ahead. 'If they're insolent, I don't think she'll know how to handle it.'

'I'm not sure I shall,' said Cassia.

'They're less likely to test your mettle. Laura's an obvious target for cheeky backchat. They'll see you as an icon.'

'Me? An icon? You're joking!'

'On the contrary. You're only a few years older. You've got your act together as far as appearance goes.' After a slight pause, he added, 'If they knew about it, they might even envy you your virginity. It's a safe bet they've all lost theirs. Sex starts early in the *barrios* they come from. According to Maria-José, it's one of the factors that keeps girls like these trapped. Only a few will break out. The rest, unless they get help, will end up as worn-out slatterns, like their mothers and grandmothers.'

At this point one of the girls who had been walking ahead of them suddenly turned round and clouted the boy behind her. When he attempted to hit back another girl jumped to her friend's defence. The incipient scuffle was nipped in the bud by Simón striding forward to grab the boy by the scruff of his tracktop and fend off the two irate girls. All three were quickly subdued, more by his innate air of command than by his physical strength, Cassia thought, watching.

The Marqués didn't come back to her, but walked the rest of the way with the now pacified combatants, leaving Cassia to mull over his conversation with her. It didn't throw much light on his current state of mind in relation to what had happened the night before his last departure.

When she got back to her room, she looked at herself in the mirror and wondered if he'd been serious with that remark about her being seen as an icon.

It was rewarding to see how quickly and positively most of the teenagers adapted to their new environment. Given a longer stay, they would soon become as healthy and hopeful as the children born and bred in the valley, thought Cassia.

One morning Jack announced that, instead of trail-clearing, they were going to be taught to abseil. No one with a poor head for heights would be forced to take part, but he hoped that everyone, including the girls, would give it a try.

Cassia was still having breakfast when Simón stopped by her chair. 'I'd like you to come with me this morning, if you will.' As she would have risen, his hand on her shoulder restrained her. 'Not yet. In half an hour. Meet me at the office.'

She could still feel the pressure of his hand when she rose from the table and, wondering what he wanted to see her about, went to the downstairs washroom to touch up her lipstick.

Simón was at his desk, with the door open, when she arrived at the office. He signalled her to sit down, said, 'I shan't be long,' and went on tapping the keyboard of a notebook computer.

Even though he was concentrating on the screen, she didn't risk staring at him in case he suddenly looked up and something in her expression gave her away. At the moment he couldn't possibly know how she felt about him. Her near-surrender proved nothing. You didn't have to be in love with a man to respond to his physical magnetism.

She had left the door as she'd found it—admitting the sound of young voices, laughter and running feet. In a few minutes they would be gone, swinging off down the back lane, with Jack shouting good-humoured orders to straighten up and speed up.

By the time Simón switched off the screen and closed the notebook the cheerful noises were dying down. He put the computer in a drawer and locked it with a key clipped, with others, to a chain attached to his belt. Replacing the keys in the pocket of his jeans, he said, 'Jack tells me you'll soon be ready for a driving test, but the testers are even busier than the professional instructors. I may be able to pull some strings for you. But before I do that I want to see how you're getting on. I brought some L-plates with me. You can have a go at driving my car.'

'Is that a good idea?' she asked nervously. 'I mean, your car is very expensive. I'd hate to damage it.'

'There's not much fear of that. I'll drive to the place where Jack gives you lessons. You can take over there.'

Cassia wasn't happy about handling his luxurious car, even on a deserted road. Recognising her dubiety, he said sardonically, 'This is not, I assure you, a scheme to lure you to an isolated spot and force my attentions on you.'

A deep flush swept up from her neck. 'I didn't think it was!'

He lifted a sceptical eyebrow. 'You tense every time I come near you, Cassia,' he said drily. 'It may not be obvious to the others. It is to me.'

She didn't know what to say. She couldn't deny it. Her nerves had been as tight as bowstrings since she had first heard his voice in the hall. Merely knowing that he was in the house made her feel deeply uneasy. Being with him like this, alone, was even more stressful. To look at him was to remember how it had felt in his arms, to be torn between regret for what she had missed and dread that he might try again—and she wouldn't have the strength to resist him a second time.

The Marqués rose from his chair. 'Most people feel strung-up whey they're taking their test. Driving with me will be a useful learning experience—how to keep calm while being inwardly *muy nervioso*.' As he came round the desk his dark eyes gleamed with malicious amusement.

She had the unnerving feeling that she was going to be punished for being the first in a long history of conquests to repulse him.

* * *

In the car, she forced herself to watch and memorise everything he did. It wasn't easy. He drove the way he made love—with a light but sure touch. Even Jack, who called his vehicle 'she' and paid more attention to the Range Rover than some men gave to their wives, did not stroke through the gears the way Simón did. The movements of his long fingers reminded Cassia how they had felt caressing her neck, her bare shoulder, her uncovered breast.

It was one of Spain's golden mornings, when the mountains were sharply outlined against a pale blue sky, every crag and cleft clearly visible as far as the eye could see.

Simón pointed out a kestrel hovering in the bright air, scanning the vineyard below it for the movement of some small prey. Some weeks ago the vines had been pruned, the rust-red clay soil rotary-ploughed. Seen from her bedroom window, the grotesquely shaped vines had looked like rows of black cross-stitch. Now the first new leaves and clusters of minuscule grapes were appearing.

In Granada she had often seen men driving aggressively, pounding their horns at the slightest delay. The Marqués's manners didn't deteriorate when he was at the wheel. When they passed through the neighbouring village he slowed down to a crawl, smiling and raising his hand to housewives who, chatting in the narrow streets on their way to and from the shops, drew aside to let the car pass.

Cassia saw by their faces that they'd got a momentary lift from eye-contact with the good-looking driver of the opulent car with a Madrid number plate. Perhaps, if they'd noticed her beside him, they'd envied her for being young and free and out with a man whose charisma was as powerful as his car.

Leaving the village, he said, 'Apropos what we were talking about yesterday—'

Did he mean her virginity? She hoped not.

'Although I have doubts about Laura, I have none about Jack...not as far as his relations with the kids are concerned. He's the man for the job. There's no question about that.'

Ignoring the implication that there were other aspects of Jack that he was less happy with, she said, 'It turns out that Roberto did his *mili* in the Spanish Foreign Legion, so he and Jack have a lot in common. Did you do military service?'

'Of course. Everyone does...or did, when I was conscripted. I was in the Navy.'

'Did you enjoy it?'

'Very much. I was based at Mahon in the Islas Baleares. Menorca's an interesting island. For a time it belonged to the British, and one of my mother's ancestors commanded the garrison in Admiral Lord Nelson's time. So I felt I had links with the place.'

Cassia had never been to the Balearics herself, although her father had spent time on Mallorca before she was born. She visualised Simón in uniform—not, perhaps, as unnervingly sure of himself as he was now, but still devastatingly attractive, especially to girls sequestered on a small island like Menorca which, so she had heard, had never been as 'swinging' as Ibiza, a mecca for drop-outs.

She wondered how many Menorcan hearts he had broken, and if most of the girls he had dated still had wistful or painful memories—memories such as she would have ten years from now.

'Why are you frowning?' he asked. 'What are you thinking about?'

'I—I was thinking about my father.'

'Sorry...I should have guessed.' He took his right hand off the wheel, reaching for her left hand and giving it a quick squeeze. 'You must often miss him.'

The sympathetic tone and gesture were immeasurably warming. She wanted to take his hand and hold it against her cheek. She wanted so much to love him and show her love. But that wasn't what *he* wanted. If and when he embarked on a long-term relationship, it wouldn't be with someone like her. She wasn't the stuff *marquesas* were made from. She might seem classy to the girls from Madrid, but she wouldn't pass muster with his mother.

Simón took his hand away. Glancing at him, she saw a tight knot of muscle showing at the angle of his jaw—usually a sign of impatience or annoyance.

Then, the road being clear, he began to point out the dials and buttons on the dashboard. There was no irritation in his voice. Perhaps she had imagined his displeasure.

When the time came for her to take the wheel she fixed her mind firmly on proving Jack a good teacher and herself a good pupil.

Half an hour later Simón directed her in and out of a small town which didn't have any hazardously narrow streets but where it was market day and there was a policeman on duty at a central roundabout.

Cassia kept her head, and acquitted herself well enough for Simón to say, 'Your road sense is excellent. I'm impressed, and I'll see what I can do to get you tested as soon as possible. I've no influence myself, but some of my friends have. Unless, of course, you have strong moral objections to queue-jumping?'

Being still at the wheel, she kept her eyes on the road, but knew by the tone of his voice that he was teasing her. She said, 'I might…in other circumstances. I wouldn't feel comfortable taking the place of someone waiting for medical treatment. But it would make life easier for Jack if he didn't have to do all the driving.'

'Your wish is my command, *señorita*.'

If only it were, she thought longingly. To have Simón at her feet—even metaphorically—was a fantasy she had forbidden herself to indulge in.

Presently they changed places, and she took it for granted that they were heading back to Castell de los Torres until, with the surrounding countryside still totally unfamiliar, she realised that they were travelling west, which must be taking them further inland.

CHAPTER TEN

'WHERE are we going?'

'I thought we'd have lunch out,' Simón said casually. 'There's a restaurant on the way to Albacete, recommended by my friend with the aeroplane. I called them this morning to make sure they were open today. You're not in any hurry to get back to the house, are you?'

'There are things I ought to be doing, but nothing which can't wait, I suppose,' said Cassia. 'Did you tell Laura we'd be out?'

'Naturally. If we weren't back when she expected us, she might think we'd had an accident.'

As it was not yet mid-morning, and an inland restaurant would be unlikely to start serving lunch before half past one at the earliest, Cassia wondered how he was planning to spend the interval.

When they stopped at a village bar for coffee, it turned out that their destination was near a large, lake-like reservoir which Simón intended to walk round. 'We shan't need boots. There's a road. I gather it's a popular picnic area at weekends and on *fiestas*.'

Later, as they strolled in the sun along a lane near the water's edge, passing one or two anglers but otherwise having the lovely place to themselves, she wondered why she was here with him. She couldn't fathom his motive for bringing her, unless, after lunch, he meant to make another pass. But he had specifically said that that wasn't his intention, and he wasn't behaving like a man with seduction in view.

Today, judging by their conversation, it seemed to be her mind, not her body that he was interested in—her favourite painters and authors, even her political opinions. He seemed to be taking her seriously and that, she discovered, could be as seductive as being flirted with. She felt herself warming, weakening, becoming dangerously happy when it turned out that they shared an enthusiasm or a dislike.

Their lunch was served at a table in the corner of a terrace. The rest of the restaurant's clientele, who all looked like travelling salesmen, ate inside in the busy dining room, which soon became noisy and, at the coffee stage, smoky.

The Marqués and Cassia could see the smokers lighting up through the window overlooking the terrace but were spared the noise, which would have made their own quiet tête-à-tête impossible.

'Not great cuisine, but very well cooked, don't you think?' he said, peeling a pear while she dipped her spoon into a crunchy topping on a home-made *flan*.

Cassia savoured the contrast between the caramelised sugar and the creamy smoothness of the custard before saying, 'I've enjoyed every mouthful. Thank you for bringing me.'

'Would you have come if you'd had the chance to opt out?'

'I don't know. Possibly not.'

'Why not?'

When she didn't speak, he answered for her. 'Because of what happened the last time I was down here.' It was a statement, not a question.

She put down the spoon, her enjoyment evaporating.

'Why did you have to bring that up?' she said in a low voice, looking towards the lake.

'Would you rather we ignored it?'

'I—I hoped we were on a different footing now. Friends.'

There was a long silence. When she flicked a glance at him, he was looking at the mountains on the far side of the water. His face gave nothing away.

Eventually he said, 'Very well, if that's the way you want it. Coffee?'

On the drive back they listened to a tape of what Simón called 'mountain music'—classical orchestral pieces.

Sitting beside him, Cassia was aware that somehow the day had gone wrong, and their pre-lunch rapport had been lost. They weren't friends. They could never be friends. It was a textbook case of a man wanting one thing and one thing only from a woman—something she wanted too, but not on the same terms.

When they got back, Laura greeted the Marqués with the news that soon after he'd left a lady had called from Madrid to say that she was paying him a visit and would arrive in time for dinner. Her name was Antonia Bretano. Laura had already prepared a bedroom for her.

Less than an hour later a loud tattoo on a horn drew Cassia to a window overlooking the *plaza* in time to see Simón coming out of the front door and opening his arms to the driver of a silver sports car.

When they finished hugging each other, his visitor drew back to reveal herself as a tall, thin redhead in her late twenties, obviously on close terms with him.

Evidently she was an artist. As Cassia watched she unlocked the boot and unloaded an aluminium easel, a collection of boards strapped together, and a motley assortment of bags—including two airline bags, three shopping carriers and a Greek-island bag.

Feeling another pair of hands might be needed, as well as being curious to meet her, Cassia ran downstairs to help.

By the time she'd emerged from the house Simón had his visitor's belongings slung over his shoulders, tucked under his arms and held in his hands.

To Cassia's surprise, he introduced them in English. 'Toni, this is Cassia Browning, whose father was an artist. Toni is also a professional painter.'

'How do you do? May I help you with your things?'

'That's kind of you. *Gracias*. I came *impulsivamente*, and packed in a hurry,' said the redhead, her English having an American accent. She was not a beauty, but she had beautiful eyes as golden as *nispero* honey.

'Tell me about your father. What sort of painter was he?' she asked, handing over a rolled mohair rug, a canvas satchel and a plastic bag full of shoes.

After Cassia had told her, Toni said, 'I paint windows...old windows. I'm obsessed by them. Don't ask me why.' She paused to look up at the façde of the Casa Mondragón. 'I expect I'll paint some of these...if I'm not going to be in the way?'

'You're never in the way,' the Marqués assured her, his voice warm, his eyes affectionate.

Suddenly Cassia had the feeling that this lanky woman, with her almost flat chest, boyish behind and wild mane of dark red hair, might be the only member of her sex, apart from his mother, for whom he felt any real warmth.

Toni flashed him a smile. Although she had none of the attributes flaunted by Isa Sanchez, she had a lot of sex appeal. In Spanish she said, 'Thank you, darling. I only wish everyone felt the same way. I always love staying with you. You let me be myself...unlike the aunts.' Turning to Cassia, she explained, 'I was brought up by two bossy aunts...both of them "ladies who lunch". They want me to join that club, but shopping and socialising bore me. How about you?'

'Cassia's life has been dominated by her father,' Simón answered for her. 'She might enjoy all the things you reject.'

'Are you being bullied by this sexist beast?' Toni asked, with a grin. 'Simón has some attitudes to women that would get him lynched by the fundamental feminists. But he isn't *all* bad.'

Considering she was talking to one of his employees, Cassia expected him to look rather put out by this disrespectful comment. But he said, 'Toni has been a thorn in my side since before she could walk. I remember her lurching into a nuclear reactor I was constructing on the Arenal beach during one of our holidays at the Jávea beach house. She's been making a nuisance of herself ever since.'

That evening Antonia Bretano came down for supper in a pair of supple suede trousers, a silver-studded belt, a tie-dyed shirt and a mirror-glass Indian waistcoat—an outfit that brought all the teenagers' eyes out on stalks. Especially as her accessories included dramatic earrings, abundant rings and bracelets all unusual and interesting—and a velvet peaked cap, worn back to front with a brooch pinned above her forehead.

Whatever her paintings might be like, it was soon clear that she had a genius for making friends with people, regardless of their ages and backgrounds.

After the meal Laura beckoned Cassia to her, saying in an excited undertone, 'I knew her face was familiar. It's suddenly come to me where I've seen her before.'

'Where?'

'In *Hola!* magazine, that's where. My friend has a stack in her flat going back four or five years. I was leafing through some of the old ones, before she threw them out, and who should I see but her…Antonia Bretano.'

'Are you sure? I thought all the people in *Hola!* were showbiz stars or royalty.'

'Most of them are. She's the daughter of a count,' said Laura. 'It's all coming back to me now. Her parents were married about the same time I was. Her father, the Conde de Bretano, was one of the richest men in Spain at the time he inherited the title. But he was a compulsive gambler. After his wife died in childbirth he gambled the whole lot away. Then he took to the bottle until his liver gave out.'

'What a dreadful thing. Are you sure?'

'I'm certain. You ask Don Simón.'

'I think he'd tell me to mind my own business,' said Cassia. 'I do know that he and Señorita Bretano have been friends since they were children.'

'Condesa de Bretano,' Laura corrected her. 'She's inherited the title.'

Cassia said, 'I shouldn't mention this to anyone else, Laura. If Toni's social status was important to her, Simón would have introduced her more formally. First and foremost, she's an artist.'

'They showed one of her paintings in *Hola!* I wouldn't have wanted to buy it. A shabby old *persiana enrollable*, some of its slats broken, hanging over a balcony. Who would want that on their wall?' said the housekeeper.

Cassia liked the old-fashioned exterior Venetian blinds, still to be seen at the windows of older houses, but rapidly being replaced by more modern aluminium blinds in new buildings. There was something typically and intriguingly Spanish about a weathered *persiana* draped over the rail of a balustrade to keep out the summer sun but admit any breath of air to the shadowy interior within.

'Those old *persianas* will have disappeared before long.'

'High time too,' said Laura. 'They might look pictur-esque, but you try keeping them clean!'

The next day Simón took Toni to revisit the beach where they had played as children.

Cassia accompanied the others on a trail-clearing outing. By now the wild flowers were out, and Roberto, a keen botanist, did his best to fire his charges with some of his own enthusiasm.

Although it would have been impossible not to enjoy the sunny day and the wild beauty of the scenery, Cassia's thoughts were often elsewhere.

She felt sure that Toni's visit wasn't merely a sudden whim to recapture the mood of carefree holidays at the seaside. She had come with a purpose, and Cassia thought that purpose might be to bring Simón to the point of pro-posing to her. It seemed likely that a marriage between them had always been on the cards. People in their walk of life chose their partners for different reasons than those whose known family history went back no further than two or three generations.

Like thoroughbred horses, Spanish grandees had blood-lines going back centuries—in Simón's case at least five centuries. The men might occasionally marry a less well-bred heiress if the family coffers were empty, but mainly they married their own kind. When they had known each other all their lives, as Simón and Toni had, and a strong affection existed, as clearly it did between them, it must work out quite well. Better, perhaps, than a passionate love match.

During the afternoon, while fooling about on some rocks, showing off to the girls, one of the boys missed his footing and fell, hitting the back of his head. For some moments he lay stunned and then staggered up, bleeding profusely.

Jack and Roberto dealt with him, while Maria-José and Cassia calmed several girls whom the sight of blood made hysterical. Others took a ghoulish interest, and had to be dissuaded from crowding round.

Cassia knew that head wounds always bled alarmingly, and she also knew that anyone who had lost consciousness, even if not for long, might be seriously concussed. She wasn't surprised when Roberto insisted on taking the boy back to the nearest village, there to telephone for a taxi to take them to the nearest hospital.

Jack drew her aside. 'Might be a good idea for you to go with them, Cass...if you don't mind?'

'Of course not. I'll see you later.'

He changed his mind. 'No, hang on. I think we'll all start back. It's a half-hour walk to the village. If that kid should start feeling woozy, he could need to be carried. I can rig up a stretcher. Roberto won't know what to do. If he'd been doing his job properly, this wouldn't have happened. Instead of watching the lads, he was chatting up Maria-José.'

'It's impossible to keep an eye on them all every second,' said Cassia.

At the time of the mishap Jack had disappeared for a few minutes. Had he been present when the showing off had started, if he had thought it risky, he would have stopped it. Both he and Simón had the ability to bring the boys to heel very quickly. Roberto was a nice man, but he lacked the steely authority of the other two.

At the village a taxi was sent for, and Jack decided that he and Cassia would escort the boy to hospital while the rest of the party returned to base on foot.

*   *   *

'We may as well go for a coffee,' he said about an hour later in the hospital, when the boy had been taken away to be X-rayed.

It was just as well that he had taken over from Roberto. They had arrived to find the casualty department crowded with people suffering from minor injuries. Having been there before, with the Belgian woman, Jack knew the drill. Even so it had taken a fierce altercation with the bureaucrat at the reception desk to get the boy seen immediately, instead of taking his turn.

'I doubt if Roberto would have put his foot down as forcefully as you did,' said Cassia, on the way to the hospital's cafeteria.

'I'm damn sure he wouldn't,' said Jack. 'But you can't afford to hang about when there might be internal bleeding.'

'I wish they had let one of us stay with him. He was rather obnoxious before, but now he looks really scared. I can't help feeling sorry for him.'

Jack put a hand on her shoulder, the one furthest from him. 'You're too soft-hearted, my love. He's been a bloody nuisance. For all you know, those expensive trainers he's wearing may have been paid for by mugging little old ladies.'

'I feel sorry for all of them,' she said. 'If my father had died when I was thirteen or fourteen, I might have taken to stealing or worse.'

'Never! You're not that kind. You've too much sense to get into that sort of trouble. Nobody with a brain in their head needs to go down that road. If these girls we've got with us now end up as whores, it won't be because they have to. Nobody *has* to make a mess of their lives. Not these days, not with do-good outfits and helplines springing up like mushrooms everywhere you look.'

Privately Cassia thought Jack's own gritty strength of character made it difficult for him to grasp how much weaker most people were. But she didn't argue with him.

The cafeteria having no *tapas* that appealed to them, Jack bought two bags of crisps to eat with their cups of coffee. The place was not full, and he carried the tray to a corner where the tables were unoccupied.

'It'll take at least half an hour for them to X-ray him and stitch up that gash on his head. Maybe longer. Suits me all right. It makes a change to have you to myself,' he said, breaking the seal on both bags and handing one to her.

'Thank you.' Cassia's concern for the injured boy gave place to a different disquiet. Why should Jack want to have her to himself?

'Do you like the job? D'you think you'll stay?' he asked, unwrapping two cubes of sugar and dropping them into his cup.

'I *need* the job, Jack,' she said drily. 'I liked my last one, but the hotel didn't have room for staff to live in and my landlord wanted the flat where I'd lived with my father. But yes, I do like this job. Don't you?'

'Sure. It suits me fine. I could do without Laura, but then she's not crazy about me,' he said, with a shrug. 'I don't think she'll stay long anyway. Women like her are more comfortable living in towns…trawling the shops…showing off new outfits at the evening *paseo*.' He stirred his coffee. 'You've looked a bit unhappy lately. Not so that most people would notice, but I've been watching you.'

This increased her unease. She said, 'If I looked down in the dumps, I expect I was thinking about my father.'

He stopped stirring his coffee to look intently at her. 'I don't think you had him on your mind. You've fallen for the *jefe*, haven't you?'

His astuteness came as a shock. She had tried so hard

not to show her innermost feelings and thought she had succeeded.

Before she could make up her mind whether to admit or deny it, Jack said, 'You can tell me to mind my own business...but I can't do that. You're the first woman I've known who mattered to me, Cass. I don't know if the way I feel about you is what people call being in love.' He reached across the table and put his hand on her wrist. 'All I know is I want to take care of you and make life easy for you.'

'Oh, Jack...' she murmured in dismay. Instinct had warned her that something like this might be coming, and she wasn't sure how to handle it.

'Listen to me,' he said earnestly. 'Before you tell me it's no go, let me tell you the way I see it.'

'All right—how do you see it?'

Jack looked at his broad-knuckled hand curled over her lightly tanned wrist. His thumb moved in a light caress and then his eyes met hers again. 'I don't see any future for you with Simón, and I don't think you do either. That's what's making you miserable. You're a lovely girl. Intelligent. Educated. A real sweetie. But you're not Spanish and you don't have the right connections.'

'His mother is English,' she said. It seemed pointless now to deny that she was in love with Simón. Jack wouldn't believe her if she did.

'She is? You surprise me. He looks completely Spanish. OK, his mum's a foreigner. But I bet she had plenty of money behind her...and a title too, I shouldn't wonder.'

'I don't know about that. You could be right.'

'I'd bet money on it,' he said. 'Those people all marry each other. It's like a private club—non-members not welcome. If you're dreaming about him making you his *marquesa*, forget it, Cass. He fancies you, yes. Anyone can see that. But, unless you're willing to be his *amiguita*, there's no future in it.'

'You don't need to tell me. I know it. In fact, I think there's a good chance Toni will be his *marquesa*. They're obviously fond of each other. They'll make a good pair.'

'She's OK…too skinny for my taste. Doesn't hold a candle to you. You're…' he searched for the right word '…magic. I get a high just looking at you.' He reached for her other hand. 'You're beautiful, Cass…just beautiful.'

It was the first time in her life that she had known herself to be loved. Her mother had deserted her. Her father had never been more than moderately fond of her. Now she saw in Jack's eyes and heard in his voice the love that she had always longed for. But she couldn't return it. She could give him affection and respect, but that wouldn't be enough. He wanted her to feel the way he did. The way she did. But not about him.

She broke the silence. 'It's funny…the first time we met, we didn't take to each other. I could see you weren't keen on me, and I was wary of you.'

'I'd had a few bad experiences with girls in the UK. When I was in the Légion, unless you were an officer, nice girls didn't want to know you. The only friendly ones were tarts. Then, when I went back to England after ten years away…my God! What a difference.'

'I've never been to England. What had changed?'

'Women had changed. Suddenly men were in the doghouse. I'm not saying we didn't deserve some comeuppance. But not that much. I expected you to be like that. Aggressive. Hostile. I'd had enough of it.'

'I had some misconceptions about you,' she said, steering him back to the point she had started to make. 'But now I like you very much, Jack. Only not in the way you want. I'm sorry; I wish I did. We have a lot in common.'

'Maybe you won't always feel the way you do now... about him,' he said. 'He's a good-looking guy... He's a *marqués*... He has all the polish, the charm...but he isn't available—not on the basis you want. You'll get over him, Cass. You'll have to. You can't waste your life on a day-dream.'

'I know. But it could take years. I really do love him. It's not just infatuation. He's a fine person...worth loving.'

'Yeah...I know he is, dammit! I like him too. If he hadn't been who he is, he'd have made a good officer—the kind you know you can depend on when things get tough.'

As he finished speaking there was a tap on the nearby wall of plate glass. Looking towards the sound, they were surprised to see Simón himself standing there. Toni was with him. It was she who had tapped on the glass and now was smiling and waving at them.

'What the hell are they doing here?' Jack muttered crossly. But he didn't show his irritation facially, just made gestures for the others to join them.

When they did, it was Toni who explained their arrival at the hospital.

'We telephoned Laura to say we would be out for dinner and she told us what had happened. So we thought we'd come to the hospital. How is the boy? Any news?' she asked in Spanish, her English not being as fluent as Simón's.

'Not yet. Can I get you a cup of something?' Jack offered.

She asked for *café solo*. Simón said he would have the same. Jack went to the counter, leaving Toni to sit down next to Cassia while Simón took the chair diagonally opposite her.

'I'm afraid our arrival is inopportune. We've intruded on

what would appear to be an important tête-à-tête,' he said, at his most sardonic.

'Not at all,' she said awkwardly, wondering what construction he had put on Jack holding her hand and wrist. Gazing into each other's eyes, they must have looked like lovers. If only they were! If Jack held her heart there would be no problem.

'If you'll excuse me, I'll go back to the desk and ask what's happening,' she said.

She thought she had escaped and gained a few moments to collect herself from the double shock of Jack's declaration and Simón's arrival. But in the long walkway connecting the cafeteria with the other parts of the hospital she heard footsteps behind her, and glanced over her shoulder.

'I'll come with you,' Simón said, catching her up.

'What about your coffee?'

He dismissed it with a shrug. 'Why was Jack holding your hand?'

'I don't think that's your business.'

They were a few metres from a corner. As soon as they turned it, and were out of sight of the cafeteria, he clamped a hand on her shoulder and forced her to a standstill.

'Is there something between you? How long has this been going on?'

'Are you crazy?' Cassia exclaimed. 'You have no right to interrogate me like this.'

'You gave me the right,' he said harshly. 'On the roof. Last time I was here.'

'I don't know what you mean.'

'I'll refresh your memory.'

His arms went round her. He jerked her roughly against him. The swoop of his head was as swift and deadly as a kestrel dropping out of the sky to snatch up its frantic prey. None of his previous kisses had prepared her for the merciless onslaught of this kiss.

CHAPTER ELEVEN

'Now do you see?' Simón said thickly, releasing her mouth but keeping her pinioned to his chest. 'You're mine. You belong to me. It's why I brought you to Castell. It's why you came.'

In her heart, she couldn't deny it. She *was* his. She always would be. But pride wouldn't let her admit it.

Then the fierce light went out of his eyes and he eased his hold on her slightly.

'My mother, who knows me very well, seems to have guessed what's been happening. She asked Toni to come down and suss out the situation. Toni also knows me very well. She spotted at once that I'd met my Waterloo, but she couldn't make out how you felt. I've spent most of the day pouring my heart out to her and being told it would be more to the point to confide my feelings to you. But yesterday you made me feel I could have been mistaken—they might not be reciprocated.'

He took one arm from around her to trace, with a gentle finger, the lips he had bruised moments earlier.

'I'm asking you to marry me, Cassia. I was going to wait…give you more time…but I have to know now. I love you. I need you. I can't get through life without you.'

'Oh, Simón…if you only knew! I've been in agony too. I love you so much it's been killing me.' The joyous relief of hearing him say that he loved her made her burst into tears.

A group of hospital cleaning staff came out of a door further along the corridor but paid little attention to the tall man giving his handkerchief and speaking soothingly in a foreign language to the weeping girl in his arms. Grief and attempts to comfort it were a common sight in the hospital.

By the time the cleaners had turned the corner Cassia was recovering herself, her world transformed by the sudden sure and certain knowledge that Simón loved her.

'We'd better go and find out what's happening to poor Paco,' she said, drying her eyes.

'After I've kissed you.' This time he held her gently, and kissed her with the tenderness which had undermined her defences on the roof.

'When I saw Jack holding your hand, I had a terrible feeling that he was telling you he loved you. I felt ready to murder him,' he said against her cheek. 'Was that what he was saying to you?'

'Yes…but he's guessed how I feel about you. I hate to hurt him. He needs loving so badly.'

'But not by you, darling girl. Someone will turn up for Jack. Maybe, on a temporary basis, Toni will ease his pain for him.'

'Toni and Jack? I thought she was marked out for you.'

'Toni is like a sister to me. She wouldn't mind a few rolls in the hay with him. She said so this afternoon. She likes macho blue-collar or no-collar guys. But I doubt if she'll ever attach herself to any man permanently. She earns enough money to keep herself and she values her independence. The only thing that might domesticate her is if, in a few years' time, she gets the urge to reproduce before it's too late. But I shouldn't be surprised if being godmother to our children isn't enough for her. I'd like to have a large family, if that's all right with you.'

'I should love to have a large family. But what if your mother doesn't approve of me? I'm not the sort of girl she must have hoped you would marry.'

'My mother will adore you. You're *exactly* the sort of girl she hoped I would marry. She's despaired of my ever finding you,' he told her, smiling.

In spite of Simón's repeated assurances that the former Marquesa de Mondragón would accept his choice of bride with enthusiasm, on the day they drove to Madrid to meet her Cassia was extremely nervous.

She knew how crucial it was to make a good first impression on the woman who, up to now, had held first place in Simón's affections, and who wouldn't be human if she didn't feel somewhat wary of the girl who had supplanted her.

If she were only half as nice as her son claimed, she would undoubtedly do her best to hide any reservations she might have inwardly and to welcome her future daughter-in-law with all the warmth she could muster. Nevertheless, it would be a daunting encounter, and one which had given Cassia several restless nights.

She had not been sleeping with Simón in the two weeks since his proposal. She had thought that he would come to her room, or take her to his, as soon as they were unofficially engaged. The official engagement had to wait until she had met his mother, after which it was his intention to marry her without delay. In the meantime he seemed in no hurry to claim the privileges that she was very willing to give him. She was still a little shy of him, and couldn't bring herself to ask point-blank why, when the embraces they did share quickly brought them both to a high pitch of arousal, he always stopped short of the point of no return.

Now that she knew he loved her, Cassia was impatient to experience every delight that love had to offer. She knew that he wanted her. She wanted him. She didn't understand

why he was postponing the moment when they would be
lovers in the fullest sense.

The Palacio de Mondragón in Madrid made the house at
Castell de los Torres seem like a cottage. It was in the heart
of the city, and as Simón slowed the car to wait for a break
in the oncoming traffic, and she saw his family's coat of
arms carved in stone above doors built to admit carriages
drawn by four or more horses, she realised for the first time
how immensely rich and distinguished he was. It made her
even more nervous.

Someone must have been on the watch for them. Before
there was a gap in the stream of cars, the great doors were
opened by two liveried manservants, revealing the patio
within, far larger and grander than any she had glimpsed
in Granada.

'Don't panic,' said Simón. 'A large part of the house is
now the administrative centre of my estates as a whole.
The grandest rooms are, in effect, a museum, open to art
connoisseurs by appointment. My private apartment is at
the back, overlooking the garden, which is where, in all
probability, we shall find my mother. She's always disliked
Madrid and only comes here to see me.'

Cassia's first sight of the former *marquesa* was from a
window in his apartment while she was in the bathroom,
freshening up after the drive from Castell. Looking down
from the first-floor window, she saw a tall, slender woman,
her hair tied back with a soft chiffon scarf, pacing the pav-
ing surrounding a fountain pool. She was simply but ele-
gantly dressed in a white shirt and navy skirt with matching
tights and shoes. Cassia knew from her movements and the
way she kept checking her watch that she was nervous too.
The knowledge calmed her own jitters.

When, a short time later, they finally came face to face,

her anxiety evaporated. She saw at first glance that Simón hadn't exaggerated his mother's *simpática* personality.

They shook hands and smiled at each other, and then the older woman looked up at her son and said, with a catch in her voice, 'I thought you had to be exaggerating, but I see you weren't. She does put them in the shade.'

Then she turned back to Cassia, saying, 'The de Mondragón wives have included many famous beauties, some with characters to match their faces and some not. Simón told me you were ravishing, but that it was your other qualities he found irresistible. I was beginning to be afraid he would never find the right girl, but at last he has, and now I can stop worrying about him. My name is Joceline.'

She let go of Cassia's hand, but only in order to give her a more demonstrative welcome—a hug, and kisses on both cheeks.

On the morning of her wedding day, Cassia woke up in a bedroom at the Parador de San Francisco, the State-run *parador* she had always loved, originally a monastery founded by the Catholic monarchs after recovering Granada from the Moors.

In her many explorations of the Alhambra she had often peeped through the gateway of the *parador*, but had never expected to find herself staying here—and especially not as the bride of a grandee.

It had been Simón's decision not to have the big fashionable wedding customary in Madrid society. Instead, they were being married quietly in a city where she felt at home and where Señor Alvarez could take the place of her father.

Simón had organised everything. Her only responsibilities had been to choose her wedding dress and a trousseau for a honeymoon on a faraway island in the sun, where the only things to do would be swimming, sailing and making love.

She had spent her last night on her own in Room 305—a very small double room with a private sitting room in the tower above it. This, she presumed, was where they would sleep tonight—their flight to their secret destination having been arranged for tomorrow.

She had had breakfast in bed, and was up and dressed when Joceline and Toni came for her. All three were going to a salon to have their hair done. Toni had driven down from Castell de los Torres the previous afternoon. She was still staying there, painting pictures of windows.

One of them she had framed and presented to Simón and Cassia as a wedding present the night before. She had not brought Jack to the wedding. He was now in charge of a second batch of teenagers, and Cassia's place had been taken by a capable local girl.

Saying goodbye to Jack had left Cassia with an ache in her heart that she would continue to feel until he found someone to love him as he needed to be loved. Whether he and Toni now had something going between them was impossible to tell.

But a sexual relationship, however enjoyable, could only ever be second-best, a substitute for the real thing, thought Cassia as, walking down the hill to the city centre, she listened to Toni telling the former *marquesa* about a wedding in Paris that she had attended recently.

'I can't wait to see *our* bride in her lovely dress,' said Joceline, giving Cassia an affectionate glance.

In one of several recent heart-to-hearts she had confided that her first wedding had been a terrifying occasion. Having lost her own mother, she had been bullied by Simón's formidable grandmother into agreeing to a Spanish ceremony of almost royal formality and splendour, made more daunting by Joceline's then inadequate command of her bridegroom's native language.

Her second husband had flown in the day before, and was now keeping Simón company at the Hotel America, also within the boundaries of the Alhambra. Joceline and Toni had hurried Cassia past it after leaving the *parador*. Although neither was really superstitious, they hadn't wanted her to be accidentally seen by her bridegroom.

Only the wedding guests were staying at the Castillo del Sultán, and there were not many of them. Simón had been ruthless in pruning the list to fewer than a dozen particularly close friends. Parties for other friends would take place at a later date. Today was to be the intimate occasion he felt a wedding should be.

It was late afternoon when Simón gave Cassia's elbow a gentle squeeze and said, 'Time to change, darling.'

Although they weren't really leaving Granada tonight, he had thought it would wind up the festivities in an appropriate way if, after changing their clothes, the guests saw them off in his car. But they would only be going as far as the cemetery, for Cassia to leave her flowers on the ledge of John Browning's vault.

Toni helped Cassia to change from her white lawn and handmade lace wedding dress into a summery frock. Although it was only just May, all Europe was having a heatwave, and here in the south the days were hot, the nights balmy.

'You look so radiant that I could almost wish someone would come and sweep me off the shelf,' she said in Spanish as she dealt with the hooks and eyes.

Even the short visit to her father's grave could not cloud Cassia's happiness. She felt that today was the real beginning of her life.

'Are you tired?' Simón asked as they drove back down the hill, past the place where the tour buses parked. By this time of day the last bus had gone, as had the rows of cars now to be seen all year round near the Generalife gardens where, only a few months ago, she had sat worrying about Simón's motive for asking her to dine with him in the Mirador suite.

'Not very. It wasn't that sort of wedding. But I'm glad the others will have left when we get back.'

Later this evening, when everyone had had time to rest, his mother and stepfather were hosting another party at a restaurant in the Albaicín.

'So am I,' he said, giving her a smile with a glint of devilment in it. 'Our engagement has been a test of restraint for me.'

She didn't pretend not to understand what he meant. From this day forward there would be no more subterfuge, no more prevarication. 'It didn't have to be, Simón.'

'I know, but it wasn't for long.' He glanced at the clock on the dashboard. 'We may just have time to look at the sunset from one of the Alhambra's *miradores*. Would you like that?'

The suggestion was unexpected, but she realised that, yes, she would like to begin their honeymoon by watching the sun go down from one of the balconies inside the sultans' palace.

'It would be lovely, but aren't we too late? I think they'll have closed,' she said regretfully.

Sometimes the Alhambra was open at night, but not always.

Simón drove through the arched gateway used by taxis and motorists staying at the *parador*. Leaving the car in a place where she didn't think cars were supposed to be left, he jumped out and locked the driver's door. As she got out she thought that he would sprint towards the ticket office. Instead he came round and, taking her by the hand, strolled leisurely towards the doors where visitors surrendered their tickets. Perhaps he was planning to slip the doorkeeper a tip.

'What about the car?' she asked. 'Won't you be fined for leaving it there?'

'You worry too much.' His dark eyes sparkled with amusement. 'Who'd fine me on my wedding day?'

'But we've nothing to prove that we are just married.'

'We shall have to hope they take our word for it.'

At the entrance, the attendant smiled and said good evening.

'I've left my car near the ticket office. Could you have someone take it up to the *parador*, please?' Simón handed over the keys.

'Certainly, Excellency.'

'How is it that he knows you?' Cassia asked. 'Do you have some connection with the Alhambra?'

'He saw me this morning, when I came here to arrange for us to watch the sunset. By special dispensation, we're going to be allowed to wander about unsupervised.'

'You arranged this! What a lovely, romantic thing to do.'

'A wedding night is a romantic occasion.'

He put his arm round her waist and they strolled through the deserted rooms with their honeycombed ceilings and walls inscribed with mysterious Arabic inscriptions.

With no one else there it was magical. No footsteps but their own. No other voices. Only the sound of the fountains and water courses, and then, faintly, somewhere far off, the music of Spanish guitars.

'As one can't rely on the nightingales, I asked some gyp-

sies to play for us,' Simón explained as they looked across
the ravine at the rooftops of the Albaicín. 'But they're not
here. They're over in the other gardens. We shan't be disturbed. The whole Alhambra is ours, from sunset to sunrise.'

Much later, after the gypsy guitarists had returned to their
caves on Sacromonte, he took her to a moonlit room where
the pools of silvery light fell from star-shaped openings in
the roof, and the diaphanous folds of a transparent tent of
fine gauze were stirred by soft currents of air. Inside the
tent was a wide divan.

It was like a scene from the *Arabian Nights*—baskets of
scented roses in every corner, their heady fragrance mingling with the exotic incense from burning pastilles which
would keep the room free of mosquitoes.

Cassia realised that these preparations must have been
made while they were drinking champagne in the Tower of
the Princesses, listening to the throbbing guitars and a fine
tenor voice singing 'Granada' which, as it died away, was
followed by another surprise. From the dark cypress groves
of the gardens on the neighbouring hill came fiery meteors
and sparkling cascades of colour—the fireworks which
were a traditional celebration at even the humblest Spanish
weddings.

When she was lying in his arms on the spacious divan,
inside the misty folds of their bridal pavilion, Simón said
huskily, 'Do you remember the night I walked you home?
The thought of you all by yourself in that gloomy house
kept me awake. Since that night I haven't wanted any other
woman. Now that you're mine, I never shall.'

She knew that it was a promise he would keep. Walking
back to this main part of the palace from the Torre de las
Infantas, pausing to gaze at the reflections of palms and

pillars in the still surface of a pool, they had both revealed thoughts and feelings not shared with anyone else.

Simón had told her how his grandfather's libertine ways had been the outcome of an arranged and loveless marriage. How he himself, as a boy, had admired and been greatly influenced by his grandfather, inheriting his attitude to women, but always with the secret hope that his own marriage would be different.

With her arms round his neck and his eyes burning with the ardour deliberately held in check until this perfect moment, she lost her last vestige of reserve and felt only a passionate longing to be his—body and soul.

'Make me yours...now,' she whispered.

As he began to kiss her, somewhere outside she heard a nightingale singing.

Modern Romance™
...seduction and
passion guaranteed

Tender Romance™
...love affairs that
last a lifetime

Sensual Romance™
...sassy, sexy and
seductive

Blaze
...sultry days and
steamy nights

Medical Romance™
...medical drama on
the pulse

Historical Romance™
...rich, vivid and
passionate

29 new titles every month.

*With all kinds of Romance for
every kind of mood...*

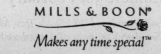

MILLS & BOON®

Makes any time special™

MAT4

Available 1st February

*Available at most branches of WH Smith, Tesco, Martins,
Borders, Eason, Sainsbury's and most good paperback bookshops.*

Treat yourself this Mother's Day to the ultimate indulgence

3 brand new romance novels and a box of chocolates

= *only £7.99*

Available from 18th January

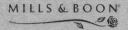

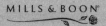

MILLS & BOON®

Tender Romance™

THE ENGAGEMENT EFFECT- *Two brand-new tantalising stories...*

An Ordinary Girl by Betty Neels
When Professor James Forsyth meets Philomena Selby
it's love at first sight. James is determined to convince
Philly *she'll* be the only wife he'll ever have.

A Perfect Proposal by Liz Fielding
Wasn't it madness to marry your secretary to provide a
baby with a mother? Jane, Mark's secretary, didn't think
so; but she wanted a marriage for love—not convenience.

THE ENGLISHMAN'S BRIDE by Sophie Weston
Sir Philip Hardesty, UN negotiator, is famed for his cool
head. But for the first time in his life this never-ruffled
English aristocrat is getting hot under the collar—over a
woman! Kit Romaine is not easily impressed—if Philip
wants her he's going to have to pay!

THE BRIDEGROOM'S VOW by Rebecca Winters
Millionaire Dimitrios Pandakis has vowed that he will
never be trapped into marriage. And he has been so true
to his word that despite his reputation as a heartbreaker
he has yet to take a woman to bed! But Alexandra
Hamilton has somehow worked her way under his skin...

THE WEDDING DARE by Barbara Hannay
As chief bridesmaid Laura has certain duties on her best
friend's hen night—like picking up the evening's
entertainment, a male stripper! But, Laura has hijacked
respectable single dad Nick Farrell, for whom taking his
clothes off in public is out of the question...

On sale 1st February 2002

*Available at most branches of WH Smith,
Tesco, Martins, Borders, Eason, Sainsbury's
and most good paperback bookshops.*

0102/02

MILLS & BOON
F REIGN
AFFAIRS
A captivating 12 book collection of
sun-kissed seductions.
Enjoy romance around the world
DON'T MISS BOOK 5
pacific passions–
Temptation in paradise...
Available from 1st February
Available at most branches of WH Smith,
Tesco, Martins, Borders, Eason, Sainsbury's
and most good paperback bookshops.
FA/RTL/5